PLAYING THE GAME

After he unlocked the backdoor and eased it open carefully, he stepped inside, and shut the door behind him. Quietly.

Listening for any sound to indicate that his entrance might have alerted her to his presence, he placed the axe against the wall, then patted his soggy jacket pocket. Ah, yes, it was still there, coated with raindrops, but otherwise unharmed. He removed the long-stemmed pink rosebud, then took the tiny key-ring flashlight from his other jacket pocket and used it to search the room. Taking hesitant steps, not wanting to bump into anything and make a noise, he paused as he passed the kitchen table and laid the rose there for safekeeping. He would need it later. A tribute. One lovely flower for another.

He felt inside his pants pocket, checking on the small digital camera. An important part of the game was photographing the kill.

The house was middle-of-the-night quiet. . . . Sonya was probably sound asleep. She had made this almost too easy for him, as if she were asking for it. But she would never suspect a mysterious stranger would use the key she thought was so cleverly hidden to enter her home.

In the dead of night.

With the intention of killing her . . .

Books by Beverly Barton

AFTER DARK

EVERY MOVE SHE MAKES

WHAT SHE DOESN'T KNOW

THE FIFTH VICTIM

THE LAST TO DIE

AS GOOD AS DEAD

KILLING HER SOFTLY

CLOSE ENOUGH TO KILL

MOST LIKELY TO DIE

THE DYING GAME

Published by Zebra Books

The Dying Game

Beverly Barton

ZEBRA BOOKS
KENSINGTON PUBLISHING CORP.
www.kensingtonbooks.com

ZEBRA BOOKS are published by

Kensington Publishing Corp.
850 Third Avenue
New York, NY 10022

All Kensington titles, imprints, and distributed lines are available at special quantity discounts for bulk purchases for sales promotion, premiums, fund-raising, educational, or institutional use.

Special book excerpts or customized printings can also be created to fit specific needs. For details, write or phone the office of the Kensington Special Sales Manager: Attn. Special Sales Department. Kensington Publishing Corp., 850 Third Avenue, New York, NY 10022. Phone: 1-800-221-2647.

Zebra and the Z logo Reg. U.S. Pat. & TM Off.

ISBN-13: 978-0-8217-7689-6
ISBN-10: 0-8217-7689-4

First Printing: April 2007
10 9 8 7 6 5 4 3 2 1

Printed in the United States of America

To Tyrone Power, Loretta Young, Sonja Henie, Richard Greene, John Payne, Maureen O'Hara, John Wayne, Errol Flynn, Olivia De Havilland, Alice Faye, Don Ameche, Bette Davis, Barbara Stanwyck, Henry Fonda, Anne Baxter, James Stewart, Cary Grant, Katharine Hepburn, Humphrey Bogart, Lauren Bacall, Greer Garson, Clark Gable, James Cagney, and countless other movie stars who shined so brightly in black and white on the old silver screen and brightened my childhood, filled my with life with romance and magic, and ignited my innate creativity.

Thank you, Daddy, for sharing your love of classic movies with me.

Acknowledgments

For their research assistance, a special thank you to:

Steven L. Romiti, M.D.
Philip L. Edney, Public Affairs Specialist, FBI
Stephen Kodak, Federal Bureau of Investigation

Prologue

The intensely bright lights blinded her. She couldn't see anything except the white illumination that obscured everything else in her line of vision. She wished he would turn off the car's headlights.

Judd didn't like her to show houses to clients in the evenings and generally she did what Judd wanted her to do. But her career as a Realtor was just getting off the ground and if she could sell this half-million dollar house to Mr. and Mrs. Farris, her percentage would be enough to furnish the nursery. Not that she was pregnant. Not yet. And not that her husband couldn't well afford to furnish a nursery with the best of everything. It was just that Jennifer wanted the baby to be her gift to her wonderful husband and the nursery to be a gift from her to their child.

Holding her hand up to shield her eyes from the headlights, she walked down the sidewalk to meet John and Katherine Farris, an up-and-coming entrepreneurial couple planning to start a new business in Chattanooga. She had spoken only to John Farris. From their telephone conversations, she had surmised that John, like her own husband, was the type who liked to think he wore the pants in the family. Odd how, considering the fact that she believed herself to be a thoroughly modern woman, Jennifer loved Judd's old-fashioned sense of protectiveness and possessiveness.

When John Farris parked his black Mercedes and opened the driver's door, Jennifer met him, her hand outstretched in greeting. He accepted her hand immediately and smiled warmly.

"Good evening, Mr. Farris." Jennifer glanced around, searching for Mrs. Farris.

"I'm sorry, something came up at the last minute that delayed Katherine. She'll be joining us soon."

When John Farris raked his silvery blue eyes over her, Jennifer shuddered inwardly, an odd sense of uneasiness settling in the pit of her stomach. *You're being silly,* she told herself. Men found her attractive. And it wasn't her fault. She didn't do anything to lead them on, nothing except simply being beautiful, which she owed to the fact that she'd inherited great genes from her attractive parents.

Jennifer sighed. Sometimes being a former beauty queen was a curse.

"If you'd like to wait for your wife before you look at the house, I can go ahead and answer any questions you might have. I've got all the information in my briefcase in my car."

He shook his head. "No need to wait. I'd like to take a look around now. If I don't like the place, Katherine won't be interested."

"Oh, I see."

He chuckled. "It's not that she gives in to me on everything. We each try to please the other. Isn't that the way to have a successful marriage?"

"Yes, I think so. It's certainly what Judd and I have been trying to do. We're a couple of newlyweds just trying to make our way through that first year of marriage." Jennifer nodded toward the front entrance to the sprawling glass-and-log house. "If you'll follow me."

"I'd be delighted to follow you."

Despite his reply sending a quiver of apprehension along her nerve endings, she kept walking toward the front steps, telling herself that if she had to defend her honor against unwanted advances, it wouldn't be the first time. She knew how to handle herself in sticky situations. She carried pepper spray in her purse and her cell phone rested securely in her jacket pocket.

After unlocking the front door, she flipped on the light switch, which illuminated the large foyer. "The house was built in nineteen-seventy-five by an architect for his own personal home."

John Farris paused in the doorway. "How many rooms?"

"Ten," she replied, then motioned to him. "Please, come on in."

He entered the foyer and glanced around, up into the huge living room and to the right into the open dining room. "It seems perfect for entertaining."

"Oh, it is. There's a state-of-the-art kitchen. It was completely gutted and redone only four years ago by the present owner."

"I'd like to take a look," he told her. "I'm the chef in the family. Katherine can't boil water."

Feeling a bit more at ease, Jennifer led him from the foyer, through the dining room, and into the galley-style kitchen. "I love this kitchen. I'm not much of a cook myself, but I've been taking gourmet cooking lessons as a surprise for my husband."

"Isn't he a lucky man."

Jennifer felt Mr. Farris as he came up behind her. Shuddering nervously, she started to turn to face him, but suddenly and without warning, he grabbed her from behind and covered her face with a foul-smelling rag.

No. No . . . no, this can't be happening.

* * *

Had she been unconscious for a few minutes or a few hours? She didn't know. When she came to, she realized she was sitting propped up against the wall in the kitchen, her feet tied together with rope and her hands pulled over her head, each wrist bound with individual pieces of rope that had been tied to the door handles of two open kitchen cabinet doors.

Groggy, slightly disoriented, Jennifer blinked several times, then took a deep breath and glanced around the room, searching for her attacker. John Farris loomed over her, an odd smile on his face.

"Well, hello, beautiful," he said. "I was wondering how long you'd sleep. I've been waiting patiently for you to wake up. You've been out nearly fifteen minutes."

"Why?" she asked, her voice a ragged whisper.

"Why what?"

"Why are you doing this?"

"What do you think I intend to do?"

"Rape me." Her voice trembled.

Please, God, don't let him kill me.

He laughed. "What sort of man do you think I am? I'd never force myself on an unwilling woman."

"Please, let me go. Whatever—" She gasped, her mouth sucking in air as she noticed that he held something shiny in his right hand.

A meat cleaver!

Sheer terror claimed her at that moment, body and soul. Her stomach churned. Sweat dampened her face. The loud rat-a-tat-tat of her accelerated heartbeat thundered in her ears.

He reached down with his left hand and fingered her long, dark hair. "If only you were a blonde or a redhead."

Jennifer swallowed hard. *He's going to kill me. He's going to kill me with that meat cleaver. He'll chop me up in little pieces . . .*

She whimpered. *Oh, Judd, why didn't I listen to you? Why did I come here alone tonight?*

"Are you afraid?" John Farris asked.

"Yes."

"You should be," he told her.

"You're going to kill me, aren't you?"

He laughed again. Softly.

"Please . . . please . . ." She cried. Tears filled her eyes and trickled down her cheeks.

He came closer. And closer. He raised the meat cleaver high over her head, then swung it across her right wrist.

Blood splattered on the cabinet, over her head, and across her upper body as her severed right hand tumbled downward and hit the floor.

Pain! Excruciating pain.

And then he lifted the cleaver and swung down and across again, cutting off her left hand with one swift, accurate blow.

Jennifer passed out.

Chapter 1

There are some things far worse than dying. Judd Walker knew only too well the agony of simply existing, of being neither dead nor truly alive. For the past three years, eight months, and two days, he had lived in a world without Jennifer. In the beginning, the pain had been unbearable. His anger and rage had nourished him, keeping him breathing, allowing him to continue from one day to the next in a fog of torment. And then a few months after his sweet Jenny's funeral, the fog had lifted and his one goal in life had become clear— to find and destroy his wife's killer.

A part of him—some far removed, distant part—still loved Jennifer. Except for that faint, lingering emotion, he felt nothing, only a goddamn, blessed numbness. Even the anger and rage had burned out, leaving him little more than subhuman, caring for nothing and no one. Wanting—needing—only one thing from life: Revenge! His goal of tracking down his wife's killer had become his only reason for living.

Judd dropped to his knees beside the snow-covered grave. He hadn't wanted to come here, had tried his best to stay away; but the overwhelming need to be near Jennifer on their anniversary controlled his actions. February the fourteenth. Valentine's Day. Jennifer had been a hopeless romantic, a trait that he'd thought silly in other women, but had found utterly charming in the woman he loved.

The woman he loved . . .

Judd reached out and ran a shaky hand over the chiseled letters on his wife's headstone. She had been laid to rest here in the Walker private cemetery, in Hamilton County, alongside his parents, his older sibling who'd died as an infant, and countless noteworthy ancestors who were a part of southeastern Tennessee history.

As his father before him, Judd had been one of the most sought-after bachelors in the state. A real catch. A former Chattanooga district attorney with a reputation as a man who genuinely cared about the welfare of the citizens of his county. The only surviving child of parents who had each inherited an ungodly fortune, Judd had known wealth and privilege all his life. But he'd wanted more—more than being Judge Judson Walker IV's son, more than being Senator Nathaniel Chisholm's grandson. And more had been expected of him. He had been brought up to believe that he was, and always would be, one of the good guys, a man destined to help his fellow man.

"Why you, Jenny? Why did it have to be you?" Judd shivered as the damp and cold seeped through his jeans, the slushy, wet snow dampening his knees. The winter wind whipped through the old, battered, leather jacket he wore.

In his mind's eye, he could still see Jennifer, the way she had looked the last time he'd seen her alive. Beautiful. Vibrant. Happy.

God help him, he should feel something—anything. He should be crying . . . ranting . . . raving. Or at the very least, his wife's memory should evoke a sentimental melancholy.

Nothing.

Dry-eyed, cold, and somber, Judd rose to his feet. Before leaving the cemetery, he gazed down at Jennifer's grave one final time. He wouldn't come back again, not even next year on their anniversary. There was no point in pretending to mourn, not when there was only emptiness left inside him, only embers of his once fiery emotions.

"You deserved better, Jenny." Judd's voice blended with the howling winter wind. "If it takes me the rest of my life, I promise that I'll find him, and I'll make him pay for what he did to you."

Judd walked down the narrow path that led to the arched wrought-iron gates guarding the family cemetery. Gazing up at the night sky, he blinked as the melting snow hit his face. With moisture coating his beard stubble and shaggy hair and beading on his leather jacket, he yanked open the driver's door on the old Mercedes that had belonged to his father. He glanced over his shoulder and took a deep breath.

"Happy Anniversary, Jenny."

He slid behind the wheel, inserted the key into the ignition, started the car, and drove away.

The only reason Griffin Powell had accepted Jillian and Gil Russell's invitation to their dinner party was a long, lean, luscious redhead named Laura Barrett. Laura and Jillian had been best friends since their sorority days at Vanderbilt, and Griff and Laura had become casual lovers when he'd invested in her father's faltering horse-breeding farm several months ago. He found Laura, as a person, mildly interesting; as a lover, she was quite talented. Even though she might have originally had a misguided idea that their relationship would lead to marriage, Griff had set her straight, in his own subtle, gentlemanly way. They both understood that this trip to Knoxville would be her last, that their affair was coming to an end.

Laura tightened her grip on Griff's arm. "There's someone you simply have to meet."

"Is there?" Griff replied.

"Yes, darling. It's Royce Palmer." Laura all but dragged Griff across the crowded room.

"Who's Royce Palmer?"

"My ex-fiancé."

"Oh."

"You're not the least bit jealous, are you?"

Before Griff could think of a diplomatic response, Henry Lewis waylaid them. The UT professor placed his thin, bony hand on Griff's shoulder. "Still getting all the pretty girls, I see."

Griff smiled at Hank despite the fact that the feel of the man's hand on his shoulder made him slightly uncomfortable. Even when they'd been students together at the university, Griff had sensed something a little off-center about the guy. They had never been friends, but now ran into each other occasionally at various functions because they both belonged to the alumni association and traveled in the same social circle. The only difference was that Hank had been born rich and thus entitled. Griff had come by his vast wealth through a combination of blood, sweat, and tears.

"Laura Barrett, may I introduce Hank Lewis." He eyed the lanky, slightly balding man. "Or would you prefer to be introduced as Professor Henry Lewis?"

Laura faked a smile. Hank removed his hand from Griff's shoulder and grasped Laura's hand, much to her surprise. She gasped softly.

While Hank babbled his way through what he probably thought was some witty repartee, Griff zoned out and leisurely scanned the Russells' massive living room. The crème de la crème of Knoxville society was in attendance, along with several out-of-towners. Interior designer Mark Crosby spied Griff, raised his hand and waved. Mark was the best in the state, and that was the reason Griff had hired him to decorate both his office suite and his home.

Who was the man talking to Mark? Griff wondered. He looked vaguely familiar, but Griff couldn't quite place him.

"Who's the fellow with Mark?" Griff interrupted the going-nowhere conversation between Laura and Hank.

Gazing up thankfully at Griff, Laura said, "That's Cary Maygarden, from Nashville. We met him at the Fentons' New Year's Eve Ball in Atlanta. Don't you remember?"

"Is he in the country music business?" Hank asked.

"Goodness, no." Laura laughed. "The Maygarden family is one of the oldest, wealthiest, and most prestigious in Nashville. Cary's great-great-something-or-other was a contemporary of Andrew Jackson."

Griff grunted.

"Please excuse us, Hank." Laura tugged on Griff's arm. "We simply have to say hello to an old friend before we leave."

"We're leaving?" Griff grinned. Nothing would please him more.

"Of course we are. I'm returning to Louisville in a few days. I want you all to myself for a little while this evening."

Hank choked on his own saliva and awkwardly excused himself.

"Very effective," Griff said, once Hank was out of earshot.

"Whatever do you mean?"

"You as good as told old Hank that you intend to have your way with me tonight."

"I do," Laura said, a wistful expression on her lovely face. Then her expression changed, hardened; and she laughed. "Let's call it what it is, shall we?"

"And that would be?"

Still smiling, she lowered her voice ever so slightly. "A farewell fuck."

Never let it be said that Laura didn't know how to make a

point. Griff placed his hand on her back and let it trail slowly downward, stopping just below her waist. When she started to speak, he grasped her elbow and maneuvered her forward, directly toward her former fiancé. Before they reached Royce Palmer, Griff leaned down and whispered in Laura's ear.

"I think a farewell fuck should always be memorable, don't you?"

As if she hadn't even heard him, Laura held out her hand to the man she had once been engaged to. "Royce, darling, how good to see you." She turned to Griff. "Sweetheart, this is Royce Palmer, an old and dear friend." She hugged closely to Griff's side as she zeroed in on the other man. "You know Griffin Powell, don't you? *The* Griff Powell, UT legend, and one of the most sought-after bachelors in the state of Tennessee."

Shortly after three in the morning, Pinkie removed his tuxedo jacket and hung it in the closet, then removed the diamond cuff links from his white shirt and placed them in the jewelry case. He'd left the party rather early because he'd been bored.

Pinkie hated being bored.

But a man in his position had to attend a certain number of these mundane affairs. It was expected.

After removing his shoes and stripping out of his other clothing, he retrieved a pair of silk pajamas from the wardrobe drawer. He stroked the luxurious fabric. Pinkie bought only the best.

Once attired in his pajamas, leather house slippers, and quilted satin robe, Pinkie went downstairs and entered his study. After pouring himself a small nightcap, he walked straight to the wall of bookshelves on the right, removed a specific book, pressed the button on the wall, and waited for the secret compartment to open. That's what he loved about this old house—the secret chambers. Like something out of a 1930s movie. How utterly delicious. There was one chamber between the study and the front parlor and another in the basement. Since he seldom went down to the basement, except when he personally retrieved a bottle of wine, he preferred the small, private, upstairs chamber.

Entering this room transported Pinkie into another world, a realm of pleasure and satisfaction that he had created for himself four and a half years ago. He flipped on the light switch. Soft, mellow illumination filled the eight-by-fourteen-foot room. He moved slowly along the back wall, studying the photographs mounted side by side. Thirty-two enlarged photos of sixteen different women, each one a true beauty. Pinkie paused in front of the most recent addition to his collection: Gale Ann Cain—*before and after.* The before photograph had been taken years ago when she'd won the Miss USA contest and gone on to compete in the Miss Universe Pageant. The after snapshot had been taken with Pinkie's tiny digital camera moments after he had killed her, less than forty-eight hours ago.

"Thank you, my pretty flower," Pinkie said. "You were worth twenty points."

After months of searching, he had specifically chosen Gale Ann because of her fabulous red hair. Redheads were the most rare and therefore worth more than a blonde or brunette.

His fingertips traced his handiwork, gliding smoothly across the snapshot, pausing on her slender ankles.

The sound of her screams echoed inside Pinkie's head.

The first kill had been the most difficult. He had hated the woman's screams. But with each kill, the act itself had become easier, and eventually, he had begun to enjoy hearing their screams.

*   *   *

"The Beauty Queen Killer has struck again."

The words were no sooner out of Sanders's mouth than Lindsay McAllister shot out of bed and ran barefoot to the open doorway of her bedroom where her boss's personal assistant stood. He had awakened her moments before with a loud knock and an urgency in his voice when he called her name.

"Have you gotten in touch with Griff?" she asked, knowing their employer had probably spent the night with his latest lady friend, a Kentucky divorcée who was visiting her sorority sister in Knoxville. The woman's family raised thoroughbred Derby winners, and Griff had invested in the faltering horse-breeding farm last fall. She often thought her boss had a white knight complex. He seemed to like nothing better than rushing in to save the day.

"Yes," Sanders replied. "He's on his way home. He should be here soon."

"Give me fifteen minutes to shower and dress," Lindsay said.

Sanders nodded. Not for the first time, she noticed the man's military bearing. Although she had worked with him for three and a half years, she knew absolutely nothing about his past, but she suspected that at sometime in his life, he had been a soldier. She had no idea how old he was, but guessed his age to be somewhere between fifty and sixty. At five-ten, he was not a large man, but stocky-built, and with his head shaved as slick as a billiard ball, he looked like a muscular, physically fit fireplug. But what set him apart more than anything else were his eyes. An intense brown so dark that they appeared black. And there was an emptiness in those hypnotic eyes that perpetually puzzled Lindsay.

"I'll have coffee ready for you when you come down." Sanders turned to leave.

She called to him, "Who, where, and how?"

Sanders paused, but kept his back to her. "Gale Ann Cain. Williamstown, Kentucky. He chopped off both of her feet."

"She was a dancer." Lindsay voiced the comment more to herself than Sanders. The killer that the Powell Agency had been tracking for nearly four years murdered his victims in various ways, each specific to the former beauty queen's talent in her pageant's contest.

Sanders's shoulders tensed ever so slightly. "Lyrical dance. She's a former contestant in the Miss Universe Pageant."

"You mean she *was*," Lindsay corrected.

"No, I mean she *is*. Ms. Cain is still alive."

"What!"

"She didn't die. Her sister found her before she bled to death."

"My God! Do you know what this means?"

Sanders nodded, then walked away.

Lindsay's heartbeat accelerated. Her pulse pounded loudly in her ears. After over three and a half years of searching for a manically clever killer, they had finally gotten a break. If the victim was still alive . . .

Lindsay closed her eyes and said a silent prayer for a woman she had never met, for a woman lying in a Kentucky hospital, missing both of her feet, the victim of a man to whom murder was some sort of sick game.

After closing her bedroom door and heading to the bathroom, Lindsay shucked off her oversized orange Vols T-shirt and slipped out of her white lace bikini panties.

When she had first moved from Chattanooga to Knox County to take a job with the Powell Private Security and Investigation Agency, she'd taken Griffin Powell up on his offer to stay at his sprawling twenty-room mansion situated on a hundred acres bordering Douglas Lake, near the foothills of the Great Smoky Mountains. She had intended to stay only until she'd found an apartment of her own, but what should have been a one-month stay had turned into three years and counting.

Lindsay turned on the shower, then gathered up a couple of towels and a washcloth. After placing the towels on the mat outside the ceramic-tiled shower unit, she stepped beneath the warm water and quickly lathered her short hair.

Some people assumed that because she not only worked closely with the big man himself but she was the only Powell agent who lived in Griff's home, the two were lovers. Nothing could be further from the truth.

Through their years together—each of them having their own agenda for being obsessed with the beauty queen murders—she and Griff had formed a bond of friendship. He had become more like a protective big brother than anything else.

Stepping out of the shower, Lindsay towel-dried her short, curly hair and hurried through her daily morning routine. She was a low-maintenance kind of woman. Short hair, short nails, a little blush on her cheeks, light lip gloss, and a whiff of fresh linen body spray. On her downtime, she dressed for comfort. On the job she preferred a casual look—slacks, shirt, and jacket, all in neutral shades. Her only jewelry, other than a sensible Fossil wristwatch, was a pair of diamond ear studs. A Christmas present from Griff.

After dressing hurriedly, Lindsay ran down the backstairs that led to the massive kitchen. Sanders stood behind the granite-topped bar, a glass coffeepot in his meaty hand. Griffin Powell, his unbuttoned overcoat hanging apart to reveal his rumpled white shirt and tuxedo, halted in the doorway leading into the kitchen from the mudroom, and wiped his snow-smeared dress shoes off on a sturdy floor mat.

Lindsay paused on the bottom step as her gaze zipped from Sanders to Griff. A silent understanding passed between her and her boss. They were both thinking the same thing— how will this affect Judd?

"Do you want me to call him?" she asked.

Griff shook his head. "I've already tried. Both his home phone and cell phone are no longer in service."

Lindsay groaned. "I'm not surprised."

"Neither am I." Griff shook the snow from his short, platinum-blond hair, then removed his overcoat and tossed it over a nearby kitchen chair. "The last time I saw him, he was just one step away from being a mad hermit."

"Will you try again to contact him or—?"

"Why don't you drive down there this morning and see what you find," Griff said. "If he's even halfway sane, tell him what's happened, stay with him and try to keep him in line as much as possible."

The thought of seeing Judd again—how long had it been, six months?—rattled Lindsay's nerves. When the Beauty Queen Killer struck three months ago, right before Thanksgiving, she had begged off working with Judd. And knowing their past history, Griff had allowed her one free pass. Apparently she wasn't due another.

"And if I'd prefer not to work with Judd, not to see him . . . ?"

Sanders cleared his throat. "Either of you want breakfast?"

"No," they both said simultaneously.

Sanders placed the coffeepot back on the hot plate, then without saying a word, walked out of the kitchen.

"You can't avoid him forever," Griff said. "Your life has been Judd Walker-free for six months. You've been dating that hotshot young doctor, so I thought maybe you might have finally worked through your personal demons."

"Getting rid of those personal demons is a work-in-progress." Lindsay went over to the coffeemaker, lifted the pot from the hot plate, and poured coffee into the two mugs Sanders had placed on the counter.

With filled mugs in hand, she walked across the room and

offered one to Griff. He accepted the mug, took a sip of the hot brew and locked his gaze to hers.

"Judd has been one of my best friends for a long time," Griff said. "If I thought we could save him, I'd move heaven and earth to do it. But Lindsay, honey, you can't save a man who doesn't want to be saved. He may be too far gone now. He lives for nothing but revenge. Not justice. Not salvation. Not peace. Just revenge."

"Then why send me down there to help him, if he can't be helped?"

"Even if neither of us can save Judd, we're the only two people left who give a damn about him. No matter what, we need to see this thing through to the end with him. It's what we both have to do." He hesitated for a millisecond, then added, "And it's the only way you'll ever be completely free."

Emotion welled up inside Lindsay, feelings she had tried so very hard to keep deeply buried, after she had realized she couldn't vanquish them altogether. "What if he wants to go to Kentucky and see Gale Ann Cain?"

"I'm flying up to Williamstown later this morning," Griff said. "I'll keep you posted on Ms. Cain's condition. And if Judd is acting like himself enough actually to give a shit about Ms. Cain, then don't try to stop him from coming to see her. As a matter of fact, drive him straight to the hospital yourself."

Chapter 2

Last night's snow had turned into a cold, relentless rain. The windshield wipers on Lindsay's two-year-old Trailblazer LT swished back and forth at high speed, barely able to keep one step ahead of the heavy downpour. She was at the halfway point between Griff's home in Knox County and the old hunting lodge in Marion County that had belonged to the Walker family for several generations. She had headed out at nine-thirty this morning, shortly after dropping Griff off at the private airstrip where he kept his personal jet. Actually, it was the company's jet—Powell Private Security and Investigation Agency—but since Griff was the sole owner, it was a moot point. In good weather, she could easily make the trip in a little over two hours, but with visibility practically nil, she'd be lucky to arrive at her destination in three hours.

Griff had known she didn't want to see Judd again, yet he'd sent her off on this assignment anyway. She could have questioned him about his decision or even refused, but she'd known Griff long enough to realize he never did anything without a reason.

And that reason would be? she questioned herself.

Maybe it was because Griff knew that if this new Beauty Queen Killer case didn't snap Judd back to life, from out of that no-man's-land where he existed, then nothing ever would. Now, with a victim who had actually survived, this was the first real break they'd gotten in tracking down Jennifer Mobley Walker's killer. If Gale Ann Cain could identify her attacker . . .

If . . . if . . . if . . .

What if she couldn't identify the madman who had chopped off both her feet? What if she never came out of the coma? What if she died? Was it fair to build up Judd's hopes, to make him believe they actually had a shot at finding out who had killed his wife?

As the windshield wipers' mesmerizing song hummed in rhythm to the drumming raindrops, and the miles along Highway 28 zipped by, Lindsay's thoughts wandered backward to a day she would never forget—her first case as a brand new homicide detective for the Chattanooga Police Department. She had been partnered with Lt. Dan Blake, a veteran cop who had been her dad's partner ten years earlier, before her father had been shot down by an escaping felon. Dan had taken her under his wing, guided her through her rise in the CPD, from rookie to detective, and had become like a second father to her.

They had arrived at the house shortly after midnight and took over from the uniformed officers—Marshall and Landers—who'd been first on the scene.

"The call came in from Ms. Walker's boss, the owner of Archer/Hert Realty. It seems Mr. Walker became concerned when his wife was late coming home and he couldn't reach her on her cell phone, so he called her boss. Mr. Archer was also unable to contact Ms. Walker on her cell, so he drove out to the house she'd been showing and found—" Officer Landers swallowed hard. "I've never seen anything like it and I hope I never—"

"That bad, huh," Dan said as he passed by Landers and entered the sprawling seventies ranch house. Lindsay followed, pausing in the foyer when Dan stopped to take a look around. Officer Marshall stood in the foyer talking quietly to a small, gray-haired man who looked as if he'd been crying.

The minute Officer Marshall heard the door open, he turned to face Dan. "Lieutenant, this is Mr. Archer. He's the one who found Mrs. Walker's body." The officer nodded the direction. "In there, in the kitchen."

"It's the most god-awful thing I've ever seen." Archer's voice quivered with emotion. "How could anyone have done something so terrible to Jennifer?"

"Take Mr. Archer outside and let him get some fresh air," Dan said. "And let me know the minute the CSI boys arrive." He turned to Lindsay. "Are you ready for this?"

She nodded.

"If you get sick, don't worry about it," he told her. "It's happened to all of us at least once."

"I'll be okay." She felt quite confident that she could handle whatever they found. After all, she had watched several autopsies and hadn't experienced more than momentary nausea, hadn't she? And she had viewed pictures of countless corpses in various stages of decomposition and hadn't even flinched.

Dan slipped on his disposable gloves and headed through the house, inspecting one room at a time. Without a moment's hesitation, Lindsay mimicked his actions. When Dan stopped abruptly in the kitchen doorway, Lindsay almost skidded into his back. She managed to sidestep him and wound up to his right, which enabled her to glance around him and into the kitchen.

Barely restraining a shocked gasp, Lindsay stared in disbelief at the slender young woman sitting on the floor, her head bowed, as if praying, her mane of long, dark hair cascading over her shoulders. Thin nylon rope crisscrossed her ankles, binding her feet together. Her arms, pulled up above her head, were bound with the same type of rope and were attached to two open cabinet doors.

"Sweet Jesus," Dan said.

The woman's hands, severed at the wrists, lay on either side of her hips, only a few inches from her thighs. Two large pools of rich, drying blood permeated the kitchen, emitting a distinct metallic scent and creating ebony-red stains where the victim's life's blood had drained from her body.

"The son of a bitch chopped off her hands." Dan glared at the discarded meat cleaver lying at the dead woman's feet.

Lindsay didn't know what to say, had no idea how to respond to her partner's comments. She wasn't sure Dan expected her to reply.

As she surveyed the dead woman from head to toe, Lindsay noted one small item that seemed totally out of place in the gory scene. "There's a flower in her lap."

"A red rose," Dan said. "Probably our killer's calling card."

Lindsay made a mental check of red rose connotations she'd heard during her lifetime. The one that came to mind first was that a red rose means *I love you.* Nope, that couldn't be it, could it? Then the lyrics to an old song hummed through her head: *Red roses for a blue lady.*

"Let's just back out of here and wait for our CSI team. If we're lucky our guy left more than a red rose behind." Dan closed his eyes, grunted and shook his head in disgust. "Why do some of them have to resort to slicing-and-dicing their victims?"

She was certain that comment had been rhetorical, so she kept quiet and took several steps backward, giving Dan room to turn around. But before Dan could close the kitchen door, a ruckus of some sort broke out from the foyer. The sound of Officer Landers's voice rang out loud and clear.

"Sir, you can't go back there," Landers said.

"The hell I can't," the agitated baritone replied.

Feet stomping. Grunts. Curses. A thud.

"Mr. Walker, come back here," Landers cried. "Stop now!"

Judd Walker, former Chattanooga D.A. and presently a successful lawyer who was expected to run for office in the next gubernatorial race, came storming toward Dan and Lindsay.

"Where is she?" Judd demanded.

"Mr. Walker . . ." Dan approached the victim's husband.

Lindsay eased backward, placing herself in front of the closed kitchen door.

Judd glared at Lindsay. "Get out of my way. I want to see my wife."

"No, sir, you don't want to see her." Dan reached out to grab Judd's arm, but Judd shook off Dan's tentative grasp and moved past him.

With Dan behind him and Lindsay in front of him, Judd paused for a split second and glowered at Lindsay. "Don't try to stop me. I've never hit a woman—"

"Then don't start now." Dan grabbed Judd from behind.

Judd whirled around and shucked off Dan's grasp. He drew back his closed fist and punched Dan in the stomach before either Dan or Lindsay realized the man's intentions. Groaning, Dan doubled over in pain.

Lindsay took a deep, bracing breath, and the minute Judd turned, she sent a swift right hook into his jaw, momentarily stunning him. Staggering slightly, obviously startled by her unexpected attack, Judd quickly focused on his single objective. While Dan managed to recover enough to draw his pistol from his shoulder holster, Judd shoved Lindsay aside, an easy feat for him since she was half his size. At that precise moment, Lindsay decided she needed to master some type of martial art.

Judd Walker thrust open the kitchen door.

"Please stop, Mr. Walker," Lindsay called to him. "Don't go in there. Don't touch anything. You'll compromise the crime scene."

Dan tromped past Lindsay, halted just inside the kitchen, and aimed his Magnum at Judd Walker's back.

"You're not going to shoot him," Lindsay said.

Shaking his head, Dan lowered his weapon. "God damn it. I should have been able to stop him, but he caught me off guard. I must be getting too old for this job."

Lindsay barely heard a word Dan said and hardly noticed Officers Landers and Marshall, who had arrived seconds too late to assist them. She watched as Judd Walker dropped to his knees and pulled his wife into his arms. He didn't cry, didn't rant and rave. He held her tenderly, his trembling fingers caressing her pale cheek.

"We've got to get him out of there." Dan motioned to Landers and Marshall.

As Dan and the officers cautiously entered the kitchen, *it* happened, stopping them dead in their tracks. Judd Walker let out an earsplitting scream, the sound so horrific that Lindsay heard it in her nightmares for years to come.

Swish, swish. Back and forth. The wipers smeared the freezing rain across the windshield of Lindsay's metallic blue SUV. Damn, that cold rain had turned into a rain/ice mix. Just what she needed. The state and county work crews would keep the main roadways clear, but the Walker hunting lodge was off the beaten path, the last five miles on a gravel road. A four-wheel drive did great in snow, but was no better than any other vehicle on ice.

Did she hope the roads became impassable? Was she looking for any excuse to avoid seeing Judd again? Probably. No, not probably. Definitely. The last time she'd had to deal with him, she'd sworn never again. The man was an unfeeling bastard. Yes, he'd lost his wife, his beloved Jennifer. Yes, the former Miss Tennessee had been murdered—her hands

whacked off—by a psycho monster. Yes, Judd had deserved
sympathy, compassion, and understanding. And she had given
him all three, in spades, as had Griff. Hell, everybody who'd
ever known him—and countless others who had never met
him personally—had felt the man's pain. But it had been nearly
four years since Jenny Walker's death, and it was way past
time for Judd to return to the land of the living.

Of course, he would never be the man he once was. How
could he be? No one expected that to happen. But where at
one time Lindsay had held out hope that Judd would go
through the grieving process and shed his crazed vigilante
persona, she now accepted the fact that his grief and rage
had sucked all other human emotions out of him. If not for
his thirst for revenge, Judd Walker wouldn't exist.

As soon as Griffin's plane landed at the small commercial
airport in Williamstown, Kentucky, he called Sanders.

"Any word on Gale Ann Cain's condition?"

"Nothing, other than she's still alive," Sanders said.

"Heard anything from Lindsay?"

"No, but we didn't expect to this soon, did we?"

"Not really."

"You're concerned about her having to confront Mr. Walker
again."

Griff didn't reply immediately, hating to admit that he actually was concerned about Lindsay. "She'll be all right.
She's tough."

"Yes, sir."

Whenever Sanders became formal enough with Griff to
say "sir" to him, he immediately understood that his assistant
was showing his disapproval. "Judd needs her," Griff said.
"She's the only one who has a prayer of reaching him on any
level."

Silence.

"It's not as if she's a lamb being led to the slaughter."

"No, sir."

Griff knew when to hold 'em and when to fold 'em, especially with Sanders. It was definitely time to fold 'em.

"If you hear from her—"

"I'll contact you, sir."

Damn it, Lindsay McAllister *was* tough. She was a former police officer who'd done a short stint as a Chattanooga PD detective. Her old man had been a cop, as had his father before him. She had grown up as a tomboy, or so she had told him, preferring to play baseball with the boys instead of Barbie dolls with the other girls. Small-boned, petite, and slender, Lindsay should have projected an image of dainty femininity. Instead, with her pale, curly blond hair cut short and very little makeup covering her freckled nose and cheeks, she came across as a no-nonsense, no frills woman. If anyone made the mistake of thinking she was fragile, all they had to do was cross her. Since he had first met her, she had acquired topnotch martial arts skills, had become an expert marksman, and hid the emotional side of her nature as well as any man.

He liked Lindsay. Respected her. And in many ways had come to think of her more as a kid sister than an employee.

They had met almost four years ago, shortly after Jennifer Walker's brutal murder. Lindsay had been partnered with Dan Blake, the lead detective on Jenny's murder case; and he'd never seen anyone more determined to solve a crime than she had been. At first, he had chalked up her perseverance in finding Jenny's killer to a rookie detective's need to prove herself. But as the weeks and months went by, he realized that the case had become personal to Lindsay. Sometime between meeting Judd at the scene of his wife's murder and becoming acquainted with him as a grieving widower obsessed with revenge, Lindsay had fallen in love with Judd Walker.

Griffin slid behind the wheel of the rental car, a two-year-old Lincoln. He'd never been to Williamstown, Kentucky, so he'd asked for directions to the hospital before he left the airport. He doubted that, in a town this size, even a direction-challenged person could get lost.

Three miles from the small airport, Griff took a left on Elmwood Street, which meant he should be less than five minutes from the hospital where Gale Ann Cain lay in a semi-coma, heavily drugged, and teetering between life and death. The former Miss Universe contestant was only one in a long line of former beauty queens who had been savagely attacked in the past four and a half years. By Griff's—and the FBI's—count, Ms. Cain was victim number twenty-nine. But neither he nor the FBI could be sure that all twenty-nine murders had been committed by the same person, and therefore weren't positive that the murders were all connected. Nor could they be certain that there hadn't been other victims.

Griff's gut instincts told him all twenty-nine had a definite connection.

The victims had not been confined to one city, county, or state, making their killer nomadic, a guy who traveled around in search of the perfect target. But these women had not been chosen at random. Not by a long shot. The common denominator in these crimes was the fact that each woman had been a winner in some kind of beauty pageant—local, statewide, national, or international. Not one victim had been older than thirty-five. And each had still been beautiful.

Jennifer Mobley Walker had possessed a flashy kind of beauty: Big brown eyes, lustrous dark hair, full lips, large breasts, and long legs that went on forever. And she had been blessed with a bubbly, enthusiastic personality that drew people to her. To know Jenny was to love Jenny.

No one had been more surprised than Griff when his old friend, Judd Walker, a confirmed bachelor, had fallen head over heels for the former Miss Tennessee and married her less than a year after their first date. Women throughout the state had mourned the loss of such a desirable catch. Rich, handsome, and charming.

That had been then—five years ago.

B.J.M.

Before Jennifer's murder.

The three-story hospital came into view as Griff neared the turnoff on to Pickler Avenue. If Gale Ann Cain lived long enough to ID her attacker, they would have a chance of catching this guy and stopping him before he killed again. Griff wasn't sure that arresting the man and bringing him to justice could save Judd's soul, but it was sure and certain that nothing else would. During the nearly four years he had worked on this case, he had done his utmost to stay detached, as much as it was possible when a friend was involved. But both he, Sanders, and especially Lindsay had become borderline-obsessed with seeing justice done.

After parking the rental car in the crowded visitors' lot, Griff slipped on his leather gloves, tightened the silk scarf around his neck, and buttoned up his water-repellent overcoat. The harsh February wind bombarded him, chilling his face, and putting a giddyup in his step.

At the information desk in the lobby area, he acquired instructions on reaching the ICU unit: Second floor; turn left coming out of the elevator; go to the end of the hallway.

As he stepped off the elevator, he unbuttoned his tan overcoat and unwrapped the scarf from his neck. He hated the sounds, smells, and sights in a hospital. Medicinal scents blended with the aroma of cleaning products and the stench of human sickness and death. Passing by patients' rooms, he tried not to glance inside the open doors, tried to avoid viewing the weak, infirm, ill men and women. His avoidance came not from empathy, but from a lack of it, and Griff hated the phlegmatic elements in his nature that were so alien to his former self. *A by-product of surviving at all costs,* he surmised.

When he entered the intensive care waiting room, a twelve-by-fourteen-foot, windowless cubbyhole filled with a small group of bleary-eyed, rumpled men and women, he removed his leather gloves and stuffed them into his overcoat pocket. A few of the people in the room appeared to have slept on the two brown vinyl sofas and in the mismatched collection of uncomfortable-looking vinyl chairs. An assortment of small pillows and blankets of various sizes and colors lay scattered about haphazardly on the furniture and the floor.

Griff had no idea if Gale Ann Cain had a husband or siblings or parents besides her sister who might be here. The information Sanders had received had been sketchy, just a brief conversation with their government contact, an acquaintance of longstanding.

Pausing in the open doorway, Griff scanned the area. Several people turned and stared at him; just as many others, engrossed in their own tragedies, ignored him completely.

A woman sitting in the right back corner, deep in conversation with a lady who was sitting in a wheelchair, seemed to have sensed his presence. Her shoulders tensed. She sat up straight. After giving the other woman's hand a gentle squeeze, she lifted her dark head and glanced over her shoulder.

Damn! Double damn! He should have known she'd be here. The bane of his existence, the thorn in his side when it came to the Beauty Queen Killer case.

She rose from the chair to her full five-ten height and faced Griff. Frowning, her pale tan eyes narrowed and her nostrils slightly flared, Special Agent Nic Baxter walked toward him, her gaze never wavering.

He stepped out into the hallway and waited for her. If there was going to be a confrontation—and there always was whenever they shared the same space—it was better for the two of them to exchange insults out of earshot of other people. Especially people with loved ones in the ICU.

She followed him into the hall. They faced each other.

"You're not glad to see me," Griff said.

"I'm never glad to see you," she replied.

"I noticed you were doing some hand-holding. Is she the sister of Gale Ann Cain or just a friend?"

"I can't order you to leave, as much as I'd like to, but I can warn you not to interfere in my investigation." She shook her finger in his face. "Sooner or later, I'll find out who keeps tipping you off and when I do—"

"Why can't you get it through that thick skull of yours that we're on the same side?" Griff understood that federal agents could be territorial, that they often had to deal with inept local law enforcement and well-meaning civilians, but he was neither.

"And why can't you get it through your thick skull that tracking and apprehending serial killers is the bureau's job, not a game for some know-it-all private dick?"

Griff cocked one eyebrow and gave her a blistering glare. "Where's Special Agent Jackson?"

When the corners of Nic's mouth lifted ever so slightly in a hint of a smile, he knew he wasn't going to like her answer. "Curtis retired last month. Didn't your mole in D.C. tell you?"

Shit!

Special Agent Curtis Jackson had been in charge of the Beauty Queen Killer case from the very beginning, heading up the FBI task force. He had liked and respected Jackson. A guy in his late fifties, with years of experience and a macho attitude that matched Griff's, Jackson and he had gotten along just fine, even though the guy never shared any info with him and had warned him repeatedly to keep his nose out of federal business. Griff kept a professional profiler on the Powell Agency payroll. But despite having a likely description of their culprit, they were no closer to apprehending this monster than they had been three years ago. He suspected it was the same for the FBI.

Nicole Baxter had come in on the case as a five-year veteran of the bureau, and although she'd graduated at the top of her class at Quantico, she'd had little field experience. From the moment they first met, she and Griff had mixed like oil and water. He didn't like women who tried to prove that they were better at everything than men were. Maybe Special Agent Baxter wasn't a die-hard feminist, but she came close enough to filling the bill that Griff grouped her in with all the other radical, man-bashing bitches.

"If Jackson retired, does that mean you've taken over the Beauty Queen Killer case?" Griff knew, but he had to ask.

She nodded. "That's right. I'm heading up the task force now."

"Is there any way we can bury the hatchet and work together?"

"Only if I can bury it in your back."

Griff let out a quiet yet dramatic groan. "You're not going to give an inch, are you, honey?" He tacked on the generic endearment because he knew it would piss her off.

She glowered at him. "I can be reasonable, honey."

"You can't prove it by me." He shouldn't have mouthed off, but couldn't help himself. She brought out the worst in him and apparently he did the same for her.

"Keep insulting me and see where that gets you."

"I guess I should apologize."

"That would be nice."

Damn, she actually expected him to grovel. "All right. I apologize."

She flopped her hand across her heart. "How sincere."

"It's all you're going to get. Take it or leave it." Griffin Powell didn't grovel. Not for anyone. Not ever again. He'd rather die first.

"Look, if you're willing to acknowledge that this is my case, that I'm the one who calls the shots and makes the decisions, I won't cut your balls off and hand them to you on a silver platter."

Go to hell, bitch had been on the tip of his tongue. "In order to safeguard my balls, what do I have to do, sign an oath in blood that I'll stay out of your way?"

"Don't tempt me."

"Believe me, Special Agent Baxter, I would never intentionally tempt you."

Nic groaned. "*Believe me*, you have nothing to worry about on that count."

He held out his hand, offering her a truce. "Let's agree to disagree. I'll stop hoping for cooperation from you, and you don't put up any roadblocks in my path."

She stared at his hand as if it were a poisonous snake, then reluctantly shook hands with him. A quick, let's-get-this-over-with exchange.

"If you start interfering, our deal is off. Understand?"

He nodded. He understood all right; he just wasn't sure how long he could play nice in the sandbox with this particular she-cat.

Seemingly satisfied, Nic nodded toward the ICU waiting area. "The woman in there is Barbara Jean Hughes. She's Gale Ann Cain's older sister and the one who found her only moments after she was attacked and left for dead."

Griff's gut instincts kicked into play. "Tell me that the sister caught a glimpse of our killer."

"I might as well tell you since I can't stop you from talking to Barbara Jean. And you are going to talk to her, aren't you?"

"Yep."

Frowning, Nic said reluctantly, "When Barbara Jean was entering her sister's apartment building over on Loretta Street, she saw a man in a trench coat and sunglasses coming down the stairway."

"Can she describe him in more detail?"

"I think she can," Nic said. "But she's scared to death—for herself and her sister."

"So, even if the sister dies, we've still got a possible witness."

"You're a cold-hearted bastard, Powell. You know that, don't you?"

"So I've been told."

"One other thing, Mr. Powell—*we,* as in you and I, don't have anything. I gave you the info about Barbara Jean because you'd get it anyway. But that's it. The sister is the bureau's eyewitness. And it will be our responsibility to protect her, if that becomes necessary. Do I make myself clear?"

Griff grinned. "Crystal clear, honey."

Nic groaned.

Chapter 3

The old hunting lodge looked deserted, as if it hadn't been occupied in a decade or longer. Actually, the place hadn't been used for its original purpose in well over fifteen years, not since Judge Judson Walker IV died. Judd had not enjoyed hunting as much as his ancestors had, instead preferring polo and tennis to killing for sport. He had turned the old lodge into a weekend getaway, and as a young bachelor had hosted numerous parties for his friends; but word had it that because his bride hated the great outdoors and roughing it in the woods, Judd had closed up the place during his brief marriage.

The road leading to the lodge had never been paved and was now little more than a winding path overgrown with snow-topped grass, weeds, and dead leaves. Towering trees surrounded the drive and the old lodge itself: Ancient hardwoods, worth their weight in gold to any lumber company, their limbs bare and coated with a thin layer of ice; huge cedars shimmering with a frozen glaze; pines tipped with small, glistening snowballs.

A two-story structure created out of native stone and

brick, the hundred-year-old building boasted numerous long, narrow windows, four chimneys, and a wraparound front porch. Out back, there was a small carriage house that had been converted into a garage in the late 1930s. Peeling paint on the eaves and window seals of both the house and garage exposed their neglected state. Two broken windowpanes on the second story of the lodge begged for repair.

Lindsay pulled her Trailblazer to a halt directly in front of the wraparound porch, but she left the truck's motor running. The freezing rain had stopped a good twenty miles back, and the sun was fighting to make its way through the thick clouds. The temperature gauge on the dashboard read thirty-four degrees, which meant it had warmed up just enough to begin the thawing process. But by nightfall, those temps would drop again, probably into the twenties, and refreeze any remaining moisture.

If possible, the place looked sadder and more dilapidated than when she'd last seen it over six months ago. Dripping icicles hung from the edges of the roof. Melting snow clung in clusters to the grassy lawn and several inches of the white stuff, hidden in corners protected from the struggling sunlight, rose several inches high. Lindsay's gaze traveled up the stone and brick front steps to the porch, then to the huge wooden door with decorative black iron bars crisscrossing the series of descending four-by-six-inch glass panes.

Inside, she remembered, just beyond the front entrance, lay a small foyer that opened up on either side to large sitting rooms. Each room boasted a massive stone fireplace, hardwood flooring, and dark wood paneling. In the room to the left, trophy deer heads hung on either side of the fireplace; in the room to the right, mounted and framed prize catches from the Tennessee River lined the walls, three fish on either side of the fireplace. She had not seen the upstairs bedrooms, but she assumed that they, too, screamed *macho domain, no women allowed.*

The thought of facing Judd, of looking into those cold, topaz gold eyes, kept Lindsay from leaving the warm safety of her SUV. Repeatedly, she had told herself that she didn't love him, that she never had. She had felt sorry for him, wanted to comfort him, tried to help him. Besides, any woman would be sexually attracted to Judd. He was so overpoweringly masculine.

All those introspective, come-to-Jesus talks she'd given herself over the past six months had convinced her that what she felt for Judd Walker was a combination of sympathy and lust, not love.

So, if she didn't love him, why was she so afraid of seeing him again?

You can't put it off forever, you know. Get out of the car and go knock on the door. Face your fears. Prove to yourself that Judd no longer has any power over you.

After donning her red knit cap and matching gloves, Lindsay buttoned her navy peacoat, shut off the ignition, and opened the car door. As she stepped down, her black leather boots hit a slushy spot on the ground, shooting muddy ooze over the one-inch heels and rounded toes. By the time she reached the porch, the wet grass she'd trekked through had absorbed most of the mud on her boots.

Taking a deep breath, she faced the front door. Stretching her gloved fingers back and forth, she garnered up her courage, then lifted her right hand and knocked. Once. Twice. Three times.

No response.

She knocked again. Harder. Louder.

Still nothing.

She banged repeatedly. "Judd, if you're here, let me in. I have some news for you. It's about the Beauty Queen Killer case."

Silence.

Damn it. Maybe he wasn't here. Maybe he'd moved away to some unknown location. A part of her prayed that he had.

Lindsay tried the front door knob, twisting it this way and that. The door didn't budge. Locked. So much for that.

She went to the nearest window and peered in through a fine layer of dirt and grime. The left parlor lay in semidarkness, the furniture still covered with protective cloths. After checking out the other parlor through an equally filthy windowpane, she walked the expanse of the wraparound porch, stopping at a side door leading through a narrow hall into the kitchen. She tried the door and surprisingly found it give. Unlocked. The door creaked loudly as she pushed it open. She hesitantly entered the dark hallway. Cobwebs shimmied along the walls.

"Judd, are you here?" she called as she made her way toward the kitchen.

No answer.

She found the kitchen empty. But a half-full coffeepot sat on the warmer, and a stained mug rested on the counter beside the coffeemaker.

He was here. Upstairs? In the basement? Taking a walk in the woods?

If he was in the house, he would have heard her calling him. Unless he was asleep or passed out drunk. The first year after his wife's death, Judd had drunk himself into a forgetful stupor on a fairly regular basis. But the last time Lindsay saw him, he'd been stone cold sober. A drunk Judd she could deal with more easily than a sober Judd. Drunk, he was hateful and belligerent. Sober he was apathetic and deadly.

"Judd, if you're here, please answer me. Don't make me search the whole house for you."

Nothing.

"The Beauty Queen Killer has struck again, but this time his victim didn't die. Not yet. She's still alive."

No reaction. No response.

"Did you hear me?"

Creak. Stomp. Creak. Stomp.

Lindsay heard heavy footsteps on the backstairs that led from the kitchen to the second floor. Her heartbeat accelerated.

"Judd?"

The footsteps grew louder as they descended the creaking stairs.

Lindsay crossed the linoleum-floored kitchen and waited at the foot of the stairs, her pulse racing as she clutched both hands into tight fists on either side of her hips.

Barbara Jean Hughes, confined to a wheelchair since a terrible car crash five years ago, responded to Griffin Powell's masculine charm the way most other women did—she practically melted into a puddle. Good grief! Nic didn't get it. Yes, he was good-looking, masculine to the nth degree, dressed like a *GQ* model, drove a fancy sports car, and was reported to be a multimillionaire. Those qualities alone would be enough to make the average female swoon. But if there was one thing Nicole Baxter had never been, it was average. She wasn't average height and weight for a woman. Her IQ wasn't average, nor was her taste in men.

Powerful, macho, overconfident men turned her off. From the time she matured early at the age of eleven, she'd had to deal with the opposite sex. Snide remarks about her breasts. Jokes about her height. Envy because she was the smartest kid in her class—even smarter than the smartest boy.

Men might like women with big breasts, but most didn't like highly intelligent women who graduated from college at the age of eighteen, stood eye to eye with many, and towered over some. She was—always had been—too tall, too big, and too smart. Not to mention far too opinionated and outspoken.

"Ms. Hughes, why don't you let us take you down to the

cafeteria and get you something to eat. A late lunch," Griff said.

Nic had been trying to convince Barbara Jean that she needed to eat, but the woman had refused to leave the ICU waiting area.

"What if Gale Ann wakes up? Or what if she . . . No, I can't leave." With Nic, Barbara Jean had been adamant.

When Barbara Jean didn't respond to Griff's suggestion, only stared up at him through a mist of tears, he reached down, grasped her hand tenderly and said, "When your sister regains consciousness, she doesn't need to see you haggard and worried, now does she? You have to eat and rest to keep up your strength." He paused momentarily to allow his comments to sink in, then added, "For Gale Ann's sake, you have to take care of yourself."

Gag me with a spoon, Nic thought. Griff was as smooth as silk. Too damn smooth to suit her. He was one of those guys who could charm the birds from the trees. A real silver-tongued devil.

It was obvious by the tentative smile on Barbara Jean's face that Griff's charisma had affected her. What would be the point in warning her about Griffin?

"You're right, I suppose." Barbara Jean sighed heavily.

Griff squeezed her hand. "Of course I am." He glanced at Nic. "Special Agent Baxter will speak to the nurse in charge of the ICU and make sure we are contacted if there's any change in your sister's condition."

Gritting her teeth, Nic managed a fake smile as she nodded her head in agreement. "I'll speak to the nurse right now." She gave Griff a blistering stare. He just couldn't help himself, could he? To him, taking charge came as naturally as breathing. In the past, the FBI had cautioned family members about cooperating with any private agency, including the Powell Agency, but legally, the bureau's hands were tied.

At one-fifty in the afternoon, the cafeteria wasn't crowded, so it was easy enough to find seating. Griff chose an isolated table in the back of the dining area and parked Barbara Jean's wheelchair so that she was not near a window and her back was to a side wall. Nic understood his reasoning. If Gale Ann's attacker had any idea that Barbara Jean had seen him and could possibly identify him, her life was in grave danger. Of course, she hadn't said that she could ID the man, although she had admitted that she'd caught a glimpse of him as he was coming down the stairs of her sister's apartment building.

"Is there anything in particular you want to eat?" Griff asked as he laid his overcoat and silk scarf on an empty chair.

"Anything will be fine," she replied.

Nic and Griff were able to go through the line rather quickly, getting coffee for themselves and a meal for Barbara Jean. No way was she leaving Gale Ann's sister alone with him. Legally, she could not prevent him from talking to Barbara Jean or offering her his big broad shoulders to lean on; the best she could do was keep a close watch on the woman. Griff handed the cashier a hundred dollar bill. The biggest bill in Nic's wallet was a twenty. The difference between being rich and simply having a good job.

After slipping the change into his wallet, Griff lifted the tray laden with a full meal, dessert, and three cups of coffee, and carried it to the back table where Barbara Jean waited for them. After removing the plates, silverware, and cups from the tray, he placed it on a nearby empty table, then he pulled out a chair and offered it to Nic. She forced another fake smile—God, her face was going to crack—and allowed him to assist her.

Charming. Gentlemanly. Infuriating SOB.

Their gazes met for half a second, a confrontational exchange. Hostility simmered just below the surface, a reality neither of them could deny. Nic suspected that Griff disliked her as much as she did him, both professionally and personally.

Barbara Jean eyed the plate of food in front of her, then glanced over at Griff. "Everything looks delicious. Thank you."

"Just eat what you can," he told her, sympathy and understanding in his voice.

"I'm afraid I don't have much of an appetite."

"It's okay," Nic said. "No one expects you to—"

"You have no idea what it was like." Barbara Jean grasped Griff's arm. "It was the most horrible thing imaginable, finding my sister like that. Her feet cut off. Blood everywhere." Barbara Jean burst into tears.

Before Nic could say or do anything, Griff slid his chair closer to Barbara Jean's wheelchair and draped his arm around her shoulders, offering her solace. She buried her face against his shoulder and wept.

Although Nic hated weepy females and had become determined at an early age to never become one, she couldn't deny that Barbara Jean Hughes had every right and every reason to cry her head off. Good Lord, who wouldn't have been devastated to find their sister mutilated and bleeding to death. It had been Barbara Jean's quick thinking that had saved Gale Ann's life.

After several minutes of sobbing, Barbara Jean lifted her head. "I'm sorry that I fell apart that way."

Griff pulled a soft cotton, monogrammed handkerchief from the inside pocket of his tailor-made jacket. The man's suit probably cost more than Nic made in a month, possibly a couple of months. He dabbed the expensive handkerchief under Barbara Jean's eyes, then handed it to her.

"You must know that you saved your sister's life," Griff said as he lifted his arm from Barbara Jean's shoulders.

"They don't think she'll live." Barbara Jean clutched the

handkerchief in her tight fist. "She lost so much blood be-fore—" She gulped her sobs. "If I'd been able to get to her more quickly . . . if . . ."

"You can help her by helping us find the man who tried to kill her." Griff's voice had softened, taking on a seductive quality that set Nic's teeth on edge.

"How—how can I do that?" Barbara Jean gulped.

"I understand that you caught a glimpse of a man leaving Gale Ann's apartment building as you were arriving. Do you feel up to talking about that or would you rather wait until after you finish your lunch?"

Barbara Jean glanced at the fried chicken, creamed pota-toes, and green beans on her plate, and Nic could almost hear the woman's stomach churn. Her right hand shook as she reached for the coffee cup, so she had to use both hands to lift the hot liquid to her lips. After several sips, she sighed.

"Ms. Hughes, I must remind you that Mr. Powell is not affiliated with the FBI or any law enforcement agency," Nic said, trying to keep her voice calm and friendly. "I must ad-vise you that it isn't in your sister's best interest for you to discuss what happened with anyone other than—"

"Special Agent Baxter is right," Griff said. "I'm a private detective, not a law enforcement officer. But one of my best friends lost a wife to the killer whom we suspect tried to mur-der your sister. I've been working on his behalf for nearly four years to try to find and stop this maniac."

When Barbara Jean looked deeply into Griff's eyes and offered him a trusting smile, Nic knew she had lost this par-ticular battle.

"I know all the residents where Gale Ann lives," Barbara Jean said. "There are only ten apartments in the building. Two are divorcées, like Gale Ann. Two are widows, one is an old bachelor, and the other four are young couples, but only two of the couples have children."

"This man you saw, he wasn't one of the residents?" Griff asked.

Barbara Jean shook her head.

"Could he have been a friend of one of the residents?" Nic inquired.

"I don't know. But I do know that in the six years my sister has lived there, I'd never seen this man before."

Nic opened her mouth to ask the all important question, but Griff beat her to the punch and asked pointedly, "Could you identify this man if you ever saw him again?"

Dead silence.

Nic gave Griff a heated glare.

"It's all right," Nic said. "If you can't ID the man—"

"What if I can?" Barbara Jean's gaze locked with Nic's.

"Can you?" Griff asked.

"You think he's the one who tried to kill Gale Ann, the one who cut off her feet?" Barbara Jean dropped her hands into her lap and entwined her fingers, trapping Griff's handkerchief between her palms.

"Possibly," Nic said.

"Does he know she didn't die?"

Nic shook her head. "The local police issued a statement to the news media that Gale Ann Cain's body had been discovered by her sister. Nothing more. But the hospital staff could let something slip, although they've been warned to be careful. And there are reporters trying to get to you to find out more details. But I or another agent will be with you twenty-four-seven. There is an agent posted at the hospital, outside the nurses' entrance to the ICU, to protect your sister."

"If this man knew I could identify him, he'd come after me, wouldn't he?"

"Yes, he might," Nic admitted.

"But we are not going to let anything happen to you,"

Griff told her. "Between the FBI and the Powell Agency, you'll be protected at all times."

Barbara Jean didn't say anything for several minutes, her mind obviously absorbing all the information and mulling over her choices. "I don't think I could identify him if I saw him again."

Nic groaned inwardly. She had been afraid of that. Either Barbara Jean really couldn't ID the guy or she was so scared that she had convinced herself she couldn't ID him.

"Could you describe him to us?" Griff asked.

"I already told Special Agent Baxter—"

"Call me Nic, please." Two could play the "let's be friends" game.

"I told Nic—" she offered Nic a fragile smile—"that as I was going in the front door of the apartment building—I always use the elevator since Gale Ann's apartment is on the second floor—that I saw a man in a tan trench coat coming down the stairs. He had on a hat and wore sunglasses. I didn't see his eyes. I think his hair was brown, but I can't be sure. He was walking pretty fast, as if he was in a hurry."

"Did he see you?" Griff asked.

"I don't know. I—I don't think so. He never looked my way. And I was already inside the elevator by the time he reached the sidewalk."

Nic's cell phone rang. Her gut tightened. She knew before she heard Special Agent Randall's voice that he was calling with news about Gale Ann Cain's condition.

"Baxter here," she said.

"Get the sister up here pronto," Jeff Randall said. "Gale Ann Cain has regained consciousness."

Lindsay's gaze traveled up the stairs and caught sight of the man's jean-clad legs. Long, lean legs. Faded, dirty jeans. Inch-by-inch, the rest of his body came into view as he trudged down the steps like a slug crawling along the ground. He wore a tattered, plaid flannel shirt over a dingy thermal undershirt. When she saw his face, she gasped. At first glance, she barely recognized Judd, and wouldn't have known who he was except for his pale amber eyes, eyes as lifeless as the world outside. Winter dead. His tawny brown hair hung almost to his shoulders, and a heavy beard obscured his handsome face.

"You look like hell." She said the first thing that came to her mind.

He stopped when he reached the foot of the stairs. "Did I hear you right—the latest victim didn't die, she's still alive?"

"That's right."

"What did he do to her?"

Lindsay hesitated. "He chopped off her feet."

Judd didn't flinch. And why should he? It wasn't as if he were actually capable of feeling any human emotion, other than his thirst for revenge.

"Where is she?"

"A county hospital in Williamstown, Kentucky."

"Is Griff—?"

"He flew up there immediately."

"And he sent you to tell me the good news." Judd walked past her and straight to the coffeemaker. After lifting the pot, he asked, "Want some?"

"Yeah, sure." She turned and faced him.

He removed another cup from the overhead cabinet, poured both cups full, and held one out to her. She went over, took the cup from him, and lifted it to her lips. The brew was strong and bitter. She suspected it had been sitting on the warmer for quite some time. Possibly since early morning.

"Can she identify her attacker?" Judd asked.

"I don't know. We were told that she lapsed into a semicoma in Recovery, shortly after regaining consciousness for a few minutes following her surgery."

"She probably won't come out of the coma."

"She might."

"Wishful thinking isn't worth a damn." Judd pulled out a chair from the table, set down his coffee cup, and slumped into the chair.

Standing behind him, Lindsay watched as he sipped the black-tar coffee. Judd Walker, multimillionaire, former playboy, former distinguished and respected lawyer, looked like a homeless bum. God in heaven, his long hair was dirty, greasy, and matted, as if it hadn't been washed or combed in weeks.

Lindsay walked over to the other side of the table so that she stood directly in front of him. "If you want to go to Kentucky—"

His vicious laughter chilled her to the bone. "Is that why Griff sent you this time? He thought you could persuade me to give a damn?"

"He sent me because he thought you'd want to know that this could be our first real break. He actually thought you might still want to see your wife's murderer brought to justice."

Judd's mocking smile vanished. "What I want is to have five minutes alone with him. Just five minutes."

"I doubt you'll ever get that chance," Lindsay said. "But if he's captured and then convicted, I'm sure it can be arranged for you to be there when he's executed."

"It won't be quite the same if I can't do the job myself." Judd downed the remainder of the liquid sludge he called coffee. "Do you have any idea how many times I've pictured this monster in my mind? I never see a face, only his hands holding a meat cleaver and chopping, chopping . . . chopping. And then suddenly he's not the one with the cleaver. I am. And I'm the one doing the chopping. I'm chopping him into a hundred little pieces."

Judd repeatedly pounded the table with his big fist. Over and over again. The table shook. Judd's heavy strikes grew harder and harder. His breathing became deeper and louder. His eyes glazed over as if he were in a trance.

Lindsay placed her cup on the counter behind her, then turned back to Judd, and grabbed his wrist. He flung her off him so forcefully that she toppled backward and landed against the refrigerator. Her back hit the fridge with a resounding thud. Judd shot up out of the chair and glared at her.

She stood there, straightening herself to her full five-four height, her gaze riveted to his as he came toward her. When he reached her, he spread his palms out flat against the refrigerator, on either side of her head, and brought his face down to hers so that their noses almost touched.

"I know why Griff sent you here," he said. "What I don't know is why you came."

Chapter 4

Lindsay hunched down just enough to slip under Judd's outstretched left arm, managing to escape his searing glare and his big, hovering body. Sucking in several deep breaths and mentally warning herself not to participate in Judd's manipulative game-playing, Lindsay psyched herself up for the inevitable battle of wills. Chuckling as if he found her actions amusing, Judd turned around to face her. She hated that cold, insincere grin he had perfected over the past few years. There was something disturbing about a smile that projected misery instead of mirth.

"What's wrong, Lindsay—afraid you can't resist me?"

She clenched her teeth, a scathing comment on the tip of her tongue. *He's baiting you. He wants an outraged reaction. Don't give it to him.*

"If you plan to go with me to Kentucky, you'll have to take a shower and—"

"I'm not going."

He's still playing his little game, she reminded herself.

"Fine by me," she said. "I'm just Griffin Powell's messenger." She reached for the cell phone clipped to her belt. "I'll call him and tell him—"

"Why did you come here? Really?"

"My boss sent me to share some information with a client we couldn't reach any other way." *That's it, Lindsay, you tell him.*

Judd studied her, his gaze raking over her insultingly. "Are you sure you didn't come back for a repeat performance?"

She felt the heat as it rose up her neck and flushed her cheeks. An involuntary reaction that she could not control. Pink-cheeked embarrassment. The curse of blondes with fair skin.

Don't tell him what you think of him. Do not give him the satisfaction of knowing what happened between the two of you the last time you saw each other devastated you. You've worked through it, have come to terms with the humiliation, convinced yourself that you never actually loved Judd.

"I'm heading back to Knoxville. I'll call Griff and tell him you no longer have any interest in the Beauty Queen Killer." Lindsay turned and headed out of the kitchen.

"Wait!"

Keeping her back to him, she paused.

"If she doesn't die . . . if she can give Griff a description . . . let me know. Okay?"

"I'll pass along the message."

"You hate me now, don't you?"

He's still playing you. Never forget that you cannot trust Judd. "That's what you want, isn't it, for me to hate you?" She glanced over her shoulder. "Sorry, but no, I don't hate you. I feel sorry for you."

She walked straight down the hall and to the side door leading to the porch.

"Lindsay!"

She opened the door and went outside, increasing her pace, wanting nothing more than to get away, to escape from this place and the man who still had the power to rip out her heart. A part of her did hate Judd, hated him as much as she loved him. And yes, damn it, she did love him. She probably always would. The heart wants what the heart wants, even if it wants something cruel and destructive.

After sitting down on the soft, gray leather seat inside her Trailblazer, she closed her eyes and willed herself under control. No tears. Not one. She had cried her last tear over Judd Walker. As far as she was concerned, he could rot in hell.

She made a quick call to Sanders for an update on the situation in Kentucky and was told she needed to contact Griff before bringing Judd to Williamstown. No point now. She inserted the key into the ignition and started the engine, then made the mistake of glancing through the side window at the lodge.

Judd stood on the front porch. Watching her.

Crap!

She hit the button to lower the window and called out to him. "Gale Ann Cain's sister discovered her in time to keep her alive until the paramedics arrived. The sister caught a glimpse of a man in a trench coat and sunglasses leaving the apartment building just as she arrived. He could have been our Beauty Queen Killer."

When Judd came down the steps, Lindsay's pulse raced. He walked over to the car and leaned down so that they were eye to eye.

He didn't say anything for several minutes, just stared right at her. As she reached for the electronic button to roll up the window, Judd said, "If you'll give me thirty minutes, I'll clean up before we head out for Kentucky."

Lindsay realized that somewhere buried deep inside him, Judd still felt something. Even if it were nothing more than an undying thirst for revenge, that was an emotion, wasn't it?

"All right. You go ahead. I'll phone Griff, get an update, and tell him we're on our way."

Pinkie was beginning to worry. He had neither read nor heard anything new about the murder in Williamstown, Kentucky—not in local or national press coverage. A few hours after the paramedics arrived on the scene, a spokesman for the Williamstown Police Department had issued a statement that a young woman, a former Miss USA named Gale Ann Cain, had been brutally attacked and her body discovered by her sister, who had immediately called 911. That had been over forty-eight hours ago. Why hadn't the local law enforcement called in the FBI? Surely they knew that Gale Ann's death could be attributed to the Beauty Queen Killer. Wasn't his signature all over the murder scene? The victim had once won a beauty contest. Her talent in the contest had been lyrical dance, so he had cut off her feet. She was a redhead, so he had left behind a yellow rose. He had used the same nylon rope to bind her hands as he always used. Were the local yokels too stupid to recognize the work of a genius?

Many criminals returned to the scene of their crime. Not Pinkie. He was far too smart to do something so stupid. But unless he could somehow find out what was going on in the Gale Ann Cain murder case, he might have no choice but to make a trip back to Williamstown. He could always come up with some legitimate reason to visit. To purchase a horse. To visit an antique mall where he would buy something outrageously expensive. Or he could simply be driving through on his way to somewhere else. Or he could simply wear a disguise and use a fake ID.

He had tried his best to dismiss a disturbing thought, one

that had plagued him since the evening he had killed Gale Ann. Just as he was leaving the apartment building using the stairs, he had noticed that a woman in a wheelchair was entering through the front door. Had she seen him? Probably not. After all, she'd been concentrating on maneuvering her wheelchair so that she could hold the door open long enough to move inside.

But what if she did see me?

So, what if she had seen him? What exactly had she seen? A man in a trench coat, hat, and sunglasses. It wasn't as if she'd seen his face and could identify him. And the clothing he wore that night had been properly disposed of, burned in the old furnace in the basement. The items he wore when he executed a game plan were inexpensive, off-the-rack items that he picked up at various chain stores. He wasn't fool enough actually to wear many of his personal tailor-made clothing or speciality items.

If only he knew what was going on, exactly how the Williamstown police were handling Gale Ann's case, he would sleep better tonight.

Pinkie removed a key from his pocket, bent over, and unlocked the bottom desk drawer where he kept a supply of disposable paid-in-advance phones. He slipped one of the phones into his jacket, locked the drawer, and pocketed the key.

He would take the Bentley out this afternoon and go for a nice long drive. Maybe a few counties over. He'd contact the Williamstown police, the newspaper, and TV station and inquire about Gale Ann's murder. If he couldn't find out anything, he'd have no choice but to rent a car, using an assumed name and fake ID and drive to Williamstown to personally check on the situation.

"I'm a distant cousin and haven't been able to reach anyone in the family." That's what he'd say. Now, what was Gale

Ann's maiden name? He always did research on his victims, learning as much as possible about them before he made his meticulous plans.

Hughes! That was Gale Ann's maiden name. Her parents were dead. She had one sister—never married—named Barbara Jean. She had no children, and she'd been divorced for over six years.

Pinkie had learned at an early age—when he was enduring his father's cruel temper tantrums—to listen to his gut instincts. Those unerring instincts had saved him from more than one beating by the old man, and had allowed him to rack up a whopping score of two hundred and fifteen points in the marvelously macabre game he referred to as "Picking the Pretty Flowers."

He should listen to his instincts now.

Something was off about this latest kill. There was a problem. He didn't know what it was, but he intended to find out.

When Griff, Nic, and Barbara Jean arrived back at the ICU waiting area, they were whisked into the inner sanctum. A nurse whose name badge read Huff stopped Nic and Griff, while another wheeled Barbara Jean down a row of cubicles and directly to the one in which her sister lay fighting for her life.

"What's going on?" Nic asked.

"Excuse me, are you a relative?" Nurse Huff asked.

"Neither of us are relatives," Nic replied as she whipped out her FBI badge and ID. "I'm Special Agent Nicole Baxter with the Federal Bureau of Investigation. I'm working with the local police department on this case. I need to question Ms. Cain as soon as possible. I spoke to your supervisor, Ms. Canton, less than an hour ago and—"

Frowning, Nurse Huff nodded. "Ms. Canton is involved in an emergency with another patient, but I'll speak to Dr. Clark. However, I don't think it will matter."

"What do you mean?" Griff asked. "Why won't it matter?"

Nurse Huff cleared her throat. "I'm sorry. I shouldn't have said anything." She nodded toward the closed door leading to the waiting area. "You two need to go back outside, please. We've been instructed to contact Police Chief Mahoney. If you have any further questions, please direct them to him."

Griff sensed Nic's heels digging in, and suspected she didn't appreciate the local law not instructing the hospital staff that the bureau—meaning Special Agent Baxter—was in charge of this case.

Griff grasped Nic's arm gently and urged her into movement, effectively leading her back through the waiting room and into the hallway. When they were out of earshot of the ICU families, she yanked free and faced him.

"What do you think you're doing?" Nic glowered at him.

"Saving you from throwing a very unbecoming hissy fit," Griff said. "You know you really should work on trying to control that hair-trigger temper of yours. It's a bad habit, especially in a federal agent."

Nic huffed. Her nostrils flared. For a minute there, Griff halfway expected her to snort and bellow and for steam to shoot out of her ears. Instead, she breathed deeply, swallowed hard, and blew out an aggravated breath.

"First of all, you are not my keeper," she told him. "And secondly, I was not about to throw a hissy fit."

"Are you saying you're not upset that the local police chief didn't inform the hospital staff that you're in charge?"

"I'm working with the local police department. This is their case as well as mine. You're acting as if I'm some rookie agent who doesn't know how to—"

"Special Agent Baxter," a female voice called.

Nic and Griff glanced at the doorway to the ICU waiting room. Nurse Huff walked toward them, a concerned expression on her face.

"Ms. Hughes is asking for both of you, and Dr. Clark has given permission for the two of you to join her in Ms. Cain's room."

"Has something happened?" Nic asked.

"I believe Ms. Cain is trying to communicate with her sister and is becoming highly agitated." Nurse Huff shook her head. "I'm afraid that if she doesn't calm down, we'll have to restrain her."

Anxious for them to see Gale Ann Cain before it was too late, Griff barely managed to stop himself from grasping Nic's arm again and rushing her into the intensive care unit. But as it turned out, he didn't need to. Nic all but ran through the waiting area, urging Nurse Huff to keep up with her.

In less than an hour, it would be dark. The days were getting a bit longer in mid-February, but with an overcast sky, night would fall early today. Lindsay was thankful that it wasn't raining or snowing, although either was a possibility before morning. They had driven straight from the Walker hunting lodge, not stopping for lunch, and were now almost to the Kentucky state line. Highway 127 would take them straight through Monticello and with only one turn onto a county road, they'd be in Williamstown no later than six o'clock this evening.

"I'll have to stop soon and get gas," Lindsay said to the somber man sitting rigidly in the passenger seat. "I'm going to pick up a burger and a Coke after I use the restroom."

"Stop at a mini-mart," Judd said. "I'll pump the gas. You go in and get the food. We can eat on the way."

"Sure. That suits me."

"Griff will call if the woman dies, won't he?"

Lindsay gripped the steering wheel tightly. "He'll call if he has any news—good or bad."

"Hmm . . ."

In the three hours they had been on the road, neither had spoken more than a few words now and then, maintaining a palpable silence, as tangible as the heavy fog that lay ahead. Damn! That's all they needed, a thick fog slowing their progress.

"By the way, how is Griffin these days?" Judd asked.

Totally surprised by the question, Lindsay snapped her head around and stared at Judd.

"Keep your eyes on the road," he told her.

She refocused on the highway. "Why are you asking about Griff? You don't really care, do you?"

"Griff's an old friend. Why shouldn't I ask about him?"

"Griff's Griff," she said. "He's fine."

"You two having sex yet?"

Lindsay clenched her teeth. So that's what it's all about— Judd just wanted to needle her.

"That's none of your business," she said.

"I could give him a few pointers, if you want me to. I could tell him what you like, what turns you on, what—"

"You can shut the hell up!"

Judd chuckled. A mirthless, cold chills-up-the-spine laugh.

"You're a real bastard, you know that, don't you."

"What's the matter, darlin'? Haven't you told Griff about us?"

"There is no us."

"There almost was. You were willing."

She'd been willing all right. God help her, she'd been more than willing. She'd been eager. She had fallen in love with Judd in those first few months after his wife's murder when she and her CPD partner Dan Blake had seen Judd on a regular basis. Dan had tried to warn her not to become personally involved. If only she had been able to take his advice. But ever since she'd been a kid, she had been the one who brought home stray dogs and cats, nursed wounded birds, and stood up to bullies in defense of those they harassed.

Her father had told her that she had a tender heart, just like her mother. She couldn't bear to see anyone—human or animal—in pain.

And Judd Walker had been in torment. Day by day she had watched him as he mourned his wife, as he became more and more withdrawn, as the anger—the pure rage—inside him had devoured all other human emotions, until nothing had been left except a burning desire for revenge.

Her heart had ached for him. Her stupid bleeding heart.

"You're awfully quiet," Judd said. "Thinking about that night?"

"No," she replied truthfully. "I was actually thinking about those first few months after Jennifer was murdered, and Dan and I worked so hard to try to find her killer."

"And here we are nearly four years and numerous beauty queen murders later, and Jenny's killer is still out there chopping off hands and feet, arms and legs, slitting throats . . . destroying lives."

"He'll be caught and punished," Lindsay said. "Griff and I made you a promise that we intend to keep. And Nic Baxter isn't going to give up until she catches this guy. She's as determined as Griff and I and—"

"And me?"

"Are you still determined, Judd? Do you still actually care?"

"I don't care about anything. You of all people should know that."

"But you want to see Jennifer's killer punished, don't you?"

"Yeah. It's the only thing I do want. My one thought, my single reason for living is the hope that one day I can kill him myself."

"And if that actually happened, if you could kill him yourself . . . hack off his hands, his feet, his arms and legs, chop him into little pieces—what then?"

"Are you asking me if I'd be at peace then?"

"No. I'm asking what then, when your single reason for living is gone?"

"I don't know," he said. "And I really don't care."

But I care. Damn you, Judd, I care.

Dr. Clark met them at the entrance to Gale Ann Cain's cubicle and motioned them to step back a few feet. Once he had them alone, he glanced from one to the other.

"Ms. Cain remains in critical condition," the doctor said. "Her chances of survival are not good. She's trying to talk, trying to tell her sister something, and has indicated she wants to speak. We've explained to her that we cannot take her off the ventilator at this point. She's highly agitated and if she doesn't calm down soon, we'll have no choice but to restrain her and sedate her. Her sister, Ms. Hughes, asked that you two be allowed to see Ms. Cain, while she's conscious. She hopes one of you might be able to help her decipher her sister's sign language."

"Sign language?" Griff asked.

"Since Ms. Cain can't speak, she's using her hands and facial expressions to try to convey a message of some sort."

"How long will it be before you can take her off the ventilator?" Nic asked.

Dr. Clark shook his head. "It's too soon to say. Maybe days or weeks. Maybe never."

"Are you saying—?"

"She has a living will," Dr. Clark said. "If she isn't able to breathe on her own after a period of time and if we see no hope for her . . ."

"We understand." Nic glanced at Griff.

"I will allow the two of you five minutes with Ms. Cain," Dr. Clark told them. "But if she becomes upset or even more agitated, I'll ask you to leave."

Nic nodded.

Griff said, "Okay."

When they entered Gale Ann's cubicle, Barbara Jean, who was holding her sister's hand, glanced up and offered them a pitiful smile. Then she leaned over and whispered, "Gale Ann, they're here. Special Agent Baxter and Mr. Powell. Tell them what you've been trying to tell me."

Gale Ann Cain's mane of shoulder-length, copper red hair contrasted sharply with the white bed linens on which she lay. Her cat-green eyes opened wide and stared upward, first at Nic and then at Griff.

She jerked her hand out of Barbara Jean's grasp, and despite the fact that both arms were connected to a series of tubes and wires, she lifted her hands in the air, palms open, fingers spread apart, then clutched her hands into fists. As quickly as she had fisted her hands, she opened them again and spread apart all ten digits.

"She keeps doing that over and over again," Barbara Jean said.

Nic moved in closer to Gale Ann and asked, "Are you trying to tell us something about your attacker?"

Gale Ann nodded and repeated the flashing fingers. Ten fingers.

"How about getting her a pad and pencil?" Griff said. "Maybe she could write it down."

"We tried that, but she can't seem to do anything except scribble," Barbara Jean explained. "And that just upset her even more."

"Ten fingers," Nic said. "The number ten?" she asked Gale Ann.

Gale Ann shook her head and repeated her flashing hands one more time.

"She's doing it twice," Griff said. "Twenty."

Gale Ann nodded.

"What does the number twenty have to do with her attacker?" Nic wondered aloud.

Gale Ann pointed to her head, slowly but surely twining her index finger around a strand of her hair.

"Your hair and the number twenty," Nic said.

"It doesn't make any sense." Barbara Jean looked from Nic to Griff, her expression one of hopelessness.

Gale Ann yanked on her hair, then pointed to the foot of the bed. When she realized that no one understood what she was trying to tell them, her actions became frantic. She grasped the ventilator tube and tried to pull it out of her throat. Barbara Jean screamed for a nurse.

"Calm down, Gale Ann," Griff said as he hovered over the bed.

Nic rushed to the cubicle entrance and cried out, "Hurry, please! Ms. Cain is trying to remove her ventilator tube."

A second too late, Griff grabbed Gale Ann's hand that held the trachea tubing she had brutally yanked from her throat. She gasped for air.

"Twenty points." She barely managed to say the two whispered words before the nurses and Dr. Clark shoved Griff out of the way. Then, Gale Ann gulped one final word, "Game."

One of the nurses shooed Griff and Nic out of the cubicle and pushed Barbara Jean's wheelchair out directly behind them. With the white curtains pulled and the door closed, they were cut off from the frantic efforts to save Gale Ann's life.

"What did she say to you?" Barbara Jean asked before Nic had a chance to ask.

"She said three words," Griff told them. "Twenty points. And game."

"Dear God!" When Nic's gaze met Griff's, she knew that they were thinking the same thing.

"Killing is a game to him," Griff said. "He must have told Gale Ann that she was worth twenty points."

Nic nodded. "She kept tugging on her hair. There has to be a connection." Nic gasped loudly. "It's because of her red hair that she was worth twenty points."

"In his sick game, redheads are worth twenty points."

Chapter 5

Lindsay and Judd arrived at Williamstown General Hospital at six-ten that evening and went straight to the intensive care unit on the second floor. As they marched straight toward the waiting area, Lindsay caught sight of Griff outside in the hallway. He stood off to the side, talking quietly with a man she recognized as Special Agent Josh Friedman, who had worked his first case with Nic Baxter and Curtis Jackson this past year. Three months ago. The last Beauty Queen Killer case: Carrie Warren. Throat slit. Tongue cut out. In the talent segment of the Miss Dixie Belle contest ten years ago, she had sung a heartrending aria from Puccini's opera, *Madama Butterfly*.

As if sensing their approach, Griff paused in his conversation and glanced down the hall. Lindsay flinched when she saw the way Griff looked at Judd. The news would not be good.

"She's dead," Judd said.

Lindsay slowed her hurried pace and glanced at Judd. "What makes you think that?"

"You saw the expression on Griff's face."

She wanted to contradict Judd, to tell him she didn't know what he meant, but what was the point in trying to give him false hope? One glimpse at Griffin Powell's tense features and she'd had the same gut reaction as Judd had. Gale Ann Cain was probably dead.

Special Agent Friedman nodded to Judd and smiled at Lindsay. "How are you Ms. McAllister?"

"Getting by," she replied. "You?"

"Yeah, about the same," Josh said. "I'm sure I'll be seeing you again soon." He turned and shook hands with Griff, then headed down the hall toward the elevators.

"The guy's got the hots for you," Judd said. "Who is he, a new Powell agent?"

Before Lindsay could reply, Griff responded. "He's Special Agent Friedman. He joined Curtis Jackson's investigative team on the last Beauty Queen Killer case. You remember Carrie Warren, don't you, Judd?"

Judd narrowed his gaze, glowering at Griff.

"You don't remember her name, do you?" Griff snorted. "Oh, that's right, you spent most of November and December drunk. How could you possibly remember anything about the last case."

"There's only one name that matters to me," Judd said. "Jennifer Walker."

Griff clenched his jaw.

Wanting to ease the growing tension between Judd and Griff, Lindsay asked, "How is Gale Ann Cain?" *Dear God, please let her be alive.*

Judd chuckled, the sound as cold as the February night.

Griff looked right at Lindsay. "She died about thirty minutes ago."

"Without identifying her killer, no doubt," Judd said.

Griff directed his gaze to Judd's bearded face. "You're

right, she didn't ID him. But she did give us some information we can use, something we didn't know about him before now."

"You've got notebooks filled with info." Grinning mockingly, Judd shook his head. "What good does new info do? What good is the profile you have of him? What good—?"

"You want me to drop this case?" Griff asked. "Just say the word and—"

"Don't feed me that line of bullshit," Judd said. "You forget, we go back a long way. I know you. You wouldn't quit this case if your life depended on it." He sneered at Lindsay. "And neither would you."

Griff glanced at Lindsay. "I've got things to do." He inclined his head toward Judd. "You keep Happy Jack here on a leash." He glowered at Judd. "If you give Lindsay any trouble, I'll—"

"He won't," Lindsay said.

Griff sighed heavily. "Gale Ann's sister found her minutes after the attack."

"Then I want to talk to the sister," Judd said.

"Not tonight," Griff told him.

"Why not tonight?"

"Damn, Judd, the woman just lost her sister."

"Yeah, and that makes her victim number what? Twenty-nine? Thirty? If I'd found Jenny only minutes after the attack, I . . ." Judd's voice trailed off. He clenched his teeth tightly and squinted his eyes as he looked at Griff. "Can she ID the guy?"

Griff clasped Judd's shoulder. "Here's the deal. I want you to leave the hospital. Lindsay will book you a local motel room for the night, or I can get Carson to drive you straight back to Tennessee right now. Or if you can behave yourself, you can come to Griffin's Rest tomorrow and meet Gale Ann's sister Barbara Jean."

Two thoughts instantly flashed through Lindsay's mind: One, she hadn't known that Griff had brought Powell agent Rick Carson to Kentucky; two, why had Barbara Jean Hughes agreed to spend a few days at Griff's home?

"Ms. Cain's sister is going to be staying with us?" Lindsay asked. How on earth had Griff managed that? *By using his powerfully persuasive charm,* she told herself. *That's how.* Griffin Powell most certainly had a way with the ladies.

"I'll bet Nic Baxter is hopping mad that you've whisked her eyewitness right out from under her nose," Judd said. "I'm sure she demanded that you back off and leave protecting a witness to the FBI."

The corners of Griff's lips twitched, a hint of amusement in the expression. "Special Agent Baxter explained to Ms. Hughes the benefits of allowing the FBI to safeguard her. But when I offered her not only the security of my home and my protection, but a job, too, Barbara Jean agreed that my offer was more acceptable to her."

Lindsay wondered just what sort of job Griff had offered the woman. Apparently, providing her a position with the Powell Agency had tipped the scales in his favor. Knowing Griff as she did, she had no doubt that he would create a position for Ms. Hughes if that's what it took to secure her safety within the Powell compound. And an added bonus would be one-upping Special Agent Baxter. Even though Curtis Jackson hadn't been happy to encounter Griff and his agents at every turn during the past three years, he and Griff had managed to remain cordial to each other. But with Nic Baxter and Griff, cordiality didn't come into play. Lindsay wondered how Griff would react if she suggested he allow her to deal with Nic during this case and for him to steer clear of the lady.

"Just answer one question for me—did the sister see the killer?" Judd asked.

Griff grimaced. "She's not sure."

"What do you mean she's not sure?"

"Look, this is not the time or the place to have this discussion."

Judd shrugged off Griff's grasp. The two men stood almost eye to eye. Judd did have to glance up a bit to make direct eye contact since Griff was a couple of inches taller.

"If you didn't want me here, why send your Girl Friday to fetch me?" Judd's upper lip curled in a snarl.

"Damn it!" Griff cursed under his breath. "If you want to take an active part in this investigation, then shape up, stay sober, and treat the people who are trying to help you as if they have feelings."

Lindsay's cheeks warmed. Griff was talking about her and they all knew it.

"And if I really just don't give a damn anymore?" Judd's tense stance eased slightly.

"You give a damn," Griff told him. "If you didn't, you wouldn't be here. So listen up—stop wallowing in self-pity and start acting like a civilized human being."

Judd bristled. Lindsay could all but hear the thundering roar of anger rushing through his body. She braced herself for the worst.

Without warning, the sound of soft weeping caught their attention, and for a split second Lindsay was grateful that something—anything—had diffused the mounting tension between the two men. The last thing she wanted was to have to put herself between Griff and Judd.

Nic Baxter escorted an auburn-haired, wheelchair-bound woman out of the ICU waiting room. Barbara Jean Hughes held her head high as she patted her damp cheeks with a handkerchief that Lindsay instantly recognized as one of Griffin Powell's. The large embroidered black "P" on the edge of the expensive linen was a dead giveaway.

As the FBI agent and the victim's sister approached, Lindsay studied Barbara Jean. Attractive, but not classically pretty. Neat. Slender. Delicate. Probably in her early forties.

In contrast, Nic was tall—very tall—with an Amazonian, hourglass-shaped body, and was a decade younger than the other woman. One thing for sure, no one would ever use the word delicate to describe Special Agent Nicole Baxter.

"That's the sister, right?" Judd said, and before anyone realized his intentions, he stepped directly in front of Barbara Jean's wheelchair and confronted her. "Did you see him? Can you can give us a description of the man who killed your sister, the same man who killed my Jenny?" Judd leaned down, grasped the arms of her wheelchair and demanded, "If you don't help us now, he'll kill another woman before we can stop him. Is that what you want?"

Reacting immediately, Nic Baxter came around the side of the wheelchair, straight toward Judd. But before she could reach him, Griff clamped his hands down on Judd's shoulders and yanked him away from Barbara Jean. She stared wide-eyed and mouth agape at the man who had accosted her.

Judd jerked free, barreled around, and lifted his fists to attack Griff. Acting purely on instinct, Lindsay stepped in between the two big men. From out of nowhere, Rick Carson appeared behind Griff. Apparently, he had been only a few steps behind Nic and Barbara Jean.

Griff bristled. The skin tightened over his sharp cheekbones and his ice blue eyes squinched with anger.

Judd froze to the spot and glared at Lindsay, her intervention acting as the deterrent she had hoped it would. Apparently, Judd wasn't so far gone that he would actually resort to hitting her.

"Get Mr. Walker under control or I will," Nic told Griff.

Griff motioned for Lindsay to move, then when she did, he locked his fierce gaze to Judd's. "Is that what you want? You want to be taken into custody by the FBI?"

Judd didn't respond verbally, simply loosened his tightly fisted hands and relaxed his battle-ready stance.

Observing Judd's withdrawal, Griff spoke to Lindsay, "Carson will take over and get him out of here. You'll fly home with me."

When Rick Carson came forward, Judd backed away, and Lindsay feared another confrontation. But Rick made no move to touch Judd, who seemed more than ready to cause an even worse scene in the hospital corridor.

Lindsay moved closer to Griff in order to speak privately with him. "Let me take care of Judd. He's less likely to resist going with me than he is if you try to send him with Rick."

"It's obvious that Judd's emotional and mental stability has worsened," Griff said. "He's dangerous now."

"I know," she replied. "But he's more dangerous to himself than to anyone else."

"Are you sure?"

"I'm sure." She had never lied to Griff, and she wasn't actually lying now. She wanted to believe that Judd did not pose a physical threat to her, despite knowing that he still possessed the power to destroy her emotionally.

Griff nodded. "Be careful."

"I will."

Griff then turned to Barbara Jean Hughes, bent down on his haunches, and clasped the woman's hands. "I'm sorry about what happened. That man is the one I told you about, my old friend who's been half out of his mind since the Beauty Queen Killer murdered his wife almost four years ago."

Meek as a lamb, Judd left the hospital with Lindsay. His submissive attitude worried her far more than if he'd been openly belligerent. She tried to think of something to say to him, but she came up blank. When they walked outside, the cold night air blasted them the minute the hospital doors closed behind them. She paused long enough to button her coat before heading to the parking deck.

Judd lifted his face to the wind, as if he liked the feel of the bitter cold. "So, what now, my little savior?" he asked, the tone of his voice strangely amicable.

Looking over the parking lot in front of them, an area reserved for doctors and VIPs, Lindsay succinctly explained her plan. "We're going to find a decent restaurant and eat supper. Then we're getting a couple of rooms at a local motel for tonight. Come morning, we're going back to Tennessee." She removed her gloves from her coat pocket and slipped them on. "I can either drive you back to the hunting lodge and dump your sorry ass off, and leave you to drown in self-pity . . ." She paused, expecting a snide remark of some type. When he didn't respond, she continued, "Or if you can behave yourself, I'll take you to Griff's and you can be part of our investigation again, the way you were in the beginning."

"Either or, huh?"

"Take it or leave it." Uncertain what Judd would do, she headed toward the two-level parking deck on the west side of the hospital.

He caught up with her before she reached her Trailblazer parked on the bottom level. "I'd like a big, juicy steak for supper. How about you?"

Lindsay released a deep breath. She hadn't known for sure how he would react to her issuing orders and giving him an ultimatum. Relieved by the normalcy in his voice, she replied, "A steak sounds great."

When she clicked the unlock button on the remote device attached to her key chain, Judd came around to the driver's side and opened the door for her. His gentlemanly action surprised her, so much so that she gasped and then glanced over her shoulder.

"I'm just showing you that I can be a good boy," Judd

said, smiling. But his smoky topaz eyes remained void of any real emotion.

She nodded. "If I take you home with me to Griff's place—"

"I'll behave myself."

"If you don't . . ." *No, don't issue him another warning. Just tell him exactly what's what.* "Griff's your friend, or at least he's tried to be. But you haven't made it easy. If you screw up this time, it will be the last time as far as Griff is concerned. You've used up all your second chances with him."

"What about you? Are you ready to wash your hands of me, too?"

Lindsay got inside her SUV, slid behind the wheel, and glanced up at Judd, who stood by the open door. "If you want me to help you one more time, let's not make it personal."

"If that's what you want."

"It's what I want."

He nodded, then closed the door, rounded the back of the vehicle, and got in on the passenger side. Once seated and belted, Judd said, "It should never have gotten personal between us. You're too nice a girl to get hung up on a guy like me. I've got nothing to offer you and I never will. You know that, don't you?"

Lindsay started the engine. Clutching the steering wheel with white-knuckled force, she closed her eyes for a millisecond, then said, "I know. You've made it abundantly clear, more than once."

She backed out of the parking place and headed the Trailblazer into the late evening traffic.

Griff had told Rick Carson to stay in Williamstown and stick close to Lindsay, to be prepared to move in and protect her from Judd if it became necessary. Although he'd known

Judd a lot longer than Lindsay had—and maybe because he
had—he didn't trust his old friend's emotional and mental
stability these days. Despite enduring everything he'd put
her through during the past three and a half years—like a
real trooper—Lindsay couldn't take much more. When everyone else had given up on Judd, she hadn't. And now, once
again, she'd persuaded Griff to give the guy another chance
to straighten up and fly right.

God, he hoped her faith in Judd wasn't misplaced.

"We need to talk," Nic Baxter said, as she came toward
Griff, a scowl on her face. A really pretty face. Too bad all
that feminine lusciousness was wasted on a hard-as-nails,
completely unlikable bitch.

The woman was relentless. She had followed them to the
airport. What part of Barbara Jean's I'm-going-with-Mr. Powell
statement didn't she understand?

Give her some slack, he told himself. Baxter's just doing
her job. Curtis Jackson would be doing the same thing. He'd
keep trying to persuade Barbara Jean to accept FBI protection instead of flying off in the night with the owner of a private security firm. It wouldn't have mattered to Curtis any
more than it mattered to Nic that Griff could provide twenty-
four-hour-a-day protection for Barbara Jean, as well as give
her a job to keep her occupied and her mind off the fact that
she was a key witness.

"Give it up, Baxter," Griff said as Nic approached him.
"Ms. Hughes has made her decision."

With a hint of pink in her cheeks—a sign of her barely controlled anger—Nic huffed loudly. A very unladylike sound.

"I understand that you want to nail this guy every bit as
much as I do, but you have to know that your interference
creates problems," Nic said. "I can't name a specific, but what
if your involvement—your agency's involvement—somehow
has already jeopardized this case? Why can't you just back
off and let us do our job?"

"My agency has done nothing to jeopardize your case," Griff said. "I've made sure of that. Besides, there have been a few instances when we've actually helped you, given you information you didn't have."

Nic rolled her big brown eyes. "If anything happens to Barbara Jean—"

"Nothing will happen to her."

"You can't be sure of—"

"Neither could you. But I think she'd much prefer living and working on my estate to being hidden away in a safe house somewhere."

"That was the clincher—the job offer. Money talks, doesn't it, Mr. Powell?"

"Is that why you dislike me so much—because I'm rich?"

Nic grunted. "I dislike the fact that you use your money to get what you want."

"No, that's not it. You dislike me, not my money and power."

"Off the record, just between the two of us?" She eyed him hostilely.

"Off the record, tell me exactly what you think."

"I think you are an annoying, know-it-all, arrogant bastard."

Griff chuckled. "And, off the record, Nicole Baxter, you're a self-righteous, irritating, wish-you-were-a-man bitch."

She simply stared at him for a full minute, then smiled. Her smile took him by surprise. There was something damned appealing about her when she smiled, something blatantly feminine.

"When Barbara Jean is ready to work with a sketch artist—" Nic said.

"I'll call you."

"Before or after you hire your own sketch artist?"

"After," he admitted. "Of course, if you were willing to

share with me the way I share with you, it wouldn't be necessary."

"You know it's against the rules."

"And you never break the rules?"

"No. Never."

Griff leaned down so that they were eye to eye and whispered, "Never say never, honey."

Pinkie had rented a late model Chevrolet, something inconspicuous so that hopefully no one would remember either him or his car. And he'd dressed in a pair of jeans, a plaid shirt, and a quilted jacket he'd bought at Wal-Mart. He hoped he looked like an average Joe.

He needed to learn the reason why there had been no recent updates in the local or national news about the vicious attack on Gale Ann Cain; so he had decided the best thing he could do was find out for himself by coming to Williamstown. Incognito.

Where better to pick up local gossip than the town's Waffle House? When he'd parked outside, he'd seen a police car and hesitated coming inside. But after reminding himself that he had nothing to fear from the local lawmen, he entered the greasy spoon as if he were just a regular guy passing through town. As luck would have it, he managed to find a booth directly behind the two patrolmen who were eating a late dinner.

A tall, skinny waitress with chopped-off blond hair, streaked with purple and pink, refilled the two cops' coffee cups, then stopped at his table.

"Want coffee?" She eyed his overturned cup.

He quickly righted the cup, smiled at her, and said, "Yes, please."

After filling the cup to the rim, she said, "Do you know what you want?"

"Uh . . ." He glanced around and saw the menu was on the table. "What would you recommend?" He smiled at the girl whose name tag read *Tammy*.

"Depends. Do you want breakfast, a sandwich, or a regular dinner?"

"Breakfast. Maybe bacon and eggs."

"Sure thing. Toast, too? Wheat or white?"

"White."

"Scrambled eggs?"

He nodded.

When she left to place his order, he added creamer and sugar to the dark coffee as he listened to the roaring hum of human voices mingling with the clatter of dishes and meal preparation. No doubt the food here would be horrible, nowhere close to his usual standards, but if he could pick up even a tidbit of local gossip about the recent murder, it would be well worth him having to go slumming.

The two policemen were discussing basketball, something Pinkie knew absolutely nothing about. He had always hated sports. Physical Education had been his least favorite subject in Hobart Military School.

The waitress returned to the booth where the policemen sat, two dinner plates in her hands. She placed the hot meals in front of the cops, but instead of leaving, she lingered, apparently flirting with the one she called Mike.

"So, has it been a quiet night?" she asked.

"Yeah, pretty quiet," Mike replied.

"Folks aren't getting out much since that Cain woman was attacked," the other cop said.

Smiling to himself, Pinkie picked up the coffee mug.

"Wasn't that just awful?" Tammy said. "You know, a Licensed Practical Nurse from over at Williamstown General was in here yesterday, and she said she heard the guy chopped off Gale Ann Cain's feet. Is that true?"

"I wouldn't know," Mike said. "That's stuff we aren't supposed to discuss with civilians."

"I understand. I just think it's odd that since Chief Mahoney made a statement a couple of days ago, there hasn't been another word about it on the local TV or in the paper. If that nurse hadn't told us any different, we wouldn't know the Cain woman was still alive."

Pinkie's hand shook so badly that coffee sloshed out of the cup and onto his fingers. He set the cup down and wiped his hand off with a paper napkin, all the while hoping no one had noticed.

"Not anymore, she isn't," Mike said.

"She died?" The waitress gasped.

"Hush up, Mike. You shouldn't be telling Tammy anything about the case."

"It's not a secret," Mike said. "The chief will be making an announcement sometime tonight."

Pinkie's heart stopped for a split second. Gale Ann Cain had lived? How was that possible? She should have bled to death rather quickly. Unless the person who had found her had gotten to her damn fast and somehow managed to keep her alive.

But what difference did any of that make now? The woman was dead.

Pinkie picked up his cup and took a sip of the bitter coffee.

"I hope she was able to give the police a description of the guy before she died," Tammy said.

Mike lowered his voice to a soft whisper. "Keep this strictly to yourself, Tammy." The waitress nodded, her eyes bright with anticipation. "The Cain woman wasn't able to ID her attacker, but they say her sister saw him and might be able to give the FBI a description."

Pinkie strangled on the god-awful coffee. Of all the local

gossip he had hoped to overhear, he'd never expected this tidbit of information. The sister? Pinkie's mind whirled, trying to make sense of what he'd just overheard. Then it hit him. Had the sister been the woman in the wheelchair, the woman who had caught a glimpse of him as he left Gale Ann's apartment building?

Chapter 6

Sonya Todd had been born and raised in Tupelo, Mississippi, so it was only natural that once she received a degree from the University of Mississippi, she would return home. It was what everyone had expected, including Sonya. But what should have been a quick and easy route from college graduation to a teaching position at her old alma mater, Tupelo High School, had instead been a long, disappointing ten-year struggle to achieve an impossible dream. She often wondered how different her life might have turned out if she hadn't won the title of Miss Magnolia. Would she have forsaken her dream of becoming a teacher to pursue a career as a concert violinist?

What was that old saying about hindsight being twenty-twenty? All the "if onlys" in the world wouldn't change a damn thing. She would never be twenty-two again. Never know that feeling of being on top of the world. But at this stage of her life, she felt lucky to have been given a second chance and she appreciated what she had now.

Being the band director at Tupelo High for the past two years, Sonya went to work each day with a positive attitude and a grateful heart. She was finally back home where she belonged, living only a couple of miles from her parents and in the same county as her two older brothers, their wives, and children. And for the first time since her divorce from Tom Harding, she was seriously dating.

Sonya glanced over at Tupelo High's baseball coach, Paul Dryer, and smiled. Like she, Paul was divorced, no children and at thirty-nine, he was ready to settle down. Sonya, too, was ready for a long-term commitment, even remarriage one of these days. She wanted kids, too, and it wasn't as if being thirty-five meant she had to rush into motherhood. Women past forty were giving birth to first babies every day, weren't they?

"The jazz band is fantastic," Paul said as he turned his vintage Mustang into Sonya's driveway. "They sounded downright professional at tonight's concert."

"I've got a bunch of really talented kids in that band. I expect each of my seniors to win scholarships."

"They all love you, you know. They want you to be proud of them."

When Paul killed the engine, he turned to Sonya, a hopeful look in his soulful hazel eyes. As she gazed at him there in the semidarkness, with light from the nearby streetlight casting shadows across his smooth-shaven face, she thought what a nice face he had. Not handsome. Not really good-looking at all. Nothing to remind her of Tom Harding, who'd been far too handsome. No, Paul was nothing like her ex-husband.

Paul was a giant-size teddy bear, with thinning brown hair, hound-dog cheeks, and a pair of big, broad shoulders she could always lean on. He was, without a doubt, one of the good guys. Like her dad. Like her brothers, Charlie and Brady.

"Want to come in for some decaf coffee or herbal tea?" Sonya knew that Paul understood she was inviting him in for more than drinks and conversation. They had been dating since the beginning of the school year, but they hadn't taken their relationship into the bedroom, not once in six months. Her choice. She appreciated the fact that he had been patient and understanding, but how long could she expect him to wait?

"Are you sure?" Paul asked.

Smiling, she nodded. "I'm sure."

Grinning like an idiot, albeit a sweet idiot, Paul jumped out of the car, raced around the hood and opened the passenger door. Before she knew what was happening, he yanked her out and onto her feet, then planted a wet, sloppy kiss on her mouth.

Laughing, she pulled away and looked up at the big galoot. "If you don't want coffee or tea, I have beer. Your favorite brand."

"Let's save the beer for later." He winked at her, then draped his arm around her shoulders and rushed her toward the porch.

"Slow down. I can't keep up with you. Your legs are much longer than mine."

Chuckling, Paul stopped, swept her up into his arms and carried her straight to her front door.

This felt so right. Being with Paul. Loving Paul. Planning a future with Paul.

He supposed he could wait a little longer, a few more days, even a few more weeks. But time was running out. Less than two months and the game would end. The points were adding up, the last kill worth twenty points.

A redhead. Damn, what luck!

Thirty women. All former beauty queens. All still attractive. Blondes, brunettes, and redheads.

He sighed as memories of his most recent kill replayed in his mind, like a technicolor movie. Red blood. Creamy, soft skin. Rich, royal blue carpet.

What an utterly delicious game. A brilliant plan from the very beginning. A part of him would hate to see it end. But no game was meant to be played indefinitely. Sooner or later someone had to win. And someone had to lose.

He had no intention of losing.

You can't rest on your laurels. Being overconfident can result in defeat. We can't have that, can we?

Time to choose another victim. If he could find another redhead . . . A blonde would do. Fifteen points would be enough. For now.

Turning around in the oxblood leather swivel chair at his Jacobean desk, he faced the computer screen and typed in the password that would open a very secret file.

With a sense of anticipation, he watched as the file opened and the list of twenty names, addresses, and personal information appeared on the nineteen-inch screen. Ten names in all. It had taken endless hours of research to find ten perfect candidates. Such a pity that there wouldn't be time to kill all of them.

Pick and choose. Pick and choose.

Which pretty flower shall I pick today?

There was only one redhead on the list.

Save her for later, just in case you need twenty points closer to the end of the game.

Five brunettes and four blondes.

A blonde this time. Definitely a blonde.

Shelly Hall. Ashley Gray. Sonya Todd. Heather Johnson.

Tapping his index finger against his chin, an amused tilt to his lips, he studied the profiles of each of the four blondes. Then he lifted his finger to the screen and counted off, eeney-meeny-miney-mo.

Griffin's plane landed shortly before eleven that evening. As instructed, Sanders had brought the limo and was waiting for them. Griff relied on Sanders in a way he relied on no other human being. He trusted Damar Sanders with his life. He could say that of no other man. Not even his old UT teammate, Jim Norton, or his former playboy friend, Judd Walker. A stint in the belly of hell could unite two men in a way nothing else could.

"Good evening, ma'am," Sanders spoke respectfully to Barbara Jean Hughes as Griff stopped her wheelchair at the right rear door.

"Hello." Barbara Jean openly stared at Sanders, not an uncommon reaction upon first meeting the extraordinary man.

"I'm Sanders, ma'am," he said.

"Pleased to meet you, Mr. Sanders."

"This, of course, is Ms. Hughes," Griff said.

"Please, call me Barbara Jean," she told Sanders.

He simply nodded.

"I'll lift you up and into the car," Griff said. "And don't be alarmed. One of my agents, Angie Sterling, is inside the limo. Angie will be one of your private bodyguards while you're our guest."

Barbara Jean's eyes widened in surprise. She gulped softly, then nodded. "Thank you. I—I appreciate everything. I really do. It's just I never imagined I'd ever be in this position and need a bodyguard. I may be a paraplegic, but I'm not helpless. I have great upper body strength, you know. I manage to live alone and can get in and out of my wheelchair without assistance. I hold down a job and can take a taxi wherever I need to go."

"We hope you won't need a bodyguard for very long and can return home soon," Griff said. "But while you do, we'll keep you so busy that you just might forget you have a guardian angel keeping watch over you."

Sanders opened the door. Griff lifted Barbara Jean into his arms and placed her inside the limousine. Griff closed the door; then Sanders folded the wheelchair and put it in the trunk.

"Are we ready to go?" Sanders asked.

Griff nodded. "Yes, and when we get inside, lift the privacy window. I have some phone calls to make and I'd rather Ms. Hughes not be bothered."

Thirty minutes later, they arrived at what many called the Powell Compound. Actually, the estate, with part of the acreage on Douglas Lake, had a name: Griffin's Rest.

Two massive stone arches flanked the locked gates, which Sanders opened electronically from within the limo. Bronze griffins, the mythological beast with the head, forepart, and wings of an eagle and the body, hind legs, and tail of a lion, had been imbedded into the stonework of both arches. The winding paved road from the highway to the house passed through a thickly wooded area before opening up to a lakefront vista. Griffin's home itself was not enormous, merely ten-thousand square feet and two stories high, but there were other buildings on the property, including a barn, stables, and three guest cottages. He supposed his estate was a compound, of sorts. Without a doubt, it was a secure area, monitored around the clock, both with surveillance equipment and manpower.

Tonight the gray snow clouds obscured the half-moon, leaving only the limo's headlights to illuminate the road. Griffin had checked in with Rick Carson and his "friend" in D.C., getting all his ducks in a row before arriving home.

Home.

He supposed Griffin's Rest was as much of a home as a man such as he would ever have. These sprawling acres in northeast Tennessee provided him with privacy, giving him a sanctuary from the world when he chose to leave business and the social scene behind him. As for family—Sanders was his brother, in spirit if not in blood. And during the past few years, he had come to think of Lindsay as his kid sister, although she did not—and never could—know the man he truly was.

As Sanders pulled the limousine up in front of the two-story portico, Griffin glanced into the back and saw that Barbara Jean Hughes had fallen asleep. He made eye contact with Angie, who nodded in understanding. Griffin had instructed Sanders to provide a mild sedative for Angie to place in a thermos of hot tea that she would provide for Ms. Hughes. He wanted his special visitor to rest, to get the first full night's sleep she'd had in more than forty-eight hours.

Sanders turned to Griffin. "Ms. Hughes's room is ready. Do you want me to take her in and put her to bed?"

"Yes, please," Griff replied, knowing that Sanders would see to it that one of the staff members took care of the limo. "And make sure Angie understands that she is to keep watch over our guest until she is relieved by another agent in the morning."

Griff emerged from the limo and went directly to the front door. He punched in the code, which was changed periodically for security reasons. After opening the double doors, he walked into the foyer, leaving the doors open behind him. Instead of going upstairs and directly to bed, he entered the room on the left, a two-story den, with a rock fireplace large enough that, if he so chose, he could walk right inside it. He went straight to the liquor cabinet, retrieved a crystal tumbler, and a bottle of The Macallan, a vintage single malt whiskey. Taking bottle and glass with him, he went over and placed both on the silver tray that topped the old tea table in front of the forest green leather sofa. He removed his coat, gloves, and scarf, then sat on the sofa and took off his shoes.

Sighing heavily, he gazed into the blaze glowing in the massive fireplace. His orders were that, in winter, a fire be kept burning in this fireplace day and night. He often slept here on this sofa. That's one reason, when he had special-ordered it, he had requested a seven-foot length. He had a perfectly fine bed upstairs in his suite. King-size. Egyptian cotton sheets that felt like silk to the touch. But more often than not, he found it impossible to rest in his own bed.

After pouring himself half a tumbler of the fine old Highland Scotch whiskey, he leaned back, burying his shoulders into the sofa, and took a hefty swig from the glass.

Life was never what it seemed to be. People were never who you thought they were. He would give every penny of his immense fortune if he could erase ten years of his life. Ten years when he had faced death and lived, been sent to hell and survived, played the devil's game and won.

Lindsay's cell phone rang. She rushed out of the bathroom, where she was brushing her teeth, and hurried into the bedroom to pick up the phone off the dresser. After checking the caller ID, she blew out a what-do-I-tell-him? breath and flipped open the phone.

"Good morning, Griff."

"I didn't wake you, did I?"

"No, I've been up about thirty minutes, had my shower, and am dressed and ready for the day."

"Where's Judd?"

"In the room next to mine," she replied. "Or at least that's where I left him last night around nine-thirty, after we had a late supper."

"How was he when you left him?"

"Sober."

"I guess that's something."

"I want to bring him to Griffin's Rest later today," she said. "Are you okay with that?"

"I'm not sure. Do you think it's a good idea?"

"I think Judd needs to be part of the investigation again.

No matter how low he's sunk—and I admit he's just about hit rock bottom—he still wants to find his wife's killer. Finding Jenny Walker's murderer is the only thing he has to live for. We can't take that away from him."

"Nobody took anything away from him," Griff said. "What's happened to Judd, he did to himself."

"Yeah. I know. Judd is his own worst enemy."

"If the guy had a lick of sense, he'd wake up and realize he has a lot more to live for than revenge against Jenny's killer."

"Don't go there, Griff. There's no point."

Silence.

"Will you let me bring him to Griffin's Rest?" she asked.

"There's something you need to know, something I want you to tell Judd and see how he reacts, then you decide if you should bring him here."

"And if he reacts badly?"

"I guess you know that Carson has been assigned to watch your back."

Lindsay smiled to herself as she crossed the room, pulled back the edge of the drapes, and looked outside. Rick Carson's car was parked next to her Trailblazer. He was inside behind the wheel and appeared to be asleep. It was so like Griff to worry about her. To protect her.

Maybe she shouldn't have told him what happened between Judd and her last year.

"I know when I'm being tailed." She let the drapes fall back into place. "Rick's parked outside. He didn't have to sleep in his car last night."

Griff chuckled.

"So, what do I need to know? What do you want me to tell Judd?"

"Barbara Jean says she can't ID the man she saw coming out of her sister's apartment building just as she was going in, only moments before she discovered Gale Ann bleeding to death. She claims she didn't get an up-close-and-personal look, but I think, if we're patient and understanding with her, she'll eventually be able to give a halfway decent description to a sketch artist."

Lindsay let out a long, low whistle.

"How do you think Judd will react to this news?" Griff asked.

How would Judd react? Would the news give him hope? Would it whet his appetite for revenge? Could he wait and give Barbara Jean Hughes the time she needed to admit to herself that she could indeed ID her sister's killer?

"I honestly don't know how he will react," Lindsay said. "I don't know Judd anymore. I'm not sure I ever really knew him."

"There are other men out there, you know. Someone who would appreciate you for the wonderful woman you are."

Griff's words created a tight knot in her belly, the one that formed whenever she thought about her feelings for Judd Walker. "Look, I don't have any false hopes where Judd's concerned. I know that he'll never love anyone except Jenny."

"He doesn't even love her anymore. Judd isn't capable of human emotions, other than hatred and revenge."

"I know."

"I shouldn't have sent you out on this case, but I thought . . . Hell, I don't know what I thought, maybe that you needed to confront your demons, conquer them, and walk away a stronger person."

"Watch out, Griffin Powell. You're on the verge of exposing your soft underbelly, and you don't want to do that, do you?"

"You know me too well."

"Not really. I don't think anyone knows the real you."

"If you change your mind, hand Judd over to Carson, and come on home alone."

"Is there anything else I need to know, anything else I should tell Judd?"

When Griff didn't respond immediately, she realized that there was more. "Griff?"

"Killing is a game to him." Griff paused. "Redheads are worth twenty points. Gale Ann was able to tell us that much before she died."

"Son of a bitch." Information swirled through Lindsay's mind. She discarded some facts and categorized others. "The roses! A yellow rose for each redhead. A pink rose for each blonde and a red rose for each brunette. We figured that out about a dozen murders ago. Now we know he's using a point system. Twenty for redheads. How much for a blonde? For a brunette? Oh, God, Griff, how many points was Jennifer Walker worth?"

Judd ordered a large breakfast—three scrambled eggs, a stack of pancakes, hash browns, and both bacon and sausage. He ate ravenously as if he were starving to death. Lindsay picked at her French toast while she watched in fascination as her companion devoured his meal. The local Waffle House had been the closest restaurant that served breakfast and since the place suited Judd, it suited her. She mostly wanted some strong black coffee. She hadn't slept more than three hours last night, so it was either prop toothpicks under her eyelids to keep them open or get a wake-up boost from caffeine.

"You're not eating." Judd eyed her plate.

"I need to ask you something."

Judd sliced off a hunk from his stack of pancakes, put them in his mouth and chewed, then washed the food down with a big gulp of coffee. He looked right at Lindsay. "So ask."

"How badly do you want to be part of the Powell Agency's investigation into the Beauty Queen Killer murders?"

Judd shrugged.

"I'm serious. If you want to go to Griffin's Rest with me,

you have to convince me that we can trust you not to come unraveled."

Judd chuckled.

The cold, unemotional sound chilled Lindsay.

"Griffin believes, if given enough time, once she feels completely safe, Barbara Jean Hughes can work with a sketch artist to identify the man she saw coming out of her sister's apartment."

Judd gripped his fork so fiercely that he actually bent it half in two. As if suddenly realizing what he'd done, he dropped the fork. It fell from his hand onto the floor, clanging against the tiled surface.

"She cannot be pushed," Lindsay told him. "She can't be bullied. Do you understand?"

His dark eyes glazed, his mind only God knew where, Judd nodded.

"There's more," Lindsay said.

"Tell me."

"Before she died, Gale Ann was able to tell Griff that killing is a game to this man." She checked Judd's face for a reaction. Deadly calm.

"Go on."

"Gale Ann said that killing her was worth twenty points to him because she had red hair."

Silence.

Judd stared at her—not really at her but through her—his jungle cat yellow gaze transfixed on something he could see only in his mind's eye.

"Judd?"

He didn't respond.

She reached out to touch him at the same moment the waitress came over to refill their coffee cups.

"Either of you need a refill?" the middle-age woman asked.

The waitress's question apparently snapped Judd out of

his mental fog. He pulled away from Lindsay's approaching touch, as if he couldn't bear the thought of her hand on his.

"Yeah, thanks," Judd told the waitress. "Fill 'er up."

As soon as the waitress finished refilling their cups and moved on to the customers in the next booth, Lindsay asked, "Are you all right?"

"Yeah, sure. Why wouldn't I be?"

He wasn't all right, and they both knew it.

"Do you want to go to Griffin's Rest with me and become an active member of the team again?" Lindsay asked. "If you do, then you have to promise me you can act like a civilized human being."

"Did Griff leave the decision up to you about whether to take me at my word or not?"

"Yes."

"And if I swear to you that I can behave myself, that I won't run around like a madman and scare the bejesus out of Ms. Hughes, will you believe me?"

"Yes. If you'll be completely honest with me about something else, too."

"What?"

"Tell me where your mind went, what you were thinking there a few minutes ago when I told you that killing was a game to this guy and that he was using some sort of insane points system."

"You know what I was thinking."

"Say it out loud."

"How many points was my Jenny worth to him?" Judd glared at her. "Is that what you wanted to hear?"

"Yes."

Judd wiped his mouth with his napkin, crumbled it in his fist, and tossed it atop his empty plate. "Can we go now?"

"Sure." She picked up the tab, left a generous tip, and headed for the cash register.

Chapter 7

He had spent the night at an inexpensive motel in Jackson, used a phony ID, and paid in cash. As he so often did on the morning of a "kill," he woke early, eager to play the game once again. The drive from the state's capital to Tupelo had been uneventful, the stretch of Interstate 55 between Jackson and Batesville desolate and dull. He'd used Highway 278 to go from Oxford to Tupelo, a medium-sized Mississippi city.

In the past, he had taken more time to study the pretty little flower before he severed her life-giving stem. But that had been in the beginning, when time had been of no importance and the years stretched before him, seemingly endless.

Odd how that five years could pass so quickly. He supposed the old adage about time flying when you were having fun was true. What had begun as a lark had turned into a passion far greater and all-consuming than he could have ever imagined. Who knew that life-and-death game-playing could be so exhilarating?

Participating in "The Dying Game" gave him a high unlike anything he'd ever experienced. And it was as addictive as any of the drugs he had experimented with over the years.

He hated to see it all come to an end, but the game would be over in less than two months. And he intended to be the winner. His life depended on it.

As he drove the Ford Taurus—rented using his fake ID—along the street where Sonya Todd lived, he recalled the information he had collected on her. She was thirty-five, divorced, no children, and lived alone. She was the high school band director, but since this was Saturday and no band contests were scheduled for Tupelo High, there was a good chance she would be at home.

Should he make contact with her today? Introduce himself into her life as a nonthreatening stranger? Or should he simply study her from afar during the day and wait for the perfect moment later on, perhaps tonight, to surprise her?

During the long, boring drive here, he had worked up a couple of different scenarios. His favorite was simply to ring her doorbell, introduce himself, and ask about houses for sale in the neighborhood. If there was one thing he knew how to do—and do well—it was playact. As a youngster, he had entertained his sisters with his antics, keeping them amused so that they wouldn't torment him with their teasing: Rolypoly. Fatty-fatty. Pudgy-wudgy.

He had learned how to turn their taunting into self-inflicting jokes that endeared him to Mary Ann and Marsha. They considered him a funny little brother. Fat and rosy-cheeked. Easily manipulated. Mary Ann never knew that he'd been the one who had poisoned her pet cat, Mr. Mackerel. And Marsha still thought one of the servants had stolen her prom dress, the one their mother had bought on a shopping spree in Paris. But he knew better. That dress, which he'd ripped to shreds, was buried in the woods near their family home, along with the bones of numerous small animals he had taken great pleasure in torturing to death.

He didn't see much of either sister these days, only at weddings, funerals, and an occasional holiday. Both had married well, reproduced darling little brats like themselves, and lived in the same type of social whirlwind their mother had thrived on.

Reciting Sonya Todd's street numbers in his mind, he slowed the car almost to a standstill when he came to 322. A woman wearing hot pink sweats and man in a heavy jacket stood on the front porch, holding hands, looking dreamily into each other's eyes. The hulk of a man kissed the woman, then headed down the steps onto the sidewalk. When he was halfway to the SUV parked in the drive, he glanced over his shoulder, grinned and waved. The woman blew him a kiss, then waved back at the guy.

Guess that big oaf got lucky last night.

Naughty, naughty of you, my little pink rose.

The midthirties' Sonya Todd bore a striking resemblance to the young woman in the old Miss Magnolia photograph he had brought with him. Still slender and shapely. Still a blonde, although the shade was now darker, richer, more golden. But a blonde was a blonde, be she platinum or dishwater. And every blonde was worth fifteen points. Killing Sonya would put him in the lead, one step closer to winning the game.

He drove past Sonya's house and glanced from right to left, as if he were searching for a street address. Then he circled the block slowly, giving her boyfriend time to leave. When he returned to 322, as luck would have it, Sonya walked out into her yard to pick up the morning newspaper. He eased the Taurus to a halt, rolled down the window, and called to her.

"Good morning, ma'am."

She looked directly at him and smiled. "Morning."

"Could I trouble you for just a minute?"

"Sure, what can I do to help you?"

"Well, I'm heading home after a business trip here in Tupelo." He stayed in the car, maintaining his distance so as not to alarm her. "It looks like I'll be transferring here, and I thought I'd take a look at some of the newer housing developments. This area looks like someplace my wife and kids would just love."

"Tupelo is a fantastic place to live, and Pine Crest Estates is one of 'the' places to live if you're an up-and-coming young professional family."

"What about the school system?" he asked. "I've got ten-year-old twins."

Sonya smiled. What a lovely smile. It was nice to see a woman who didn't let herself go just because she was past thirty.

Such a sweet, friendly lady. Unsuspecting. She had no idea that she was conversing with the man who had come to town expressly to add her to his collection of pretty flowers. Pretty dead flowers.

As she rubbed her hands up and down her arms in an effort to warm herself from the chilly air, she walked to the edge of her driveway. And while she talked, telling him that she was the high school band director and that the school system in the area was one of the best, if not *the* best in the state, he noticed how she used her hands as she spoke. Long fingers. Sculptured pink nails.

She was a violinist, wasn't she? She'd even had aspirations of being a concert violinist. Unfortunately, her talent was limited, and she had never reached the heights of success about which she had once dreamed.

As he studied those beautiful, animated hands, he thought about tonight and how he would hack off those slender hands she used to play the violin in such a mediocre way. Actually, he would probably chop off both of her arms entirely.

Judd adjusted the passenger seat to recline slightly, closed his eyes, and dozed off not long after they crossed the Kentucky state line and entered Tennessee. When he awoke, he glanced out the side window and realized they were going through Knoxville. Roadwork seemed to be the norm in this city. Expansion always creates the need for bigger and better. He hazarded a quick glimpse at Lindsay. Focused on the heavy traffic, she didn't glance his way.

Judd closed his eyes again.

It was better for both of them if Lindsay thought he was still sleeping. That way neither of them had to make an effort at conversation. From the very beginning of their relationship, things had been strained between them. Now more so than ever.

Judd grunted silently.

Relationship? Could you actually call whatever existed between them a relationship? They weren't friends or lovers. Nor were they enemies. But if he was completely honest with himself, he'd have to admit that he often hated Lindsay. She didn't deserve his hatred; she had done nothing to warrant such an extreme reaction from him. For a man whose emotions were pretty much dead, the very fact that Lindsay could elicit any emotion from him bothered him on a gut-deep level.

Each new murder—now totaling twenty-nine that they knew of—evoked thoughts of those first few weeks after his wife had been killed. Last night in the Williamstown motel, he'd been unable to rest. Memories of his Jenny had plagued him.

And thoughts of Lindsay.

Yeah, thoughts of Lindsay McAllister.

He'd spent nearly four years telling himself that the reason his recollections about those first few horrific days, weeks, and months after Jennifer was murdered centered as much on Lindsay as they did on Jenny was because Lindsay had been involved with the murder case on a day-to-day basis. She'd been partnered with the lead detective.

He knew she'd been there that night at the scene of Jennifer's murder when he barged in like a madman. But to him that evening was little more than a blurred nightmare. Even now, he could still feel the deadweight of Jenny's slender body as he sat on the floor and held her in his arms. Not all the time in the world would ever erase that bloody scene from his mind. Jenny's hands lying beside her, her perfectly manicured nails a bright coral. He had loved her hands, those long fingers that stroked the piano keys with such expert ease.

Odd how he could now think about her, even about her brutal murder, and not get a knot in his belly or a lump in his throat. Odd that despite having once loved her madly, he now felt practically nothing. Just a vague numbness. And an occasional twinge of bittersweet memory. Odder still was the fact that the only person, living or dead, who made him feel much of anything was Lindsay.

In those early days, she'd been around almost all the time. At Jennifer's funeral, in his home, at the police station where he'd been questioned repeatedly. Always in the background, always with Lt. Dan Blake. He'd been aware of her presence, but little more than that—until about a month after his wife's murder when he'd been called to police headquarters one more time. His lawyer had explained that the husband is always a suspect. Being a lawyer himself, intellectually he understood the reasoning behind such an assumption. But being a mourning widower, half out of his mind with grief, he couldn't understand how anyone could think he would have harmed a hair on Jennifer's beautiful head. He had adored her, worshipped her, loved her insanely. And yet even weeks after her murder, the police were still questioning him. Looking back, he realized the reason had been desperation on their part because they had no other suspects, just the unknown, unseen "client" whom Jennifer had supposedly met that night.

During that final interrogation, he truly saw Lindsay for

the first time. Not as Lieutenant Blake's shadow, not as just some woman whose face he could barely recall, but as a person.

He hadn't slept all night through in weeks, not since Jenny's death less than a month ago. And every waking moment was sheer torture. If he wasn't remembering her smile, her laughter, the feel of her lying next to him, he was recalling the way she had looked in death, her arms bound above her head, her hands missing. Some nights he woke up in a cold sweat after dreaming of her. Her masklike face lying against the pale pink satin lining her casket. Her arms reaching out to him, hands missing, pleading for him to save her.

Sleep deprived and grief-stricken, he showed up at the police station that day accompanied by his longtime friend and fellow lawyer, Camden Hendrix. He and Cam had met in law school—the two of them exact opposites in nearly every way. Cam had grown up poor, fatherless, and determined to one day be rich. Very rich. They had become fast friends immediately. Cam had been the best man at his wedding.

"You've got to be the luckiest damn son of a bitch I've ever known." Cam had slapped him on the back and shook his hand when he told him that Jennifer had accepted his proposal.

Cam had loved her just as Griff had. Everyone who knew his Jenny had loved her.

As usual, when Lieutenant Blake questioned Judd, Sergeant Lindsay McAllister was present. Cam had mentioned, just in passing, that he thought the young officer was mighty cute, and he just might ask her out. Judd had been oblivious to Lindsay's attractiveness, and that day was no different. He barely glanced at her.

Lieutenant Blake threw question after question at Judd, going over the same tired old material. Judd managed to reply in a reasonably calm manner for the first half hour, but suddenly the detective's tone changed and he began hammering away at Judd.

"You don't have an alibi for the time your wife was killed," Blake said. "And we have two witnesses who saw you and your wife in an argument the day before she was murdered. What were you arguing about?"

"Damn it, I've told you over and over again. The argument was about nothing," Judd said. "I wanted to reopen the family's hunting lodge for the weekend and she didn't want to. She didn't like the country. She wanted to go to a party some friends were having. We ended up deciding to do neither, to just stay home and spend some time alone together."

The same honest explanation he'd given repeatedly didn't satisfy Lieutenant Blake. "Your wife was very beautiful and men adored her, didn't they? That must have bothered you, knowing your wife was such a flirt—"

"Jennifer was not a flirt!" Judd came up out of the chair and lunged at the detective, whose combative reaction spurred Judd on.

Cam reached for Judd, who was by that time halfway across the table separating him from his tormentor. Cam grabbed hold of Judd's shoulders just as Lindsay McAllister plopped herself down on the table right in front of her partner, creating a barrier between Judd and the lieutenant.

"My God, Dan, stop this! Enough's enough. Mr. Walker shouldn't have to go through this insanity." Lindsay defended Judd in a loud, authoritarian voice, as if there was not one doubt in her mind that he was an innocent man. "Any fool can see that this man loved his wife, and he's suffering unbearably."

Judd allowed Cam to yank him back into his chair. All the while his gaze focused on Lindsay, seeing her for the first time as more than a nonentity.

"That's quite enough, Sergeant McAllister," Lieutenant Blake said, his tone calm and even.

Lindsay slid off the table and stood at attention, her cheeks flushed bright pink, and her jaw tightly clenched.

She wasn't beautiful. She didn't have a knockout figure. But Cam had been right—she was cute. Short, slender, with an all-American girl wholesomeness. The strangest notion went through Judd's mind. He bet she liked the great outdoors, probably enjoyed camping and fishing and . . .

Suddenly he realized that he was thinking of her the way a man does a woman he's interested in getting to know. His wife had been dead for less than a month and he found another woman attractive and interesting.

His gut clenched painfully.

He hated Lindsay McAllister. Hated her because she made him feel something besides grief.

As mile after mile of Tennessee roadway passed by outside the SUV, Judd opened his eyes, came back to the present, and looked out of the side window of Lindsay's Trailblazer. They had gone through Knoxville and were now on Interstate 40, heading toward the turnoff for the Douglas Lake area. He glanced at the dashboard clock: Ten to twelve. Nearly noon. They should arrive at Griffin's Rest in another thirty minutes or so.

"When's the last time you saw Cam?" Judd asked, realizing he hadn't even thought about his old buddy in at least six months and hadn't gotten in touch with him in nearly a year. Like everyone else, including Griff, Cam had pretty much given him up as a lost cause.

Lindsay gasped. "I thought you were still asleep."

"Nope."

"I saw Cam last fall. He came up to Griffin's Rest and spent a few days," she said. "We went fishing."

"I'm surprised you two didn't hook up. He's always liked you."

"Hmm . . ."

"Don't want to discuss your personal life with me, huh?"

When she didn't reply, he should have let the subject drop, but instead he said, "If you're not screwing around with Griff, and Cam isn't your latest lover, then you must still be—"

"Carrying a torch for you," she finished for him.

"Are you?"

"I'm dating a very nice man. A doctor from Knoxville."

"Are you serious about him?"

"I could be."

"Good for you. You deserve to be happy."

"Gee, thanks, Judd," she said sarcastically. "I'm glad you think so."

He chuckled. "It's always going to be there, isn't it? That tension between us."

Silence.

"It's the reason I hate you, you know," he told her.

She didn't even flinch, which surprised him. There had been a time when he could get to her, irritate her, and hurt her so easily. Guess she'd grown a thick skin, at least where he was concerned.

"I suppose I should be flattered that you're capable of feeling anything for me, even if it is hatred," she said.

"I don't want to feel anything."

"Hurts too much, huh?"

"I really hope things work out for you and the doctor."

"Thanks."

Liar. You don't want Lindsay to care about another man. To want another man. To love another man.

Even if he didn't love her, he didn't want any other man to have her.

Barbara Jean found it difficult to accept what had happened to her in the past few days. Nothing seemed real, least of all losing her only sibling. She and Gale Ann had been close since childhood, always best friends as well as sisters, despite the differences in their ages and personalities. She was seven years Gale Ann's senior and had been her sister's caretaker and protector most of their lives—until the car wreck five years ago. Then their roles had reversed and Gale Ann became the caretaker for a while.

"Good morning, Ms. Hughes," Sanders said when she entered the kitchen.

"Good morning." She tried to offer him a smile, but the effort failed.

As the stocky, tan-skinned Sanders nodded in a curt, polite manner, she studied him for a few moments. Last night, she had been half-asleep when he had lifted her from the car and carried her up a flight of stairs to an incredibly lovely guest room. At the time, she had thought how very strong this man was to be able to carry her one hundred and forty pounds without breaking a sweat or even breathing hard.

Odd that although she usually hated being catered to or fussed over because of her handicap, she had felt only cosseted and protected in Sanders's strong arms.

Her streamlined, motorized wheelchair allowed her access to all the downstairs rooms in Griffin Powell's mansion, but she had been forced to rely on one of his agents, a big, burly man named Shaughnessy Hood, to carry her downstairs and place her in her chair this morning. At home, she maneuvered around in her one-bedroom apartment without any assistance, but unfortunately all the bedrooms in this huge house were on the second floor. She liked being as independent as possible, liked living on her own, and holding down a job. But due to circumstances beyond her control, she'd been forced to take an indefinite leave of absence from her position at Honeywell, Inc.

Powell agent Angie Sterling had explained that Mr. Hood would take over bodyguard duty today, and she would be returning this evening. Apparently, the two were rotating twelve-hour shifts.

"I'm sorry we don't have another female agent available until tomorrow," Ms. Sterling had said. "Griff is calling in someone and sending out one of the guys to replace her, but it'll be tomorrow before she arrives."

Male or female, the agent didn't really matter, but it was nice of Griffin Powell to try to accommodate her by having women as her bodyguards. It was the fact that she actually needed to have protection twenty-four-seven that bothered her, not the sex of her protector.

"What would you like for breakfast?" Sanders asked.

She glanced around at the huge, state-of-the-art kitchen. "Are you the cook, Mr. Sanders?"

"Just Sanders, ma'am." His dark eyes settled on her, but without the look of pity she so often recognized when people saw her handicap instead of her. "And yes, in a way, I am the cook. One of them anyway. I often prepare breakfast for Mr. Powell and any guests who might be here at Griffin's Rest. We do have a regular cook who comes in to prepare the other meals and occasionally also does breakfast."

"Have you worked for Mr. Powell very long?"

"We've been together nearly eighteen years."

Been together, not worked for. Barbara Jean understood the subtle difference in the two statements. Was this his way of telling her that he was more than an employee, more than a mere servant?

Realizing she was gawking pointedly at Sanders, she quickly said, "Griffin is a very persuasive man, isn't he?" When Sanders continued staring at her with those expressive black eyes, she cleared her throat and added, "I mean he's charming and understanding and—"

"He is a good man. He wishes to keep you safe and do all he can to help you."

"I think he and Special Agent Baxter both assumed that my sister's killer would come after me, but since I can't identify him, I doubt he'd risk being caught by trying to kill me just because I might have gotten a passing glimpse of him."

"Mr. Powell had pancakes this morning and I still have batter," Sanders said, as if he hadn't heard what she'd said. "Will pancakes suit you?"

"I don't want to be any trouble."

"No trouble." He indicated the coffeemaker on the counter. "There is coffee prepared. Would you prefer to serve yourself or—"

"I can do it myself," she replied. "Thank you."

She wheeled herself to the counter, reached up, and managed to lift the glass pot and pour the steaming black liquid into one of several mugs near the coffeemaker. Clutching the mug between her hands, she brought it to her lips and took a sip. Delicious.

"The coffee's really good."

"Hmm . . ." Sanders removed a plastic bowl from the refrigerator.

"Where is Griffin . . . Mr. Powell this morning? You mentioned that he'd already had breakfast."

"He's in his office."

"Would it be possible for me to see him? I need to discuss making arrangements for my sister's funeral and—"

"I believe he has already taken care of that. I'm sure he'll speak with you later this morning. Right now, he is quite busy."

Sanders had a unique accent. He spoke English quite well, with a slight British accent, yet there was a hint of something else, as if perhaps he had grown up in a bilingual home.

"Do you happen to know what type of job he has in mind for me to do for the Powell Agency?" she asked.

"No, ma'am, I have no idea."

Had she been wrong to trust Griffin Powell, to accept his offer of protection and a job to keep her busy as well as pay her bills? She could have allowed Special Agent Baxter to put her under FBI protection, but she couldn't bear the thought of being whisked away and kept hidden. She needed to bury her sister. She needed to work. And she needed to be somewhere she was not only protected, but where no one would pressure her to identify the man she'd seen leaving her sister's apartment.

"Would you mind if I prepare my own breakfast?" Barbara Jean asked. "I like to take care of myself as much as possible."

"Certainly," Sanders replied. "I am here to help you in any way I can. Just tell me what you need and I will see that you have it."

"I don't have much of an appetite right now." She had done little more than nibble at her food since she had discovered Gale Ann's almost lifeless body. Had that really been four days ago? Yes, four days ago this afternoon. "I'd like to fix myself a couple of pieces of toast. And if you have orange juice, I'd like a glass of that, too."

Sanders pointed out where everything could be located— the pantry, the refrigerator, the toaster behind one of the closed counter cupboards. When she dropped the loaf of bread on the floor, Sanders picked it up, handed it to her, and smiled. Not an overly warm or friendly smile and not a you-poor-thing smile. Just a cordial tilt to his wide mouth.

His dark hand brushed her pale fingers as she took the loaf of bread from him. She tried not to stare, but she found him fascinating. And handsome in a very exotic sort of way. An image of Yul Brynner as he looked in the old movie, *The King and I*, flashed through Barbara Jean's mind.

Glancing away hurriedly, she concentrated on preparing her breakfast. A few minutes later, when she placed her buttered toast on a plate and wheeled over to put it on the table alongside her coffee and small glass of juice, Sanders removed one of the kitchen chairs so that she could park her wheelchair close to the table.

"May I join you?" he asked as he poured himself a mug of coffee.

"Please do."

When he sat across from her, neither of them spoke for several minutes. She nibbled on the toast and sipped the coffee.

"You must not worry about anything while you are here," Sanders said. "Whatever you need will be provided."

"Since you've known Mr. Powell for such a long time, perhaps you can tell me something about him." When Sanders didn't reply, she continued. "I agreed to come here with him instead of going with Special Agent Baxter because I believed he wouldn't pressure me about identifying the man I saw leaving my sister's apartment building the day she was . . ." Barbara Jean swallowed hard. "What will Griffin do if I can't give him a detailed description of the man, if I can't give him more of a description than I already have?"

"You are under Griffin Powell's protection and will remain so as long as you might possibly be in danger. Griffin knows that if you can identify this man, you will because you will want to do all you can to help find the person who murdered your sister and stop him before he can kill again."

"And if I can't identify him?"

"Then you cannot."

I can't. I swear I can't.

She really hadn't gotten a good look at the man. But the truth—the whole truth—was that she didn't want to remember what he looked like, didn't want to recall any specific facial features or distinguishing marks. How could she ever make Griffin or anyone else understand how terrified she was at the thought that this maniac might kill her the way he had her sister? As long as she lived, she would never be able to forget the sight of Gale Ann bound and gagged, both of her feet severed at the ankles.

Suddenly she felt a large, warm palm covering her trembling hand. Through a sheen of fresh tears, she looked from where Sanders's hand clasped hers up to his face. Without saying a word, he pulled a linen handkerchief from his pocket and gently wiped away her tears.

Chapter 8

Judd hadn't been to Griffin's Rest since early last year, right after the twenty-third beauty queen had been murdered. For the life of him, he couldn't recall her name. Hell, he didn't remember any of their names.

Only Jenny's.

Former Miss Tennessee, Jennifer Mobley Walker, twenty-nine, wife of prominent Chattanooga lawyer, Judson Walker V.

Strange how he could no longer see her clearly in his mind's eye. The visual image of Jenny that he'd carried around in his head and in his heart had faded so gradually that he hadn't realized it was happening. Not until one day a few months ago when he'd thought of her and had been unable to conjure up a sharp, clear image of the woman he had once loved so deeply. He had searched the old lodge for a photo of her, looking in all the desks, every cupboard, every drawer. But only after he'd torn the house apart in one of his drunken rages had he realized that there were no photos of Jenny at the lodge.

After only one visit to the Walker hunting lodge, she had

stated adamantly that she hated the place. "God, Judd, it's ancient and creaky and out here in the middle of nowhere."

People had thought he and Jennifer were an ideal couple, and in many ways they had been. They'd certainly looked good together. Chattanooga's Golden Couple. Society's darlings.

And they'd been in love. Passionately in love.

But their personal interests often hadn't meshed and more often than not, he had wound up doing whatever Jenny wanted to do. She had loved parties; he'd hated them. He had loved weekends in the country; she'd despised the great outdoors. He'd enjoyed quiet evenings at home, just the two of them; she had thrived on socializing.

"It's been awhile, hasn't it?"

Lindsay's question snapped Judd out of his thoughts, thoughts better left in the past . . . with Jenny. Only recently had he allowed himself to admit the truth, that if his wife had lived they would have had to work hard at their marriage. Sometimes love just wasn't enough.

"Yeah, it's been awhile since I've been to Griff's place."

"Nothing much has changed," she said.

"I suppose Sanders is still running the show."

"Griff depends on Sanders. He trusts him implicitly." Lindsay pulled up in front of the house. "You can get out here, if you'd like, and go on in. I need to park in the garage."

"Got your own space in the garage, huh?"

"Don't make anything of it," she told him. "It's a ten-car garage. Any agent who stays here at Griffin's Rest parks in the garage."

"But you're the only one who lives here."

She stopped the Trailblazer directly at the foot of the steps leading up to the porch. Ignoring his comment, she said, "Griff will want to see you first thing."

"The big man wants to lay down the law to me, huh?"

"Something like that."

Judd opened the door and got out, then leaned down so that he could look back inside the SUV. "How much does Griff know about what happened between us six months ago?"

"As much as he needed to know."

Judd grunted. "You didn't tell him everything, did you?" When she simply stared at him with just a hint of pain in her baby blues, he wanted to tell her that he was sorry, but instead he said, "If you'd told him all of it, he'd have beaten the shit out of me."

"Is that what you wanted—for Griff to beat you senseless? Is that why you did it?"

"No. That was just an afterthought. If there was any reasoning behind what I did, it was to scare you off once and for all."

Judd pulled back, stood up, and slammed the door. Before he had time to turn around, Lindsay drove off, leaving him standing there staring after her.

He had scared her off. Just not permanently. But they'd taken a six-month breather from each other. Six months that should have made him hate her less, fear her less; and six months for her to realize loving him was the most self-destructive thing she could ever do.

Judd walked up the steps, crossed the porch, and rang the doorbell. While he waited, he rubbed his hands together to warm them. The wind off the nearby lake kept the temperatures in this area several degrees colder than in Knoxville. And the weather during the month of February in northeast Tennessee could be unpredictable. Rainy one day, sunny the next. The temps could be in the sixties one day, then a cold front could pass through and bring snow with it the following day.

While he blew his warm breath on his chilled hands, the front doors opened. Sanders nodded. "Good morning,

Mr. Walker. Please come in and go to Griffin's study. I believe you know the way. I'll tell him that you have arrived."

"Thanks." Judd entered the foyer. "So, how have you been doing, Sanders?"

"Quiet well, thank you, sir."

"Want to let me in on just what Griff has in store for me?" Judd asked. "Is he going to put me on the rack and tighten the screws or just ask me to bend over and give me a swift kick in the butt?"

Sanders didn't crack a smile as he closed the doors and turned to face Judd. "I wouldn't know, sir. But if I were to make an educated guess, I would say he plans to speak to you about how to conduct yourself around Ms. Hughes. And . . ."

"And?"

"And anything else is none of my business."

"I thought everything to do with Griff was your business, especially Lindsay McAllister, since both of you are quite fond of her."

Avoiding direct eye contact with Judd, Sanders walked away. "I'll tell Griffin that you are here."

Judd knew the way to Griff's study. He'd been in the house on numerous occasions, both before his marriage and after Jennifer's death.

But not once during his brief marriage.

The door to Griff's den stood partially ajar. Judd nudged the heavy wooden door with his hand and walked into the two-story study. A chunk of burned wood crumbled in the massive rock fireplace. The antique clock on the mantel struck eleven times, announcing the hour.

He had always liked this room—a man's room, with wood paneling, sturdy leather sofa and chairs, hardwood flooring— because it was totally void of anything remotely feminine. Every man needed one room in his home that was his. In the family mansion on Lookout Mountain, a home built by his grandfather, there was a room similar to this one. It was a room he'd loved as a boy when he'd spent time there with his dad and a room he'd loved as a man when he had inherited the house. But Jennifer hadn't wanted to live in "that stuffy mausoleum" and had insisted they purchase a downtown penthouse, which had reflected the sleek, modern, minimalist style she preferred.

"You need a haircut," Griffin said.

Judd turned to face his old friend. "A lot of men wear their hair long these days. I hear that women think it's sexy."

Griff snorted. "You don't give a damn how you look. That's why your hair is shaggy, why you're wearing those old clothes, and why you didn't shave this morning."

"Hey, at least I'm clean. I did take a shower."

"Should I be grateful?"

"Look, if you don't want me here, I'll go," Judd said. "I realize you've given me more chances than I deserved. If I've used them all up, just say so."

"If you stay, there are a few rules you'll have to follow. Are you willing to do that?"

"If the rules have anything to do with Lindsay—"

Griffin glowered at him, a fierce expression tightening his jaw. "How could you have hurt her that way? You knew how she felt about you."

"I didn't ask her to care about me, did I? It's not my fault that she—"

"Bullshit! You've depended on her caring, wanted it, craved it."

Standing face-to-face with the six-four former UT quarterback, Judd glowered at Griff. He wanted to deny the accusation, the words were on the tip of his tongue, but he couldn't respond. Had he been using Lindsay for the past few years? Had he really craved the tender loving care she had lavished on him?

"I never realized that I might have subconsciously needed her to care," Judd admitted. "Look, I can't change the past, but what if I swear to you, here and now, that I won't ever hurt her again."

"Then cut her loose, let her go."

"I tried. Six months ago."

The anger in Griff's steely blue eyes sent an undeniable warning. "You should be horsewhipped for what you did."

"She said she didn't tell you everything."

"She didn't."

"Then how—"

"I know Lindsay," Griff said. "And I know what an unfeeling bastard you've become. It didn't take a genius to figure out that you nearly raped her."

"Rape is an ugly word. I did not . . ." Judd cleared his throat. He didn't want to think about how he had mistreated Lindsay, how cruel he'd been to her. "I stopped before it went that far."

"You humiliated her. You broke her heart." Griff glared at Judd. "Being a grieving widower whose wife was murdered is no excuse for becoming the kind of man you are now. Do you think you're the first man who ever lost the woman he loved?"

"I take it that I can't play the sympathy card with you any longer."

"You got that damn straight. If you want to be a part of this investigation, from here on out, you'll have to prove to me you deserve this one last chance. And make no mistake about it. As far as I'm concerned, this is your last chance." Griff's gaze linked with Judd's. "Do you understand?"

"I understand."

"Cut your emotional ties to Lindsay," Griff told him. "And a couple of other things—"

"You really want your pound of flesh, don't you?" Judd managed an unsteady smile.

"At the very least." Griff's tense stance relaxed. "Barbara Jean Hughes is staying here, under my protection. You are not to confront her or bother her in any way. If you do, I'll personally throw you out."

"Has she told you anything else? Has she given you a description of the man she saw leaving her sister's apartment?"

"No. Not yet. And I have no intention of pushing her. If she's not pressured, she might be able to remember more and be less afraid to confront the truth about what she does know."

"I'll steer clear of Ms. Hughes." Judd lifted his hand in a Boy Scout's honor signal. "That's two rules down and how many more to go?"

"Would I be pushing it too far to ask you to get a haircut, wear some decent clothes, and shave every day?"

When Judd noted Griff's mouth lift in a hint of a smile, he realized that there might be hope for their friendship. He had taken old friends for granted—friends like Griffin and Camden. He had abused their trust. Had tested their patience. Had driven them away. All in the name of self-pity.

"How about we compromise," Judd said. "I'll shave every day."

Griff grunted. "There is one more thing—I want you to apologize to Barbara Jean."

Judd eyed Griff curiously. "All right."

"You're wondering why I'm not asking you to apologize to Lindsay, aren't you?"

Judd nodded.

"It would be too little too late."

A soft rap on the partially closed study door announced the end of their private conversation.

"Ms. Hughes to see you," Sanders said.

Judd and Griff turned and faced Sanders and the wheelchair-bound woman in front of him. Although he'd gotten right up in her face last night, Judd hadn't really looked at her. He now realized that she was a very attractive woman, probably in her early forties, with short, curly red hair, and kind, hazel eyes. He saw grief in her eyes, the kind of grief he had once known.

"Please, come in," Griff said.

Sanders followed Barbara Jean as she wheeled into the den, then stopped abruptly when she saw Judd.

"Ms. Hughes, I'm Judd Walker." He made no attempt to approach her. "I want to apologize to you for acting like a madman at the hospital last night. I'm sorry that I frightened you."

She stared at him, surveying him from head to toe, then she settled her gaze on his face. "You think the man who killed my sister is the same man who killed your wife. I can understand how much you'd want to find this man and bring him to justice."

"Thank you for being so kind," Judd said.

"Please, come on in," Griffin repeated, then looked at Judd. "Why don't you go with Sanders. He'll show you to your room and you can settle in. Lunch will be at one. I'd like for you to join us."

Realizing he'd been dismissed, Judd nodded, smiled at Barbara Jean, and walked out of Griff's den, with Sanders only a few steps behind him.

"Where's Lindsay?" Judd asked Sanders.

"She's in a meeting with several of the other Powell agents."

"Big powwow going on, huh?"

"I believe they're making arrangements for Ms. Hughes to have around-the-clock protection and preparing for a meeting with Griffin this afternoon," Sanders said. "I assume you'll be included in that meeting."

"Only if I'm a good boy and play by the rules."

"That's as it should be." Sanders marched around and in front of Judd. "This way, please."

"Just tell me which room," Judd said. "No need to put yourself out."

"Where is your luggage?" Sanders asked.

"Didn't bring any."

"Very well. Just make a list of what you'll need and I'll—"

"Start with a shave kit," Judd told him. "I promised Griff I'd shave every day."

"Very well, sir. Please follow me."

Judd shrugged, then went up the stairs behind Sanders. "You don't like me very much these days, do you?"

"No, sir."

Judd chuckled. "Because of Lindsay?"

"Yes, sir."

"Why she'd bother giving me the time of day, I don't know, not when she has you and Griff wrapped around her little finger."

Ignoring Judd's caustic comment, Sanders opened the second door on the right. "I will bring back a shave kit so that you can shave before lunch. What about clothes?"

"I'll have some things sent down from Chattanooga." Judd clicked his heels and saluted Sanders, who gave him a withering glare, then turned and walked away.

Sanders was an odd one. Judd had once asked Griff how the two had met and why they had become fast friends. He had been surprised by Griff's reply.

"Sanders and I met in hell and joined forces to fight the devil."

Griffin situated Barbara Jean across from the sofa in his den, then sat so that they were eye to eye. With her head slightly bowed and her gaze cast downward, she cleared her throat several times.

"Do you like your room?" Griff asked.

"Yes, very much. Thank you."

"Is there a problem with your having Shaughnessy acting as your bodyguard just for today?"

She shook her head. "He seems like a very nice man."

"If you want or need anything, all you have to do is ask."

"Sanders mentioned that you were making arrangements for Gale Ann's funeral. Is that correct?" She looked at him then, a thousand questions in her misty eyes.

"I took the liberty of contacting a funeral home in Williamstown," Griff told her. "Your sister's body won't be released until after the autopsy, which hopefully will be fairly soon, so there is no real rush. Whatever decisions you wish to make, you may certainly do so. And anything you'd like for me to handle, I will."

"Thank you. It was difficult enough when Gale Ann and I had to take care of everything when each of our parents died, but I never thought I'd have to—" A sob caught in her throat. "I'm the older sister, so naturally I thought I'd die first."

Griff reached out, engulfed Barbara Jean's trembling hands in his steady grasp and said, "Please spare no expense in the funeral arrangements. Judd and I will pay for whatever you want."

"You and Mr. Walker? I—I don't understand."

Judd had not paid for the funeral of any other victim, but Griff intended to make him help foot the bill for Gale Ann's. One more way to help bring his old friend back to the land of the living.

"Judd and I are both very wealthy men," Griff explained. "Your sister's funeral will be only one of several we have paid for." A small white lie. He had paid for ten funerals. This would be the first for Judd.

"But why would you—?"

"In memory of Judd's wife, Jennifer, who was also my friend." *And because I have more money than I could spend in ten lifetimes. Blood money.*

"That's very kind of you . . . and of Mr. Walker." She searched Griff's face, as if suspecting he had a hidden agenda, some dark secret reason he would make such a generous offer.

Griff squeezed her hands, then released his hold. "There are no strings attached."

"I'm so sorry if I gave you the impression I didn't trust you. You've been more than kind and generous and . . . I can't identify that man. Really, I can't. I barely saw him and—"

"And we won't mention it again. Not unless you remember something else. No one here at Griffin's Rest will pressure you, Barbara Jean. You're here to rest and recuperate from a harrowing experience. And when you're ready to go to work, just say the word."

She took a deep breath, then released it quickly. A heavy sigh of relief. "I'll go crazy without something to do. Whenever you're ready to put me to work, I'm ready."

"You don't want to rush yourself. Take all the time you need to deal with what happened to Gale Ann."

"Working will help me cope. Please, I'd like to start first thing tomorrow."

Griff nodded. "All right. Then first thing tomorrow, you can begin Sanders's instructions."

Leaning her head to one side in an inquisitive manner, she looked directly at Griff. "You've hired me to instruct Mr. Sanders in what way?"

"On the computer. He's totally computer-illiterate."

"Oh, I see."

"No, you don't. Not really."

Her gaze widened.

"Sanders is not a servant in my home. He is my right arm. I need a man in his position to be computer savvy. He has resisted going near a computer for years now, but I've finally persuaded him that in order to assist me even more than he does now, it is necessary."

"Well, since my job with Honeywell was as a computer programmer, I don't think I'll have any trouble teaching Sanders the basics rather quickly. He seems to be a highly intelligent man."

"Sanders is a brilliant man," Griff assured her. "Just a bit old-fashioned and set in his ways."

"It would be my pleasure to be his teacher."

"Good. Good." Griff stood. "I'll turn you over to Shaughnessy. You're welcome to go anywhere at Griffin's Rest, as long as your bodyguard is with you." Griff walked to the door, opened it, and motioned for Shaughnessy Hood, who stood waiting at the end of the hallway. "If you need anything, anything at all, just let us know."

As she wheeled herself through the doorway, she said, "Thank you, Griffin. You've been very kind to me."

Griff watched as she maneuvered her chair down the hall toward the solarium, Shaughnessy following several feet behind her. Once they were out of sight, he sought out Sanders, whom he found at one of the three computers in Griff's fully-equipped home office.

When Sanders started to rise from the swivel chair, Griff motioned him down. "Don't get up."

"You've spoken to Ms. Hughes?" Sanders inquired.

"Yes, I have."

"And?"

"And you start computer lessons first thing tomorrow, so do your best to act like you don't know the first thing about computers."

"Of all things for you to have hired her to do—why teach me how to do something that I know how to do?"

"Because I needed to offer her a job and since there are none available at the agency or here at home, the only thing I could think of was something in her field."

"I shall try not to give myself away," Sanders said.

"I have every confidence in you."

"As I do in you."

Griff nodded. "We have three wounded souls under our roof. I'd like to think we can somehow help all three of them."

"I leave Mr. Walker to you," Sanders said. "I find his

treatment of Lindsay unforgivable. And as for our Lindsay . . . she must heal herself by accepting Mr. Walker for who he is and not the man she wants him to be."

"What about Barbara Jean?"

"It would be my honor to do all I can to help her through the next few weeks. I believe beneath all that innate shyness and the sadness caused by her recent tragedy, there is a special lady."

Griff eyed his friend speculatively. "You like her."

"She is a likable person."

Griff smiled. In all the years since he had returned to the United States and brought Sanders with him, this was the first time he'd ever seen his friend show any special interest in a lady, other than Lindsay. But Lindsay was like a daughter to Sanders and it was apparent his interest in Barbara Jean was not fatherly.

Chapter 9

Divided into three separate areas, Griffin's home office rivaled any modern, well-equipped office space. Boasting every conceivable state-of-the-art device and furnished with the best money could buy, the impressive setup reflected the man himself. Although Judd had admired Griff Powell, the star UT quarterback, as had the entire state of Tennessee, Judd hadn't known the young Griff. They hadn't met until eight years ago at a social function of some type, only a few months following Griff's reappearance after a mysterious absence of ten years. Rumors had flown like debris in a hurricane; rumors about where Griff had been and how he had acquired an amazing fortune that matched or exceeded some of the wealthiest men in the country, if not the world. Over a period of a couple of years, Judd and Griff had discovered they had a great deal in common, the least of which was the fact they were considered the two most eligible bachelors in the state. A genuine friendship had formed gradually and eventually reached the point where Judd had considered Griff one of his best friends.

Sometimes, on a clear, bright day when he took long walks

in the woods around the family's hunting lodge, his mind would wander back to those good old days when he and Griff and Cam Hendrix had raised high-class hell. They had often gone after the same woman, sometimes just to see who would be the first to win a date with the lady. Jennifer Mobley had been one of those women. God, she'd been so beautiful. She had known just how gorgeous she was and had used that knowledge to her advantage. He wasn't sure why she'd accepted a date with Griff first. Judd had never been jealous of either of his buddies—not until Jenny entered their lives. Oddly enough, she had dated Cam second, which only whetted Judd's appetite for her all the more. He didn't know if she'd had sex with either of his friends. Didn't want to know. Had never asked them or Jennifer. But she hadn't gone to bed with him until their fifth date. By that time, he was half out of his mind, so hungry for her that he would have walked over hot coals to get to her.

"Everybody come on in and take a seat." Griffin Powell's instructions brought Judd back to the present moment, to the here and now.

A large rectangular table took center stage in front of a wall lined with shelving that contained two plasma televisions, a DVD player, a CD player, and neatly organized books and magazines. Lindsay and Rick Carson sat across from each other in two of the plush, leather swivel chairs surrounding the table. Griff took a seat at the head of the table. Judd walked toward the empty chair beside Lindsay, but paused, noted the disapproving expression on Griff's face, and backtracked a few steps. He pulled out the chair at the other end of the table. Griff nodded approval. Judd sat.

Griff lifted a small stack of file folders from where they had been placed on the table, probably by Sanders, who had a knack for not only being one step ahead of everyone else, but seeming to know in advance exactly what Griff would want or need.

"These files contain the most pertinent facts about the Beauty Queen Killer case that the Powell Agency has compiled during the past three and a half, nearly four, years."

Griff placed all except one of the folders back on the table, then opened the file in his hand, pulled out several crime scene photos and passed them around, one by one. Lindsay shoved the pictures across the table to Judd, who in turn, sent them on to Rick Carson with little more than passing glances. Each showed a different redheaded victim. One with her throat slit, another missing her feet and legs up to her knees, a third with her tongue cut out and a knife embedded in the center of her chest. Each woman had been savagely mutilated and left to bleed to death.

"These women were worth twenty points to our BQ Killer," Griff said. "Gale Ann Cain, the latest victim, was able to tell us that she had been worth twenty points to him because she had red hair." Griff glanced around the table, from Lindsay to Judd to Rick. "What does that bit of info tell us?"

"That this guy is using a points system," Rick said.

"That if redheads are worth twenty points, that means blondes and brunettes are worth certain points, too." Lindsay shook her head. "This man is playing some kind of sick, perverted game."

"How does this information help us catch him?" Judd asked.

Griff's gaze locked with Judd's. "I don't know that it will."

"But it makes sense that the more we find out about him, the better our chances of finding out who he is," Lindsay said.

Judd harrumphed.

"Do you have something else to say?" Griff looked point-blank at Judd.

"Nothing new," Judd said. "It's just that after three and a half years, neither the Powell Agency nor the FBI is any closer to catching this guy than they were when this psycho killed Jennifer."

"That's not necessarily true." Griff glanced at the photos

lying on the table, neatly arranged by Rick before he placed them between him and Griff. "Do we know the man's name? No, we don't. Do we know where to find him? No, we don't. But we do know a great deal about him, and Derek Lawrence, the former FBI profiler who works for my agency, has updated his profile of our BQ Killer."

"For all the good that will do." Judd blurted out his opinion, then thought better of being so negative. "Sorry." He looked from Griff to Lindsay, who didn't even glance his way. "It's just that you—" he focused sharply on Griff "—have a woman right here at Griffin's Rest who can probably identify this man."

"Barbara Jean Hughes may or may not be able to identify the man she saw leaving Gale Ann's apartment," Griff said. "First of all, we can't be a hundred percent sure he's our guy. And secondly, it's possible that Barbara Jean will never be able to tell us more than she already has. A medium size, medium height man, wearing a hat, a coat, and sunglasses, maybe with brown hair, was leaving the building where her sister lived just as she arrived."

"Crap," Judd said. "Okay, I'm sorry. Again. I'll behave myself, but you can't expect me not to question your decisions."

"Left alone and allowed to feel safe and secure here at Griffin's Rest, Barbara Jean may well begin to recall more details about this man." Griff gathered up the photos of the redheaded victims and placed them back in the file folder.

"Just how long do we wait for this woman to remember?" Judd asked.

"As long as it takes."

"And in the meantime, while you're coddling her, the BQ Killer is out there choosing his next victim."

"More than likely," Griff said.

"Too bad we can't figure out how he chooses his victims," Rick Carson said. "I mean other than the fact that they've all been former beauty contest winners and are still under the age of forty and have retained their good looks."

"Before the information Gale Ann gave us, we were looking for a reason he's chosen only former beauty queens," Lindsay said. "We had wondered if there was a connection in his past to someone who had been a beauty queen, and, of course, that's still a possibility. But we now know that he has concocted some sort of game that involves using a points system according to the woman's hair color."

"One question comes to mind about his game-playing." Griff scanned the room, pausing briefly on each of the other occupants, and when no one made a comment, he asked, "Is he the only player in this deadly game?"

Silence.

Nerve-racking silence.

For the first time since they had entered the office, Lindsay looked right at Judd. "My God, do you think—?"

"So far, there's been no evidence that we're dealing with more than one person," Rick reminded them.

"Maybe he's got a split personality, and he's playing against his other self," Judd suggested sarcastically.

"Or he could be playing the odds, pitting his skill and cunning against the FBI," Rick said. "Some games don't require two players: Solitaire, Russian roulette, many video games."

"Good point." Griff picked up another file folder, opened it, and reviewed the contents. "For now, let's continue to assume the BQ Killer is acting alone, that he's playing this 'Dying Game' where he racks up points with each murder. So is there a final score goal, a certain number he plans to reach before he stops?"

"I didn't think serial killers *could* stop," Lindsay said. "I thought the compulsion to kill never goes away, that the desire to murder has to be satisfied over and over again."

"Who's to say this is the first game he's played or, if it is, that it will be the last." Griff waited for a reaction from the others.

"We hadn't—" Lindsay paused. "Well, at least *I* hadn't thought of that possibility. If that's the case, then he would end this game when he reaches a specific score and simply start a new game."

"Are we trying to figure out what his perfect score would be?" Judd asked. "If we could narrow it down to say five-hundred points, what would that prove? How would that get us any closer to him?" Judd scooted back his chair, stood, and shoved his hands into the pockets of his tattered jeans. "Got any coffee in here? I could use a stiff drink, but I'll settle for a shot of caffeine."

Hitching his thumb in the direction, Griff said, "Sanders keeps a fresh pot ready when he knows anyone will be using the office."

Spotting the stainless steel coffeemaker, Judd left the others, using the excuse of needing caffeine to get away from just one more fruitless discussion. He'd been directly involved in this investigation from the day he hired the Powell Agency to conduct a private inquiry into Jennifer's murder. For nearly three years, he had lived and breathed the investigation, believing that each new tidbit of information brought them one step closer to finding his wife's killer. Then midyear last year, he'd given up shortly after another senseless murder. He couldn't remember her name or the details, only the fact that after she'd been killed, he had shut down, gotten drunk, and stayed drunk for days. Then he had attacked the one person who had never given up on him.

Two months after Jennifer's murder and Judd being hauled down to the police station for questioning, Judd had hired his old friend Griffin Powell. He had asked Griff to head up a long-term investigation, to use all of Judd's wealth, and both his and Griff's power and connections to keep track of what the FBI was doing. And to move heaven and earth to find the man who had killed Jenny.

It hadn't taken a genius to figure out that Sergeant Lindsay McAllister believed Judd was an innocent man, a bereaved widower who had loved his wife and wanted to see the real killer brought to justice. But it had taken Griff's intuitive observations to figure out that Lindsay had fallen in love with Judd. Even after she'd quit her job on the Chattanooga PD and gone to work for the Powell Agency, Judd hadn't suspected the career change had been solely because of him.

He remembered the day, a couple of years ago, when Griff had shared his insight into Lindsay's motivation for joining Griff's staff.

"She's in love with you," Griff said.

"What?"

"The reason Lindsay wants to work for me is so that she can participate in the Beauty Queen Killer case."

"Yeah, sure, I figured as much. It was her first case as a detective and when the police and the FBI botched the job of finding Jenny's killer, Lindsay decided to join us and help solve the crime."

Griff shook his head. "That's only the half of it. Why do you think it matters so damn much to her? It's because she's done the unthinkable and fallen in love with a man who is still in love with his dead wife."

"You're nuts. Lindsay isn't—"

"She is. And sooner or later, both of you will have to face that fact and deal with it."

"There's nothing to deal with," Judd said. "I like Lindsay. She's been in my corner all along, and I appreciate it, but as for anything else . . . Not now. Not ever. All I want is to find Jenny's killer and make him pay for what he did to her. Nothing and no one else matters."

"You know that and I know that, but a woman in love sees

and believes what she wants to. You might not realize it, but in the past year, you've been leaning pretty heavily on Lindsay, counting on her to rescue you when you dive off the deep end. She probably thinks that once Jennifer's killer is caught and punished, you'll be able to start fresh, maybe with her."

"I don't think Lindsay's that big a fool," Judd said. "She knows that my life ended the day Jenny died."

Griff snorted. "You're the fool. You didn't die the day Jennifer did. Your life didn't end. It just changed. For the worse. I understand all about seeking revenge, believe me. But sooner or later, you have to move on, build a new life and—"

"Don't preach to me! Don't tell me what I should think and how I should feel." He grabbed the lapels of Griffin's sports coat and glared right into his eyes. "Don't you get it— except for anger, I'm as good as dead inside."

"Then I feel sorry for you, my friend. I know only too well that anger, hatred, and a thirst for revenge can sustain you for only so long—and then you have to reach out for life again. If you don't . . ."

Judd released his tenacious hold on Griff's jacket and smoothed the lapels. "Talk to her, will you? Make her understand that she shouldn't waste herself waiting for me to care about her."

The tender touch of Lindsay's hand on his shoulder jerked Judd out of the past and back to the present, away from an old conversation to face the here and now.

She possessed a gentle yet firm grip.

"Are you all right?" she asked.

Keeping his back to her, he shrugged off her hand, reached out and removed the glass pot from the warmer. "Want some coffee?"

"No, thanks."

Judd poured the black java into one of several orange and

white mugs on the table, then lifted the bright orange UT cup to his lips, and sipped the strong brew.

"If you'd rather not sit in on this initial session, I can fill you in later," Lindsay told him. "We'll go over all the old info and the new to see if anything sparks an idea."

Judd gazed past Lindsay to the rectangular table where Griff and Rick sat, deep in conversation. "What's the point? I don't even know why I'm here. I should have stayed at the lodge."

"Don't go back there." Her sincere look implored him. "Stay here. Help us. Help yourself."

"Stop caring so damn much," Judd spoke quietly through clenched teeth.

"You stop being such a jackass."

Judd grinned. "You're a lot tougher than you used to be. Is that my doing?"

"Feel free to take credit for it."

He inclined his head toward the conference table. "Why don't we leave the hashing over old facts and blending them with new ones to those two? I'm going to put on my coat and take a long walk. Want to go with me?"

She studied him intently, as if trying to decide whether or not to trust him.

"Forget I asked," he told her. "I guess it was a bad idea."

"No, it's just that you surprised me. Do you need somebody to talk to or do you just need some silent company?"

"Talking is overrated. And in this situation, it certainly hasn't solved anything."

"You go on," she said. "I need to let Griff know I'm leaving, then I'll catch up with you after I grab my coat."

Judd headed for the door, then paused and called to Griff, "See you at supper."

Griff looked up, stared at him for half a second, and returned to his conversation with Rick. Judd closed the office door behind him, then went through the kitchen to the back-stairs. He really didn't understand why he'd invited Lindsay to take a walk with him. The words were out of his mouth before he realized he really did want her company.

He had gone to his motel room, changed into a nonde-script gray jogging suit, gray wool cap, and white athletic shoes, then driven back to Pine Crest Estates. He parked his car several blocks from Sunrise Avenue and jogged up the side of the street, nodding and speaking to those who acknowledged him. He figured that in a housing development as large as this one, most people probably thought he was just a new neighbor that they hadn't met. Most wouldn't even remember him. He didn't slow down as he passed 322, but he noted that Sonya Todd's boyfriend was back. If that big oaf wound up staying the night, he'd have no choice but to alter his plans. He hated when things didn't go to suit him. But he was not going to leave Tupelo without earning those fifteen points he so desperately needed.

If not tonight, then tomorrow night.

After dark, he'd come back, take a good look around her house and figure out a plan of action.

Sweaty and slightly winded, he got back in his car, wiped the perspiration off his face with a towel he'd borrowed from the motel and revved the Taurus's motor. Just as he reached for the gearshift, his cell phone rang out a familiar tune.

Who the hell?

Only one person had this cell phone number.

He lifted the phone from the cup holder where he'd stashed it.

Why is he calling me?

Don't answer it.

As the tune to the song Bert Parks made famous years

ago when he had emceed the Miss America Pageant kept playing, he stared at the phone in his hand. His mind recited the
words, "There she is, Miss America." When the game had
begun nearly five years ago, he had chosen this particular
music for his cell phone ring after his first kill. Such an appropriate tune. In a couple of months, when the game ended,
he would choose a different ring, perhaps something to celebrate his victory.

Lindsay walked alongside Judd down the gravel road that
went through the woods and ended at an old boathouse on
the lake. Griff didn't use that dilapidated boathouse, but hadn't
bothered with tearing it down. He'd also left an old, shabby,
weathered barn on the property. Except for the new road that
led from the highway to his house and the house itself, little
had been altered since he'd purchased the acreage.

The crisp winter breeze shimmied through the treetops,
swaying them gently, as it assaulted Lindsay's pale cheeks
and nose. They were probably pink from the cold, a curse for
anyone such as she with an extremely fair complexion. Her
guess was that the temperature hovered somewhere around
forty, but once the sun went down, it would quickly fall into
the thirties, probably to freezing before daylight tomorrow.

She'd been an outdoor girl all her life and had spent many
happy tomboy hours fishing and camping out with her dad.
She could remember several times when it had snowed enough
in Chattanooga so that they could build a snowman. And there
was enough snow or ice at least every other year, for them to
take her dad's childhood sled out of attic storage and sail
down a steep hill near their house.

Happy memories.

Even though she had lost both of her parents before their
time, at least she had grown up in a home filled with love and

laughter. Someday, she would like to have children of her own and give them the kind of happy and secure childhood she had known.

But before she could think about marriage and children, she had to stop loving Judd Walker.

Neither of them had said a word for the past fifteen minutes. She had kept in step with his long strides and had occasionally stolen sidelong glimpses of him. Why was it that no other man affected her the way Judd did? Although no great beauty like Jennifer Mobley Walker, Lindsay had always been popular and well liked. And she'd had boyfriends ever since kindergarten. But she'd never been madly, passionately, insanely in love until Judd entered her life.

Strong emphasis on the word insanely.

Her love for Judd bordered on the insane, didn't it?

If any other man had done to her what he had, she not only would have hated him forever, she probably would have stuck his butt in jail. But loving Judd the way she did, she had forgiven him for being such an ass. And in a way. she understood why he'd treated her so badly. He had wanted to scare her off; and he'd accomplished just that, at least temporarily.

During the past six months, she had tried to put the incident out of her mind, tried to pretend it hadn't happened. By staying away from Judd, she'd been able to deal with the situation and even started dating Dr. Nathan Klyce. She really needed to end things with Nathan before it became serious. It wasn't fair to lead him on, not while she was still in love with another man.

Fool!

Any woman in her right mind would run like hell from a renegade like Judd, a man teetering precariously between sanity and madness. And that same smart, sensible woman would pursue a relationship with a great guy like Nathan, a stable, dependable, sweet man.

She supposed that made her neither smart nor sensible. And probably emotionally unstable.

But what can you do when you can't stop loving a man who is bad for you?

If what happened six months ago couldn't bring her to her senses, apparently nothing could. Late last summer, after he'd spent two weeks here at Griffin's Rest during the heat of the investigation into the most recent beauty queen murder, Judd had asked her to drive him home to the hunting lodge, as she'd done numerous times in the past. And like in the past, she had spent the night. But that night turned out to be different in ways that haunted her, in ways that disturbed her, in ways that broke her heart.

Don't think about it.

It hadn't really changed anything between Judd and her, at least not on a permanent basis.

"Is it safe to go inside?" Judd asked as he paused in front of the boathouse.

"What?" The fact that he'd spoken after such a long silence startled her.

"I've walked out this way a couple of times before, but I've never gone inside the boathouse. If we go inside, it won't fall in on us, will it?" He inclined his head toward the rickety building.

"I don't think so," she told him. "But why do you want to go inside?"

He shrugged, lifting and dropping his broad shoulders clad in his battered brown leather jacket. "Just something to do."

When he jangled the hinge and lifted the heavy wooden latch, she watched him. And when he opened the door and went into the dark interior, she hesitated. The last time they had been alone in the dark . . .

"Are you coming in?" he called to her.

"Sure." Garnering up her courage, she walked into the boathouse, then paused several feet past the entrance.

Soft afternoon sunlight shot through the numerous cracks in the loose wooden walls and crumbling cedar shingles on the roof. Lindsay inspected the empty interior, noting the galaxy of shimmering cobwebs and taking in the damp, musty scent that permeated the air.

"It doesn't look like anybody's been inside for years," Judd said.

"It's kind of creepy, don't you think?" Feeling oddly chilled, Lindsay crisscrossed her arms and hugged herself.

Judd turned around and stared at her. "Is it the place that's rattled you or is it being alone like this with me?"

"I'm not afraid to be alone with you."

When he came toward her, it took every ounce of her willpower not to back away from him. Instead, she stood her ground, and when he stopped less than a foot from her, she tilted up her chin and looked him right in the eyes.

Judd laughed. "You remind me of a little Chihuahua who thinks she's a Rottweiler."

Lindsay bristled. "Don't make the mistake of letting my size fool you."

Judd closed the minuscule gap between them, coming so close that they were almost touching.

Steady, girl, Lindsay warned herself.

He lowered his head until his breath fanned her mouth and mingled with her breath. "I swear that I will never again do anything intentionally to hurt you." He lifted his head and took a step back.

Lindsay released the chest-aching breath she'd been holding. Forcing back the tears that threatened to dispel the tough image she was trying to project, she swallowed hard and nodded. It was all she could manage at the moment.

"I'm a rotten bastard, and I don't deserve friends like you and Griff."

Answer him, damn it! "You're right, you don't. But you need us."

"Yeah, I guess I do."

"Griff talked to you, didn't he? Was the apology his idea?" she asked. "Did Griff make it one of the stipulations of your being allowed to stay here at Griffin's Rest and take part in the investigation?"

Before she realized his intentions so that she could side-step his move, Judd reached out and ran the back of his hand across her cheek. "The apology was sincere." He eased his hand away from her face. "But don't read too much into it. It was only an apology, not a declaration of love."

Just when she thought nothing he said or did could hurt her, he proved her wrong. But this time, the wound had been inflicted unintentionally.

"I understand," she told him. "The apology was more than I expected."

Chapter 10

The next day, Judd sat in on another meeting. This time, he tried to act as if he was paying attention, as if he thought going over the same old information might actually prove useful. It wasn't Griff's fault that the Beauty Queen Killer hadn't been apprehended. God knew the Powell Agency had used every resource available—legal and slightly illegal—to track down the man who had killed Jenny. Neither Powell nor the FBI had been able to pick up the madman's trail, although both had extensive profiles that narrowed down suspects. But that was the problem—they didn't have any suspects.

In the past three and a half years, Judd had learned more about serial killers than he'd ever wanted to know. He could easily recite the rhetoric. Memorized facts and figures. Eighty-five percent of American serial killers are male, eighty-two percent are white, eighty-seven percent are loners, and most range in age from twenty-two to fifty.

While Judd did his best to stay focused on the conversation taking place, Griff explained how he had three Powell agents in Williamstown, Kentucky, right now, keeping track of everything that the local law enforcement and the FBI were doing. "These men have built a professional rapport with the police department, and the chief has been very cooperative, despite Nic Baxter's disapproval."

"Does anybody involved in Gale Ann Cain's murder case have even one tiny lead?" Judd asked. "Other than Barbara Jean, who either cannot or will not give a detailed description of the possible killer."

"We've been here before," Griff said. "Our guy is nomadic. Once he kills, he leaves town. He either moves often or he travels a lot. And because this type of killer isn't stationary, doesn't kill in just one area, he's more difficult to catch than one who stays close to home."

"And until now, he's been invisible," Lindsay said. "He manages to kill and disappear without anyone seeing him. Except this time, Barbara Jean saw him."

"We believe she saw him," Griff corrected. "We can't be certain the man she saw is our killer."

Propping one elbow on the desk, Judd leaned forward. "Okay, let's say she can ID him and finally agrees to work with a sketch artist. What happens then?"

"We share the sketch with the FBI," Griff said. "And that sketch will be sent to every local law enforcement agency in the country. Sooner or later, somebody will see the sketch and recognize our guy."

"Then for God's sake, use your powers of persuasion on Barbara Jean." Judd's gaze collided with Griff's. "While you're giving her time to come around on her own, this guy is out there plotting another murder. Tell her that her fear and uncertainty could very well cost another woman her life."

He hated cheap motel rooms, but staying in an inexpensive place where he could pay cash and the clerk probably wouldn't remember him the next day made sense. It would be foolish to flash his money around, to say or do anything that might make him stand out and cause someone to re-member him. Keep a low profile was the number one rule in this game. Victories were not for public celebration. They were to be savored privately.

Early this morning, long before daylight, while Sonya had entertained her boyfriend, he had taken the opportunity to check out the houses on either side of and across from hers. He had inspected her backyard. No fence. No large shrubbery. Exposed on all four sides to the prying eyes of neighbors. His best course of action was to enter her home late tonight, when there was less chance of anyone being awake and peeking out the window. He didn't think she had a security system. There were no signs posted and ninety-five percent of people with private security posted warning signs. And quite a few people without security systems stuck stickers on their doors or signs in their yards as a deterrent to thieves.

Of course, the one thing that would make entering Sonya's house as easy as taking candy from a baby was the fact that she, like a lot of other idiots, kept a key "hidden" under a fake rock in her front yard. He'd taken that key around one this morning, while he'd been examining the layout of her house and yard.

He clutched the brass key in his hand and smiled as he drove into downtown Tupelo to look for a decent restaurant, preferably a crowded establishment. He would eat a good supper, go back to the motel, and think about the night that lay ahead, a night of horrible pain for Sonya and unforget-table pleasure for him.

Sometimes he found a suitable weapon in the woman's home, but he never left anything to chance. He always went prepared. He had a bright, shiny new axe that he had bought at a Wal-Mart in Monroe, Louisiana, lying under a plastic painter's tarp in the trunk of his rental car.

* * *

Judd paced back and forth in the two-story living room that spanned the width of the house. A wall of floor-to-ceiling windows and three sets of French doors dominated the back wall; the doors opened onto a deck that overlooked the lake.

Although when Griffin was at home, dinner was usually served at seven, it was five past seven and Griffin hadn't shown up nor had Sanders announced dinner. After the end of their afternoon meeting, Lindsay had stayed on in Griff's home office and gone over the most recent reports from the agents in Williamstown. She hadn't seen or talked to Griff since then, and until they had met in the living room ten minutes ago, she hadn't seen Judd either.

Judd moved around the room like a caged animal searching for an escape route. Whenever he paused, he stuck his hands in his jacket pockets and stared out into the darkness; then as if jolted by an electrical prod, he would start moving again. Edgy. Unsettled. Nervous energy.

Lindsay knew the signs. She had seen them all too often. Judd was restless. He had little patience, expected immediate action, and was the type who snapped his fingers and thought everyone should jump. Perhaps, in part, that came from having been reared in the lap of luxury, accustomed to issuing orders and having them instantly obeyed.

With each murder case, Griff and the FBI had gathered information. Sometimes, it was nothing more than an insignificant tidbit that didn't further the investigation one iota. Other times, it was info that helped them add to, build on, or alter the profile of the Beauty Queen Killer. But it all seemed meaningless to Judd because compiling information and building a profile had not produced results. While the Powell Agency, local law enforcement agencies in various cities, and the FBI investigated, the man who had murdered Jennifer Walker continued killing. Woman after woman after woman.

"Want to play cards or chess or watch a movie after dinner?" Lindsay rattled off a list of possible temporary cures for Judd's restlessness.

"You don't have to babysit me," he told her. "I'm not going to do anything stupid, like drown myself in the lake . . . or corner Barbara Jean."

"You gave Griff your word about not pressuring Barbara Jean, didn't you? That's good enough for me."

Judd harrumphed. "You shouldn't be too trusting. There was a time when I was a man of my word. That Judd Walker doesn't exist anymore."

Before she had a chance to think of an appropriate response, Griffin entered the living room; but he was not alone. He escorted an exotic woman with luminous black eyes and blue-black hair cut in a shoulder-length pageboy style. She wore cream white slacks and an oversized matching sweater. Diamond and gold hoops dangled from her small ears.

"Dr. Meng." Lindsay walked across the room to greet their guest, an old and dear friend of Griff's. "How wonderful to see you again." Lindsay shook hands with the woman Griff had first brought into her life six months ago. She had no idea how old Dr. Meng was, but if she were to guess, she would say late thirties, although she looked younger.

"How are you, Lindsay?" Dr. Meng asked. "Quite well?"

"Yes, quite well, thank you."

Judd approached them, but kept his distance, a leery glint in his eyes, as if he suspected Dr. Meng was his enemy.

"Judd, come over and meet Yvette Meng," Griff said.

Judd took several tentative steps forward, but didn't come close enough to shake hands with Dr. Meng.

"Yvette, this is Judd Walker," Griff told her. "Lindsay and I have mentioned him to you on several occasions."

"Mr. Walker." Yvette nodded cordially, but respected Judd's wariness and made no move to approach him.

"Almost perfect English, which means you were probably

not born and raised here," Judd said. "Yvette Meng." He examined her as if she were a specimen under a microscope. "Eurasian?" he asked.

"Yes, very astute of you, Mr. Walker. My father was Chinese, my mother French."

Judd eyed Griff suspiciously. "Is Dr. Meng's visit merely social or have you brought her here in her professional capacity?" Judd immediately focused on Yvette. "Do you have a medical degree or simply a PhD?"

"A medical degree," she replied in a voice that dripped with honey. Delicate and sweet.

As Lindsay knew—personally—that sweet voice was deceptive. Yvette Meng might look like a geisha doll, delicate and subservient, but the woman possessed the heart of a tiger and the courage of a lioness.

"Somebody here sick?" Judd asked sardonically.

But Griff didn't get a chance to reply. Sanders appeared and announced dinner was ready. Yvette took Griff's arm, and he led her toward the dining room.

Judd looked at Lindsay and offered her his arm. "Shall we?"

When she took his arm, he paused and asked, "Did Griff bring her here for me?"

"If he did, would you talk to her?"

Chuckling derisively, Judd glowered at Lindsay. "No way in hell."

Taking in and releasing a deep breath, Lindsay replied, "I'm sure Griff brought her here to talk to Barbara Jean. It's quite possible that she's suffering from some form of traumatic stress syndrome, an area in which Dr. Meng has specialized."

"Hmm . . . I have to hand it to Griff. He's gone above and beyond the call of duty to try to find Jenny's killer. And he's still doing everything he can."

"Maybe you should tell him that." Lindsay tugged on Judd's arm.

He didn't budge. "You've met Dr. Meng before. When?"

Just tell him the truth. There's no reason why he shouldn't know. So what if it makes him uncomfortable at dinner this evening, realizing that Dr. Meng knows all about him.

"Griff brought her here to help me through a rough patch . . . about six months ago."

"Goddamn! Did I fuck you up so badly that you needed a shrink?"

"Yeah. Yeah, you did." She released his arm and walked away. Head held high. Shoulders straight.

Sonya walked Paul to the door, kissed him, and reluctantly said good night. She didn't think either of them were quite ready for the next step in their strong and steady relationship—marriage. Here in Tupelo, there was no way they would ever get away with living together without the bonds of matrimony. Not with them both employed by the school system. So, for now, they would have to settle for him occasionally staying the night. Not too often or people would talk.

"See you tomorrow," he told her just before he kissed her one final time.

She stood in the open doorway and, despite the frigid night air, watched him until he got in his car and drove away. Sighing dreamily as she recalled the great sex they'd just had, she closed and locked the door.

Since she had to get up at six in the morning because it was a school day, she should take a shower and go to bed. But she wasn't sleepy. Paul had stayed overnight last night and they had slept late this morning, skipping both Sunday school and church, wicked sinners that they were.

Sonya giggled and twirled around and around. The belt on her housecoat loosened and the quilted robe slipped apart across her legs. The feel of the material as it raked across her flesh sent shivers through her, reminding her of the way Paul's mouth had created a moist trail up the inside of one thigh and down the other, then traveled the same path back again. That man sure knew how to eat pussy. How many times had she climaxed?

Three times!

Humming happily, Sonya went into the kitchen, retrieved a bottle of white zinfandel from the refrigerator, removed the cork from the half-full bottle, and poured herself a glass of wine.

Suddenly a horrific boom of thunder shook the house, rattling the windows and scaring the holy crap out of her. Her hand holding the glass trembled so badly that a few drops of wine splattered over onto her fingers.

She hated winter rain. It was always so cold and made the world look even more dismal than it already was. But she supposed rain was preferable to snow. They didn't get much snow in Tupelo, but she'd heard that parts of Tennessee had gotten blanketed with the white stuff a few days ago.

As she carried her wine into the living room, she paused to pick up the remote and turn on the TV before sitting down to relax. The evening news had just come on. Sitting alone in the semidark room, lightning streaking the night sky and thunder roaring, Sonya shivered. Odd, she wasn't scared of storms so she shouldn't be nervous.

By the time the weather report came on, she had finished the wine and felt a little sleepy. She'd better get a shower now before she relaxed even more.

Once in the bathroom, she removed her robe, hung it on the door hook and set the showerhead to spray, then turned on the water. Just as she stepped beneath the warm mist, the lights flickered. Once. Twice. Then everything went pitch-black.

Damn!

Don't panic.

She had candles in the kitchen and a flashlight in her nightstand drawer. But her hot water heater was electric, as was her heating unit.

Get out of the shower carefully, dry off, put on your robe, and get your flashlight, then double-check the front and back doors.

More than likely the electricity wouldn't stay off more than an hour, two at the most. She could crawl into bed, cover up, head and ears, and go to sleep. The house would cool off quite a bit in a couple of hours, but by morning it would have warmed up again, and she should have plenty of hot water to shower and wash her hair.

Feeling her way out of the shower, she reached for a towel, finally found it, and dried off hurriedly. Why didn't this bathroom have a window? At least a flash of lightning now and then would give her a little illumination.

After she managed to put on her robe, Sonya went into the bedroom. Even though she moved slowly and thought she was being careful, she stubbed her toe on the edge of the dresser. Cursing under her breath while her big toe throbbed, she made it over to the nightstand, pulled open the drawer, and rummaged around inside for the flashlight.

Found it!

She sighed with relief when the yellow-white beam streamed across her bedroom. She just hoped the batteries weren't low. She didn't think she had any replacements.

First she checked the front door—locked—and then headed for the kitchen. Just as she passed the double windows over her sink, a flash of brilliant lightning zipped across the sky, catching her immediate attention. When she glanced out the window, she screamed. Had that been a face peering into the window, looking right at her?

She pointed the flashlight at the window. There was no one there. Another loud clap of thunder rumbled. Trembling from head to toe, she blew out a shaky breath. What was the matter with her? Why was her imagination working over-time? It wasn't like her to be a Nervous Nellie.

Hurrying, she tried the backdoor to make sure it was locked. It was.

She walked over to the sink and looked outside again. Utter darkness. Nothing. No one. Certainly no faces staring in at her.

Suddenly another zigzag of lightning brightened the sky. When she looked outside, she saw only her driveway and her neighbor's three-year-old son's tricycle. Cody was always leaving his toys strewn about in his yard and often in hers.

Get a grip, Sonya. There is no one out there.

For some unknown reason, she was as jumpy as a cat in a room full of rocking chairs.

Judd ate only to live, but occasionally, like tonight, he actually enjoyed a good meal. Griff's cook, Inez, wasn't a world-renowned chef, just a woman who knew how to pre-pare good, old-fashioned country meals, Southern meals, like the fried chicken, fried potatoes, and cornbread she had put on the table tonight. To top off dinner, she had served a mouth-watering blackberry cobbler. Wild blackberries, not the cul-tivated ones with huge seeds. When he complimented her on the dessert, she informed him that she had personally picked the wild berries on Griffin's land last year and canned them herself.

During dinner, Judd had found himself actually interested in those in attendance: Griffin Powell, Lindsay McAllister, Sanders, Dr. Yvette Meng, and Barbara Jean Hughes. Three men, three women, almost as if they were paired into cou-ples. Sanders seemed unusually interested in Ms. Hughes, something that puzzled Judd because he'd never actually thought of Sanders as an ordinary man who had a perfectly natural interest in the opposite sex. In truth, he'd seen the quiet, reserved man as little more than Griffin's shadow. Griff's attitude toward Yvette Meng intrigued Judd. It was apparent the two were old friends, probably lovers, if not now, at sometime in the past. He suspected that the lovely Yvette knew some of Griff's deep, dark secrets.

And then there was Lindsay. His Lindsay. Odd how he thought of her that way. His. As if she belonged to him. She didn't, of course.

He had observed her periodically, all through dinner, and as if seeing her for the very first time, realized she was cute and funny and sexy. Not sexy in the obvious way that Yvette was, but in her own more subtle way.

In the past he had used her, abused her, taken advantage of her, and had expected her to take every cruel, thoughtless thing he dished out and still be there for him, even when he tried to send her away. If she had loved him once, surely she didn't any longer. But then, he didn't want her love. Love was wasted on him.

After dinner, Sanders escorted Barbara Jean to Griff's office to show her the lay of the land, so to speak. Apparently, the lady was going to teach Sanders basic computer skills. He supposed, considering the fact that the man could probably build a computer from scratch, this ruse had been something Griff was using to keep his houseguest occupied.

Griff excused himself, saying he needed to contact his agents in Williamstown and asked Lindsay to accompany him. Naturally, this left Judd alone in the living room with Dr. Meng.

"Do I have a stain on my sweater or food between my teeth?" Yvette asked.

"Neither," Judd replied. "I'm staring at you because I'm trying to figure out a gentlemanly way to tell you I'm not interested in being psychoanalyzed."

After offering him a mysterious smile, she turned her back on him and went to the bar area. "Would you care for an after-dinner drink, Mr. Walker?"

"Sure. I'll have whatever you're having."

"Whiskey. Neat." She poured some of Griffin's expensive liquor into two glasses.

Judd grinned. "I wouldn't have pegged you for the type of woman who drank whiskey."

She turned, handed him one of the glasses, then saluted him with her glass, and took a sip of the liquor. Not one gasp or cough. The lady was accustomed to the hard stuff.

"I'm not here to psychoanalyze you," she told him. "Griffin asked me to help Ms. Hughes."

"Yeah, he probably did, but didn't he tell you that if you got a chance, to study his crazy old friend Judd?"

"Are you crazy?" She sauntered across the room, like a sleek little black cat who knew she was beautiful and far smarter than the average feline.

When she sat down on one of the two overstuffed sofas that faced each other, Judd sat across from her, crossed his legs, and took a hefty swig of his whiskey.

"Haven't you heard—I'm mad as a hatter. Mad with grief. Mad with anger and a thirst for revenge."

"Wanting to see your wife's killer caught and punished doesn't make you mad."

He downed the remainder of the liquor, blew out a hot breath, and set his empty glass on the floor at his feet. "How about wanting to do the job yourself? I have dreams of chopping the guy into pieces."

Yvette scrutinized him, her dark eyes seeming to see beyond the physical realm. Sensing that she had invaded the darkness of his soul, Judd shivered involuntarily.

Squinting calculatingly, he gazed into her black eyes. "Did anyone ever tell you that you're downright spooky?"

She smiled. "I was born with a gift that few understand and many ridicule."

"Don't tell me—you're psychic," Judd said cynically.

"All right, I won't tell you."

Judd didn't believe in any of that woo-woo nonsense. If he couldn't experience it with his normal, five basic senses, it didn't exist. Yeah, so a time or two when he'd been out of his mind drunk, he had thought he felt Jenny's presence. A hint of her Chanel No. 5 perfume. The whisper of her voice. The light, tender touch of her hand. None of it had been real, just liquor-induced wishful thinking.

"Where the hell did Griff find you?"

"If you really want to know, you should ask Griffin."

"Okay, then when did you two meet?"

"Many years ago, when we were both very young." She sipped the whiskey, then set the glass on one of the soapstone coasters resting on the large mahogany and iron coffee table between the two sofas. "And if you wish to know more, only Griffin can tell you." Her gaze met Judd's head-on. "Such questions as were we once lovers, do I know where he was those ten missing years of his life, and do I know how he acquired his vast fortune?"

"I see part of your special gift is reading minds."

Her full, red lips parted, the edges lifting in a curious smile. "I find you interesting, Mr. Walker, especially knowing what I do about you."

"I'm flattered that Griff and Lindsay would bother filling you in about a hopeless case like me."

"Shortly after your wife was murdered, Griffin told me that you needed help, but he knew you would refuse to see me or any psychiatrist. And I met Lindsay only six months ago. I was her doctor for a brief period of time. I tell you this only because I know she has already mentioned it to you."

"She told you all about what happened, didn't she?" When Yvette did not respond, he slid to the edge of the sofa, lurched forward, and focused directly on her. "I'm not going to open up to you and spill my guts. If you were able to help Lindsay realize that I'm no good for her and that she should give me up as a lost cause, then I'm grateful. Beginning and end of story as far as I'm concerned."

Judd shot to his feet, accidently knocking over his empty whiskey glass. "Good evening, doctor. See you around."

"Good evening, Mr. Walker."

He made his escape. Almost. Just as he exited the living room, Yvette Meng's soft, compelling voice called to him, "You must not be afraid of your feelings for Lindsay. Allow yourself to love her. She is your salvation."

Judd froze to the spot for a millisecond, then fled as if the hounds of hell were on his heels.

Chapter 11

He loved storms. The loud, rumbling thunder. The danger-ous lightning. The torrential downpour. Storms were power-ful and deadly, just as he was. He felt a strong kinship with tonight's violent tempest. Carrying the shiny new axe in one hand, the weapon held against his thigh, and the key to Sonya Todd's house in the other hand, he scanned the area around her backdoor. Who in their right mind would be outside after midnight when it was raining like crazy? He didn't mind get-ting wet, didn't care that his clothes were drenched, that his skin was cold and damp. Somehow it all simply heightened his excitement, added to his anticipation. After he unlocked the backdoor and eased it open carefully, he stepped inside, and shut the door behind him. Quietly.

Listening for any sound to indicate that his entrance might have alerted her to his presence, he placed the axe against the wall, then patted his soggy jacket pocket. Ah, yes, it was still there, coated with raindrops, but otherwise unharmed. He removed the long-stemmed pink rosebud, then took the tiny key-ring flashlight from his other jacket pocket and used it to search the room. Taking hesitant steps, not wanting to bump into anything and make a noise, he paused as he passed the kitchen table and laid the rose there for safekeeping. He would need it later. A tribute. One lovely flower for another.

He felt inside his pants pocket, checking on the small digital camera. An important part of the game was photographing the kill.

The house was middle-of-the-night quiet. Only the hum of the electric heat pump and the ticking of a rather loud clock disturbed the stillness. Sonya was probably sound asleep. She had made this almost too easy for him, as if she were asking for it. But she would never suspect that a mysterious stranger would use the key she thought was so cleverly hidden to enter her home. In the dead of night. With the intention of killing her.

Wouldn't she be surprised.

A gleeful chuckle escaped his lips.

Shh . . . Must be quiet. Don't want her to scream. Can't have her telephoning for help.

Using the tiny flashlight to guide his steps, he crept through the house, into the living room and down the hall. Two doors lay on either side, one door closed, the other open.

His heartbeat accelerated, his breath quickened. He passed through the open doorway and straight into Sonya's bedroom. He could barely make out the dark shadow that rested under the covers in her bed. The power had stayed off for a little over an hour, but it was on now and with a flip of a switch he could cover her room in light. No, that wasn't what he wanted. When he had her subdued, then he might turn on a bedside lamp to provide just enough light so that she could see what he was going to do to her. So that he could watch the terror in her eyes as he chopped off her arms.

Apparently, she had left a nightlight burning in the bathroom, because a glimmer of illumination wafted beneath the closed bathroom door.

On tiptoe, he made his way to the side of the bed, then eased one knee down on the edge.

She was such a sound sleeper.

He smiled to himself.

Easy. So easy.

He slithered into the bed alongside her. She grunted and flopped over, from her side onto her back. He propped himself on one elbow and stared down at her. Lovely, even at thirty-five. Her shoulder-length blond hair draped her oval face. He barely resisted the temptation to curl a strand of her hair around his finger.

The covers clung to her from the waist down, leaving the upper half of her body exposed to the night's chill and to his scrutiny. As his eyes adjusted to the darkness, his night vision improved, enough so that he could see she wore nothing under the silk robe that had parted just enough to reveal the inner curve of her luscious breasts.

His penis twitched. Hardened.

He would not have to be inside her to experience pleasure. That would come later, once the deed was done, the pictures taken, and he was safely away.

In one swift, calculated move, he rose up, threw one leg over her body and straddled her; simultaneously, he covered her mouth with one hand and pressed himself on top of her, trapping her beneath him.

Her eyelids flew open and she stared up at him in shock and disbelief.

For the first few terrifying moments, Sonya thought she was asleep and having a horrible nightmare. But she quickly realized that the man bearing down on her, his breath hot on her face, his warm, damp hand on her mouth, was all too real. She struggled against the force of his weight and shook her head from side to side. He lay down on top of her, his mouth at her ear and spoke in a whispery yet threatening voice.

"Be very still and very quiet."

She tried to speak, tried to beg him not to hurt her, but all she managed was a jumble of mumbling sounds caught under his open palm.

"Shh . . . my pretty little flower. Don't fight me."

He was going to rape her. She could feel the outline of his erect penis as it twitched against her through the sheet and thin blanket.

Dear God, help me!

Although he wasn't as tall and big as Paul, he was not a small man. From the weight of his body pressing against hers, she suspected that he was rather heavy. A detail she needed to remember to tell the police. Later. When it was over and he was gone.

As his cheek brushed against hers, she noted that he was clean-shaven. Another detail not to forget.

He squirmed around, but kept her completely trapped beneath him until he moved one shoulder, just enough so that she managed to free her right hand. When she did, he yanked the pillow from the other side of the bed and pressed it down over her face as he lifted his hand from her mouth.

She tried to scream, but it was useless. The pillow muffled the sound.

Was he going to smother her?

She felt him jerk something out of his pants pocket; then he grabbed her wrist and lifted it above her head.

No, don't. Please don't. She struggled when he yanked first one and then her other wrist over her head.

He pressed the pillow against her face with his elbow, effectively cutting off her air. So panicked at the thought he was going to suffocate her, she didn't realize at first what he had done. Not until he lifted the pillow. She gasped for air, but before she could cry out, he placed his hand over her mouth and tossed the pillow onto the floor.

He had tied both of her wrists with some type of cord and had secured each to opposite sides of the intricately carved headboard.

Now he would rape her.

Sonya's heart beat wildly. Her pulse throbbed in her temples.

Suddenly, before she realized his intent, he stuffed a rag in her mouth, then fastened a piece of cloth around her face to hold the gag in place.

While she stared at him pleadingly, he eased up and off her. She tried to make out his face in the semidarkness. He turned his back to her as he stood.

What was he doing? Removing his clothes? Unzipping his pants?

She wiggled about, testing the sturdiness of the ropes that bound her. Ouch. There was no give in the rope. She wasn't going anywhere, not until he chose to release her.

He switched on the bedside lamp, casting a forty-watt glow over the room. The man turned around and smiled at her. She tried to scream, but the wad of thick cotton in her mouth made it impossible.

She stared at him. *Memorize his face. For later. The more you remember, the more help you'll be to the police when they—*

He had no qualms about her seeing his face.

That was a bad sign, wasn't it?

"Hello, Sonya. You're such a lovely blond flower. And worth fifteen points to me."

What was he talking about? How could she be worth fifteen points?

Dear God—was raping her part of a sick game he played with his victims? Did he keep some kind of score of his conquests?

He removed the covers, shoving them to the foot of the

bed. She shivered from head to toe. He reached out, loosened the belt on her robe, and spread it apart, revealing her naked body.

Why hadn't she put on her pajamas or at the very least a gown? Why had she simply toppled into bed wearing only the robe?

"You're as lovely as you were when you were crowned Miss Magnolia, oh so long ago."

Had he known her back then, when she was Miss Magnolia? Had he been infatuated with her? Had she spurned his advances?

She inspected him as best she could in her awkward position, half sitting and half lying. He was about five-nine and hefty. His belly hung over his belt and his face was round and full. He was indeed clean-shaven, his cheeks smooth and soft-looking. His brown hair was short and neat. And, at the moment, slightly damp.

He studied her with a set of large hazel brown eyes. "You stay put, my sweet pink rose. I'll be right back and then the fun will begin."

Where was he going?

She tugged on her bound wrists until she groaned with pain.

Gone only a few minutes, he returned hurriedly, plodding into the room with heavy feet. She turned to look at him and gasped, the sound trapped by the gag. He carried a sinister-looking axe.

Dear God in heaven, he's going to kill me!

"Which shall I remove first?" he asked as he gazed at her, an expression of absolute glee on his fat face. "Your right arm or your left?"

She shook her head. The sound of her silent screams echoed in her mind.

"It takes both hands and arms to play the violin, doesn't

it, so I have no choice but to remove both arms." He lifted his weapon. "Hmm . . . I think the right arm first. Is that okay with you?"

Help me! Help me! The prayer repeated over and over in her heart as her attacker came closer and closer, the axe lifted and ready to strike.

When he swung the axe, she closed her eyes.

Unbearable pain. Blood everywhere. Terrifying realization.

Then Sonya passed out before he struck the second blow.

He stood under the warm shower, washing away Sonya Todd's lovely red blood. As the crimson water swirled down inside the floor drain, he sighed with a delectable sense of pleasure. Taking a human life gave one a feeling of God-like power. There was nothing else like it, no experience equal to it, no drug capable of creating the astounding sensation of absolute control. He chose who died, when she died, and how she died.

With each kill, the thrill increased, leaving him only temporarily satisfied and longing for a new conquest.

After drying off, he donned his silk pajamas and robe, then entered the run-of-the-mill motel room on the outskirts of Tupelo. He hated staying in these working-class places, with no room service and no down comforters.

He lay on the king-size bed, atop the horrid floral spread and stared up at the popcorn ceiling. The lonesome wail of a train whistle pierced the silence of early morning, and within minutes a speeding locomotive rumbled along the nearby train tracks.

Like so many of his other victims, Sonya had been an easy kill. By leaving a door key hidden under a fake rock in her front yard, she had all but invited him into her home, into her bedroom.

He loved surprising his victims, and usually settled for simply seeing the shocked expression on a woman's face when she realized he wasn't who she thought he was. But with Sonya, the experience had been even better because she had awakened to find him in bed with her, on top of her. He shivered with the memory of the way she had felt lying beneath him, her slender body trembling with fear. Closing his eyes, he allowed his thoughts to take him back to the very moment Sonya had seen the axe in his hand and had realized he was going to kill her. Involuntarily, his hand rose from his side, his fingers curled as if clutching the axe handle and once again he swung the deadly blow that severed her right arm.

His penis hardened.

He groaned deep in his throat.

Sonya had passed out, so he had waited until she regained consciousness before he took off her left arm. Knowing it would be only a matter of time before she bled to death, she had stared at him, and he had triumphantly watched the expression of pain and helplessness in her eyes.

Recalling her agonizing moans as she died and savoring the moment, knowing he could relive it again and again once he printed the photos he'd taken with his digital camera, he reached inside his pajama bottoms and touched himself. With the image of a dying Sonya in his mind, he climaxed.

Shuddering.

Quivering.

Alive in a way he was only after a fresh kill.

Chapter 12

As she walked down the hall toward the kitchen, Lindsay wasn't sure if she dreaded or was looking forward to seeing Judd this morning. Perhaps both. Being near him was sweet torture. There was no better way to describe her feelings. She both loved and hated Judd. Loved him because she couldn't stop loving him. And hated him for the same reason. It wasn't his fault that he didn't love her, that he couldn't love anyone. But it was his fault for treating her badly. She might forgive him for his cruelty, but she would never be able to forget.

Stop thinking about that night!

For six months, she had fought the memories. She had undergone therapy with Dr. Meng and had come through stronger and more determined than ever to give up her hopeless dreams about Judd Walker. It would be easier if she didn't have to spend time with Judd. But if she gave up on him entirely, what would happen to him?

Preparing herself to face him with a friendly greeting, she entered the kitchen. She halted abruptly when she saw the crowd congregated in the room. Inez stood at the stove, flipping pancakes. She smiled and nodded when she saw Lindsay. The two had become fast friends, almost since the first day they met. Inez was sixty, fat, blond, and motherly. With a coffeepot in hand, Sanders moved around the table filling one empty cup after another. He didn't seem to notice her, but that was just Sanders, a man who focused on one thing at a time.

Lindsay didn't miss the way Barbara Jean offered Sanders a fragile smile and whispered "thank you" when he poured her coffee. Sanders's gaze lingered on Barbara Jean, as if the sight of her pleased him.

Wouldn't it be wonderful if those two fell in love?

Mercy, Lindsay Leigh McAllister, you're a romantic fool.

When Lindsay approached the table, where a place had been set for her, Yvette Meng spoke to her first, "Good morning. Did you sleep well?"

"Fair," Lindsay replied. "You?"

"Quite well, thank you, but I always sleep well when I visit Griffin's Rest."

Although Lindsay was curious about Dr. Meng's relationship with Griffin and Sanders—she appeared to have known them both for quite some time—Lindsay never asked. She suspected that Yvette Meng had somehow been a part of their lives during the missing ten years of Griff's life.

"How many pancakes do you want?" Inez called. "I've put a sausage-and-egg casserole on the table, along with some banana nut muffins, and I'm working on the pancakes."

"None for me, thanks," Lindsay said. "The casserole and muffins will be more than enough." Before she had a chance to request coffee, Sanders made his way around the table quickly to fill her cup.

He leaned down and said quietly, "Griffin is in the den, taking a phone call, and Mr. Walker hasn't come down yet."

Lindsay said, "Okay."

No one else seemed to have paid any attention to Sanders's private comment to her. Everyone was too busy either eating or talking.

Three other Powell agents were here this morning, two of them other female agents, Angie Sterling and Maleah Perdue, who would take alternating twelve-hour shifts guarding Barbara Jean around the clock. Rick Carson was pulling two-week duty here at Griffin's Rest, in charge of security for the estate. Griff rotated Powell agents for this duty, changing them out every couple of weeks. It gave each agent a chance to take a break from outside assignments and at the same time familiarize himself—or herself—with the workings of Griffin's Rest. At any given time, Griff had between fifteen and twenty agents on the roster. They worked out of a downtown Knoxville office building that Griffin owned. Occasionally, an agent moved on to another type of job, and two had even opened up their own small detective agencies in other states. But the turnover at the Powell Agency was minimal and the death rate among agents very low. In the seven-year history of the agency, only one had died in the line of duty and one in an off-duty car accident. The risks depended upon the individual assignment. The pay was excellent and the fringe benefits superior to those found anywhere else. Griff even had a retirement program in place for those who stayed with the agency twenty years or more. A third of his agents were married and another third were in committed relationships. Lindsay, Maleah, and Rick were part of that final third—single and alone. Angie was engaged to another Powell agent, Jason Blaine, and their wedding set for this June.

Just as Lindsay took her first sip of coffee, her telephone, which she kept in her pocket, vibrated and rang simultaneously. "Sorry," she told the others, who had actually paid very little attention to her ringing phone.

She set her cup down on the saucer, pulled her phone

from her pocket, and noted the call was from Griffin. Odd. Why hadn't he simply used the house's intercom system?

She flipped open her phone. "Yes?"

"Come to the den. Now," Griff said. "Simply excuse yourself without any explanations."

"All right." She slipped the phone back in her pocket, scooted back her chair, and stood. "If y'all will excuse me."

Lindsay and Sanders exchanged pensive glances before she exited the kitchen. Sanders knew Griffin had called. She wasn't sure how he knew, but he did. Sometimes she felt as if Griff and Sanders communicated telepathically.

Two minutes later, she reached the den door, which was closed. She knocked.

"Come in," Griff said. When she did as he requested and entered the den, he told her, "Close the door behind you."

She closed the door. "What is it?" She could tell by the stern expression on his face that the news was not good.

"He's struck again. In Tupelo, Mississippi. Sometime last night or early this morning."

Lindsay's empty stomach soured, a feeling of nausea pulsating through her. "It's too soon, isn't it?"

"I think that what we've feared is happening—he's narrowing the time between kills, escalating the game plan."

"Who was she? How did he—?"

"The son of a bitch chopped off both of her arms."

Salty bile rose up Lindsay's esophagus. Even after knowing the details about so many gruesome murders the Beauty Queen Killer had committed, each time brought new disgust, anguish, and anger.

"You're okay, aren't you?" Griff asked. "You look a little green."

"I'm okay. I just haven't had my coffee yet."

Griff nodded. "Her name was Sonya Todd, former Miss Magnolia. She was a violinist." Griff positioned his big arms in the stance a violinist would take when holding the musical instrument. "The method always matches the woman's talent in the contest, and it's just a part of the game to him. He thinks it's clever. He thinks he's clever."

"He is," Lindsay said. "This woman is his thirtieth kill, that we know of, and he hasn't been caught."

Griffin slammed his fist down on his desk. "I want that bastard. I want him dead or alive."

"You sound like Judd."

He looked directly into Lindsay's eyes. "Do I?"

"Yes, you do. And that bothers me."

"What does—the fact that I could kill the man with my bare hands or that you think my attitude borders on the unstable?"

"I don't know. Both. Neither. It smacks of vigilante justice. As a former police officer, that goes against everything I was taught. By my dad, at the police academy, and while on the force."

"Theoretically, allowing our legal system to punish criminals is the right thing to do. But sometimes, a man has no choice but to take the law into his own hands." A far-off, detached expression on his face told her that Griffin was thinking of something other than the most recent murder.

"Are we going to Tupelo?" she asked.

"Yes, I've called Jonathan and told him to have the jet ready to leave this morning."

"Who's going with us?"

Griffin grinned. "You assume you're going?"

"I've been working on this case with you since the beginning. My going with you to Tupelo wasn't an assumption, it was a statement of fact."

"Just the two of us and Judd are going."

"Nic Baxter will break her neck to get there before us," Lindsay said.

"All the more reason for us to get a move on," Griff told her. "Do you want to tell Judd or shall I—"

"I'll tell him. He's still upstairs."

When she turned to leave, Griff reached out and grasped her arm. "Just because he's doing his best to play nice doesn't mean he's changed in any way. Remember that."

Swallowing hard, she nodded, then hurried out of the den.

Judd stood by the windows gazing down at the bleak winter landscape. He had gotten, at most, four hours of sleep. Four hours was a lot for him, at least in one stretch. There were nights when he didn't sleep at all and stayed up prowling around the old lodge or taking midnight walks in the woods. Other nights, he'd fall asleep at two or three in the morning and sleep until daylight. And then there were the nights when he passed out drunk.

Had he actually become an alcoholic during the past few years? Were his drinking binges more than sporadic self-pity parties? When the pain became too great to bear, wouldn't anyone choose whatever method possible to alleviate some of the pain, if only temporarily? Sure they would. That's how people became drug addicts—and how they became alcoholics.

What did it matter? It wasn't as if his life meant a damn thing to him or to anyone else.

That's not true, he reminded himself. *Lindsay McAllister cares.*

His life meant something to her.

The woman had to be crazy to waste her time on him. He'd tried to convince her to forget about him, to write him off. It's what he wanted.

Or was it?

Griff's words echoed in his mind. *You've depended on her caring, wanted it, craved it.*

He hated admitting that his old friend was right, but God damn it, he *had* depended on Lindsay. He had needed her to care. For nearly four years now, he had used and abused her, and she'd always come back for more. Until six months ago. But even after what had happened then, she hadn't completely given up on him.

You do want her, Judd told himself. *You want her so bad you can almost taste it. Taste her. You crave her the way a man dying of thirst craves water.*

That night six months ago when he had come close to raping her, he had told himself that he was doing it to scare her, to force her to see him for the sorry son of a bitch he was. But that wasn't the only reason.

You wanted to have sex with her.

Un-uh, no half-truths, he told himself. *Be completely honest with yourself. You wanted to make love to Lindsay. And that scared the shit out of you. The way she makes you feel scares you.*

Hell, the very fact that she made him feel anything at all was enough for him to hate her.

As if on cue, Lindsay called his name as she tapped softly on his bedroom door. "Judd? Are you awake? I need to talk to you."

"Come on in," he said, not giving his state of undress a thought. Not until she opened the door and stood there staring at him, her eyes wide, her full, pink lips slightly parted.

"You've seen me in less," he told her, then reached over on the floor and picked up his discarded jeans where he'd tossed them last night.

She didn't respond until after he had pulled his jeans on over his briefs and zipped them. "He's killed again. A former Miss Magnolia in Tupelo, Mississippi."

Judd's guts twisted into knots. "When?"

"Last night or early this morning." She stared at his naked

chest, but when she realized what she was doing, she cleared her throat and looked right into his eyes. "Griff's ordered the jet readied for us. We need to leave immediately."

He inspected her briefly, noting that she wore a jogging suit. "Do I have at least ten minutes? You don't look like you're ready to travel."

She glanced down at her baggy gray jogging suit. "I'm heading to my room to change and pack an overnight bag. We leave for the airport in thirty minutes."

Judd ran his hand over his face. "I'll need to grab a quick shave. My being clean-shaven is one of Griff's stipulations for being allowed to participate in the investigations again."

The corners of Lindsay's lips lifted marginally, just a hint of amusement. "I'll meet you downstairs in thirty minutes or less."

He walked toward her. She backed up, out into the hall. It was then that he realized that when she had entered his room, she had stopped just over the threshold and stayed there. By the time he reached the door, she was outside, obviously keeping several feet between them.

"Was she a blonde, brunette, or a redhead?" Judd asked.

"I don't know."

"What was her talent?"

"She was a violinist."

"So, how did he kill her? Cut off her hands or—"

"He chopped off both of her arms."

Judd clenched his teeth. He and Lindsay stared at each other, but neither of them spoke again. She turned and walked down the hall. He closed the door, shut his eyes, and leaned his head against the door as memories of Jenny engulfed him. Jenny sitting on the kitchen floor, her arms tied above her head, her hands hacked off and lying on either side of her body.

God in heaven, would he never be able to erase that memory from his mind?

* * *

The Powell jet landed at the Tupelo Regional Airport shortly before noon. A Town Car, ordered by Sanders, waited in the parking lot, and the chauffeur met them inside the terminal. Their driver was a tall, lanky black man named Devin Chamness, who owned and operated his own limo service in the Tupelo area. He often escorted wealthy visitors and politicians. Lindsay knew that if Sanders had hired Mr. Chamness, the man was topnotch, the best in his field, and the type to keep his eyes and ears open and his mouth shut as far as his client's business was concerned.

The short drive from West Jackson Street, where the airport was located, into downtown Tupelo took them along Madison and straight onto Court.

"I spoke to Chief Winters before we left Knoxville," Griff had told them during the flight. "Lieutenant Bobby Skillman is the CID detective in charge of the Sonya Todd case. The chief told me that his department would cooperate with us, up to a point."

Up to a point could mean that local law enforcement would share no more with them than what they told the press or it could mean they would share almost everything with them. On past Beauty Queen Killer cases, Lindsay had seen the locals clam up completely and resent the Powell Agency's presence. She'd also seen police chiefs or sheriffs who were very forthcoming with information—until the FBI showed up and took over the case. If Nic Baxter was already on the scene, she would be doing all within her power to lock Griff out of the inner circle.

Griff, who was sitting up front with the driver, turned and looked into the backseat at Lindsay and Judd. "Lieutenant Skillman is set to make a statement to the press at noon outside the crime lab on Court Street."

Lindsay checked her watch. "It's five till."

"We're only a block away," Devin informed them, but kept his gaze focused straight ahead.

A horde of people, mostly local and state press, congregated on the sidewalk at 324 Court Street, many of them spilling out into the street. Camera crews zeroed in on the plainclothes detective at the makeshift podium, a guy in his early forties, with thinning black hair and a slight stoop to his broad shoulders.

Devin slowed the Town Car, but didn't stop. Griffin rolled down his window to get a better look. Cold air seeped into the car's interior. Despite the warm noon sunshine, the temperature hovered near fifty. The loudspeaker broadcast the detective's deep, aw-shucks, Mississippi drawl.

"Park up the street," Griff said. "We'll walk back."

Within minutes, Devin had pulled the Lincoln into a parking place a block away; and before he killed the engine, Griff swung open his door and got out. He was several steps ahead of them before Lindsay and Judd caught up with him. The three of them hung back, staying on the periphery of the assembly, listening to the completion of the officer's statement, waiting for their chance to approach him after the press conference ended.

"There have been no arrests in this case," Lieutenant Skillman said. "And at this time we have no suspects." He took a deep breath. "Ladies and gentlemen, I'll now take a few questions, but please make them brief. Y'all have five minutes."

The news people bombarded him with questions, which seemed to fluster him greatly. No wonder. A brutal murder occurring in Tupelo was hardly an everyday event. It wasn't as if the detective was accustomed to answering these types of questions. Finally, Lieutenant Skillman pointed to a man closest to the podium. "Yeah, you, Joe Mitchell."

Mitchell barked out his question, "How was Sonya Todd murdered? We've heard she was hacked up into little pieces."

"I am not at liberty to reveal that information at this time," Lieutenant Skillman replied.

A collective groan spread through the reporters, along with a couple of boos and one distinct hiss.

A petite redhead shoved her way through the throng, all the while shouting her question. She might be little, but she had a big voice. "Is it true that the police department suspects that the notorious Beauty Queen Killer is responsible for Sonya Todd's death?"

"No comment." Lieutenant Skillman's cheeks flushed and perspiration dotted his forehead despite the February chill.

The Powell Agency already knew more than the press did. The fact that Griffin had been given details that were not being revealed to the press told Lindsay that Griff had somehow persuaded the local chief to divulge classified information.

Lindsay stood on tiptoe and, in order to be heard over the den of the crowd, shouted into Griff's ear, "What did you do, use the 'I'm Griff Powell, former UT football star' to make brownie points with the chief?"

Griff frowned at her. "You underestimate my notoriety as a rich and famous private investigator. Chief Winters was very interested in the fact that I was hired by one of the victim's husbands to search privately for the Beauty Queen Killer."

"Well, I'm impressed. You didn't have to bribe him or anything, huh?"

Before Griff could respond, another reporter managed to shout louder than the others and make his question heard above the clamor.

"Has Chief Winters called in the FBI?" The tall, skinny, forty-something TV reporter had a cameraman behind him taping everything.

Lieutenant Skillman had that deer-trapped-in-the-headlights expression, and he stuttered when he tried to respond.

"At this time . . . er . . . we . . . that is Chief Winters . . . has . . . er . . . has—"

"The FBI was notified," a strong, clear feminine voice called out from the back of the crowd, on the opposite side from Griff, Lindsay, and Judd.

All but strutting, Nic Baxter parted the reporters, like Moses parting the Red Sea. "I'm Special Agent Baxter, and as of now, the lieutenant will not be answering any further questions. This is officially a federal case."

"Shit," Griff mumbled under his breath.

"She's not going to let us get anywhere near Lieutenant Skillman," Lindsay said.

"Probably not," Griff replied. "But as we all know, there's more than one way to skin a cat."

Chapter 13

Yvette Meng understood grief, from a personal stand-point as well as from her years of training and experience as a licensed psychiatrist. And she understood fear in a way only the victim of cruelty and abuse could comprehend it. She knew what it was like to have her life hanging in the balance, to be at the mercy of another for the very air she breathed.

Barbara Jean Hughes grieved for the sister that she loved, but her grief was in the first stage, where one cannot fully comprehend that the other person is truly gone. Forever. It is as if nature protects a person's fragile emotions for days, sometimes for weeks, after the event. If not for this, one might go mad.

As Judd Walker had done?

She had seen it happen before, with strong, aggressive people, especially men who were accustomed to being in complete control of their own lives and the lives of others. Not madness in the truest sense of the word, but an anger and thirst for revenge that bordered on madness.

Over three years ago, Griffin had wanted her to help Judd.

But first, one must want to be helped. Judd had spurned all offers. Even now, he was not ready to free himself from the past. He had become comfortable with his pain, had embraced it above all else.

"Would you care for more tea?" Sanders asked as he held the teapot over Yvette's china cup.

"Yes, thank you." Yvette loved Damar Sanders, as she loved Griffin Powell, as one loved brothers. "More tea would be nice and perhaps a few more of Inez's delicious little cakes."

Taking his cue to leave, Sanders replied, "I will see if she has more. If not, I am sure there are some of her homemade oatmeal raisin cookies." He nodded curtly, the motion showing gentlemanly deference to her and Barbara Jean.

Once Sanders left, Yvette turned her attention on the woman who had been sitting quietly, her hands in her lap, watching the interchange between Yvette and Sanders. "You are wondering about our relationship?"

"No, I—your relationship is none of my business," Barbara Jean said.

Smiling, Yvette reached over and laid her hand on the other woman's arm. "Sanders is a brother of my heart. We have known each other for many years."

"He—he's a good man? I mean, he seems to be very kind."

"He is more than kind."

Barbara Jean nodded.

A marked silence fell over the room. Barbara Jean avoided eye contact with Yvette.

Sometimes the direct approach is best. This woman was not stupid. She had to at least suspect why Griffin had brought a psychiatrist to Griffin's Rest.

"I will be staying here for a few weeks," Yvette said. "I am available to you, day or night, whenever you may need me. If you wish to talk, we will talk. If you prefer that I—"

"I can't identify him." The declaration whooshed from

Barbara Jean in one gasping breath. "I've told Griffin all that I remember about the man. I swear that—"

Yvette patted Barbara Jean's arm. "It is all right. There is no need to upset yourself. I am not here to pressure you, only to be at your service should you need me."

Barbara Jean stared skeptically at Yvette, apparently wondering if she could trust her. "I won't remember anything else. I know that for sure and certain. I–I can't."

Keeping a pleasant expression on her face, Yvette pulled back and picked up her cup of tea. "Sanders makes delicious tea. My favorite is this Earl Grey. I remember my mother drinking it when I was a child."

The change of subject seemed to relax Barbara Jean. "Gale Ann liked our Grandma Hughes's sassafras tea. When we were girls, she'd make it for us. I detested the stuff. It tasted too much like licorice to me and I can't stand licorice."

"I never knew either of my grandmothers," Yvette said. "I was an only child, as was my mother. And my father's sister died as a young girl. So you see, when my parents died, I had no family."

"Gale Ann and I were so lucky to have each other." Tears gathered in Barbara Jean's eyes. "It's so unfair that she . . ." A soft gulp. "It should have been me. I'm older and I'm . . ." she glanced down at her useless legs. "I'm crippled. If one of us had to die, it should have been me."

Yvette waited. Tears trickled down Barbara Jean's cheeks.

"If you could have, you would have died for your sister." Yvette spoke softly, sympathetically. It was simply in her nature to be caring. And it was in her unique makeup to share the emotions another person felt more intensely than the average person did.

"Yes. Yes, I would have. I wish—wish I could have." Barbara Jean wept, releasing some of the emotions she had been keeping bottled tightly inside her.

Facing reality could be a devastatingly painful experience, but it was necessary. Acceptance was cathartic and could lead to the next stage of grief.

"I'm sure your sister knew that you would have exchanged places with her," Yvette said. "And I'm certain that, had the situations been reversed, she would be feeling now, just as you are."

Barbara Jean continued crying.

Yvette sensed his presence before she glanced at the door and saw Sanders standing there with a platter of tea cakes and oatmeal cookies in his hand. He hesitated. Yvette shook her head. He eased backward and disappeared down the hall. He would return, of course, in five minutes or so, when Barbara Jean was no longer crying.

Griffin watched Nic Baxter as she took over the press conference and succinctly ended it with one statement. "The Sonya Todd murder is now a federal case. I will issue a press release tomorrow morning, at the earliest. Until then, do not approach any federal or local officer with questions."

The crowd grumbled. Loudly. But everyone seemed to understand Special Agent Baxter's take-no-prisoners attitude. All except the ferocious little redhead who apparently wasn't as intimidated by Nic as the rest of the press corps. Or perhaps she simply wasn't smart enough to know when to back down.

"Are we to assume that since the FBI is now involved that this is another Beauty Queen Killer murder?" the redhead asked.

Nic's hot gaze melded with the redhead's. "What's your name?"

"Brigit Henson, the *Memphis Commercial Appeal*."

"Well, Ms. Henson, I suggest that you assume nothing." Finale. Complete. Over and out.

Brigit opened her mouth to speak again, but before she

got out a word, Griff interceded. "Special Agent Baxter!" Griff's deep baritone voice rumbled like thunder in the hush of the dispersing crowd. Like in a freeze frame, no one moved.

Nic searched and found him in the crowd, not difficult to do since he stood a tad over six-four and weighed a good fifty pounds more than he had when he'd played ball for UT. Muscle, not fat. He prided himself on keeping fit.

She glowered at him, but didn't respond.

"Why make these people wait?" Griffin said. "Within an hour, every one of these reporters can find out that you're the special agent in charge of the Beauty Queen Killer cases. And any idiot can put two and two together and come up with four."

Nic bristled. Her brown eyes glimmered with anger. "Now they won't have to wait, will they, Mr. Powell, since you've shared the information with everyone present."

He knew he'd pissed her off. He didn't care. Getting a rise out of Nic Baxter had become one of his favorite pastimes. She would put up every possible barrier to keep him out of the loop. Of course, that was part of her job. He understood. Yet he resented the hell out of her attitude.

"Why not make a statement now?" He was playing with fire and he knew it. She could arrest him for interfering in a federal case. And she was just the type who would.

If Griff thought playing nice in the sandbox would get him anywhere with Nic, he'd be the nicest guy she'd ever met. But he had tried charming her. Hadn't worked. Wouldn't work. Apparently, she was not only immune to his charm, she had an aversion to it.

While the dispersing crowd lingered, waiting for Nic's re-action, she ignored Griff completely. She turned, grasped Lieutenant Skillman's arm and led him toward the front door of the Tupelo crime lab. Nic's assistant, Special Agent Josh Friedman followed, but kept glancing over his shoulder, his gaze connecting with Griff's a couple of times.

A few reporters zeroed in on Griff. One had recognized him, remembered him from his UT days. The two men and one female reporter—Brigit Henson—questioned Griff about his connection to the case.

"My client, Judd Walker, lost his wife to the Beauty Queen Killer almost four years ago. Mr. Walker hired me to do an independent investigation, but unfortunately, I have had no more luck than local and federal law enforcement agencies in tracking down this monster. However, when this psychopath killed Gale Ann Cain in Kentucky last week, he was seen leaving the woman's apartment complex."

"Are you saying there is an eyewitness, someone who can identify the killer?" Brigit asked.

"Yes, that's exactly what I'm saying."

"Who is this person?" This question came from one of the male reporters.

"She is the sister of the murder victim."

All three reporters shot question after question at Griff, who told them that he could give them no further information. "Not at this time."

Griff made the finality of his statement clear by walking away, back to where Judd and Lindsay waited several feet down the sidewalk.

"You all but invited the killer to come after Barbara Jean Hughes," Judd said.

"Yes, I did, didn't I?"

"But you didn't mention where she was," Lindsay said.

"I will." Griff smiled. Unless he missed his guess, Brigit Henson was heading straight in his direction.

Barbara Jean was as safe as the gold in Fort Knox. No one could possibly harm her as long as she was at Griffin's Rest. But he had no qualms about using her to tempt this madman into making a wrong move. It was highly unlikely that he would be stupid enough to try anything. They couldn't get that lucky. But Griff wanted him to sweat, to spend sleepless nights worrying about an eyewitness being able to identify him.

"You could have asked my permission before you gave the press my name." Judd looked past Griff. "Here comes your little pigeon, homing in on you."

"The fact that you're my client is old news." Griff kept his gaze focused on Judd, acting as if he had no idea Ms. Henson was directly behind him. "But it was worth repeating. You inherited the vast Walker fortune. You're always newsworthy. But the real news is that I have Barbara Jean Hughes safely tucked away in my home outside Knoxville."

Brigit Henson cleared her throat.

Griff turned around slowly, only a hint of surprise on his face. He didn't want to overplay his hand. "Ms. Henson, I trust that you won't repeat what you've just heard."

Her hazel green eyes rounded wide and sparkled with mischief. "Why not give me an exclusive, Mr. Powell, and we'll discuss terms."

"Please, call me Griff." He offered her one of his cocky, self-assured smiles, the kind that made unspoken promises to a woman. And in this woman's case, the promises were both professional and personal. He'd never been a man adverse to mixing business with pleasure.

Brigit laced her arm through his. "Well, Griff, why don't we go somewhere for a cup of coffee and talk things over."

Griff glanced at Judd. "You two take the car and I'll meet up with y'all later, at the Wingate."

He walked up Front Street and then onto Barnes Street where he had parked his Ford Taurus. Smiling at his own cleverness, he unlocked the door, then removed his hat and coat and tossed them into the backseat. Losing himself in the throng of reporters had enabled him to be front and center when the lead detective on Sonya Todd's murder case made a statement to the press. Not that he had revealed anything of importance. But that was to be expected. The police always liked to keep things under wraps.

When both Special Agent Baxter and Griffin Powell had shown up, it had been like old home week. He hadn't always been able to stay in a town the day after a kill, but more and more often now, he delayed his departure just long enough to savor his victory. These local yokels didn't have a clue. And even the FBI had no idea who he was.

Laughing, he started the engine and pulled out into early afternoon traffic. He would drive home today, take his time, make a few necessary stops, but he would not stay overnight anywhere. There was too much to do when he got home. Photographs to print out and place in his gallery. Memories to savor while they were fresh. And one all-important phone call to make.

Perhaps I should also call Nicole Baxter.

He had been tempted to telephone the lovely FBI agent in the past, if only to hear her voice. She had fascinated him from the first moment he saw her, when she had worked with Curtis Jackson before his retirement.

If only she were a former beauty queen . . .

Don't get sidetracked. Nicole is an opponent, not a victim. She might be an extremely attractive woman, but she is not a pretty flower who needs to be picked before she begins to wither. No, Special Agent Baxter's part in this game was that of a worthy adversary, not a victim.

But when this game ended . . .

He could not believe that the end was near. Only a couple of months until the five years would be over and the winner would claim the ultimate victory. He and his cousin had been friendly opponents, sharing the thrill of each victory in a competition neither had realized in the beginning would become a game they lived to play. And what made their little game all the more fun was that no one had figured out that there were two of them—two Beauty Queen Killers.

He would miss the game, the rivalry, the quest to achieve the highest points. And he would miss his cousin most of all. But there could be only one winner and he intended for that honor to go to him. The alternative was to lose—not only the game, but his life.

Lindsay and Judd picked up burgers at a fast food restaurant before having their driver drop them off at the Wingate Inn on Stone Creek Boulevard. Sanders had booked a junior suite for Lindsay and an adjoining double for Judd and Griff. Luckily, the rooms were actually ready for them when they arrived at one-thirty. Despite check-in being at three, they were welcomed and given their keys.

"Will Mr. Powell be checking in soon?" the desk clerk asked.

"Yes, later this afternoon," Lindsay replied.

When they reached the suite, Lindsay invited Judd to come inside.

"We can share lunch," she said, as she unlocked the door.

Judd brought the two sacks of food into the room and placed them on the coffee table in front of the tan sofa. Lindsay parked her wheeled overnight bag in the corner. Judd dropped his carryall from his shoulder and let it fall beside her bag.

"I don't know why I bothered to come along." Judd removed the two large iced colas from one sack, stripped the paper wrapper from a couple of straws and stuck them through the plastic lids. "I've done this too many times to think anything will come from our being here."

"Call me an optimist, but I still hope that sooner or later he'll screw up and give himself away."

Lindsay went into the bathroom and washed her hands.

When she came back out, Judd had their burgers unwrapped and their fries emptied onto the inside of the spread-apart wrappers. Sitting on the sofa, he held up a packet. "Ketchup on the side. Right?"

She nodded. He tore open a couple of packets and emptied the contents alongside her fries; then he opened two more and spread the ketchup over his fries.

Neither said much while they ate. She supposed there wasn't much for them to talk about, nothing that wouldn't be a repeat of past conversations.

Just as Lindsay removed her piece of apple pie from the cardboard container, her cell phone vibrated. She had turned off the ringer at the press conference and had forgotten to turn it back on. When she pulled the phone from her pocket, she checked the caller ID.

Griff.

"Hello."

"How's it going?" Griff asked.

"Fine. Judd and I just shared a delicious meal of burgers and fries."

"Yummy."

"Do I need to ask where you are?"

She had seen "That Look" in Griff's eyes before, and she knew that he had chosen Brigit Henson as his next conquest. Lindsay respected Griff, liked working for him, adored him really. But she knew him for the predator he was. The seemingly cultured, well-mannered gentleman's façade he presented to the world masked the cunning, deadly warrior that lay beneath the exterior trappings. In every aspect of his life business and personal—Griffin Powell was a conqueror.

"I'll have you know that Ms. Henson and I are at the local Olive Garden," Griff said. "She's gone to the ladies' room."

"Will you be joining us later?"

"The verdict is uncertain. The jury's still out on that one."

Lindsay laughed.

Griff got down to business. "Sonya Todd had a boyfriend. His name is Paul Dryer and he's the baseball coach at Tupelo High."

"Are you going to—?"

"No, I want you to get in touch with him, see if he'll talk to you. He's more likely to open up to a woman."

"Okay. When?"

"Not today. It's too soon." Griff paused. "Contact him tomorrow. Play the Judd Walker card. Men in the same situation. See if Judd will go along."

"Oh, sure, give me the easy assignment."

"Brigit has done her homework. The lady is a fount of information. But I don't think she would readily share what she knows with you. You're not her type."

"So, she likes the big, hairy-chested, burly type, huh?"

"Yep. And that would be me."

"Why is interviewing the boyfriend going to do us any good?" Lindsay asked.

"He's the one who found the body," Griff said. "And he's the one who, like Judd, compromised the crime scene."

"Great," Lindsay said sarcastically.

Flashes of memory rattled Lindsay.

Judd holding his dead wife in his arms. Judd tenderly caressing Jennifer's face. His earsplitting scream.

"Lindsay?" Two male voices called her name.

The flashback of the night Jennifer Mobley Walker had been brutally murdered ended as abruptly as it had begun.

Lindsay glanced at Judd, then spoke to Griff. "Yeah, I'm here."

"Sanders contacted me right in the middle of my veal parmigiana," Griff said. "It seems a little research has turned up a possible contact within the police department."

"Why am I not surprised?"

"Now, now, don't be that way. We may be bending the law just a little, but we're doing it for a good cause."

"So you keep telling me whenever you bribe someone."

"He's an assistant technician at the crime lab. Sanders will contact him tonight, at home, and see if he can persuade the gentleman to give me a few minutes of his time tomorrow."

"If Nic Baxter gets wind of—"

"You let me worry about Nic," Griff said.

"Sure thing, but it's your funeral if she catches you."

Griff chuckled, then hung up.

Lindsay turned to Judd. "Griff wants me to contact Sonya Todd's boyfriend and arrange a meeting with him tomorrow." When Judd simply stared at her, she continued. "He found her body this morning."

"Griff wants me there when you question this guy, doesn't he?"

"Yes."

Judd looked past her, off into space. "You were remembering, weren't you? When you were talking to Griff and you zoned out, you were remembering the night Jenny was murdered."

"Yes, I was remembering."

"It's odd, but I don't remember much of anything before I arrived at that house or what happened afterward. I remember seeing Jenny lying there, her hands cut off—" Judd closed his eyes and clenched his teeth. "That memory is branded inside my head. Nothing short of a lobotomy could erase it. That's what you remembered, wasn't it? The sight of Jenny . . ."

"Yes."

The sight of Jenny in your arms.
The way you touched her so tenderly.
Your agonizing scream.

Chapter 14

Griffin had known the first minute he saw her that Brigit Henson would be a really good fuck. Experience had taught him a great deal about the opposite sex, their strengths and weaknesses. For the most part, women were all similar, but it was those subtle differences that defined them, that made some worth the effort and others not. He wasn't looking for love. Didn't want it. Didn't need it.

But he did want and need sex. On a regular basis.

And not since he turned fifteen had he ever had a problem getting laid. In high school, he'd been captain of the football team and had dated various cheerleaders. In college, as the star quarterback for UT, he'd had his pick of girls. And women. Older women, who had taught him a great deal. In his youth, he'd broken a few hearts because he'd made promises he never intended to keep. Horny young men tended to be callous and unfeeling, focused on only one thing.

As a man, he made no promises to his sexual partners.

Griff lay in the bed beside Brigit, staring up at the ceiling, his mind wandering. He could have left after they'd made love, but instead, he'd cleaned up and come back to bed, knowing how women liked attention afterward as much as they enjoyed foreplay.

Cuddling against him, she traced her long nails over his chest and sighed contentedly. "You don't have to leave, do you?" she asked. "It's early—" she lifted up and looked past him to the digital bedside clock "—only ten-thirty."

Skimming his open palm over her naked hip, he grinned. "I could be convinced to stay."

She smiled, whipped back the covers and danced her fingertips from his chest to his thighs, then back up to circle his penis. When she lowered her head and kissed his belly, Griff cupped the back of her head, urging her in the right direction. Her tongue wet a path downward. Slowly. Maddeningly.

She licked him from tip to shaft, then repeated the maneuver a couple of times before taking him into her mouth.

Anticipating a really good blow job, he groaned deep in his throat.

Within minutes, Brigit proved for a second time that Griff's instincts about her were correct. She was a lady with a great deal of experience, a woman who knew how to pleasure a man. His last coherent thought, before the whole world centered on his dick, was a question. Just how many men had divulged classified information to this talented reporter after she went down on them?

When Griff came in her mouth, he released his solid grip on the back of her head. She swallowed a couple of times, then licked his penis. He shivered involuntarily. She came up and over him, running her tongue over her lips, as if savoring every drop.

She kissed him, giving him a taste of himself.

As she lay on top of him, her small, perky breasts flat against his chest, she whispered in his ear. "I always like to wash out my mouth with some good liquor."

"Do you now?" He swatted her butt.

Laughing she rolled off him and over onto the bed. "I have a bottle of Jack Daniels in my suitcase." She started tapping her fingernails up his chest again. "And I really like my whiskey on the rocks."

"Is that a hint for me to go get some ice?"

"That's the problem with motels. No room service." She propped up in bed, completely comfortable with her nudity. "We could have a few drinks, talk, screw around some more." She sighed dramatically. "If only we had some ice."

"I'm willing to make a trek down the hall for some ice." He rolled out of bed. Once on his feet, he grabbed his slacks off the nearby chair and slipped into them. "I'm all for drinking and screwing . . ."

"But not for talking?"

"That depends on the subject." He put on his wrinkled shirt, leaving it unbuttoned.

"I thought maybe we could share information about the Beauty Queen Killer."

"What makes you think I know more than you do?" Griff picked up the empty ice bucket on his way to the door.

"You've been investigating this killer for nearly four years. You've been involved ever since Jennifer Mobley Walker was murdered in Chattanooga and her hubby hired you. My guess is that you know as much, maybe more, about the killer than the FBI does."

"Maybe I do." With the ice bucket in his left hand, he opened the door, then glanced over his shoulder and grinned at Brigit. "But what I know isn't for sale, not even for a damn good blow job."

Brigit's self-satisfied smile vanished. "Name your price. We've got all night."

Griff winked at her, then fixed the lock to keep the door ajar and headed down the corridor toward the ice machine. He had noticed the ice-maker at the refreshment center in a small alcove earlier when he had walked Brigit to her motel room door and she'd invited him in.

When he approached the alcove, he heard ice rattling and figured someone else was using the machine. So, he'd wait his turn.

He rounded the corner, intending to nod cordially to the guy ahead of him, and came face-to-face with a tall, statuesque brunette in a pair of fuchsia sweats. His gaze traveled over her from head to toe, then back up to look her right in the eyes.

She glowered at him, taking in his appearance, staring at his unbuttoned shirt and bare feet.

"Good evening, Special Agent Baxter," Griff said.

They danced to the soft, jazzy tune, Jennifer following his lead as he nuzzled her neck. She smelled like Chanel No. 5, the only perfume she wore. The same perfume that her mother and grandmother had worn.

When he slowly drifted his hand from her waist to her hip, she grasped his hand and led it back up to her waist. "People are watching us," she told him.

"So what? We're married," Judd replied.

Offering him that famous smile that some said had won her the Miss Tennessee title a few years back, Jennifer pressed herself against him. "Behave yourself. We're in a public place. There will be time enough later for what you have in mind."

He stopped on the dance floor, grasped her hand and said, "Let's leave now. We put in an appearance. No one will miss us."

She gazed at him, a pouting expression on her beautiful face. "Thirty more minutes and then we'll leave."

As much as he wanted to take his wife home right now and make love to her all night long, he could deny her nothing.

He had never loved anyone the way he loved Jennifer. His entire world began and ended with her.

As those thirty minutes ticked by and he watched from the sidelines as she danced with the mayor, a state senator, and his old friend Cam Hendrix, Judd thought about making love to his wife.

She lay beneath him, her lush, damp body accepting him inside her, lifting up to meet each thrust, whimpering with pleasure, begging him for more.

On the verge of climaxing, Judd gazed into her blue eyes and saw the look of love, deeper and more profound than ever before.

Blue eyes? No, not blue. Jennifer's eyes were brown.

But the body lying beneath him, giving him an exquisite orgasm was not Jennifer. And the look of love was not in Jennifer's eyes.

"Lindsay," Judd moaned.

Suddenly, Lindsay disappeared. As quickly as his mind had drifted away from thoughts of lovemaking, it returned to the gala event he and Jennifer were attending. But everything began to change. The dance floor turned red. Red with blood. Jennifer lay on the floor, her severed hands turned upward, the fingers reaching out. For him? He tried to go to her, but he couldn't move. Naked and aroused, he stood immobile as dark shadows closed in around Jennifer, separating him from her. He tried to reach her, to stop the shadows from enveloping her, but someone was holding him back, preventing him from going to his wife.

"Judd, help me," Jennifer cried as she lifted her bloody, handless arms.

Lindsay held him fiercely about the waist, stopping him from saving Jenny.

Let me go. I have to save her. Don't do this. Don't hold on to me.

Jennifer . . . Jennifer!

* * *

"I had no idea you were staying at this motel." Nic Baxter glared sharp daggers at Griff.

"I'm not," he replied.

She raised a damning eyebrow. "Let me guess—the little redheaded reporter?"

Griff smiled. Nic didn't.

Griff eyed the filled ice bucket she held. "Late night drinks with a friend?" he asked.

She bristled. "Unlike you, Mr. Powell, some of us do not mix business with pleasure."

Griff chuckled. "Too bad. If you did, I might be persuaded to give you a few lessons on how to relieve work stress. Getting rid of all that tension might help erase those frown lines at the corners of your eyes—" he pointed at her pensive brown eyes, his index finger only inches from her face "—and it would probably work a few inches off your hips." His gaze appraised her curvaceous body.

"Hell will freeze over before I'll ever let you give me lessons of any kind," Nic told him quite adamantly. "But I'm sure Ms. Henson can't wait for another *lesson*. You shouldn't keep her waiting."

"She'll be okay without me for a few more minutes."

Why didn't he just get his ice and go back to the room? Why couldn't he pass up this opportunity to ruffle Nic's feathers?

Because she was so easy. All he had to do was look at her to piss her off.

Griff moved in closer until his ice bucket clinked against hers, neither of them moving aside to accommodate the other.

"Your intimidation tactics don't work with me," Nic told him.

He shrugged. "I've tried charm, reasoning, and intimidation without any success. So tell me, Nicole—" he lowered his voice to a whisper when he said her name, and leaned down just enough so that they were almost nose to nose "—what does work with you?"

Taking a deep breath, she stepped back, putting a little distance between them. "Respect works with me."

"I respect you," Griff said.

"I could care less how you feel about me personally. What I was referring to was respect for the law, respect for me as an FBI agent."

"Respect works both ways you know. If you'd stop thinking of me as the enemy and start thinking of me as a friend—"

"If you wouldn't interfere with my investigation every time there is a new murder, I might see you in a different light. You shouldn't even be here in Tupelo."

"If you'd cooperate with me just a little, I wouldn't have to make a pest of myself. We're on the same side, you know."

"No, we're not," she said. "I'm a federal agent. I'm on the side of law and order. You're a P.I., hired by a man who is obsessed with revenge."

Griff focused his gaze on her and asked, "Can't you understand why Judd is consumed with the need to find the man who killed his wife and bring him to justice?"

"He doesn't want justice. He wants revenge."

"So your motives differ from Judd's," Griff told her. "The bottom line is that your goal is the same as mine and Judd's—to find this guy and stop him from killing."

Just as Nic opened her mouth to respond, they heard a woman's voice calling in a loud whisper, "Griff, honey, where are you?"

Glancing around the side of the alcove, he saw Brigit— with her midthigh-length robe loosely tied at the waist— coming up the corridor.

"You're being summoned," Nic said. "Apparently she couldn't do without you for another minute."

"Apparently." Griff grinned.

Clutching her ice bucket, Nic snapped around, walked out of the alcove, and headed back up the hallway toward her room.

Brigit came up to him and slipped her arm through his. "Was that Special Agent Baxter?"

"Yeah."

"I'm surprised she didn't shoot you on sight."

Brigit's attempt at humor fell flat, but Griff forced a weak smile. "She got in a few shots during our conversation."

Brigit looked at the empty ice bucket he held. "How much do you know about her?"

"Who?"

"Nicole Baxter, silly."

"All I need to know."

"Then you know about her husband."

Husband? What husband? "Yeah, sure."

Brigit hugged up to him. "Forget the ice, honey." She took the bucket from him and rubbed her breasts seductively against his chest. "I think I might like to lick my whiskey straight out of your navel . . . or maybe off your flat belly . . . or . . ."

After dinner together, Lindsay and Judd had parted company, each retreating to the privacy of their separate hotel rooms. She should be thankful that he had left her alone. Instead, she found herself repeatedly staring at the connecting door between her junior suite and the room Judd shared with Griff. She had done everything she could think of to get Judd Walker off her mind. Taking a warm shower, watching a couple of hours of mindless TV, reading several chapters in the latest Linda Howard novel, making a phone call to Sanders.

Now here it was going on eleven o'clock and she'd spent the past half hour in bed, tossing and turning. Her mind wouldn't shut off. Sleep wouldn't come.

She flung back the covers, got up, and walked over to the windows. After pulling back the edge of the drapes and peering out into the night, she heaved a deep sigh. Not much of a view.

Why had she flushed the remainder of those sleeping pills that Dr. Meng had prescribed for her months ago down the toilet? For several weeks six months ago, she had been unable to sleep without them.

She had disposed of the pills because she wasn't the type who liked to use medication as a crutch any longer than necessary. She'd actually thought of the sleeping pills as a sign of weakness, but Yvette Meng had made her realize that sometimes even the strongest people needed help.

"Be as kind and understanding with yourself as you would be with a friend. With Griffin or with Sanders," Dr. Meng had said.

Lindsay flopped down on the sofa, stretched out, and stared at the tiny light on the fire alarm above the door.

I wonder if Griff is back yet? Probably not. He'll drag in here around daylight.

Lindsay smiled to herself. Brigit Henson was a lucky woman tonight. Griff had his pick of women and he'd chosen her.

If Lindsay was the type who went in for brief, meaningless flings, she might risk her job for one night with Griff. But God help her, she was the one-man woman type. And Griffin Powell was not that man.

A loud, unnerving yell startled Lindsay. Jerking when she heard the unexpected sound, she listened carefully.

Silence.

Then another cry, not as loud. A mournful, terrified voice coming from the next room.

Judd!

She shot up off the sofa and raced to the connecting door, unlocked it, and flung it open. She shoved on the door leading into the adjacent room. To her surprise, the second door gave way. Apparently, Judd had not locked it from his side. After entering the dark room, she paused at the foot of the one occupied bed—the other empty, the covers undisturbed—and saw Judd thrashing about as if he were fighting someone in his sleep.

He cried out again, but this time he uttered a name.

"Jenny!"

Lindsay froze to the spot.

Judd mumbled several incoherent words.

Lindsay forced herself to take a few tentative steps toward the bed.

Obviously, he was having a nightmare about his dead wife. Should she wake him or let him wrestle with his subconscious thoughts of Jenny?

"No, God, no!" Judd moaned, then began to weep in his sleep.

Lindsay's heart ached for him.

And for herself.

How could she have ever thought that he would eventually get over Jenny, that someday, somehow, someway, he might be able to love again?

It had been nearly four years since that tragic night, and it seemed plain to Lindsay that Judd would never recover from losing his wife.

"Lindsay."

When he growled her name, she shivered, then as if her feet had a mind of their own, they carried her across the dark room, illuminated only by the light seeping in under the door from the well-lit hallway. She went straight to the side of his bed.

She sat beside him, reached out and caressed his face. "Judd. Wake up. You're having a nightmare."

His hand shot up lightning fast and manacled her wrist. Startled, she inhaled sharply and struggled to free herself.

He opened his eyes and looked up at her. "Let me go, Lindsay."

What was he talking about? He was the one holding her, not she him.

"Judd, are you all right?"

He yanked her down on top of him so that they lay face-to-face. Her breathing quickened. "Damn you, why wouldn't you let me go?"

"I don't understand . . . what are you—"

He reached up and circled her neck with both hands. When his fingers tightened, biting into her larynx, Lindsay gasped for air.

What the hell was wrong with him? Was he trying to choke her?

His deadly grip around her neck loosened. He eased one hand to the back of her neck and forced her head down to his while he placed his other hand on the small of her back and pressed her lower body against his erection.

"Judd?"

He took her mouth hungrily.

Don't let him do this again. Stop him now before it goes any further.

But she could no more stop herself from responding than she could prevent the sun from rising in the morning. Pure feminine instinct ruled her as she opened her mouth for his invasion.

He kissed her until she was breathless. Then he shoved her aside, almost toppling her off the bed as he stood up and walked across the room. With his naked back to her, he said, "Get out. Go back to your room."

"Judd?"

"I'm sorry." His broad shoulders slumped. "I was dreaming. When you touched me, I was half-asleep. I thought you were Jenny."

No, you didn't, she wanted to scream. *You called my name.
You knew you were kissing me. Why lie about it?*

"Yeah, sure," she said, then turned and ran back to her
suite, hurriedly closing her door and locking it.

He had driven from Tupelo to Jackson before stopping for
the evening. He had left his rental car parked at the airport,
changed clothes in the men's room, and taken a taxi to the
closest Holiday Inn Express. No one would pay any attention to just one more businessman staying overnight. He had
paid cash for his room, explaining to the desk clerk that his
credit card had been stolen and he was waiting for a new one
to be issued.

He put on a pot of the god-awful hotel coffee before he
showered. He preferred not to sleep the night after a kill. He
liked staying up all night and recalling every delicious moment. Of course, part of the fun of reminiscing was in sharing the details with his cousin.

Naked, freshly bathed, and cleanly shaved, he yanked the
spread off the king-size bed and draped it over the armchair
by the windows. He lifted his jacket from the foot of the bed
and removed the cell phone from the pocket. After sitting in
the chair, he dialed Pinkie's home phone.

Pinkie answered on the second ring. "Hello."

"Call me back at this number." He rattled off the cell
phone number.

Whenever they shared information about their latest victim, they always used disposable prepaid cell phones. Little
if any chance of ever being traced. The main rule of their little game was don't get caught.

In less than two minutes, his phone rang.

"She was a blonde," he told his cousin. "Sonya Todd. A
violinist."

"Fifteen more points for you," Pinkie said.

"We're neck and neck now, aren't we, Cousin?"

"It seems we are."

He chuckled. "Have you chosen your next pretty flower? Remember, she can't be a redhead. You've already had your redhead for this year."

"I won't need another, but you need one desperately, don't you, Pudge?"

He could hear the laughter in Pinkie's voice. *Let him laugh now, but in the end I'll have the last laugh. No way in hell will I let him win our little game.*

"I wouldn't say desperately, but yes, I rather think the next pretty flower I pick will have to be a redhead."

"All I need to win our game is one more brunette and one more blonde."

Pudge didn't reply. His cousin Pinkie was right. The only way he could win was if he found a redheaded former beauty queen as quickly as possible, then be ready to move in for the kill within hours after Pinkie took his turn next.

"So, are you going to tell me about her?" Pinkie asked. "Did she put up much of a fight? Did she suffer a great deal before she died? Tell me. Tell me. And don't leave out anything. I want to hear every gruesome detail."

Chapter 15

Griffin joined Lindsay in the junior suite for coffee. She didn't ask what time he'd gotten back to his room because it was none of her business. He certainly didn't look any worse for wear. His short platinum hair appeared to be slightly damp, probably from a recent shower. As usual, his appearance was impeccable. Navy blue suit, white linen shirt, and maroon and navy striped tie. His suit alone probably cost more than her monthly salary. And he was always clean-shaven. She'd known him to shave twice a day, often enough that she'd wondered if he had some sort of hangup about it.

"I don't have time for breakfast this morning," he said. "I have an early meeting with Johnson Rivers."

"The technician at the crime lab?"

"Yeah. He's nervous about talking to me, so I agreed to meet him outside of town where we're less likely to be seen together."

Lindsay handed Griff a cup of black coffee, then the two sat down facing each other. She took a sip from her second cup of the morning. She doubted Griff had gotten any more sleep than she had, but for an entirely different reason.

He looked great. A new conquest always seemed to agree with him. She, on the other hand, had dark circles under her bleary eyes, hadn't showered or put on any makeup and wondered if Griff could tell she'd cried herself to sleep.

He took a sip of coffee, checked his watch and said, "I've got ten minutes before my rental car arrives, if you want to tell me what happened last night."

"What is it with you? Are you psychic or something?"

He shook his head. "Nope, not my thing. If you want a psychic reading, you'd better call Yvette."

"Yeah, like she'd give me one." They smiled at each other, then Lindsay cleared her throat. "You seem to have a knack for making pretty good guesses."

"It doesn't take a genius to figure out something happened between you and Judd. When I got in an hour ago, I met him on his way out. He was going for a run and didn't say two words to me. And all I have to do is look at you to tell you had a rough night."

"Before you make any wrong assumptions—"

"You don't have to give me any details," Griff told her. "All I need to know is if I need to send Judd home."

"No, you don't need to do that." Lindsay took another sip of coffee, then held her cup between her open palms. "Long-story-short, Judd had a nightmare about Jenny. I went to check on him when I heard him hollering, and he kicked me out of his room."

Griff gave her a skeptical look, then changed the subject when he asked, "What time is your appointment with Sonya Todd's boyfriend?"

"He's supposed to come here to the Wingate at ten this morning."

"If Judd's okay—and I mean really okay—have him sit in on the meeting. Introduce him to this Dryer guy and let him know that Judd lost the woman he loved to the same killer.

Common ground is always a good place to start a conversation."

"After we meet with Paul Dryer, I plan to talk to some of Sonya's neighbors this afternoon," Lindsay said. "There's always the possibility that someone knows more than they think they do."

Griff nodded in the direction of the bathroom. "Why don't you go ahead and take your shower? When Judd comes back, you two can go out for breakfast."

"Are you suggesting a breakfast date?" She forced a smile.

Griff studied her closely as he finished off his coffee, then set the cup aside. "Judd is a damn fool."

"Yeah, I agree. But he's a damn fool still in love with his dead wife, and without some sort of miracle, I don't think that will ever change."

"Miracles happen."

"Ooh, watch it there, Mr. Powell, you're sounding rather philosophical this morning."

Griff chuckled.

Lindsay placed her half-full cup beside Griff's empty cup on the desk; then made her way over to her open suitcase sitting on the luggage rack. "How long are we going to be here in Tupelo?"

"I'm not sure. A couple more days at most. Unless we get a break in the case, there's no need to stay."

"Wouldn't it be great if we actually caught him this time." She removed a pair of clean panties and a bra from her suitcase before heading for the bathroom.

"Yeah, it sure would be great. And if Nic Baxter is the one to get him, that's fine with me, but something tells me that if we're the ones who crack the Beauty Queen Killer case, she won't feel the same way."

"She might. You never know."

Lindsay went into the bathroom and closed the door before she realized she'd forgotten her toiletries case. Just as she opened the door, she heard Griff's voice, low and deep. She peered into the suite. He was talking on his cell phone.

"How's everything there?" Griff asked. "That's good. I'm glad Barbara Jean seems to like Yvette."

Lindsay started to interrupt, say excuse me, and retrieve her toiletries case, but Griff's next comment stopped her.

"Run a check on Nicole Baxter for me," Griff said. "Dig as deep as you need to. I want to know everything there is to know about her husband."

Her husband? Lindsay didn't know Nic was married.

"Yeah, it was a surprise to me, too," Griff said. "Look, keep this just between us. Understand?"

Lindsay eased the bathroom door closed. How did Griff know Nic was married? And why was he so interested in information about her husband? Surely he didn't intend to use the info as leverage of some sort in dealing with Nic.

No, he wouldn't do that. It wasn't Griff's style to use blackmail.

Are you sure? she asked herself.

Just because she didn't know of any instances where Griff had resorted to blackmail and intimidation, it didn't mean he wasn't capable of both. She had worked with him long enough to know he possessed some hidden depths, and she suspected something unspeakably horrific had happened to him during those ten mysterious missing years of his life, from twenty-two to thirty-two. Something that had irrevocably changed him. Strengthened him. Hardened him.

Judd couldn't say that he and Paul Dryer had bonded, but he understood what the guy was going through, and for the first time in a long time, he actually felt someone else's pain. Dryer was still in that mind-fogged denial stage, where you were numb most of the time and still found it impossible to believe the woman you loved was dead. Dryer was in pain now, but it was nothing compared to the agony he'd feel in a few weeks. Judd had never actually spoken to a victim's husband or boyfriend until now. After sitting in on this interview, he had an idea of what it was like for the police officers and FBI agents who had worked the various cases, what it was like for Griff and Lindsay, for anyone who had to see firsthand the devastation murder created in the lives of those left behind.

He knew what it felt like on the other side, from the victim's husband's point of view. But now he had an inkling of the toll it probably took on the people trying to solve the crimes.

Judd followed as Lindsay walked Dryer to the door of the motel suite. With tears glazing his eyes, the guy looked right at Lindsay.

"I hope y'all find him," Dryer said. "When you do . . ."

Damn it man, don't cry, Judd thought.

Lindsay grasped Dryer's hand and squeezed. "Thank you for talking to us."

He nodded. "I'm just sorry I couldn't be of more help."

"You've done all you can do," she told him.

Dryer turned to Judd and held out his hand. Judd hesitated, then shook the guy's hand.

"Tell me it gets easier," Dryer said. "Tell me that somewhere down the line the pain will go away."

How the hell was he supposed to answer that? Was he supposed to be honest and tell this man that the pain would never go away?

Or was that actually the truth? He was no longer certain of anything.

When Judd didn't reply, Lindsay said, "You'll find a way to deal with what happened. It'll take time, and you'll never forget Sonya, but . . ."

"If you focus on the rage and hate, it will destroy you," Judd said. "She wouldn't want that for you, would she?"

Where the hell had that bit of wisdom come from? From the depths of your twisted soul, Judd told himself.

Dryer swallowed hard and clenched his teeth in an effort not to cry. With his face contorted in a agonized frown, he nodded, then hurried out the door and down the hall.

Lindsay didn't respond as Judd had thought she would. She didn't say, "Jenny wouldn't want that for you either, would she?" Instead she said, "Since we skipped breakfast, I'm heading out for an early lunch before I have Devin drive me over to Sonya's neighborhood. You can go with me or—"

"Lunch sounds good."

"Okay." She grabbed her shoulder bag off the bed.

"If you don't mind, I'd like to go with you this afternoon."

"Sure, it's fine with me, but more than likely it won't amount to anything." Lindsay headed for the door. "But there's always a chance that some stay-at-home busybody might have seen something."

"Lindsay?"

"Huh?"

"About what I told Dryer . . ."

With her hand on the door handle, she paused and glanced back at him. "You gave him some good advice." She opened the door, entered the corridor, and hurried away.

Was that all she intended to say? No lecture? No sermon?

Judd caught up with her when she was halfway to the lobby. "Wait up, will you?" When she slowed her pace, he added in a light tone, "You sure are in a hurry to eat."

She didn't respond, but waited until he was at her side, then immediately rushed through the lobby and outside to the waiting limo. Devin Chamness smiled and said good morning, then closed the limousine door after both Judd and Lindsay had slipped inside.

Judd waited for her to speak, waited for her to give him

one of her famous lectures on straightening up and flying right. For nearly four years, she had been preaching the same sermon, doing her best to convert him to her way of thinking. Life is for the living. Her pleas had fallen on deaf ears. But after spending six months apart from Lindsay, he had come to realize just how much he had missed her. Missed her caring about him, worrying about him. Hell, he'd even missed her get-on-with-your-life speeches.

"About last night . . ." Judd said.

She kept her gaze focused straight ahead, apparently determined not to make eye contact. "You had a nightmare. I startled you. You thought I was Jenny. Beginning and end of story."

She entwined her fingers together and placed her hands in her lap. Judd inspected her from head to toe, all the while wondering what she was really thinking. Lindsay possessed the fresh, wholesome looks of an all-American girl. A young, healthy, blue-eyed blonde. Petite and trim. Not beautiful, but pretty. Her clothing was always simple. Understated. Never sexy.

But she didn't need to dress provocatively to be sexy.

"I knew who you were when I kissed you," he told her.

She snapped her head around and glared at him, her gaze questioning him, silently accusing him of lying.

"The nightmare I had was about Jenny," he admitted. "But it was about you, too. It was like most nightmares, all mixed up and screwy. It didn't really make any sense."

"Let's just forget it, okay?"

"Yeah, sure. Fine with me."

I hurt you again, didn't I? And this time, I didn't mean to. I'm sorry. Honest to God, I'm sorry.

Pinkie enjoyed the lobster bisque almost as much as the delicious spice cake Cook had prepared for his lunch. One of the perks of being a multimillionaire was fine dining, even at home. He picked up the half-empty bottle of Stella Artois, a premium dry beer from Belgium that he especially liked, and carried it with him to his study. After closing and locking the door, he went straight to the bookshelves, removed one of the books, and pressed the button that opened the shelves to reveal his secret chamber. He flipped on a light switch that created instant illumination to this private "trophy room."

But he wasn't here to bask in past glories, to fantasize about all the kills he'd made. No, he was here to do some research, to seek and find the next pretty flower, ready to be plucked before she withered. If possible, he would prefer a blonde this time, but a brunette would do. After all, he had scored twenty points with Gale Ann Cain. She'd been his redhead for this year.

Only one redhead per year. That's what he and Pudge had decided when they set the rules for their little game, almost five years ago. Redheads would be worth the most since they were rare. Blondes would be worth fifteen points and brunettes ten. With less than two months remaining until they tallied five years' worth of scores, all he needed to win was twenty-five more points: One blonde and one brunette. It really didn't matter in which order, did it? After all, even if Pudge found himself a redhead next time, he wouldn't stay in the lead for long.

Pinkie picked up his laptop from the desk and carried it with him over to the comfy brown chenille armchair. He lifted up his feet, decked out in size ten Cole Haan shoes, on the matching chenille ottoman, and opened his computer. He loved modern conveniences, little things like wireless Internet.

As he played around with various sites, searching for just the right woman, Pinkie's mind began to wander, back sixteen years ago. He had always hated family reunions, had thought them a useless plebeian pastime. But he'd been sixteen that year, still under his parents' rule and had been given no choice but to attend the event. Every five years, the maternal side of his mother's family met to celebrate their revered ancestors, those men and women who had first set foot in the New World in the late eighteenth century. One of his austere, four-times great-grandfathers had been a revolutionary war hero, a contemporary of Washington, Franklin, and Jefferson.

Absorbed in his memories of the past, his senses came into play. The sights, scents, and sounds of a weekend spent with relatives he barely knew and for the most part disliked. April in Louisiana was preferable to any of the summer months, but the moist heat of springtime had been unpleasant enough that year. Pinkie recalled his first glimpse of the antebellum mansion belonging to his mother's third cousin. The structure hadn't been all that impressive, just one more old house where distant relatives lived. His mother had an absolute passion for visiting aunts, uncles, and cousins, and she never missed a reunion. He had found the older generation little more than doddering fools; his parents' age group social-climbing gossipmongers; and his own peers nothing but silly pea-brains.

All except Cousin Pudge, the owner of the old Louisiana mansion's grandson. The fat, dark-eyed sixteen-year-old had appraised Pinkie as judgmentally as Pinkie had him. However, five minutes into their first conversation, they had known they would be friends for life.

Hmm . . .

Friends for life.

How odd that they actually thought of each other that way, especially considering the terms of the deadly game they had been playing. Winner take all. Loser . . .

Pinkie preferred not to even consider the possibility of losing.

Losing was unthinkable.

If he lost . . .

But what if I win? Can I actually claim the ultimate prize?

Perhaps a better question to ask himself was if he lost, would Pudge follow through and demand payment on their wager?

Tall, thin, with a birdlike appearance, silver-haired Janice Nix lived across the street from Sonya Todd. Out of half a dozen neighbors Lindsay had questioned, Janice was the first one to mention seeing a stranger jogging along Sunrise Avenue the day that Sonya was murdered.

"You'd never seen this man before?" Lindsay asked.

"No, I hadn't seen him before and I haven't seen him since. And I know everyone who lives in Pine Crest Estates." Janice's dark, beady eyes peered over the rims of her wire-frame glasses, her gaze riveted to Lindsay's. "I'm the president of the Homeowners' Association, so I keep close track of who moves in and who moves out."

"Can you describe this man?" Lindsay held her breath. What if the man Janice had seen was the Beauty Queen Killer?

"Sure can." Janice huffed. "He wasn't much to look at. Not ugly, mind you, but very ordinary."

When Judd asked, "How do you mean ordinary?" Lindsay glanced at him, silently cautioning him not to push this woman, not to frighten her the way he had Barbara Jean.

"You know, ordinary. Not short or tall. Not real fat or skinny. Maybe a little on the hefty side." Janice looked from Judd to Lindsay, then back to Judd again. "It was hard to tell in those bulky sweats he wore. As for his age, I'd say late twenties, early thirties."

"Can you describe him in more detail?" *Even if she can*

give you a detailed description, that doesn't mean he's the man who killed Sonya, Lindsay reminded herself.

"I didn't see him close up, just through the window over there." Janice nodded to the living room's double windows that faced the street. "I don't know about his eyes or his hair. He wore a cap of some kind and a jogging suit, but he had fair skin. His face was pink, maybe chapped from the wind, but he definitely had plump, rosy cheeks."

"If you saw him again, would you recognize him?" Judd asked, his voice calm.

"I'm not sure. Maybe. If he was wearing the same getup."

Lindsay rose from the sofa. "Thank you, Mrs. Nix. I appreciate your taking the time to tell us about this man."

Judd got up quietly, kept his composure, and acted like a normal, rational human being. She wasn't accustomed to seeing him act in a logical manner.

Janice came up out of her easy chair. "Do you think he might have been the man who killed Sonya?"

"We don't know," Lindsay replied. "It's possible."

As Janice walked them to the front door, Judd asked, "Did you tell the police about this man?"

"I haven't. Not yet. No one from the police department has asked me anything, but some FBI agent knocked on my door first thing this morning. Real nice lady named Baxter. She was as interested in hearing what I had to say as you two were."

Lindsay and Judd exchanged glances. Neither were surprised that Nic had gotten here first.

Five minutes later, when they were heading out of Pine Crest Estates, resting comfortably in the back of the limo, Lindsay sent a text message to Griff.

Stranger jogging on Sonya's street day of murder. Neighbor's description similar to one BJH gave you. Nic knows.

"Contacting Griff?" Judd asked.

"Uh-huh." She closed her cell phone and turned to Judd. "The description Janice Nix gave us of the jogger is similar to the one Barbara Jean gave Griff of the man she saw leaving her sister's apartment."

"And just as worthless." Judd grimaced. "An average-looking white male, medium size and height. That really narrows it down for us, doesn't it?"

"It's more than we've had in the past."

"But not enough to help us catch this monster."

Lindsay wanted to reach over and take Judd's hand in hers. She wanted to promise him that eventually they would catch Jennifer's killer and bring him to justice. But in the end, would it really make a difference? Once Jennifer's murderer was behind bars, would Judd be free from the past? Could he ever recover from losing his wife?

"You were good with Mrs. Nix," Lindsay said.

Judd huffed. "You mean you're thankful I didn't lose control, shake her until her teeth rattled, and demand she give us an exact description."

Lindsay managed a weak smile. "I wish she could have given us a more detailed description, just in case the jogger was our murderer, but a witness can only tell us what he or she remembers."

"What about Barbara Jean—do you think she really can't remember any more about the man or do you think she's blocked it out of her mind because she's afraid he'll come after her?"

"I have no idea. But I feel certain that if she'll allow Dr. Meng to work with her, she'll eventually remember if she knows anything else."

"You have a high opinion of Dr. Meng, don't you?"

What was Judd really asking her? "She's good at her job. And she's a kind, understanding person."

"She helped you, didn't she? After . . ." Judd frowned, his

expression filled with pain. "I'm a real bastard. What I did was unforgivable."

"Do you want forgiveness?"

"What?"

"I asked if you wanted my forgiveness."

He glanced away quickly, terminating their connected gazes. "Would you believe me if I said yes?"

"Forgiveness is earned," she told him.

He nodded.

Silence.

Lindsay leaned her head against the back cushion and closed her eyes. *Don't make too much of this. It isn't a declaration of love. It's nothing more than Judd's conscience bothering him. Once he finally realized that his actions had achieved the desired effect six months ago, maybe he actually had second thoughts about cutting me out of his life. After all, without me, he truly is all alone in this world. Even Cam has given up on Judd; and Griff would have, too, if not for my intervention.*

Griff drove his rental car into the parking lot of the Wingate at three-forty-two. Just as he killed the engine and reached to open the door, his cell phone rang. From the caller ID, he knew Sanders was contacting him.

Griff flipped open his phone. "Yeah?"

"We received notification from the Williamstown PD that Gale Ann Cain's body will be released tomorrow," Sanders said. "Everything has been arranged for the funeral. All I need is a day and time to let the funeral director know when to plan the service."

"What are Barbara Jean's wishes?"

"I believe she would prefer to have the funeral as soon as possible."

"Day after tomorrow?" Griff asked.

"Yes, I think that would be suitable."

"How is she?"

"As well as can be expected."

"Is Yvette with her now?"

"Yes, they've taken an afternoon walk, with Angie, of course."

"Does Barbara Jean have any idea that I've revealed to the press that she is an eyewitness, that she saw her sister's killer?"

"No. We have done as you requested and made sure that she hasn't seen any news reports on television, the radio, or in the paper."

Griff heard a hint of disapproval in Sanders's voice.

"She's safe there at Griffin's Rest," he assured Sanders. "You must know that I would do nothing to put her in danger."

"I know that is what you believe."

"If there is the slightest chance we can lure the killer—"

"I have the information you requested on Special Agent Baxter's husband." Sanders cut him off, abruptly changing the subject.

Griff knew better than to press the matter about Barbara Jean or to try to placate his old friend in any way.

"Okay. Let's hear it."

"To begin with, Nicole Baxter's husband is dead."

Chapter 16

Pilkerton Funeral Home in Williamstown, Kentucky, provided their most expensive and elaborate service for Ms. Gale Ann Cain. Money had not been an object since Griffin Powell and Judd Walker were picking up the tab. A local Baptist church choir had provided the music in the chapel for the main service and a soloist and violinist had accompanied the large crowd of mourners to the graveside. Lindsay wondered how many of the several hundred onlookers were local and national reporters and curiosity-seekers and how many had actually known Gale Ann.

While Griff and Sanders sat on either side of Barbara Jean and Angie Sterling stood directly behind her, five other Powell agents mixed in with the crowd. Lindsay stood on a rise above the burial site, near an ancient cypress tree that shot a good thirty feet into the sky. From this vantage point she not only had a perfect view of the service, but also of the mourners and a large section of the small cemetery.

Judd stood beside her, stiff as a poker, his gaze riveted to Gale Ann's pale pink, metallic casket.

Jennifer Walker's casket had been white, with pink satin lining.

Lindsay had been startled when Judd asked to accompany them here for the funeral. In the past, he had never attended a victim's funeral, not once since he had buried his wife. Lindsay would never forget Jennifer Mobley Walker's funeral, attended by the Who's Who of Tennessee society. It had been a lavish affair, which she later learned had been planned and orchestrated by Camden Hendrix. Cam was Judd's friend, and he, like she and Griff, had gone that extra mile for Judd these past few years. But eventually, Cam had had enough and called it quits. Judd had pushed Cam away, as he had his other friends, as he'd tried to push her and Griff away.

The wind howled mercilessly, and although the sun kept peeking out from behind the clouds, rain threatened. Lindsay glimpsed at Judd, not wanting him to catch her doing it because he'd realize she was concerned about him. Although he was shaving every day now, he still needed a haircut. But at least this morning he had combed his thick, jaw-length mane of honey brown hair back out of his face and behind his ears. He wore dark slacks and a tan turtleneck sweater under his leather coat. Just looking at him, no one would ever believe that he was one of the richest men in the South.

Lindsay saw the pain in Judd's golden eyes, noted the tightness in his features, and knew he was remembering Jenny's funeral. Why had he come here with them today? Why put himself through this torment?

The heart-rending strains of the violin music rose up and away on the winter wind, the tune one she remembered from her own mother's funeral: "In the Sweet By-and-By." The soprano's voice carried through the cemetery, a mournful promise that loved ones would be together again in the distant, heavenly future.

Tears sprang instantly to Lindsay's eyes. Damn it, why that song, of all songs? Swallowing hard, she blinked away her tears and took a deep breath. Suddenly, unexpectedly, Judd grasped her hand and squeezed. Startled by his actions, she whipped her head around and stared at him. Dry-eyed and somber, he looked at her as he squeezed her hand again. Unaccustomed to any kindness from him, she didn't know what to think or how to feel. Telling herself not to overreact, she glanced away, back at the scene below. But she clung to his hand as they stood there and watched while the song ended and the minister quoted the Twenty-third Psalm.

Griff hated funerals. In the past few years, he had been to far too many, almost all of them for victims of the Beauty Queen Killer. He always wondered if the murderer was there at the service, mixing and mingling with the mourners. Pretending to be someone he wasn't. Keeping a low profile. As he glanced across the closed casket and past the minister, Griff saw Nic Baxter standing in the second row of the crowd on the other side from the canopied tent where he sat with Barbara Jean.

What was Nic thinking right now? Was she remembering her husband's funeral six years ago? Remembering how he'd died? Feeling guilty, possibly blaming herself? Or was she thinking as he was that maybe the killer was here today, getting some kind of perverse pleasure out of attending the funeral of the woman he had hacked to death.

Barbara Jean wept softly, her slender shoulders trembling. She held Sanders's hand discreetly between their side-by-side thighs, their shoulders and hips almost touching. It had been a long time since he had seen Sanders show deep feelings of any kind. Griff understood. A man does what he must do to survive, in order not to lose his mind. The closest

Sanders had come to expressing emotions in recent years had been his concern for Lindsay's welfare. But Griff suspected that his old friend was beginning to care about the soft-spoken, gentle Barbara Jean. Of all the women in the world, why this one? But then again, why not? Griff was not an expert on love. Far from it. He'd thought himself in love a couple of times when he'd been much younger, back in college. But both relationships, based mainly on sex, had fizzled out rather quickly.

Was Sanders worried about Barbara Jean's safety? Probably. The man was a worrier. A silent worrier, one who kept his concerns mostly to himself.

If the murderer was somewhere in the crowd of mourners—at least a hundred and fifty or more—Griff doubted that the man was stupid enough to try to kill Barbara Jean here and now. A man smart enough to commit nearly thirty murders and not get caught wasn't the kind of man to take foolish chances. But then again, after so many successful kills, he might be getting cocky, might be feeling a little too self-assured.

If the killer was here and if he tried anything, he'd be surrounded within seconds. Not only were there five extra Powell agents, other than Angie and Lindsay, in attendance, but there were a number of police officers and FBI agents here, too. Nic hadn't shared that information with him, but he didn't need her input to know what was going on.

Scanning the cemetery beyond where he sat, Griff surveyed the crowd, then looked up toward the knoll where Lindsay and Judd stood, at least a dozen other people near them, including Chief of Police Mahoney.

What was it like for Judd being here today? Griff had been as surprised as Lindsay when Judd had asked to come to Kentucky with them to attend the funeral. The more he thought about Judd's request, the more he wondered if this was a good sign, maybe a healthy sign of recovery. It couldn't be easy for him. He had to be thinking about Jenny. Remembering her funeral.

Griff thought about Judd's wife every time he attended a victim's funeral. And with each new murder he questioned the existence of a God who would allow such a thing to happen. Twenty years ago, as a recent UT graduate, he had believed in the Almighty, had been thankful for the blessings he had received in his life. It had been easy to have faith back then when every day, every week, every year, his life had gotten better and better. His mother had been a devout Christian and dragged him to church and Sunday school when he was growing up in the little town of Dayton, Tennessee.

His father had been killed in a logging accident when he was ten, and his mother had died—some said of a broken heart—when Griff had gone missing when he was twenty-two.

I'm so sorry, Mama. If I could have gotten word to you that I was alive, I would have.

But if she had known where he was and what was happening to him, would she have been any better off? If there is a God and if there is a heaven, he knew his mother was there, behind the pearly gates, walking on streets paved with gold, listening to the heavenly choir. If anyone ever deserved eternal peace and happiness, it was his mama.

After the minister ended the graveside service with a prayer, the soloist and violinist joined for a final song. Sanders stood and took charge, wheeling Barbara Jean from underneath the canopy and away from the grave. Angie stayed at her side. The minister came over and offered Barbara Jean his deepest sympathy, as did several of the bystanders, those who had known Gale Ann or knew Barbara Jean. Most of the crowd began to disperse, a few nodding and speaking to one another, others heading directly for their vehicles.

Griff had noticed several people snapping photos and

suspected quite a few were local and national reporters who had slipped in. He figured that the local morning newspaper would display a photo of the grieving sister.

Griff spoke quietly to Sanders. "Wait here for a few minutes until I contact the others and have them join us, then you can take Barbara Jean to the car. I'll follow with Lindsay and Judd in a few minutes."

Barbara Jean looked up at Griff and lifted her hand. "Thank you. I couldn't have given Gale Ann a funeral like this without your help. It was everything I wanted for her . . . and more." She glanced back at the open grave surrounded by numerous floral arrangements, over half of them provided by the Powell Agency.

Griff grasped Barbara Jean's hand. "I'm just glad I could do something."

Tears streamed down her face. She dabbed her eyes and cheeks with the handkerchief Sanders had provided for her.

Griff had never carried a handkerchief before he met Sanders. He had learned everything he knew about being a gentleman from his friend.

Griff called Rick Carson to inform him that he wanted all the Powell agents to go with Angie when she took Barbara Jean to the limousine. Once that was done, Griff walked through the disbanding crowd and up the hill to where Judd and Lindsay waited.

Judd didn't like what was happening to him, but his gut instincts told him that being able to feel again wasn't a bad thing. It might hurt like hell actually to give a damn, but at least now he knew he was still alive, that there was something left of him other than a revenge-crazed shell of his former self. It wasn't that he had changed overnight. He hadn't. And it wasn't that he'd changed all that much. Six months ago he hadn't given a damn that he'd hurt Lindsay, that he had ripped her to shreds and sent her running.

That had been what he'd wanted.

At least that's what he'd thought at the time. He had convinced himself that she didn't matter to him, that no one mattered. But there had been a few niggling moments during the past six months when he'd thought of her, wondered what she was doing, who she was with. And in those moments, he had damned her, determined not to care, not to feel.

Asking to come along today to attend Gale Ann Cain's funeral had been a spur-of-the-moment decision, not something he'd thought about or agonized over. Two seconds after he'd made the request, he'd wanted to take it back. He could have. Griff hadn't questioned Judd's reasoning, though he had been somewhat surprised by the request.

"You'll have to stay with Lindsay during the services," Griff had said. "And if you say or do anything inappropriate, I'll have your ass hauled away so quick—"

"I'll be on my best behavior."

"You'd better be."

Griff was a man of his word. Judd didn't doubt for a minute that his old friend would follow-through on his threat. Griff had his own set of rules by which he lived, but in Judd's estimation, Griff was honorable and loyal. Yet at the same time, he was capable of being ruthless and dangerous.

During the past four years, Judd had both relied on Griff's friendship and had resented it. He had abused their relationship time and again, which spoke to the depth of Griff's affection for him. He hadn't deserved that kind of loyalty. Not from anyone, especially not from Griff. Or from Lindsay.

He glanced at Lindsay, who stood beside him on the knoll overlooking the cemetery. Apparently her cell phone had vibrated. She flipped it open and spoke so softly that he could barely hear her.

"We'll wait here for you," she said.

"Griff?" he asked.

She nodded, but avoided touching Judd or looking at him.

Lindsay had to know that during the service in the chapel and the one here at the cemetery, he'd been thinking of Jenny. Of her funeral. What little he could remember. Cam and Griff had somehow slipped some prescription medication into him the day of Jenny's memorial service. He'd been not only numb with grief, but doped to the gills. He recalled bits and pieces of the service, which he'd later learned Cam had arranged. Someday, he'd have to thank Cam for taking over and doing what he'd been unable to do.

Judd did remember that Cam and Griff hadn't left him alone for several weeks after Jenny's murder. One or the other was with him twenty-four-seven. When he'd come out of that initial numbness, he had realized that his two best friends had been afraid he'd kill himself.

God knew he'd thought about it, but the anger inside wouldn't let him die. Concentrating on revenge had given him a reason to live. He had been damned by his own hatred, embracing the agony of losing Jenny, wallowing in the mire of unrelenting grief.

You shouldn't have died, sweetheart. And neither should any of his other victims. It was wrong. It was unfair.

How had the families of the other victims dealt with their deaths? How had the men who had loved them survived? Had they drowned in their anger and bitterness, as he had, or had they found other reasons to live?

If he and Jenny had had a child . . .

She had wanted a baby. Someday.

And he had wanted whatever Jenny wanted.

"Let's go," Lindsay said, bringing Judd out of his melancholy thoughts. "Griff's ready to leave."

Judd glanced at her and then a few feet away where Griff

had stopped to speak to a stocky, sandy-haired man in uniform, a high-ranking police officer.

"Who's Griff talking to?" Judd asked.

"Chief Mahoney."

Judd watched the interchange between the two men and surmised that the Williamstown chief of police didn't share Special Agent Baxter's animosity toward Griff. The two shook hands before the chief walked off and Griff motioned to them.

When they caught up with Griff halfway to his rental car, he stopped, glanced around and said in a low voice, "Someone else saw our mystery man leaving Gale Ann's apartment the day she was killed."

"What!" Lindsay said a little too loudly.

"One of the other tenants was taking out his garbage and caught a glimpse of Barbara Jean entering the building and this guy leaving."

"When did the witness come forward?" Lindsay asked.

"Only a few days ago," Griff said. "It took him awhile to build up his courage and go to the police."

"Can he ID the man?"

"No, not really. His description is less detailed than Barbara Jean's. But I want to tell her that she's not the only witness, that someone else saw the guy. That might reduce some of the pressure on her to remember."

"But it doesn't help us, does it?" Judd knew the others understood his comment was rhetorical and required no response.

"Do we need to stay on in Williamstown and question this witness?" Lindsay asked.

"We can't," Griff replied. "It seems Nic Baxter has him in protective custody."

* * *

Pinkie had never attended a victim's funeral. Not until today. He had been unable to resist the overwhelming urge to come back to Kentucky and watch Gale Ann Cain being laid to rest. She'd been a lovely woman. And such an easy kill. He would never forget her, just as he wouldn't forget any of the others. They were all precious to him, especially the red-heads.

Pausing in the midst of the mourners, he watched while the Powell agents descended on Barbara Jean Hughes like a swarm of locusts, surrounding her as Griffin Powell's man, Sanders, wheeled her away from the graveside.

Did these fools actually think he would try to kill her today?

He knew that Griffin had intentionally released the infor-mation that Gale Ann's sister had seen a man who might be the killer.

It was possible that Griffin had hoped he would be lured in by the information, that he would try to kill Barbara Jean and they could trap him. But after being a part of his and Pudge's little game for nearly four years now, surely Griffin knew better.

He has to know I'm too intelligent to fall into a trap. I haven't been caught yet and I won't be. Part of the fun is out-smarting not only the local lawmen and the FBI, but in elud-ing the famous private detective Griffin Powell.

Pinkie had enjoyed the service at the church and also this graveside farewell. If he had known how entertaining these events were, he would have gone to the previous ones. He could have brought along a small hidden camera and taken pictures and added the photographs to his collection.

Next time.

He wouldn't have to wait long. He had already chosen the next pretty flower. A brunette. Only ten points. But ten points would keep him ahead of Pudge, enough so that he didn't have to worry the least little bit.

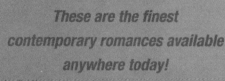

To start your membership, simply complete and return the Free Book Certificate. You'll receive your Introductory Shipment of FREE Zebra Contemporary Romances, you only pay $1.99 for shipping and handling. Then, each month you will receive the 4 newest Zebra Contemporary Romances. Each shipment will be yours to examine FREE for 10 days. If you decide to keep the books, you'll pay the preferred subscriber price (a savings of up to 30% off the cover price), plus shipping and handling. If you want us to stop sending books, just say the word... it's that simple.

FREE BOOK CERTIFICATE

Yes! Please send me FREE Zebra Contemporary romance novels. I only pay $1.99 for shipping and handling. I understand that each month thereafter I will be able to preview 4 brand-new Contemporary Romances FREE for 10 days. Then, if I should decide to keep them, I will pay the money-saving preferred subscriber's price (that's a savings of up to 30% off the retail price), plus shipping and handling. I understand I am under no obligation to purchase any books, as explained on this card.

NAME _____

ADDRESS _____ APT. _____

CITY _____ STATE _____ ZIP _____

TELEPHONE (____) _____

E-MAIL _____

SIGNATURE _____

(If under 18, parent or guardian must sign)

Offer limited to one per household and not to current subscribers. Terms, offer and prices subject to change. Orders subject to acceptance by Zebra Contemporary Book Club. Offer Valid in the U.S. only.

Thank You!

CN047A

THE BENEFITS OF BOOK CLUB MEMBERSHIP

• You'll get your books hot off the press, usually before they appear in bookstores.

• You'll ALWAYS save up to 30% off the cover price.

• You'll get our FREE monthly newsletter filled with author interviews, book previews, special offers and MORE!

• There's no obligation – you can cancel at any time and you have no minimum number of books to buy.

• And – if you decide you don't like the books you receive, you can return them. (You always have ten days to decide.)

Be sure to visit our website at www.kensingtonbooks.com.

Zebra Book Club
P.O. Box 6314
Dover, DE 19905-6314

PLACE
STAMP
HERE

He supposed he could have continued searching until he found a blonde, but the moment he saw LaShae, he knew she was the one. Her photo on her Web site probably didn't do her justice. A former Miss Birmingham who went on to model professionally for a few years in her early twenties, LaShae was tall, slender, elegant. At thirty she had her own successful talk show on a local TV station, was happily married to an up-and-coming lawyer with political aspirations, and had a four-year-old son.

So much to live for. Pinkie sighed.

But better for someone as lovely as you are, my dear LaShae, to die young and leave behind memories of how beautiful you were. You would hate growing old, losing your looks, becoming withered and wrinkled.

Pinkie hurried along, keeping himself surrounded by the scattering mourners all the way to the parking area at the nearby Baptist church. Although he wore a disguise, he didn't want to risk anyone noticing him in particular. And he certainly didn't want to come face-to-face with Griffin Powell and risk Griff recognizing him.

Chapter 17

LaShae Goodloe loved her house in Mountain Brook in a way she loved little else, except her son Martin. This beautiful home represented her success in life, her climb from poverty to riches. She had never been ashamed of her humble beginnings, had in fact used her own life story in the inspirational talks she gave to various organizations in and around Birmingham. The fact that her father had been a school janitor and her mother a cook at another school in her hometown of Bessemer had been a source of pride for her and her brother, Tony, who both now held Master's degrees from the University of Alabama.

As LaShae made her way up the staircase to the second floor, she sighed deeply, weary from a long day at the station, and then dinner with her husband to discuss the terms of their legal separation. Rodney had moved out only a week ago, after another of their heated arguments. Neither of them wanted to rush into a divorce. For many reasons, they wanted to try to make their marriage work. Martin being the main reason. They both adored their son. Another reason was because Rodney had plans to run for state senator. He understood that a family would be a benefit for him in any election. And LaShae had her own selfish reasons for wanting to remain Mrs. Rodney Goodloe. Her husband was quite wealthy and she enjoyed the lifestyle they shared. Although her local TV show was fairly popular, she had no false hopes of ever hitting the big time, of becoming the next Oprah Winfrey. No, she was lucky just to be doing local TV in a big city like Birmingham and she knew it.

As she passed Martin's open bedroom door, she paused and glanced inside. Her four year old slept soundly in the antique spindle bed that had been his grandfather Goodloe's. LaShae wasn't all that fond of antiques, but Rodney loved them. One of their many differences. Differences that seemed unimportant five years ago when they married, but now those tiny molehills had become mountains.

LaShae tiptoed into her son's room and paused by his bed. Looking down at him, she smiled. He was such a beautiful child. Long, lean, and sturdy, his body build a great deal like hers. His black hair was thick and coarse like Rodney's, and his face round, his cheeks full like his father's.

She wanted to wake him, lift him into her arms and hug him. She had never realized she could love anyone so much, not until she'd given birth to this perfect little boy. Another thing she could thank Rodney for. He'd given her so much. She should love him.

She did love him. Just not as much as she should. Not in the way she should.

What will it do to you, sweet baby, if your daddy and I get a divorce?

Lying there in innocent bliss, he knew nothing about his parents' marital problems. When Rodney moved out, they'd told Martin that Daddy had to work at night for a while. Being a partner in one of Birmingham's most prestigious law firms was time-consuming for Rodney and occasionally she felt that he neglected Martin as much as he neglected her.

"I won't make a selfish decision," she whispered to her son. "I promise I'll do what I think is best for all of us, but especially for you."

As she crept silently out of the room, she didn't hear her aunt Carol approaching. When she came face-to-face with her mother's sister, she gasped.

"I didn't mean to scare you, child."

"You didn't," LaShae said. "You just startled me."

Her aunt, now nearly seventy, had moved in with them shortly after Martin was born. Neither LaShae nor Rodney had wanted to put their child in daycare or allow a stranger to come into their home to raise him. Having Auntie Carol as Martin's nanny had been a godsend for the entire family.

"Did you and Rodney have a nice dinner?" Aunt Carol asked.

Towering over her by a good seven inches, LaShae put her arm around her five-two aunt. "Dinner was very nice. But before you say anything else—no, we are not going to get a divorce. And yes, we are going to try a trial separation."

"Separations ain't no good. His eye will start wandering and before you know it, he'll take up with another woman."

LaShae smiled indulgently. She could hardly tell her aunt that it wasn't Rodney who had a wandering eye. She was the one who had had an affair. The sexual attraction between her and the morning-and-noon news anchor at WBNN, Ben Thompson, had exploded a couple of months ago.

Frustrated to the breaking point, Ben had put out feelers about a job at other stations: In Nashville, Knoxville, Mobile, and even in Louisville.

Walking her aunt to her room, LaShae said, "Don't worry so much about Rodney and me. We just need some time apart. We both need to reevaluate our marriage, our careers, and decide what is best for everyone involved."

"Staying married is what's best for all of you, especially

little Martin. Babies need their mama and daddy together. Think about your own dear mama and your good daddy."

After stopping at her aunt's bedroom door, LaShae leaned down and kissed her on both cheeks. "Have I told you lately how much I love you, Auntie?"

Grinning broadly, her aunt gave her a big hug. "I love you, too, child. Like you was my own."

After saying good night, LaShae walked down the hall and entered the master suite, an eighteen-by-twenty-five foot room that boasted a king-size mahogany bed with matching chest and dresser on one side and a sitting area on the other. She had decorated this room herself, without the assistance of the interior designer Rodney had hired. She had wanted their personal retreat to reflect her own personality.

LaShae removed her jacket and unzipped her dress, then kicked off her heels. Just as she lifted her dress up and over her head, the phone rang. Tossing her dress on the bed, she checked the caller ID on the bedside telephone.

Her heart lurched to her throat. She picked up the receiver. "Hello, Ben."

"How are you?"

She loved the sound of his voice.

"I'm okay. You?"

Silence.

"Ben?"

"I . . . uh . . . I've been offered a job as evening news anchor at WMMJ in Mobile."

"Oh. Are you going to—?"

"Cherie and I talked it over and we decided that if we're going to make a move, now is the time. While the girls are still in preschool."

"When?"

"I'm going to hand in my notice Monday, after I call and accept the offer."

Silence.

"LaShae?"

"I'm here."

"This is the best thing for both of us. You know that, don't you?"

She swallowed the lump of tears lodged in her throat. "Yes, I know."

"I wish things were different."

"You know what Auntie Carol says—wish in one hand and shit in the other and see which one fills up the quickest."

He chuckled softly, then sighed and said, "I love you."

Tears gathered in her eyes. Oh, God, she was going to cry like a baby if she didn't end this conversation now.

"I love you, too," she told him, then hung up.

The morning after Gale Ann Cain's funeral, Judd left the house at dawn. He hadn't gotten more than three hours sleep last night and felt like total crap. As he'd tumbled about restlessly during the night, he'd told himself that he shouldn't have gone to the funeral, that it had dredged up too many memories of Jenny's funeral. But that was a lie. He couldn't remember a great deal about his wife's funeral and what he did recall stayed with him all the time and resurfaced without the least provocation. He hadn't needed Gale Ann's services to remind him of what he'd lost.

He had lost everything the night Jenny was murdered. For nearly four years, he had felt as if his life had been ruined that night. Ruined forever.

How many times had he wished that he had died with Jenny?

As he jogged along the endless trails at Griffin's Rest, Judd tried to block out the memories, even the happy ones. But Jenny's laughter echoed inside his head.

She'd been such an exuberant person, so bubbly and energetic. A true extrovert. He had loved just being with her, watching her, listening to her.

But sometimes all that effervescent vitality had gone too far.

Don't think about it!

Why not? Jennifer wasn't a saint. She made mistakes. She was human.

It wasn't her fault. It was never her fault. She couldn't help herself, the way she flirted, the way men were always coming on to her.

But she enjoyed it. You know she did.

Judd's lungs burned with exhaustion. He had no idea how many miles he had run. Two? Five? More?

Unfortunately, no matter how many miles he ran, how far or fast, he could never escape the past. All those walks and jogs he'd taken at home, at the hunting lodge, had accomplished little more than to make him so tired he'd been able to sleep for a few hours at a time.

Stopping by the boathouse he'd first seen with Lindsay, Judd slumped down on a nearby tree stump, dropped his hands between his knees and stared at the dead leaves beneath his feet. Sunlight flickered softly through the towering trees, creating a patchwork of light and dark over the ground.

Despite the wintry chill, perspiration moistened Judd's forehead. He gulped in air, filling his aching lungs. As he sat and rested, his breathing gradually returned to normal and his mind cleared. He forced himself to concentrate on the moment, on appreciating the solitude, the brilliant sunlight, the still waters of the lake.

How long had it been since he'd allowed himself to enjoy something as simple as feeling the sun on his face?

The crunching of dried leaves alerted him that someone or something was approaching. Lindsay? She had probably followed him to make sure he was all right. How many times did he have to tell her to stop worrying about him?

He wished she'd leave him alone.

No, you don't.

He looked over his shoulder, expecting to see Lindsay, but instead Yvette Meng walked toward him. She was a beautiful woman: Exotic and alluring. The heavy moss green sweatpants and matching fleece-lined jacket hid her sensuous curves.

Looking back at the ground, he waited for her to speak first.

"Good morning," she said.

"Morning."

"You were expecting someone else." A statement of fact, not a question.

"I wasn't expecting anyone," he said. "I just heard a noise and turned to see what it was."

"Do you lie to yourself all the time?"

He looked up at her then, into her dazzling black eyes, and felt as if she could see through him, that she was probing inside his mind. The thought unnerved him.

"As a general rule, I try not to be judgmental," she told him.

Wanting to change the subject he said, "You're out and about awfully early."

She smiled, her mouth closed, the corners of her lips lifting delicately. "I saw you leave and followed you."

He rose from the stump and turned to face her. "Dare I ask why?"

"I thought perhaps, after yesterday, you might need someone to talk to about—"

"Which one of them sent you after me—Griff or Lindsay?"

"I haven't seen either of them this morning. The decision to find you and offer my help was my own idea."

He eyed her skeptically.

"I have no reason to lie to you."

He studied her face for a couple of minutes, then nodded. "Sure. Fine."

"Griffin has a beautiful estate."

"Yeah, he sure does." Now what? Idle chitchat? Lulling him into a false sense of ease?

"You are a very wealthy man, also."

He grunted. "Old money. Generations of millionaires."

"What do you do with your money?"

"Pardon?"

"Do you share your wealth? Do good deeds with it? Give to charity?"

"Oh, I see. No, I don't personally do anything with it. I haven't in quite some time. I have lawyers and accountants and administrators who have been handling all the Walker family business for me."

"Since your wife died?"

"Yeah, since Jennifer was murdered."

"I've seen photographs of your wife. She was lovely. And I understand she was also a very talented pianist."

"Is this our first session, Dr. Meng?"

She took several steps away from him, toward the lake, her gaze focused on the gently rippling surface of the water as the morning breeze danced lightly over it. "If you'd like for it to be."

He closed his eyes to shut her out, to close himself off, trying to sidestep the truth. Why he was tempted to take her up on her offer, he didn't know.

"How about a trial run?" he asked.

"Meaning?"

"Give me some advice and I'll see if I like my advice."

She laughed, the sound filled with good humor and . . . tenderness. "And if you do not like my advice?"

He shrugged. "We'll see."

"Very well. I advise you to do something good for someone else."

"Anyone in particular?"

She shook her head. "It doesn't matter."

"I'm not much into good deeds."

"You asked my advice. I gave it to you. It is up to you whether or not to use it."

He walked up beside her. "Tell me something?"

"Yes?" She continued looking at the lake.

"Is Lindsay really all right? I mean after what happened between us, what I did to her, is she okay?"

"I never discuss my client's privileged information with anyone else."

Before he realized her intention, Yvette reached out and laid her hand on his arm. He felt the warmth from her touch through the thickness of his jacket. Odd.

"Fair enough."

"You are sorry that you hurt her," Yvette said. "You care about her. You—"

Judd jerked away from Yvette and glared at her. "Haven't you heard? I don't give a damn about anyone or anything except finding my wife's killer."

"You're lying to yourself again."

When he stomped away from her, heading deeper into the woods, he halfway expected her to follow him.

She didn't.

Griff had slept in this morning and was still in his robe when Sanders knocked on his bedroom door.

"Yeah, come on in. I'm awake."

Sanders entered carrying an insulated carafe of coffee and a single china cup and saucer on a small silver tray. He placed the tray on the large leather ottoman in the sitting room.

"How is Barbara Jean this morning?" Griff asked.

"She is quite well, all things considered," Sanders replied. "I was concerned that yesterday might have been too difficult for her, but I am learning what a remarkably strong woman she is."

"You admire her."

"Yes, sir."

"And like her?"

"She is a likable person."

"So she is."

"Will there be anything else?"

"What effect do you think it had on Barbara Jean my telling her about the other witness?" Griff asked.

"The effect you desired. She seems quite relieved to know that someone other than she can describe the man to the authorities."

"I prefer that she not know his description was as sketchy as hers."

"Yes, sir. I understand."

Sanders nodded, then walked to the door. Just as he reached the hallway, Judd spoke to him in passing as he entered Griff's room.

"Got a minute?" Judd asked.

"Come on in. I was about to have my first cup of coffee." Griff sat down on the sofa in the sitting area, opened the carafe, and poured the steaming black liquid into his cup.

Judd came over and sat down in the chair to the left of the sofa. "I talked to Dr. Meng this morning."

"Hmm . . ."

"She's an interesting woman."

Griff lifted the cup to his lips and took a sip. Delicious. He savored that first morning cup of coffee. He had hated coffee in his teens and early twenties, preferring colas and beer. Sanders had taught him to appreciate coffee when the drink had been a delicacy for both of them.

"Yes, Yvette is interesting, intriguing, beguiling."

"Where did you meet her?"

"Long ago and far away," Griff said, then took several more sips from his cup.

Judd grunted. "I guess you know that sounded like the beginning of a fairy tale."

"Believe me, it was not a fairy tale."

"You met her while you were out of the country, didn't you?"

"Yes."

"Are you ever going to tell anyone where you were or what happened?"

"No." Griff finished off his coffee, then poured a second cup.

Silence.

After several minutes, Judd said, "I'm probably going to talk to her. Just talk. See how it goes."

Don't react too quickly, Griff told himself. *If Judd thinks you're pushing him, he'll balk.* "Yvette's a good listener."

"She gave me some advice this morning."

"Are you planning on taking it?"

"Maybe."

Griff nodded, then started on his second cup of coffee.

"Aren't you going to ask what advice she gave me?"

Griff shrugged. "I figured you'd tell me if you wanted me to know."

Judd said, "She suggested that I try doing something good for someone else."

"Got anything in mind?"

"No. I'm not even sure I want to do anything. I'm not sure I can."

"You won't know until you try," Griff said. "You're a little out of practice. But there was a time when you were a pretty decent guy."

"Yeah, that was the other Judd Walker. The guy who thought he had the world by the tail."

For all his money, Griff didn't think he'd ever again be as happy as he'd been when he'd been the star quarterback for UT. Back when he'd been young and cocky and, like Judd, had thought he had the world by the tail. "Do you think we only get one chance at that?" Griff asked, dead serious.

"Probably," Judd said.

"Yeah, that's what I figured."

"Whatever happened to you, you seemed to have come out of it okay."

"Give yourself a chance and one of these days I might be saying that to you."

"What, that I came out of it okay?"

"That you seemed to have."

Judd narrowed his gaze and studied Griff. "Run that by me again?"

"Nothing will ever be the same again. Accept that fact. But you can recover enough to become a productive member of society. You can enjoy life again. You can learn to put the past behind you."

"Right now, I'm not even sure I can do that."

"At least you're thinking about it." Griff wanted to ask Judd why the change of heart. What had prompted him to talk to Yvette. Besides the fact that Judd would probably lie to him, Griff figured he already knew the answer.

And her name was Lindsay.

Chapter 18

Staring at her ringing cell phone, Lindsay debated whether or not to answer it. She had avoided returning any of Nathan's phone calls lately. They had been dating on and off for a couple of months, and although she truly enjoyed being with him, she wasn't sure she could ever love him. Dr. Nathan Klyce was handsome, intelligent, and an all-around nice guy. If only she had met him before she'd fallen in love with Judd. But Judd was not emotionally available and probably never would be. Nathan was.

She answered on the sixth ring. "Hello, Nathan."

"Well, hello to you, too." As always, he sounded genuinely pleased to hear her voice. "I'd begun to think you'd left the country."

"I've been super busy."

"I realize your job demands as much of your time as mine does of me, but when you don't return my calls . . . Look, I need to know where we stand."

Crap! How did she reply? She could hardly say that she was, unfortunately, still in love with Judd Walker. And she couldn't ask Nathan to be patient and understanding, couldn't tell him that she really wished he'd be there for her while she tried to work through her feelings for Judd.

"As far as I'm concerned, nothing has changed," Lindsay said.

"Does that mean we're still dating?"

"Yes, if that's what you want."

"Is it what you want?"

"Nathan, you know I'm not ready for anything serious. Not yet. But I'd very much like to continue seeing you."

She imagined him smiling. He had such a pleasant smile, one that always reassured her.

"In that case, I'd like to invite you to be my date for the upcoming fund-raiser for the new free clinics we're hoping to open next year. It's a dinner dance, followed by an auction. It's this weekend, and I realize this is short notice, but—"

"I'd love to be your date."

"Wonderful."

Hearing the pleasure in his voice created pangs of guilt in Lindsay. Was she using Nathan? By continuing to date him, was she giving him false hopes about their future? But she'd been up front with him, hadn't she? No lies, no pretenses. At least she wasn't lying to Nathan.

What about to yourself?

"Give me the details so I can arrange for the day off." She needed this date, needed to be with a man who appreciated her. Needed to get away from Judd.

"Saturday at seven-thirty. I'll drive out there and pick you up around five-thirty."

"No, don't do that. I'll drive into Knoxville and meet you."

"All right." He paused, then asked, "I suppose I'd be pressing my luck to ask you to stay overnight."

She had known this moment would come, that sooner or later Nathan would want them to have sex. Maybe she shouldn't say no. Maybe she should think about it. After all, she couldn't spend the rest of her life celibate.

"Let's wait and see," Lindsay told him. "If it seems right for both of us, I might stay."

"In that case, I'll do everything in my power to make the evening as perfect for you as possible."

"That's so sweet of you." Nathan was a kind, gentle, loving man. He was almost perfect. So it should be easy to fall in love with him, right? "Look, give me the address and any other details I'll need."

After they said their good-byes, she jotted down everything on a notepad she kept on the desk in her room: Saturday night. Seven-thirty. The Willows Country Club. 1018 Bonaventure Avenue. Evening attire.

What on earth would she wear? She owned two gowns, one a black floor-length and the other a beige tea-length. Until she'd come to work for the Powell Agency, she hadn't owned an evening gown since she'd been a high school senior. She had two gowns now because, on occasion, her assignment as a Powell agent required evening wear.

Lindsay opened her closet, looked in the back and removed both dresses, then hung them side by side on the open closet door. Each had been dry-cleaned, each ready to wear. As she inspected the gowns, she realized that either would do. She had heels and evening bags to match both.

Perhaps I should be more concerned with my lingerie. If I spend the night with Nathan . . .

That was a big if.

After checking his social calendar for the next couple of weeks, Griff remembered he was obligated to attend a fundraiser at the Willows Country Club this Saturday night. One of the problems with being so damn rich was that everyone wanted a piece of the pie. And once you became known as a generous giver, your name automatically went on every invitation list known to God and man. Sometimes he simply wrote out a check and declined the invitation. Other times, after checking out the charity organization and finding it fraudulent, he notified his lawyers and turned the matter over to them.

A fund-raiser to build much needed free clinics struck a personal note with Griff. He'd been a poor kid who had been dependent on the kindness of others. He had grown up living in rental houses that were little more than shacks, wearing hand-me-down clothes, and often going to bed hungry. If it hadn't been for local churches, the Masonic lodge, and good-hearted neighbors, he would have found nothing under the Christmas tree many a year. He knew what it was like to need a helping hand.

Griff tapped his finger on the calendar. The event was this Saturday. Although it was only a few days away, he could probably arrange for a date without much trouble. The problem was that he really couldn't think of anyone he wanted to spend an entire evening with.

What about Sara Burcham? She was a good lay, but a lousy date. The vivacious brunette had an obnoxious giggle.

Candace Ragsdale was a possibility. An attractive, fifty-year-old widow with the body of a thirty year old. But hadn't he heard somewhere recently that she was seriously dating Bradford Hern, the president of Tennessee Savings and Loan?

A soft knock at his study door interrupted Griff's musings.

"Yes?"

"Griffin, may I speak to you?" Yvette Meng asked.

"Come on in." He rose from the desk and walked across the room.

Yvette opened the door and entered.

"Would you care for something to drink?" he asked. "I can have Sanders bring some tea."

She waved her hand in a no-no gesture. "I am fine, thank you."

"Please, have a seat."

She sat in one of the two chairs flanking the fireplace, placed her folded hands in her lap, and waited for him to take the seat across from her.

"I believe Barbara Jean will soon be ready to recall everything about the day her sister was murdered," Yvette said. "Perhaps in a few days."

"And you ascertained this by what method?"

Yvette possessed a smile that implied hidden depths, secrets that she shared with no one. But Griff knew her secrets, as she knew his, their lives connected in a way few would understand.

"If you wait for her to be able to tell you what you need to know, you could well be waiting for years," Yvette told him. "But I believe that she is close to remembering, even if only on a subconscious level."

"Does she have any idea that you are capable of sensing what she's feeling and thinking?"

Yvette shook her head.

"Obtaining the information we need by using your special abilities won't pose a moral dilemma for you, will it?" he asked.

"I would prefer that Barbara Jean know I am probing her thoughts. But I am afraid if she knew, she would resist and close me out."

"Then you'll do what needs to be done."

"Yes, of course. I always do, don't I?"

They sat together quietly for several minutes, then Yvette rose to her feet. "We will speak later."

"Wait." Griff stepped in front of her, blocking her path. "I have a fund-raiser that I have to attend this Saturday evening. Would you be interested in going with me?"

"If you would like."

"I'd like very much." He stepped aside, clearing the way to the door.

He noted a particular glint in her eye, as if she'd suddenly been struck with a brilliant idea.

She laid her hand on his arm. "Would you mind if I invited someone to go with us?"

Her question took him off guard. "I beg your pardon?"

"Since our attending this event together will not actually be a date, I would like to invite another person to go with us. Is that all right?"

Griff eyed her quizzically. "Yeah, sure. But who—?"

"If he accepts the invitation, I will tell you."

Without another word, she slipped from the room, like a silvery vapor floating away. She moved with grace and dignity, an otherworldly quality about her. He had the greatest admiration and respect for Yvette Meng, and prized her friendship for the special gift it was.

Just as he was closing the door, Griff's cell phone rang. It lay on his desk, where he'd placed it after making a couple of calls earlier. Having used one of the phone's many features, he had programmed it to various ring tones for several different people, especially those he occasionally preferred to avoid. He immediately recognized the tone he associated with Special Agent Nicole Baxter.

He considered letting voice mail pick up, but curiosity got the better of him. Taking long, hurried steps, he reached his desk in a matter of seconds and picked up his phone.

"What can I do for you, Special Agent Baxter?" He kept his tone light and friendly.

"You can let me speak to Barbara Jean Hughes."

"I'm not stopping you from talking to Ms. Hughes."

"Then will you please tell your assistant that it's all right to put me through to Ms. Hughes the next time I try to contact her?"

"I can assure you that if Sanders didn't put your call through, it was because Ms. Hughes prefers not to speak to you."

Nic groaned. "You've probably brainwashed her with all that Griffin Powell charm."

Griff chuckled. "I'm not sure whether to be flattered or insulted."

"Believe me, I'd never flatter you."

"Now, now, let's not be nasty. Don't you know that honey catches more—"

"Just tell me one thing—can Barbara Jean give us a positive ID of the man she saw leaving her sister's apartment the day Gale Ann was killed?"

"What's wrong—didn't your Williamstown eyewitness come through with a detailed description?"

"How the hell did you know about him?"

"I have my ways."

"Yes, and one of these days, you're going to get caught using some of those unlawful ways," Nic told him. "And when that happens, I hope I'm the one who's around to slap the cuffs on you personally."

"I had no idea you were into anything kinky. If I'd known you were, I would have invited you over to play with my handcuffs. But it's never too late. If you're interested . . ."

Apparently thinking his brand of humor was not funny, Nic growled in disgust.

"Ah, come on, can't you take a joke?" he asked.

"I don't find anything about the Beauty Queen Killer case the least bit amusing."

"Nor do I. But I wasn't joking about the case. I was just poking some good-natured fun at you."

"Fine. Ha-ha. Very funny." Nic snapped the words succinctly. "Now, tell me what I have to give you in exchange for an answer to my question."

"Unlike you, Special Agent Baxter, I willingly share information," Griff said. "If and when Ms. Hughes is able to provide us with a more detailed description of our possible killer, you'll be the first person I call."

Silence.

"Are you still there?" he asked, knowing full well she hadn't hung up.

"Yes."

"Anything else you want to know?"

"I want to know who he's chosen as his next victim so that we can stop him before he kills again."

"Yeah, me, too."

"Griffin?"

"What?"

"Thanks."

Silence again. This time she had hung up.

Griff closed his cell phone and laid it back on his desk.

Since their first encounter, when she'd still been one of Curtis Jackson's underlings, Griff had wondered what made Nicole Baxter tick. Almost from the moment they met, he'd felt her animosity. She had taken an instant dislike to him. And the fact that she'd bucked him at every turn hadn't endeared her to him.

If he had known about her husband, about the way the man had lived and the way he had died, would he have cut her some slack? Maybe. Maybe not. But knowing about Gregory Baxter's final days certainly explained a few things about Nic.

Pudge both loved and hated the hundred-and-sixty-year-old, money-sucking mausoleum of a house he had inherited from his grandfather. As the only male child of an only male child, he had been the heir to a rather sizable fortune. He had grown up in what many referred to as the lap of luxury, a spoiled child who seldom heard the word no, and to this day demanded his own way in everything. One of the perks of being wealthy. He avoided most things over which he had no control, things his money couldn't buy for him.

He hired and fired servants on a regular basis. Few could live up to his standards, and he refused to pay good money for sloppy work. At present, he had no live-ins, only a weekly cleaning service and a cook who came in at eight each morning and left at five in the afternoon. Whenever he was out of town, she prepared meals and froze them for him. And she didn't work weekends.

As he walked the length of the front veranda, he thought about his cousin Pinkie and the game they had been playing for nearly five years. And although this would be their final competition, it was hardly their first. They had met when they were both sixteen, and over a period of time—letters, phone calls, and visits—they had become best friends. He knew that Pinkie loved him, as much as his cousin was capable of loving anyone. And he cared about Pinkie.

He would sorely miss his dear cousin when their game was over.

But all good things must come to an end.

Pudge sighed wearily.

He chose his favorite spot on the porch, a huge wicker rocker that had been his grandmother's. She had died when he was two. Drowned in one of the numerous ponds on the property. Ruled an accidental death. But family rumor was that she had killed herself.

Wrapped in a decadent fur coat that he'd purchased on his last trip to New York City, Pudge rocked steadily back and forth. Watching the sunset, he breathed in the fertile Louisiana air, rich with the scents of nature. Even in winter, there was a hint of the lushness that springtime would bring to the land.

Rocking back and forth, enjoying the invigorating cold air, Pudge contemplated what had to happen in the near future. No doubt Pinkie had already chosen his next victim. They both knew they had no choice but to accelerate the time period between kills now that the end was near. In four weeks one of them would win their five-year game.

On April Fools' Day.

Smiling at his own cleverness, he remembered that he had been the one who had decided that they should begin and end their game on the first day of April. They had flipped a coin to see who would pick the first pretty flower from the garden of former beauty queens. He had won the toss.

He would never forget his first human kill.

A blonde. Worth fifteen points.

Brooke Randolph. Former Miss Baton Rouge.

He would always remember the terrified expression on her face when she realized he was going to kill her.

Sweet Jesus, what a feeling!

Despite the fact that he and Pinkie had agreed that redheads were worth the most points because there were fewer of them, Pudge actually preferred brunettes. Tall, exotic, dark-eyed beauties.

But one of his next two kills would have to be a redhead. And he had already chosen the first of the two: Sandi Ford, a former Miss Teen USA, who now lived in nearby Parsons, Louisiana. Of course, he couldn't let Pinkie know that he had jumped the gun, so to speak. He really wasn't supposed to choose his next victim until after Pinkie took his turn.

Humming softly to himself as he pulled the lapels of his fur coat around his neck to block the cool breeze, he thought about what his life would be like without his cousin. He supposed they could change the rules, even this late in the game, so that the loser didn't have to pay such a high price. He had spent the past fifteen years competing with Pinkie, the only person whose intelligence and cunning matched his own. A truly worthy opponent.

What will you do when this game ends? You'll be bored to tears without Pinkie.

But there can be other games. Other opponents.

Recently he had been thinking about a rather intriguing game, one in which his competitors would also be his victims.

Judd found Dr. Meng in the sunroom facing the lake, exactly where Sanders had told him she would be. He had spent the entire day mulling over her suggestion of doing something good for someone and had drawn a blank. He supposed he could instruct his accountants to issue a check to some worthy cause or other, but that would require no real participation on his part. The less personally involved he was with other people the better he liked it.

Maybe he should rent a car and drive home to the hunting lodge and stay there permanently. Stay away from Lindsay. That would be a good deed, wouldn't it?

He couldn't allow things to continue the way they were. It wasn't fair to her. If she wasn't able to cut her ties to him, then he should do it for her.

But no repeats of what happened six months ago.

There was a kinder, less traumatic way to end their relationship.

And yeah, he'd finally admitted they did have a relationship. One that oddly enough had been good for him. But bad for Lindsay.

She deserved so much better than anything he could ever offer her.

You can't offer her a damn thing except more misery.

As Judd entered the sunroom, he cleared his throat.

Without turning to see who had come into the room, Yvette said, "Please come in, Judd."

Now how the hell had she known it was he who had walked up behind her?

"How did you know?" he asked.

"Your walk. Your scent. Your aura."

Had she said his aura? "Just how do you pick up on a person's aura?"

She glanced over her shoulder and looked directly at him. "I can see the aura surrounding you, but I can also sense it."

Judd walked over and sat down beside her on the rattan sofa. Looking out at the lake instead of at her, he asked, "What would therapy involve?"

The corners of her mouth lifted the merest bit, an almost smile. "It would involve doing something that you men hate to do."

He glanced at her then.

"Talking," she told him.

"Oh." He grunted.

"It would be at your own pace. I never press a patient to move faster than he or she is ready to go."

"Patient, huh? I guess if I do this, I'm admitting that I need help."

She nodded. "More than that—you will be admitting that you want help."

"That's just it, you know. I'm not sure I do want to be helped."

"Shall we put you to the test and see?"

Judd turned sideways on the sofa and stared at Yvette, wondering just what sort of test she had in mind.

"What sort of test?"

"I made a suggestion to you this morning," she said. "Have you given it any thought?"

"Yeah. Too much thought."

Beverly Barton

She smiled in earnest. "I appreciate your being honest with me. That is the first step in building a good working relationship with your therapist—honesty."

"Does that work both ways—will you be honest with me?"

"Yes. Always."

"Okay. So tell me what the test is?"

"It is a way in which you can take my advice and do something good for someone else, and at the same time find out if you truly want to return from your self-imposed purgatory to the land of the living."

"You don't pull any punches, do you, doctor?"

"Honesty, remember?"

"Okay, so what do you want me to do? Walk over hot coals? Eat glass?"

"I would like for you to accompany me to a fund-raiser this Saturday night." Her dark gaze scrutinized his face, gauging his reaction.

Judd chuckled. "Dr. Meng, are you asking me for a date?"

"In a way. I am asking you to join Griffin and me for a dinner dance and auction that will benefit a worthy cause."

"Why can't I just write them a check?" She shook her head; he grimaced. "Yeah, yeah, I know. That would be too easy."

"You haven't taken part in any social activities since your wife died," Yvette said. "I know that this will not be easy for you. But if you accept my invitation, we will both know that you truly want my help."

Chapter 19

Pinkie rented a cabin on the lake in Guntersville, Alabama, Thursday evening. At this time of year, almost all of the surrounding cabins were empty. Staying here instead of a hotel in Birmingham gave him more privacy. And yet he could easily drive into the city and fly in and out of the Birmingham airport. When he'd made the reservations, he had used a fake ID in the name of John Chapman. A nice enough name. And as usual, he had paid in cash.

"I'll be staying a week," he'd said when he arrived, but gave no other information and wasn't asked for any.

When he'd checked in yesterday, he had worn a cap, scarf, and heavy coat. He'd also allowed his beard to grow just long enough for a scraggly stubble, and he had put on a pair of clear glass, black-rimmed glasses. Not much of a disguise, but he doubted that anyone would make a connection between the man staying in the lake cabin in Guntersville and the man who killed LaShae Goodloe in a Birmingham motel.

Of course, he hadn't killed LaShae. Not yet. But soon. Very soon. Time was running out. Four weeks. If Pudge chose a redhead when it was his turn again, then he would have to kill a blonde next time to win the game.

Resting comfortably in the bed, several pillows propped behind his back, Pinkie clicked on the TV. He reached over on the nightstand and picked up the coffee cup he had placed there. He despised cheap coffee. This time, he had remembered to bring one of the gourmet brands he preferred.

"Good Morning, Birmingham," the television announcer said. "Welcome to Wake-Up Call, featuring WBNN's own LaShae Goodloe. It's six o'clock, the first Friday in March."

The camera focused on the beautiful black woman, the host of the local six o'clock talk show. He noted LaShae's fashionable attire. A crimson red wool dress clung to her curves, but wasn't too tight. A pair of small gold hoops shimmered on her earlobes and a heavy gold bangle bracelet hung on her slender right wrist.

Everything about LaShae was perfect, from her thick, shoulder-length black hair to her long, lean body. Her skin was like a fine brown marble—smooth and flawless. But it was her eyes—a pale, milky brown, so light they were almost translucent—that captured one's attention.

A woman such as she should be worth more than ten points. She was as rare as any redhead, possibly even more so.

But rules were rules and a brunette was worth only ten points.

Realizing that he hadn't been listening to the monologue between LaShae and her guest, a counselor who worked with adults who had been sexually abused as children, Pinkie upped the sound a bit as he sipped his first cup of morning coffee.

"Dr. Woodrow Landers will be back this coming Monday for a week-long session," LaShae told her audience. "We are in the process of lining up guests who are willing to share their stories. If they choose to use their real names and go on camera live, we'll do that. However, if they prefer to be in silhouette and have their voices disguised, we will give them that option."

The camera zoomed in on her face. "If you have a story to tell, we want to hear it. If you know the name of the person who molested you when you were a child and wish to press charges now, we will help you by hiring a lawyer to represent your interests. After this morning's show, please call me here at WBNN. I will be at the studio to take your calls personally until noon today."

Pinkie smiled. Why did they always make it so easy for him?

He and Pudge had laughed about the naivete of the women they had killed. Women left "hidden" keys. They opened their doors to deliverymen, to telephone repairmen, to utility department workers. They had taken both Pinkie and Pudge at face value. It never ceased to amaze him how stupid these women had been. How trusting.

So often he and Pudge were able to use a woman's profession against her.

Jennifer Walker, a Realtor, had been more than happy to meet a potential client, with his nonexistent wife, alone at night in an isolated house.

Erin Murphy, a private duty nurse, had gladly allowed him to come to her home to interview her for the job of caring for his elderly, nonexistent mother.

And here LaShae Goodloe was inviting him to call her, to set up a private appointment, to discuss his fake memories of having been molested as a child.

Getting LaShae to open her home to him would have proved problematic since she was unlikely to allow just anyone into the house where she lived with her family. However, it should be fairly easy to lure her to another destination. All he had to do when he called her was to sound pitiful and helpless.

* * *

During the past three hours, LaShae had spoken to only two people willing to appear on her show next week: A twenty-year-old girl who had been molested at ten by an older neighborhood teenager and a fifty-year-old woman, whose father had molested her when she was a child. Neither wanted their true identity revealed. The station had received a flood of calls, a few from pranksters, a few from people protesting airing "such trash," and numerous messages from viewers who simply wanted to speak personally to LaShae.

"You might want to take this one," LaShae's assistant, Mindy, told her. "He sounds genuine."

LaShae nodded, then took the call. "Hello, this is LaShae Goodloe."

"Ms. Goodloe, I–I saw your show this morning." The voice was decidedly male. "You seem to really care about people. You're not a phony like so many other TV people."

"I do care," LaShae assured the caller. "Especially about this subject—children who are molested. I had a childhood friend who was raped and killed by her cousin."

"The man who . . . I trusted him. Everyone trusted him. He—he was the youth minister at our church," the man said, his voice a mere whisper. "The man who raped me when I was twelve."

"I'm so very sorry."

This poor man.

As long as LaShae lived, she would never forget the heartbreak of learning that her best friend in sixth grade had been brutalized and killed by a twenty-five-year-old cousin that everyone in the neighborhood had known all their lives.

"I'm not sure I have the courage to appear on your show," the caller said.

"We will protect your identity. No one will see your face or hear your real voice."

"I want to have the courage to do this, but—I'm scared."

"Is your molester still alive?"

"Yes. And he's the minister of a large church now."

"You do realize that if he molested you, he's molested other boys. By identifying him and bringing charges against him, you can save countless other young boys from suffering as you did."

"I know. It's just . . . Could we talk privately?"

"Yes, of course we can."

"I can be in Birmingham Sunday evening. Could you meet me in some public place and let me tell you my story, face-to-face?"

"Yes, we can arrange to do that." LaShae's heart went out to this man. He sounded as if he were on the verge of tears. How heartbreaking that memories of being molested years ago tormented him so strongly to this day.

"My name is . . . I'm Sammy. I'll call again when I arrive in Birmingham."

The line went dead.

LaShae hung up the phone and looked over at Mindy. "I believe he'll be the one who will actually press charges against his molester."

"Want me to put a call through to your husband?" Mindy asked.

"Yes, call Rodney and see if he has time to talk to me right now. Since he'll be acting as our legal representative for all of the people appearing on our show next week, I'll need to keep him up to date on everything."

As Mindy dialed Rodney's office, LaShae stilled her nerves, preparing herself to talk to her husband. If only she didn't feel so terribly guilty about her affair with Ben. Although he'd given her no indication that he suspected her of infidelity, LaShae wondered if Rodney didn't know, at least on some level, that there had been another man in her life.

* * *

The weather had turned nasty about fifteen minutes ago, a blustery thunderstorm, with cold rain pouring down and streaks of lightning brightening the dark evening sky. She had caught the Saturday noon news and the weather fore-caster hadn't mentioned rain for tonight. Lindsay brought her Trailblazer to a stop at the canopied front entrance of the Willows Country Club, got out, and was very thankful for valet parking.

This was her first time here at the swanky private club frequented by the Who's Who of local society. She'd heard the yearly membership fee was fifty thousand dollars. For most people that was the equivalent of a year's salary.

As she passed along a row of floor-to-ceiling mirrors, she forced herself not to stop and inspect her appearance. She had chosen the black evening gown. Simple and understated. After debating what to do with her hair and finally deciding to brush her curls away from her face to expose her diamond earrings, she had faced the makeup dilemma. In the end, she had kept everything light and natural. Her own personal style all the way.

Three days ago, Lindsay had asked Griffin for Saturday and Sunday off.

"I have a date with Nathan," she'd told him.

"Good for you." Although he'd seemed genuinely pleased, he had looked at her with concern.

"No, I haven't mentioned it to Judd and I don't intend to."

"I didn't ask, did I?"

"No. No, you didn't."

Their conversation had ended on that note, neither of them taking it a step further. Each respected the other's pri-vacy. She understood that Griff was simply concerned about her relationship with Judd.

Lindsay had spent the past few days in the Powell Agency office at Griffin's Rest. She was in charge of all information on the Beauty Queen Killer cases, and with two recent murders adding to the long list, she'd been busy updating the agency's files. She had spoken with former FBI profiler, Derek Lawrence, sharing information with him, so that he could provide them with an up-to-date profile of the killer.

"I don't have to tell you that these last two murders happened much closer together than any of the previous ones," Derek had told her. "I think you can expect another murder very soon."

When she'd spoken to Griff about Derek's prediction, they had discussed the possibility that the killer was on the verge of a murderous rampage.

"Since we know he's playing a game, we have to assume that for some reason, the rules have changed," she'd told Griff.

"Possibly. Or he may have given himself a deadline to end the game and that date is fast approaching. It could be that he hasn't reached his goal."

"You think he started out planning on killing a specific number of women in a certain time span?"

"It's just a theory," Griff had said.

A darn good theory.

She had been totally absorbed with work, so that although she hadn't consciously avoided Judd, she hadn't sought him out since their return from Tupelo. She had seen him at breakfast one morning and at dinner each evening, but other than that, their paths hadn't crossed. She had no idea how he filled his days and tried to convince herself that she didn't care. As long as he left her alone, he could do whatever the hell he wanted to do.

Actually, she was surprised that he hadn't gone home by now, back to solitary confinement at his hunting lodge.

Why was she thinking about Judd today of all days? She should be concentrating on Nathan and the evening ahead. Unless she managed to get Judd off her mind, she would ruin any chance she might have of actually enjoying her date.

Not to mention that it would be terribly unfair to Nathan for her to be thinking about another man most of the time she was with him.

Following the small signs placed on stands at various intervals, Lindsay made her way from one carpeted hallway to another, steadily heading toward the ballroom. Just as she turned the final corner, she saw Nathan in the corridor, along with several other people, all deep in chitchat conversations. Nathan was talking to two other men, one about his age— probably another doctor?—and one around sixty—possibly a wealthy contributor? The moment he caught a glimpse of her, he smiled warmly and excused himself, then came toward her with his hands held out in front of him.

As he grasped her hands, he leaned over and kissed her on the cheek. "You look lovely."

"Thank you. I'm not used to dressing up like this."

"I appreciate your being my date tonight. I'll be the envy of every man here."

She smiled, flattered by his words, yet oddly uneasy. Nathan expected her to spend the night with him. And although she had packed a small overnight bag, just in case, she wasn't sure how this night would end.

"I'd like to introduce you to a few people." He tugged on her hand, urging her to follow him. When she did, he took her directly to the two men he'd been speaking with when she arrived.

Both men responded in a cordial manner when Nathan introduced her as his date. As it turned out, the younger man was Davies Carlton, who had, only this past year, taken over as CEO of Carlton Pharmaceuticals. And the sixty-something gentleman was Dr. James Stafford, a local cardiologist.

As more and more people gathered for tonight's event, the corridor grew crowded and attendees began overflowing into the ballroom, many finding their assigned seats while others worked the room.

Nathan worked the room.

And as his date, he expected her to stay at his side. After they entered the ballroom, she finally saw a familiar face. Sighing with relief, she exchanged eye contact with Mark Crosby, who made a beeline straight to her. He lifted her hand, kissed it, and beamed with delight, as if he'd found a long-lost friend.

"Lindsay, my darling, you look absolutely delectable," Mark said.

"Thank you. You look pretty delectable yourself."

Dressed impeccably in a tuxedo, white shirt, and bow tie, Griff's interior designer possessed a suave, sophisticated appearance. His brown hair was cut very short, a style that downplayed the fact that he was going bald. And a flashy, two-carat ruby ring glimmered on his left pinkie, his only concession to his slightly flamboyant personality.

"Griffin didn't mention that you would be here tonight," Mark said as he held onto Lindsay's hands.

"Is Griffin here?" she asked. "I didn't know he planned to attend. I'm afraid our only conversations for the past few days have been about business."

"All work and no play." Mark shook his finger at her. "Griffin's here, somewhere. And with the most devastatingly exotic woman I've ever seen."

"Dr. Meng?"

"Yes, Yvette Meng. Even her name has a mysterious and romantic sound, doesn't it?"

"She's a lovely person."

"So, just how long has Griffin been hiding her away? Inquiring minds most definitely want to know. Is it serious between them? Or is she involved with that other fellow?"

A tight knot formed in the pit of Lindsay's belly. "What other fellow?"

"Judd Walker, of course," Mark said. "I mean, who would believe it? After nearly four years living as a hermit, the man has resurfaced socially at this little dinner dance."

"Judd is here—tonight?"

"Yes, he is. And I must say that grief and despair certainly agree with him. He's every woman's—and some men's—living, breathing fantasy. My dear, he's being fawned over by half the women here."

Lindsay thought she might be sick. A churning sensation agitated her stomach. "Mark, I'm sorry. If you'll excuse me . . ." She turned and walked away, going in search of the nearest ladies' room.

Nathan caught up with her before she exited the ballroom. Clasping her arm, he asked, "Is something wrong? Mr. Crosby thought perhaps you were ill. You're not, are you?"

Putting a phony smile on her face, she glanced up at Nathan. "No, I'm fine. Mark mentioned that Griff is here and I thought I'd find him and say hello."

"Why don't you let that wait? Dinner will be served shortly and my speech is one of the first of the evening. You don't want to miss that, do you?"

"No, of course not."

Struggling to control the panic she felt knowing Judd was here tonight, Lindsay allowed Nathan to escort her to their table.

Why was Judd here? The man had been avoiding most human contact for years, so what had prompted him to attend this social event? She would have bet everything she owned that no power on earth would ever persuade him to give up his reclusive lifestyle, not even for one evening.

LaShae whimpered loudly as Ben took them both over the edge.

They came simultaneously.

Quivering uncontrollably as the orgasm radiated through her, she clung to her lover, wanting to hold on to this moment—and to him—forever.

"I love you," he moaned in that final moment. "God, how I love you."

"Ben . . . oh, Ben . . ." She kissed him hungrily, as needy as she'd been when she met him at this motel half an hour ago.

He rolled over onto his back and closed his eyes.

She cuddled against him.

When he said, "I don't want this to be our last time . . ." she placed her index finger over his lips.

"It has to be," she told him. "We've thought about it, talked about it, agonized about it, but in the end we know what we have to do."

Turning to face her, he slipped his arm beneath her head and brought her close enough so he could kiss her. As they lay in each other's arms, she listened to his heartbeat and knew that as long as she lived she would never love another man the way she loved Ben.

"Maybe someday," he said. "When our children are older . . ."

"It's a lovely thought."

"Once we leave Birmingham, can I call you? Not often, just once in awhile, to hear your voice."

She tensed, every muscle in her body reacting.

"LaShae?"

He knew her too well, understood her in ways her husband never had.

"No," she said. "We need to make a clean break." She pulled away from him and got out of bed. "It's the only way."

"I don't know if I can do that. Never see you again. Never talk to you again." He rose from the bed, as naked as she was, then walked over to her and wrapped her in his arms. She loved the feel of him. The strength in his muscular arms, the power of his touch. When he pulled her backward and tumbled them both into the bed, she didn't protest, wanting him again, as much as he wanted her.

"Tonight has to be the last time," she told him as he pressed down on top of her and kissed her again.

Within minutes, all rational thought left her, and Ben became the beginning and end of her world.

Lindsay managed to avoid any contact with Griff, Yvette Meng, and Judd during dinner and caught just a glimpse of them after the auction began, and only because Griff bid on and won several items. Of course, he paid outrageous amounts for the items because this was, after all, a charity event. The only person who had been the highest bidder more often than Griff was a man named Cary Maygarden. Nathan mentioned that Mr. Maygarden lived outside Nashville, but because of various business interests, he visited Knoxville regularly.

Lindsay would rather be just about anywhere other than here. And not just because of Judd. She wasn't the society gala type and felt uncomfortable rubbing elbows with the city's rich and/or famous. On a cold, drizzly Saturday night like this, she would much rather be curled up in front of the fire with a cup of hot chocolate.

If Nathan hadn't been one of the organizers of tonight's function, she would have asked him to leave an hour ago. And she probably would have gone home with him. Anything to escape from the inevitable moment when she would come face-to-face with Judd Walker.

Damn the man!

Just when she'd given up all hope of him showing any signs of recovery, he did something like this.

What did it mean?

The auction came to a close when Henry Lewis successfully bid on the final item, paying what Lindsay suspected was three times its worth. Although she didn't really know the UT professor, she had heard Griff make several negative comments about the pompous ass. Griff's term. It didn't surprise her in the least that Griff had bid against the professor, raising the price again and again. Knowing Griff as she did, she'd bet he had done it on purpose, figuring that the man was determined to outbid him.

When the band struck up a slow jazzy tune, Nathan asked her to dance. At least that was something she enjoyed. But a few minutes later, she realized that her date had two left feet. The poor guy kept stepping on her toes.

"Sorry. Maybe you should give me a few dance lessons," he said.

"It's all right. Really. We can sit the next one out."

Thankfully, they managed to finish the dance without Nathan doing any permanent damage to her toes, but she felt certain her black heels were ruined.

"Good evening, Lindsay," Griff said as he came up behind her when she started to leave the dance floor. He nodded to Nathan. "How are you, Dr. Klyce? Would you mind if I steal Lindsay for the next dance?"

"Hello, Mr. Powell," Nathan said. "I'm sure Lindsay would appreciate another partner. I'm not much of a dancer."

As soon as Nathan excused himself, Griff put his arm around her waist and led her onto the middle of the dance floor just as the band's next tune began.

"I didn't know you'd be here tonight," she told him.

"And I didn't realize your Dr. Klyce was one of the organizers, not until after we arrived here this evening."

"Since we don't compare social calendars, I guess we have to chalk this up to coincidence." She had to tilt her head backward to see his face because she was short and Griff was very tall.

"If I'd known, I would have warned you," he told her.

"You mean about Judd being here?"

"His coming along with us was Yvette's idea. And to be honest with you, I'm not sure how she persuaded him."

"Maybe hell has frozen over."

Griff smiled. "Maybe it has."

"Do you think it means anything? Is it a first step or—"

A deep voice interrupted her midsentence. "May I cut in?" Judd tapped Griffin on the shoulder.

Griff paused, looked at Lindsay for a decision, then when she nodded, he turned her over to Judd and walked away.

The moment Judd eased his arm around her waist, a series of tiny explosions erupted along her nerve endings. They stared into each other's eyes. Neither of them spoke. He was so devastatingly handsome that he took her breath away. And the fact that he hadn't cut his hair, that it touched his collar in the back, only added to his roguish appeal.

For years, she had longed to be in Judd's arms like this. But after what had happened between them six months ago, she didn't trust him and found herself questioning his motives. What was going on inside that mixed-up mind of his?

When the dance ended, Lindsay tried to pull away from him, but he held on to her. She looked at him, her gaze questioning his actions.

"Let's get out of here," he said.

"What?"

"You're as bored as I am. Why should either of us stay?"

"I happen to be on a date," she told him.

"With the esteemed Dr. Nathan Klyce," Judd said. "I suppose he's a nice guy. Reliable. Safe."

"Yes, as a matter of fact, he's all those things."

"Do you love him?"

"I don't think that's any of your business."

When the next tune started, Judd pulled her back into his arms. She went willingly, not wanting to make a scene. She had noticed quite a few people staring at them, trying to eavesdrop on their private conversation. No doubt everyone was curious about Judd Walker's first public appearance since his wife's murder nearly four years ago.

Judd held her much too close. But her body loved being next to his.

These were moments out of time. Not real.

It was unfair of him to do this to her.

His mouth hovered over her ear as he whispered softly. "Don't settle for Dr. Perfect just because you're running from me. You deserve better. You deserve nothing less than the real thing."

Closing her eyes, she laid her head on his chest as he pressed her close, so close she could hear his heartbeat. Damn, you, Judd. Damn you!

When their second dance ended, she pulled away from him. And he let her go. As she escaped from Judd, she glanced over her shoulder, taking one final look. Their gazes joined for a brief second, then she marched back to the table where Nathan sat talking to the other guests. When he saw her, he jumped to his feet and smiled.

As she slipped her arm around his waist, she kissed his cheek, then whispered, "When can we leave?"

A perplexed expression crossed his face. "Are you all right?"

She urged him several feet away from the table and looked directly at him. "Do you still want me to stay the night?"

"Yes, of course."

"Whenever you're ready to go, I can follow you home. I want to be with you tonight."

Chapter 20

At one-forty-five, Judd went upstairs to his guest room at Griffin's Rest, changed out of his tuxedo, one he'd had over-night delivered from his home in Chattanooga, and took a quick shower. He lay down in bed and spent the next half hour staring up at the ceiling, doing his level best to get Lindsay McAllister off his mind. Images of Lindsay in Dr. Nathan Klyce's arms kept flashing through his mind. The harder he tried to stop thinking about Lindsay, the more vivid his thoughts became.

Lindsay in her simple, little black dress. Both elegant and sexy, without even trying. She probably didn't have any idea how appealing her fresh, wholesome type of beauty was. Nothing false, nothing overdone. Natural. That's what Lind-say was—a natural beauty.

At two-fifteen, Judd got up, yanked a pair of jeans from his still unpacked suitcase and put them on. Then he donned a ratty, seen-better-days sweatshirt and, in his bare feet, padded out of the bedroom and downstairs. He headed straight for the bar in Griff's study, poured himself a glass of bourbon and sat down in front of the fireplace. The last embers of yesterday's fire blinked reddish gold as the heat from the burning logs diminished.

Judd sniffed the bourbon. Liquor had been his companion over the past few years, neither a friend nor an enemy, just there when he needed it. Then sometime last year, his drinking had gotten out of hand, going from bad to worse, as it had in those first few months following Jennifer's murder.

After what happened with Lindsay six months ago, he'd gone cold turkey for weeks, proving to himself that he could kick the habit, that he was not an alcoholic. But his sobriety hadn't lasted. At the first sign of trouble, he had turned to his trusty companion.

Face the truth. You can't drink. You shouldn't drink.

His hand trembled. The bourbon sloshed around inside the glass.

Judd cursed under his breath.

He brought the glass to his lips. Lindsay's blue eyes stared at him. Eyes filled with heartbroken tears.

Judd threw the glass into the fireplace. The bourbon sizzled as it hit the simmering hot wood, creating sparks, and the tumbler shattered into pieces.

Leaning forward, he cupped his hands together behind his head and rocked back and forth for a couple of minutes, then shot out of the chair.

Why had he let her walk away from him? Why hadn't he gone after her?

And said what? Don't date Dr. Klyce. Don't date anyone. Don't even think about having sex with your nice doctor or any other man for that matter.

She was with Nathan Klyce right now, lying in his bed, in his arms.

Judd hated the very thought of Lindsay with another man. She belonged to him. She was his.

When had he started thinking of her as his? When had he become so possessive of her?

You can't give her what she wants and needs. It wouldn't be fair to use her as you've used other women. Women without names, without faces. Lindsay isn't a woman for a one night stand, someone to provide you with sexual release.

Judd left Griff's study and prowled the downstairs hallways. Walking off his frustration. Trying not to think about Lindsay.

As Lindsay exited off I-40 at two-thirty Sunday morning, she questioned her sanity. Nathan had tried to persuade her to stay the night, but she had known she couldn't. Not after the way she had treated him.

"I'll sleep on the sofa," he'd told her. "It's still raining, maybe sleeting a little. Besides, I don't think you should try to drive home at this time of night. Not in your condition."

Her condition?

That had been Nathan's kind way of saying she was an emotional wreck.

Nathan was a kind man. An understanding man. God, any other man would have been angry with her, and would have had every right to be.

She had shaken her head, lifted her hand to caress his face and thought better of the idea. "I am so sorry. I didn't mean to lead you on, to be a tease." She'd swallowed her tears. "I–I need to go. Please, don't worry about me. I'll be all right."

Yeah, sure.

She had lied to him and lied to herself.

She wasn't all right.

What should have been a beautiful evening of lovemaking with a wonderful man had turned into a fiasco. And it was all her fault. Nathan had been patient; he hadn't pushed her into a sexual relationship. No, she'd been the one who had made the decision to spend the night with him, for them to move beyond friendship and become lovers.

Right now, she felt like the biggest fool on earth.

With one hand on the wheel, she reached up with the other and swiped the tears from her cheeks. She'd been crying on and off for over an hour. *Enough already.* What was done was done. She couldn't change the sequence of events. But if she could . . .

She would go back to that moment when she had fled the dance floor, trying to escape from Judd. What on earth had possessed her to fly straight into Nathan's arms and all but beg him to take her home right then and there and make love to her?

Because you were running scared.

Scared of her feelings for Judd. Worried that he might use her and then discard her. Puzzled by the very fact that he had attended the dinner dance at the Willows Country Club when, for nearly four years, he had avoided socializing as if it were a plague.

So, what should she do now? What if she went home and Judd was there waiting for her?

Why would he be up waiting for her? A man had to actually care about a woman to give a damn if she had sex with another man.

Oh, Nathan. If only . . .

After they had gone to Nathan's home, she had gotten as far as stripping down to her panties and bra; but when Nathan had released the front hook on her bra, she had balked. He had kissed her neck while he cupped one hip and hadn't immediately realized she was withdrawing from him. She'd wanted to be with him, had wanted them to make love, but something inside her shut down when the moment of truth arrived.

Nathan had been frustrated and hurt. But not angry.

Dear sweet Nathan.

Lindsay wouldn't be seeing him again. There was no point in putting either of them through the hell of trying to make a going-nowhere relationship work.

Not as long as she was in love with Judd Walker . . .

Whenever Pinkie had difficulty sleeping, he took a hot bath and soaked until the water turned tepid. Tonight had been such fun that he'd found himself on an adrenaline high afterward. But the bath had helped relax and soothe him, enough that perhaps he could catch a few hours of restful sleep before heading to the airport to catch his Sunday noon flight to Birmingham. The very thought of meeting with LaShae at an out-of-the-way bar and restaurant on the out-skirts of the city excited him. He had chosen a very simple disguise for their first encounter. A dark blond wig and bright sky-blue contacts. After all, who would remember him if he was with LaShae. If they were noticed, all eyes would be on her.

Pinkie had gone to great lengths to cover his tracks. John Chapman, the alias he used to rent the cabin in Guntersville, was for all intents and purposes still in Guntersville. The real Pinkie had been seen by hundreds at the charity auction in Knoxville tonight. Flying back and forth from Birmingham might be time-consuming, but well worth the effort. He didn't think the FBI or Griffin Powell would ever figure out who the real BQ Killer was, but just in case . . . Besides, he enjoyed creating a tangled web of lies. It simply added to the thrill of the game.

The more convoluted and confusing he made things for the authorities, the better. John Chapman wasn't in Birming-ham nor was Pinkie. But LaShae Goodloe's killer would be. Tonight.

He would practice his story on the flight from Knoxville

to Birmingham. While others slept, read, or talked to one another, he would close his eyes and mentally go over not only everything he would say to LaShae, but the way he would say it. Humble. Slightly uneasy. Needy. Sympathetic. A sweet, pitiful young man whose life had been ruined because a minister he and his family had trusted had raped him.

As he wrapped the white robe around him, savoring the delicious warmth, Pinkie smiled.

His first meeting with LaShae would set the groundwork for their second meeting. Once they were together this evening, he would be able to decide if it would take one more or two more secret meetings with her before she trusted him enough to come to his motel room.

Quivers of anticipation rippled through him as he walked into the adjoining bedroom. In his mind, he could see LaShae in a seedy motel room with him, there because she wanted to help him, and all the while she would be walking into a trap.

He would have everything waiting for her. If she didn't drink the doctored cola he would provide for her, then a whiff of ether on a handkerchief would render her groggy long enough to subdue her without any noise.

Pinkie removed his robe, folded it neatly over the nearby chair and got into bed. As he pulled the down comforter up to his chin, he sighed with contentment.

How would he kill LaShae?

So many of the pretty flowers had had pretty voices. And there was only so many ways to silence a singer: Throat slit; vocal cords severed; tongue cut out; head chopped off. In the past, he had chosen the former three, but his cousin Pudge hadn't had a problem with chopping off heads. Two heads to be exact. The most recent had been last year—a former Cotton Queen who'd lived in Cullman, Alabama.

Perhaps he should try it. Now would be the time if he was going to do it. After all, only one more kill after LaShae and he could win the game. Their scores were so close now that it could easily go either way. If something went wrong . . .

Things would never be the same again when this game ended. Pudge would be gone and he'd be left all alone.

Why oh why had they decided to make the end of this game so final—for one of them? It had been Pudge's idea, hadn't it? Or had it been his? For the life of him, he couldn't remember. They'd been discussing the rules, making them up as they went along, not deciding definitely on everything until after the first few kills. And it had been almost a year into the game before they'd added that one last stipulation.

"To keep us on our toes," he remembered saying.

"To keep the game from becoming dull," Pudge had countered.

Pinkie's eyelids grew heavy. He yawned. Sleep. He needed sleep.

But how could he rest, when his mind wouldn't shut off, wouldn't let him stop thinking. *If you must think, think about more pleasant things than the fact that the end of our five-year game is near. Think about how much fun you had at the dinner dance last night. You mixed and mingled with every-one of any importance in Knoxville, a few of them even old friends from out of town and out of state. You even had a conversation with Griffin.*

Pinkie chuckled to himself, loving the irony. Griffin Powell had spent almost four years searching in vain for the Beauty Queen Killer. If only the man knew how many times their paths had crossed, how many times they'd shaken hands and indulged in idle conversation.

Too bad you'll never know that I'm the man you're seeking. You'd be so surprised.

Lindsay parked her Trailblazer in the garage, used her key to the backdoor, hurriedly tapped in the security code, and closed the door behind her. She rearmed the system and quietly walked through the kitchen. The silent stillness assured her that no one was awake, that neither Judd nor Griff would meet her and ask for explanations. *Where have you been young lady? What are you doing coming home at this hour of the morning?*

Making her way through the house, down the hallway toward the staircase, she breathed a sigh of relief. Almost home free. If she could make it upstairs to her room, no one would know what time she had arrived home.

It wasn't Griff that concerned her, although she knew he worried about her. Like a big brother. He had encouraged her to start dating and had approved of Nathan. But he'd also had reservations about her rushing into a commitment, even a temporary one. Now, she realized that Griff had been right to have concerns.

If she could make it to her room, no one would know that she hadn't spent most of the night with Nathan.

Admit it, you don't want Judd to know.

And just why is that?

Because her personal life was none of Judd's business.

That's not the reason.

Okay, so she wanted Judd to think she'd had sex with Nathan, that she'd spent the entire night in another man's bed.

When Lindsay was only a few feet from the foyer and the stairs that led up to the privacy and safety of her bedroom, she made the mistake of glancing into the dark living room. Her breath caught in her throat when she saw the black silhouette of a man standing by the expanse of windows, his body illuminated by the distant security lights outside along the lakeshore. It wasn't Griff. The shadow wasn't tall enough to be Griff, nor was it short enough to be Sanders.

"Judd?"

She didn't realize she had said his name aloud until the dark shadow turned around and faced her.

"Hello, Lindsay."

Damn it, Judd, what are you doing up at this time of night, alone down here in the living room?

Say good night and go to bed, she told herself. Instead she walked into the living room. Just a few feet. *Don't go any farther. Keep a safe distance away from him.* But it was already too late. She had deliberately entered the danger zone.

He came toward her, a few hesitant steps at a time.

Run like hell. Now!

"You didn't stay all night," Judd said, his voice deep, low, and frighteningly soft.

"No, I didn't."

Silence.

He took several more steps toward her.

Her heartbeat accelerated.

"I don't usually stay the night when I go home with Nathan," she lied.

"Why not?"

Her erratic pulse pounded so loudly inside her head that she barely heard his succinct question.

She opened her mouth to speak, but nothing came out, not a single word. After all, what explanation could she give him that wouldn't ring false?

Judd moved closer until only a few feet separated them.

Thank God, I can't see him clearly and he can't see me. If he could see her eyes, the expression on her face, he would know the truth. Over the years, Judd had learned to read her, as if she were an open book. No mysteries. Nothing hidden. All revealed.

"Is he a good guy?" Judd asked. "Does he make you happy?"

She swallowed hard. "Nathan is a very good guy. He's kind and considerate and caring."

"You deserve someone like that."

"Yes, I know I do."

"Then he does make you happy, doesn't he?"

"Why wouldn't he?"

Judd moved in for the kill. Odd that she thought of it that way, but that's how she felt when he stood directly in front of her, so close that their breaths mingled.

"He'd probably make a good husband . . . a good father." Judd spoke quietly, but there was a surly gruffness in his tone.

"Why all the interest in Nathan?" she asked boldly.

Despite the darkness, Lindsay could tell that Judd was looking right at her.

Please, don't touch me. If you do, I'll crumble into pieces.

"I'm interested in Dr. Klyce because I want you to be happy, and I don't think he can make you happy."

Clenching her teeth in a determined effort neither to cry nor lash out at Judd, Lindsay stood there glaring at him, her body quivering with anger and pain.

"Lindsay?"

She couldn't reply. Not without crying. Not without flying into a rage.

And then he did the unthinkable. He touched her. God help her, he eased his fingertips across her cheek and down her neck to her shoulder.

Lindsay trembled.

"You slept with him tonight to hurt me, didn't you?" His hand tightened around the side of her neck, his thumb biting into her jaw. "Well, you got what you wanted."

"You're lying." The words rushed out of her. Hot and angry. "Why would you care if I slept with Nathan or a dozen other men? You're not jealous. You have to care about someone before you can be jealous."

"Do you honestly think I don't care?" He lowered his head enough so that his lips hovered over hers.

She couldn't think, couldn't breathe. "Please, don't do this to me."

He yanked her close, so that her breasts pressed against his chest. "I want you so much I hurt."

Tears misted her eyes. How could he do this to her?

"I swear that I'll never hurt you again."

He kissed her. Gently. Tenderly.

And she was lost.

Her traitorous body melted into his, surrendering without putting up even a token resistance. When she lifted her arms up and around his neck, he wrapped her in a possessive embrace and deepened the kiss.

He kissed her hungrily, devouring her, ravishing her mouth; and all the while she gave him all he asked for and more. As hungry for him as he was for her.

When they were both breathless, they broke apart. Judd pressed his forehead against hers.

"I care too much about you," he told her in a hushed tone. Soft. Almost loving.

He lifted his head. "I'm no good for you, sweetheart. I'm no good for anyone."

Lindsay felt as if she'd been doused in ice-cold water. "Judd?"

"The best thing I can do for you is leave you alone. It's not what I want, but it's what you need. If I stay—"

"Shouldn't I be the one to decide what's best for me?" She clung to him, her words and actions desperately pleading.

He shoved her gently away from him. "I'm leaving later this morning, going home to the hunting lodge."

"No, Judd, please . . ."

He walked past her, then paused and glanced back. "Don't settle for anything else but the real thing."

He disappeared into the dark hallway, leaving her alone in the living room. Tears trickled down her cheeks.

"You're the real thing, Judd," she whispered. "You and no one else."

Chapter 21

At his request, Lindsay joined Griff in the Powell Agency office at Griffin's Rest that Sunday. Business, no doubt. But also something to keep her busy, to help her not think so much about the fact that Judd was leaving today, going home to the hunting lodge. To be alone. To escape from human emotions. To hold on to what was dearest to him in the whole world—the memory of Jennifer.

Carrying a small pot of coffee and a mug on a silver tray, Sanders had knocked on her door at eleven-fifteen this morning. When she had answered the door wide awake and fully dressed, Sanders hadn't seemed the least bit surprised. He had carried the tray over to her desk, set it down, and said, "Good morning."

"Good morning to you, too," she'd replied.

"Griffin would like to see you in the office at noon."

"All right. I'll be there."

He had simply nodded.

"Have you seen Judd this morning?"

He'd given her a blank stare and said, "No, I haven't seen him."

Sanders had then made a hasty retreat.

Lindsay checked her watch. Twelve noon on the dot. She opened the office door and walked in. Griff sat alone at the head of the conference table, a slew of papers scattered about, an ink pen in one hand. When he heard her enter, he glanced up and motioned to her.

"Come on in. I want to go over some facts with you."

She sat on the right side of the table, in the chair closest to him. "Is there something new?" she asked as she turned one of the many sheets of paper around so she could see it. "This is a computer printout of all the Beauty Queen Killer's victims."

"Yes, it is. And to answer your question—no, we're not working with any new information. I just want to look back at some basic facts and filter them through what we've learned about our killer in the past few weeks." Griff picked up another sheet and handed it to her. "Take a look at this."

She scanned the page quickly. "Okay, so what am I supposed to see? Am I looking for something in particular?"

"Look at the dates of each murder."

She ran her gaze over the dates, top to bottom, beginning almost five years ago on—"April first," she said. "There has been a murder every April first for the past four years. And we're less than a month away from April the first this year." She shrugged. "But this is old news. Last year, we noted that the one and only recurring date for any of the murders is April first."

"We can be pretty sure he'll kill again this April first."

"I realize that, but what good does that information do us? We don't know where he'll strike or who his victim will be. So the date is useless to us."

Griff handed her another sheet of paper. "Check this out. Note the dates, the year to be specific, that corresponds with the victim's description."

Once again, Lindsay scanned the page. "Blondes, brunettes, and redheads, with fewer redheads."

"Look closer."

She did, then gasped. "Starting nearly five years ago, he has killed various numbers of blondes and brunettes per year but only two redheads each year." She looked at Griff. "Why only two redheads when we now know they're worth twenty points?"

"One of the rules of the game?" Griff suggested.

"He limits himself to two redheads a year, but blondes and brunettes are fair game, no limit on either."

"And he limits himself to women who live in the South," Griff said. "Anywhere from Texas to Florida, from North Carolina to Arkansas."

"Derek surmises that he lives somewhere in the South and either moves around a lot or travels extensively."

"Derek's profile suggests that our killer has money and education, probably a job that pays well and entails traveling or—"

"Or he has accumulated a fortune in some way—work, marriage, or inheritance."

Griff reared back in the swivel chair in which he sat, lifted his arms, and cupped his hands behind his head. "Yvette thinks Barbara Jean is on the verge of remembering more about the man she saw leaving her sister's apartment."

"If anyone can help her remember, Dr. Meng can."

"I want you to talk to Yvette this afternoon," Griff said.

Lindsay eyed him questioningly. "For any specific reason?"

"Judd left this morning. Around eight."

A tight fist solidified around Lindsay's heart. "Oh. I—I knew he was going home. I just didn't realize he would leave before I could say good-bye."

"Talk to Yvette."

"I don't need to talk to her. I'm fine."

Narrowing his gaze, Griff studied her. "Talk to her anyway."

Lindsay huffed. "This meeting to hash over facts about the Beauty Queen Killer case was just a ruse, wasn't it? You wanted to check me out, see if I was holding it together, help me cope with Judd running back to his solitary misery." She shoved her chair from the table and stood. "I need a few days off to decide what I want to do with my life. I've wasted nearly four years trying to help you track down a phantom and believing I could help Judd stop loving a ghost. I've failed on both counts."

Griff got up, walked over to her, and placed his arm around her shoulders. "Take a few days, take a week." He hugged her. "But before you go, talk to Yvette."

"Damn it, Griff, I told you that I don't need to—"

"Humor me," he said. "If you talk to Yvette before you leave, I won't worry as much about you while you're gone."

After blowing out an aggravated breath, she acquiesced. "Oh, all right. I'll talk to Dr. Meng."

At her invitation, Rodney had joined them for church this morning and had followed them home after the services for a midafternoon lunch. Before their separation, Sundays had usually been the only day of the week LaShae and Rodney spent together, the two of them with little Martin. But often, after things became so strained between them, Rodney had slipped away after lunch and stayed in his home office until bedtime.

In the beginning of their marriage, they had been happy. Working together, planning their future, having a baby. And then Rodney had become obsessed with his job, determined to succeed at all costs. She had been lonely, had felt neglected. And had eventually turned to another man.

But Ben wasn't just any man. He was the man she loved. And the man she could never have, except for stolen moments in motel rooms.

"Auntie Carol, that was a delicious meal," Rodney said. "Pork chops are my favorite and nobody can fix them the way you do."

"Ah, go on with you." Carol beamed with pride. "I had help with dinner today. Would you believe that LaShae actually baked that chess pie. She used her mama's recipe."

Rodney focused on LaShae, offering her a warm smile. "The pie was very good. If I wasn't so full—" he patted his flat belly "—I'd ask for a second piece."

"I want another piece," Martin piped in. "I like pie."

Everyone laughed.

"We know you like pie," Rodney said. "You like anything sweet."

"Just like his mama. When LaShae was little she would have eaten dessert for every meal and left off everything else."

Martin cocked his head to one side and looked at LaShae. "Mama, when were you a little girl?"

"Years ago," she told her son.

"Before I was born?"

They all laughed again.

Rodney shoved back his chair, stood, and walked over to Martin. "It's about time for your nap, isn't it, son?"

"Do I have to take a nap today?" Martin whined.

"You most certainly do, young man," Aunt Carol told him as she stood and held out her hand. "You come along with me." She glanced at Rodney and smiled. "Why don't you help LaShae clear off the table. Just put everything in the kitchen and I'll load the dishwasher later."

Once her aunt had taken Martin out of the room, LaShae started stacking dirty dishes. "In case you didn't figure it out, Auntie Carol made herself scarce so we could be alone."

Starting at the other end of the table, Rodney picked up the used silverware. "I appreciate your inviting me for lunch today. I miss Martin." He paused, then added, "I miss you, too, LaShae."

"I miss the way things used to be," she told him. "If we could go back . . . But we can't."

"We could try."

She carried a load of dishes toward the kitchen. With his hands full of silverware, Rodney followed her. While she placed the dishes in the sink, he came up behind her and laid the silverware on the counter. When she turned to go back into the dining room, she found Rodney blocking her path.

"I'm not ready to give up on our marriage," he said. "I still love you."

She took a deep breath. "I'm not giving up on our marriage, but we need a little time apart."

He scowled. "You need time apart."

"Yes."

"Because of Ben Thompson?"

LaShae gasped.

"Did you think I didn't know?" Rodney glared at her.

"Ben is leaving Birmingham. He's moving his family to Mobile in a couple of weeks. He's turning in his resignation tomorrow."

"Is he leaving you or did you send him away?"

"I—I don't feel comfortable talking to you about . . . Please, Rodney. I'm sorry. I never meant for you to find out."

"Do you love him?"

Oh, dear God!

"Let's not do this," she said. "Not now. Not today."

Rodney grabbed her upper arms, his grip painfully tight. "Answer me, woman, do you love him?"

Looking down at the floor, she shook her head. "How I feel about Ben doesn't matter. In two weeks, he will be out of my life . . . forever."

Rodney jerked her toward him, anger burning in his dark eyes. Then he shoved her away, releasing her abruptly as he turned and walked away. She let out the breath she'd been holding and choked back threatening tears.

"I'm sorry. Oh, Rodney, I'm so very sorry," she said.

A couple of minutes later, she heard the hum of her husband's Mercedes as he backed out of the driveway.

LaShae brushed the tears from her face, squared her shoulders, and checked the time on her wristwatch. She had two hours until she met Sammy at the Blue Water Bar and Grill. If only she could see Ben tonight, talk to him, hold him, make love with him.

No, that part of your life is over. And you know as well as Ben does that it is for the best.

Maybe when Ben was gone and she could think straight again, she and Rodney could work at saving their marriage.

If Rodney can ever forgive me.

Late that afternoon, Dr. Meng asked Lindsay to join her in the sunroom. Lindsay agreed because she had promised Griff she would.

It would be dark in about an hour, and she really wanted to get on the road soon. Chattanooga was a little over two hours away, so she could easily make it to her cousin's house well before bedtime. Callie was the only relative she kept in touch with on a regular basis. They had been best friends as children, and she'd been the maid of honor at Callie's wedding ten years ago. No matter how much time passed between telephone conversations and visits, when they were together, it was as if no time at all had gone by. Of course, exchanging e-mails a couple of times a week kept them up to date on each other's lives.

But there was one thing she'd never told Callie, one secret she'd kept, one she planned to share while she visited. And although she suspected that talking to Callie might do her more good than talking to Dr. Meng, she wouldn't go back on her word to Griff.

"You're reluctant to talk to me," Yvette said as she indicated for Lindsay to take a seat opposite her. "Why is that?"

"Because I don't need to be psychoanalyzed. I'm fine. I just need a few days vacation. I'm going to Chattanooga for a visit with my cousin."

"Judd's home is in Chattanooga."

Lindsay bristled. "I'm not going anywhere near Judd Walker. I am washing my hands of that man once and for all."

"Interesting."

"You don't believe me, do you?"

"What I believe is unimportant. It is what you believe, truly believe, that matters."

"I hate him. I wish I'd never met him." Lindsay sat down in the rattan wingback chair across from Yvette. Heaving a deep sigh, she shook her head. "I'm protesting too loudly, aren't I?"

"There is no disgrace in loving someone."

"No, but there's plenty of heartbreak in loving someone who doesn't love you back."

"And you believe that Judd doesn't love you?"

Lindsay laughed sarcastically. "Judd love me? Hell, no. He wants to screw me, but the only woman he'll ever love is Jenny. His damn precious Jenny."

"What if I told you that I believe Judd does love you . . . perhaps more than he ever loved his wife."

As Yvette's words echoed inside Lindsay's head, she stared at the woman. She was so startled by what Yvette had said that she couldn't speak.

"He doesn't know how much he loves you." Yvette's gaze connected with Lindsay's. "He is confused and in pain. He truly believes that you are better off without him."

"Did he tell you that—"

"No, not in so many words."

"Then how do you know? What makes you think he loves me?"

Yvette slid to the edge of the sofa and held out her hands to Lindsay. Understanding what Yvette wanted, Lindsay placed her hands in the therapist's gentle grasp, trusting her completely.

"You did not have sex with Dr. Klyce last night, but you let Judd think you did."

Lindsay shivered.

"You are going to tell your cousin, Callie, what happened between you and Judd six months ago."

Lindsay gasped.

"You believe she can help you now, more than I can." Yvette smiled. "And you're right. She can."

"How did you know all that? It's as if you read my mind."

"I did." Yvette's smile diminished, changing, becoming fragile, bittersweet.

Chapter 22

LaShae's first meeting with Sammy at the Blue Water Bar and Grill had gone well. Her instincts told her that with just a little more gentle persuasion, she could not only get him to appear on her show this week, but she could convince him to press charges against the minister who had raped him when he was a boy. Although Sammy hadn't told her his exact age, she guessed he was no more than thirty-one or two. The poor man was extremely shy and reserved and had made direct eye contact with her only once. She'd never seen such blue eyes. Beautiful blue eyes. He was not a handsome man, but he could be. If he cut his shaggy blond hair, learned how to dress better, and built up a bit of self-confidence, he would be quite appealing.

When she had asked for a second meeting, he had agreed. Reluctantly. That's why she had told him she would come to his motel room this evening. Normally, she wouldn't meet someone she didn't know—male or female—under circumstances that might prove dangerous to either of them. But her instincts told her that Sammy needed her trust; otherwise, he would never return that trust.

She pulled her Lexus into the parking area at the Triple Eight Motel in Bessemer, not the nicest place to stay or the safest neighborhood. But she kept a pistol in her glove compartment and carried pepper spray on her key chain. And her cell phone stayed clipped to her purse strap practically twenty-four-seven.

Just as her hand grasped the car door handle, her phone rang. Groaning, she released the handle, grabbed her phone, and checked the caller ID: Rodney. Why was he calling her? Sunday dinner had ended badly, with him storming out in anger. She had thought about contacting him today, but decided to allow him time to cool off first.

She could let the call go to voice mail and call him back later tonight or even in the morning. After all, what could he possibly have to say to her that couldn't wait.

Go ahead and talk to him. No point in putting it off.

She flipped open the phone. "Hello."

"LaShae . . . I'm sorry," Rodney said.

Regret welled up inside her. He had nothing to be sorry about; she did. "You had every right to be angry. After all, I'm the one who had an affair."

Silence.

"I'm the one who should be saying I'm sorry," she told him.

"You can't take all the blame. If I'd been a better husband . . . If I hadn't neglected you so much . . ."

She couldn't bear hearing him beg for her forgiveness, not when she and not he had broken their marriage vows. "Why don't you come for Sunday dinner again next week and we'll try again?"

"I'd like that. Thank you for giving me another chance."

"I'm not promising anything. It's just Sunday dinner," she said. "I want us not only to do what is best for Martin, but what's best for the two of us as well."

"LaShae . . ."

"Yes?"

"I love you. No matter what."

She swallowed hard. "I love you, too."

She closed the cell and slipped it into the pouch clipped to her purse handle. Loving Rodney was not the problem. She would probably always love him. No, the problem was that she was *in love* with Ben Thompson.

LaShae opened the car door, stepped out, and searched for Room Ten. When she reached Sammy's room, she paused, opened her purse, clicked on the small tape recorder she used for interviews, closed her purse, and knocked on the door.

No response.

She waited for several minutes, then knocked again.

Nothing.

She knocked louder and harder. "Sammy? It's LaShae Goodloe." Not wanting to disturb other guests or bring undue attention to herself, she kept her voice low.

The door opened just a crack and Sammy peered through the minute opening, his bright blue eyes staring at her. "I–I wasn't sure you'd come."

"I'm here and I very much want to talk to you again." She waited for him to respond, and when he didn't, she said, "I want to help you."

He unhooked the chain and opened the door several inches, but didn't invite her into his room. "I don't think you can help me. I don't think anyone can."

"Please, Sammy, give me a chance."

Silence.

He eased the door open slowly. With his head bowed and his gaze downcast, he stepped back to allow her enough space to enter.

The maternal part of her nature wanted to put her arms

around him, hug him, and tell him she truly did want to help him. But common sense kept her from acting on motherly instinct.

She entered the dingy, dismal room, the last room on the end of a U-shaped, sixties motel that should have been condemned years ago. No doubt the other residents were local hookers, drug addicts, and down-on-their-luck men who paid for a room by the week. Shivering at the thought of cockroaches in dark corners, rusted sink and shower faucets in the bathroom, and mold growing beneath the smelly carpet, LaShae wished that she could turn around and leave.

"This place is actually cleaner than it looks," Sammy told her, as if he'd read her mind. "There aren't any bugs or anything. And the sheets are clean." He kept wringing his hands together nervously.

She reached out and placed her hand over his. He jerked away from her. Their gazes met for a brief second before he looked away.

Poor, pitiful man.

"It's all right," she said.

He nodded.

She glanced around the room, spotted two chairs on either side of a small table, and noted the three liter plastic bottle of cola on the tabletop. Apparently, Sammy had already poured himself a glass because one of the two glasses was empty where the other was half full.

"May I sit down?" she asked.

"Yes, please."

When she sat in one of the two chairs, he came over, and sat across from her. With his gaze downcast, he asked, "Would you like some Coke?"

"Yes, thank you." She placed her purse in the chair beside her.

"I've got ice," he said, then got up to retrieve the ice bucket from where it sat on the cheap, scarred wooden dresser.

While Sammy busied himself adding ice to his drink and putting it into her glass, LaShae snapped open her purse, just enough to enable the recording device to better pick up their conversation.

"I hope Coke is okay," Sammy said as he unscrewed the cap and poured the cola into her glass. "I didn't know if you preferred Coke or Pepsi or maybe RC."

"Coke is fine."

He picked up his glass, took a sip, then holding it with both hands brought it down to rest above his lap. He sat there quietly, shyly, not saying a word, just staring at the floor.

"I'd very much like for you to come on my show and talk about what happened to you," LaShae said. "Even if you don't want to name your rapist—"

"Reverend Boyd Morrow," Sammy blurted out.

LaShae breathed in deeply. "I know how much courage that took—to tell me the man's name."

Saying nothing, Sammy lifted his glass to his lips and took another sip of cola.

Taking her cue from him, LaShae picked up her glass and took several sips of Coke, then put her glass down, and held out her hand to Sammy. "If you decide to press charges against this Reverend Morrow, I and WBNN will stand by you and help you in every way possible."

Nodding as he listened, Sammy continued sipping on his cola. "Maybe, I will press charges. If you . . ." He looked up at her with those incredible blue eyes. "If you promise that you won't desert me."

LaShae smiled at him, then hesitantly reached over and patted his arm. He stared down at her hand on his arm.

"I promise," she said.

He nodded again.

She leaned back in the chair, lifted her glass, and told him, "Whenever you're ready to tell me more about what happened, how Reverend Morrow abused you, I'm ready to listen."

"You won't hate me or judge me or think I'm terrible, will you?"

She took a hefty sip of Coke, set the glass down, and smiled at him again, hoping her friendliness translated into caring. "You're the victim, Sammy. You were an innocent young boy. I'm very proud of you for having the courage to tell me about what happened."

Suddenly, LaShae's vision blurred. Just for an instant. She shook her head. Her vision cleared momentarily.

"Are you all right?" he asked.

"Yes, I–I think so. I feel odd. A bit dizzy."

"Maybe you're hungry," he said. "Did you miss lunch or—"

"Sammy, I–I'm . . ." She tried to stand, but couldn't manage to get to her feet. She flopped back down into the chair. "I don't know what's wrong—"

She tried to focus on him, but when she did, she realized two things: Sammy loomed over her, staring down at her with an odd smile on his face, and she knew she was going to pass out. Right now.

Judd removed his muddy boots and left them on the back porch. He had stomped through the woods until well after dark, trying his best to work off some of the frustration that plagued him. He had left Griffin's Rest Sunday morning, running away from Lindsay and the emotions she evoked in him. Life would be much simpler if he could continue to deny the fact that he had feelings for her. Damn it, he didn't want to care. Caring for someone was too painful. Loving someone and losing them was a fate worse than death.

After entering the kitchen, he removed his leather jacket, flung it across the back of the nearest chair, and headed toward the cupboard where he kept his whiskey stored. Yesterday, he'd drunk himself into a mindless stupor, finding a few hours of forgetfulness in his alcoholic haze. In the past, when he'd gotten drunk, he had been trying to forget about Jennifer, about how much he had loved her, about how she had died. But last night, he'd been trying to forget Lindsay.

He opened the cupboard, reached in, and yanked out the three-quarters' empty bottle of Jack Daniels. Gripping the bottle in one hand, he stared at it, seeing it for what it was— his friend and his enemy. A friend who could ease the pain inside him. But only temporarily. An enemy that made false promises.

He set the bottle on the counter.

He wanted a drink.

No, he needed a drink.

Six months ago, he wouldn't have thought twice about drowning his sorrows. Hell, a few weeks ago, he would have gotten drunk and stayed drunk for a week. But that was before . . .

Before he realized that he hated himself for having hurt Lindsay. Before he admitted to himself that after almost four years of being incapable of caring about himself or anyone else, he actually cared about Lindsay McAllister.

He didn't want to care, but God help him, he couldn't stop himself.

Judd left the bottle of Jack Daniels on the counter.

As he prepared the coffeemaker, his hands trembled.

He had gone cold turkey six months ago. He could do it again.

This time for good.

He stood and watched as the black liquid drained down into the glass coffeepot. Staring sightlessly, his mind wandering, his thoughts taking him away from the present moment, Judd didn't fight the inevitable memories that were gradually replacing the memories of his wife.

Lindsay smelled fresh and clean, like Ivory soap and baby powder. Her scent filled his nostrils, floating through him, enticing him in a way expensive perfume could not. Chanel No. 5 or any other heavy perfume reminded him of Jennifer.

Nothing about Lindsay reminded him of his wife. They were as different as night and day. Comparing them would be like comparing apples to oranges.

He had loved Jennifer. God in heaven, how he had loved that woman. She had been exciting, flirtatious, effervescent, and lusciously beautiful. With her on his arm, every man who saw them envied him, wanted to be him. Until she came into his life, he had never truly been in love, had never known what it was like for one person to be the other's sole reason for living.

Whatever problems they'd had in their brief marriage, they would have worked out. He had never doubted for a minute that they would have spent the rest of their lives together, had children together, grown old together.

Anguish stabbed through him, a pain so severe that he doubled over as tears misted his eyes. It had been years since he had felt this intensely.

Jenny . . . Jenny . . .

Snapping straight up as the pain subsided, Judd glanced from the coffeemaker to the bottle of whiskey.

Damn you, Lindsay McAllister. Damn you for making me feel again.

He grabbed the bottle, opened it, turned it upside down over the sink, and poured the reddish brown liquid down the drain, then tossed the empty bottle into the topless trash can halfway across the room.

With the coffee brewing, his stomach knotted and his hands shaky, Judd checked the refrigerator. Empty, except for a couple of moldy items that could have, at one time, been something edible. When he rummaged in the pantry, he found two cans of soup and a half-full box of crackers. Probably stale.

Soup, crackers, and coffee tonight. Tomorrow morning, he'd make a trip to the nearest store for more supplies. And he'd call Dr. Meng. If he couldn't manage to stay sober on his own, he wanted to have a backup plan. He might need her help.

LaShae's eyelids fluttered. Despite feeling lethargic, her limbs heavy, her mind foggy, she managed to open her eyes. The room was dimly lit and eerily quiet, except for music. Instrumental. No words. The tune unfamiliar. Classical. Mozart, perhaps.

Where was she? Not at home.

Think, LaShae. Try to remember.

I left the station and drove to Bessemer to meet with Sammy.

Sammy!

Where was Sammy?

She looked around the empty room. Sammy's motel room. Was she alone? Where was he?

When she tried to sit up, she realized she couldn't.

Why couldn't she get up?

Her arms were spread out wide on either side of her and her wrists were bound with rope that disappeared under the bed. Attached to the bed railing? She struggled against the confinement, but couldn't escape her bondage. The ropes held her bound tightly.

She lifted one foot and then the other. Her legs were free. She raised her left leg, then her right leg, finally kicking as hard as she could, thrashing about uselessly.

Who had done this to her? And why?

And where was Sammy? What had happened to him? Had someone killed him?

She searched the room again. Empty. She was alone.

Scream! She opened her mouth to yell for help and realized she couldn't. A thick rag tied across her open mouth effectively gagged her.

Had someone raped her and then left? She looked down at her body. She was fully clothed, could feel her bra against her breasts, could feel her panties still in place, and could even feel the shoes on her feet. No one had undressed her.

She heard a noise. What? Where?

The bathroom door opened. Her gaze focused on the shadowy figure moving toward her. Slowly. Precisely.

Whoever he was, he wasn't in any hurry.

What was he holding in his hand?

As he approached LaShae, her heartbeat went wild, adrenaline pumping through her rapidly. He stopped several feet away and looked at her. She studied him closely, her eyesight slightly fuzzy and her brain foggy. She had no idea what had happened or what was going to happen. Managing one coherent thought at a time, she wondered if she would live long enough to give this man's description to the police. If his intent was rape, she might survive. If not, if he killed her . . .

No, God, please. No! I don't want to die.

Don't punish me. I swear I'll be good for the rest of my life. I'll make my marriage to Rodney work. I'll be a faithful wife, a loving mother . . .

Her gaze focused on the object the man held in his hand, the handle a light wood or a plastic that looked like wood. LaShae's heart stopped when she recognized the tool he clutched.

A shiny new axe.

Merciful Lord!

Talking, trying to make him understand her words through the gag in her mouth, she struggled against the ropes that trapped her.

Please, don't kill me.

He moved closer, stopping at the side of the bed. She

gazed up at him, pleading with him, letting her eyes speak for her. He returned her stare. The man's eyes were brown, as was his hair, and his cheeks flushed pink. He looked familiar, but she couldn't quite place him. She had seen him somewhere before, hadn't she?

"Hello, my pretty flower," he said.

LaShae gasped. The man standing beside the bed, holding an axe in his hand was Sammy. And yet he was not Sammy. Where were his blue eyes? His blond hair?

A wig? Contacts?

She mumbled incoherently through the gag, trying to ask him why? Why was he going to kill her?

Was he really a victim of childhood rape or had he lied to her, lured her into a trap? God, she felt like a fool. She hadn't been naive since she'd been a teenager, if then. Why had she been so trusting?

"Don't fret, my lovely LaShae," he told her as his free hand reached down and stroked her cheek. "You'll never grow old and ugly. I'm picking you before you wither, while you're still fresh and beautiful."

She tried again to talk to him, but her words came out garbled.

He stroked her cheek, her neck, her shoulder. "I've been practicing, so I should be able to take off your head with one powerful chop." He grasped her chin between his fingers and thumb, then squeezed. "I don't want you to suffer."

LaShae keened loudly, the sound muffled beneath the thick gag.

Don't. Please, please don't!

Griffin felt her presence before he glanced up and saw Yvette standing in the doorway of his den. He had known many stunningly attractive women over the years, but none as completely beautiful as this incredible woman whose heart and soul were as beautiful as her face and body. He admired Yvette, respected her, loved her.

He owed her his life.

"Good evening," she said in that soft, mellow voice he had first heard eighteen years ago. An angel's voice in the depths of hell.

"Come in." He invited with a wave of his hand.

She entered the den like a puff of smoke, her walk so graceful that she seemed to float as she moved.

"I've spent the last hour with Barbara Jean," Yvette told him.

Griffin nodded.

"I can tell you what she remembers. In detail."

"Is it enough for me to send for a sketch artist?"

"Perhaps."

"Tell me."

Yvette thought for several seconds before she spoke again. "He was average height and probably average build, just as she has said. He was wearing a tan overcoat and a hat and sunglasses."

"None of this information is new." He eyed her knowingly. "There's more, isn't there?"

"His hair was brown. His cheeks very pink. Either flushed or chapped. He was clean-shaven. She's very certain of those facts. His clothing was inexpensive, but his gloves were fur-lined leather and she believes the scarf around his neck was silk."

"He wore a combination of his own expensive clothes and cheaper apparel."

"He was quite fair, his face round and full, his nose large, rather prominent. Not handsome, but not ugly."

"Anything else?" Griffin asked, knowing that even with an artist's sketch, it was unlikely anyone could ID the suspect from this description. But it was far more than they'd ever had. And there was always the off chance that even a sketch showing a guy in sunglasses and wearing a hat might be of some use. After all, they now had a partial description.

"Does Barbara Jean have any idea that you were—?"

"No. When we spoke, she simply repeated what she had already told you in the past," Yvette said. "The rest, I gained by invading her private thoughts."

Griff took Yvette's small, slender hands into his, lifted them to his lips and kissed first one and then the other. "Don't feel guilty for using your special talent. You did it for the right reason, for a good cause."

"The end always justifies the means." Her voice held a tone of self-condemnation.

"Not always," he told her. "But sometimes."

Curling her fingers around his hand. "Damar is very protective of Barbara Jean."

Griff nodded.

"She reminds him of his wife."

"Damn! I should have known it was something like that. He hasn't shown any interest in a woman in all these years, now suddenly . . ." Griff eyed Yvette speculatively. "He didn't tell you that, did he?"

"No."

"He wouldn't want either of us to know, would he?"

"He hasn't admitted it to himself."

"Then how did you . . ." Griff groaned. "You probed his subconscious?"

"Not intentionally. But it happens sometimes. Especially with you and Damar. I've told you that our connection is quite strong. The three of us."

"Three tortured souls spit out of the bowels of hell together. That would tend to bind people together, wouldn't it?"

With only a slight hesitation, a glimmer of remembrance behind those luminous black eyes, Yvette said, "Send for your sketch artist and I'll work with him alone, without Barbara Jean knowing."

"Very well. I'll have someone here by morning."

When Yvette left him alone in his den, Griff tried not to think about the past. Eighteen years ago, fifteen years ago. Ten years ago.

Damar Sanders and Yvette Meng would be a part of his life from now until they died. He was as bound to them as if they were blood kin, his brother and his sister. Spirit siblings, their relationship forged in fire and brimstone.

Pinkie fed off her fear, devouring it the way a starving man consumes food. He wished he could remove the gag from her mouth so that he could hear her scream, but he couldn't risk it. Someone might hear. He had brought along a CD player with a favorite Mozart CD to muffle any noise he or LaShae might make.

She thrashed about on the bed, fighting to free herself. Poor darling. Like an animal caught in a snare. If she could, she would no doubt chew off her hands at the wrists to escape.

"If you lie still, it will be easier for me to take off your head with one chop," he told her, and loved the terror he saw in her eyes. "If you keep squirming, it might take several tries. We don't want that, do we? You don't want to suffer and I don't want you to suffer."

Tears flooded her eyes.

Such pretty pale brown eyes.

"I've never chopped off a head before, but I decided that since time was running out and the game would soon end, that I should try it. On a human, that is. I've practiced numerous times on various animals. Cats and dogs mostly."

She went still suddenly, her gaze fixed on his as tears streamed down her face. She was begging him for her life. Silent begging. Not as satisfying as hearing her plead and beg and bargain, but it would do. This time.

He knelt down, reached under the bed and pulled out a large wooden chopping block that he had picked up at the local Dollar Store. Resting the axe against the nightstand, he reached over, lifted LaShae's head, and slid the block beneath her neck. She continued staring up at him, silent and still.

"I'll make it quick," he said. "I promise."

He lifted the axe over his shoulder, then brought it down with all his strength. The first blow severed her head, which rolled sideways on the block. Two arteries in her neck sprayed blood at least eight or nine feet, all the way across the bedspread and onto Pinkie's slacks. He would simply remove this pair and leave them. He had bought them at the same time he'd bought the axe, the chopping block, and the other necessities this morning.

He noted that her head itself didn't bleed much, but her eyes moved around some while her body trembled for only a few seconds. Then it was over.

He went into the bathroom, stripped out of his bloody clothes, tossed them into the shower, then washed his hands, and put on clean slacks and a shirt. When he went back into the bedroom, he flipped open the black vinyl duffel bag and removed his digital camera. He took several pictures. Hurriedly.

He would stay only long enough to savor the kill. The photos would allow him to enjoy this moment over and over again. For days, weeks, months.

After placing the camera back in the duffel bag, he removed the single, long-stemmed red rose he'd gotten at a local grocery store this afternoon.

Pinkie laid the rose between LaShae's lovely breasts.

Chapter 23

Lindsay and Callie sat on the sofa in Callie's den, their feet on the coffee table, a small glass of chilled fig vodka in each of their right hands. The grandfather clock in the foyer struck eleven. Callie's husband and kids were in bed, snug and safe for the night. For the past twenty-four hours, since she had arrived here in Soddy-Daisy, a small town outside Chattanooga, Lindsay and Callie hadn't had a moment alone. Now, Lindsay and her cousin, who was like a sister to her, could share some one-on-one time. They could talk, laugh, cry. They could share. Men didn't understand the concept of sharing the way women did. They had little comprehension of the necessity of sharing feelings, that innate need a woman has to confide in another woman. Sometimes that type of sharing was the only thing that kept a woman sane.

And God knew that for the past six months, Lindsay's sanity had been in question. Thanks to Judd. And to her own stupidity.

"So, are you going to tell me or not?" Callie asked.

Lindsay took a sip of the smooth vodka, a deceptive liquor

that could knock you on your ass before you knew you were drunk. "I'm a fool."

Callie lifted her brows in an inquisitive manner.

Heaving a deep sigh, Lindsay confessed, "I'm still in love with Judd Walker."

"That's a given, honey. When you kept telling me in your e-mails and phone calls that you were finally over him, I knew you were lying to yourself." Callie shook her head. "No, that's not it. There's something else. What is it?"

How could she tell her cousin about something she didn't want to remember, something she wished she could forget?

"Late last summer, something happened between Judd and me." Lindsay set her glass on the coffee table.

"I figured it had."

"It made me hate him," Lindsay said. "I walked away severely wounded, but I survived." She scooted around on the sofa until she faced her cousin. "I spent several months in therapy with Dr. Meng, a psychiatrist friend of Griff's."

Callie studied Lindsay. "What happened? What did Judd do?"

"Other than breaking my heart?"

I will not cry. I can tell Callie about what happened without falling apart. Judd has apologized. He's genuinely sorry.

"Judd knew I was in love with him. He wanted to scare me off and he did. At least for awhile. Half a year."

"This doesn't sound good." After Callie set her glass on the table, she reached over and grasped Lindsay's hand. "Tell me what he did."

"He's told me he's sorry. He's explained that he wanted to scare me off for my own good, that he wanted me to see him for the bastard he is."

"If it's too difficult to talk about, then—"

"Judd almost raped me."

"My God!" Callie squeezed Lindsay's hand tightly.

Tears gathered in Lindsay's eyes. "We were alone to-gether at his family's old hunting lodge, the way we'd been together a dozen times before. I was trying to help him . . . trying to get him to go to bed so he could get some rest. You know there are nights when he can't sleep at all."

"I know. You've told me."

Lindsay pulled her hand free and looked Callie right in the eyes. "Judd came on to me. He touched me. Kissed me. And I responded." She could still feel his hands cupping her breasts, his lips pressed against hers, his tongue probing in-side her mouth.

"He pulled me into bed with him and when we were both naked and . . . He said terrible things to me. Told me that I wasn't the first woman he'd had since Jennifer died. That when he screwed me, he'd be thinking of her, pretending I was her, the way he had those other women."

"Oh, Lindsay, honey . . . I'm so sorry."

"I tried to get out of bed, tried to pull away from him, but he wouldn't let me."

"The man's a real bastard."

"He said things . . . did things . . ." Lindsay sucked in air, trying her best not to cry. "He frightened me. I thought he was going to force me to have sex with him. I fought him, crying like a baby the whole time. And just when I thought—" Lindsay swallowed her tears. "He rolled off me and shoved me out of bed. Then he laughed at me."

Callie pulled Lindsay into her arms and held her.

It was what she needed.

Why had it taken her all this time to realize that she should have come to Callie sooner? *Because you weren't ready,* an inner voice told her. Now was the right time. Now that the wounds were not so fresh, now that she had forgiven Judd. Now that she knew she had to let him go. Somehow. Someway.

Crying softly, Lindsay didn't respond when Callie asked,

"Want me to take one of Jimmy's rifles and hunt Judd Walker down?" Her humorous question instantly lightened the mood. Callie had always been able to make Lindsay smile.

Gulping down her tears, Lindsay lifted her head from her cousin's shoulder and offered her a weak smile. It was the best she could do. "I don't want you to shoot him. I just want him out of my life."

"So, get away from him and stay away from him. You did it for six months. Do whatever you have to do to keep him out of your life."

"I'm thinking about quitting my job."

"You're kidding?"

"No, I'm serious. As long as I continue working for Griff, continue trying to help him find the Beauty Queen Killer, I'll never be free of Judd."

"Then quit. Do it tomorrow. Call Griffin Powell and resign."

Heaving another deep sigh, Lindsay faced Callie. "I can't."

"Oh, honey, why not?"

"I want Judd out of my life, but I can't bear the thought of never seeing him again. I love him more than I hate him. I'm such a fool."

"You can't waste your life wanting a man you can never have. You're too good for him. You know that, don't you?"

"I know, but . . ."

"What about Dr. Nathan Klyce? I had hoped things would work out for you two."

"Oh, Lord. Nathan's another story entirely."

"You blew it with him, didn't you?"

Lindsay picked up her glass and took a sip of the sweet vodka. "Oh, yeah. I blew it big time. It's over between Nathan and me. Permanently over."

"Well, we're just going to have to find you another man. Someone who can make you forget Judd Walker."

"The man doesn't exist who can do that," Lindsay said.

Callie picked up her glass, tucked her legs beneath her on the sofa and said, "What you need is an extended vacation. You've always wanted to go to Italy, to Tuscany. You should go. Take a leave of absence from Powell's and fly to Europe. Who knows, you might meet some delicious Italian guy who'll sweep you off your feet."

"That happens only in the movies."

"Sometimes movies are based on real life."

"Real life sucks, at least for me."

Callie sipped the vodka. "Okay, enough—let's pretend we can fix this problem and get down to the honest-to-God truth. You don't want to go to Italy right now. You don't want to take a leave of absence from Powell's or quit your job. You don't want to wash your hands of the BQK case and you certainly don't want to leave Judd Walker."

"I do want to leave him. I want him out of my life."

Waving her index finger back and forth, Callie said, "You're lying to yourself if you really believe that."

"Damn it, Callie, what am I going to do? I love him so much it hurts. And the worst part of it is that I know he cares about me. He admitted that he did."

"Merciful Lord, gal, what are you doing here with me? You should go to Judd and—"

"He cares about me, wants me sexually, but he still loves Jennifer."

"Son of a bitch!"

"Yeah, I know. The man I love will always love his dead wife. So what do I do?"

"That depends," Callie said.

"Depends on what?"

"On whether you're capable of sharing him with her memory, of letting him love both of you."

* * *

Judd woke at dawn, after maybe three hours of sleep. He had fought the desire to take his father's old Mercedes out of the garage and drive to the nearest liquor store. He had needed a drink last night. Needed one now. His stomach churned. His hands shook. His head ached. His skin crawled.

He flung back the covers, sat up, and put his feet on the cold, wooden floor. *Damn, it's freezing in here.* Since he kept the gas heat turned low at night, the old lodge felt ice-box cold. Outside, the wind moaned, its northeastern force flapping the old shutters and scraping nearby towering tree branches against the roof. March had come in like a lion. Roaring with blustery strength.

Naked and sporting a morning hard-on, he got out of bed and padded barefoot toward the bathroom down the hall. After taking a leak, he turned on the shower and waited for the water to go from cold to hot before stepping under the warm spray. He lathered and rinsed his hair, then soaped his body, his hand lingering over his erection.

Flashes of Lindsay zipped through his mind. The way she had looked lying beneath him, flushed, aroused, and ready to give herself to him.

Damn it, why hadn't he just taken what she offered and had sex with her? God knows he'd wanted her, wanted her so badly that even now, six months later, thinking about it made him painfully hard.

Judd circled his penis, closed his eyes, and thought about screwing Lindsay. As he jerked off, he imagined what it would feel like to be buried deep inside her. Within a couple of minutes, he came.

Taking deep, shuddering breaths, he pressed his forehead against the tiled shower wall. Why was he fantasizing about Lindsay and not Jennifer? In the years since his wife's death, when he'd jerked off or had sex with a woman, Jenny had been in his heart, in his thoughts. Then six months ago, everything had changed. More and more often, sexual thoughts of Lindsay had replaced his thoughts of Jenny.

That doesn't mean you love Lindsay. You want her. You need her. But you don't love her.

Judd hurried through his shower, then returned to his bedroom and dressed quickly in old jeans, thermal undershirt, and flannel shirt. Once in the kitchen, he put on a pot of coffee and checked the time. Five-thirty. Too early to call Griffin's Rest. As he waited for the coffee to brew, he walked out onto the back porch and breathed in the fresh, frigid morning air.

I don't need a drink to get through the morning. I can live without it.

So why did he feel as if a freight train were running through his body right now? Why did he want to ram his fist through the wall? Why did he want a drink so badly?

Cursing himself for allowing alcohol to get such a powerful hold on him, Judd went back inside, poured himself a cup of black coffee, and downed the entire cup, all the while staring at the telephone.

He'd had the service to both his landline and his cell phone disconnected a couple of months ago. But while he'd been at Griffin's Rest, Lindsay had had both reconnected.

He continued staring at the phone.

Call for help.

He hated asking anyone for anything. It went against his basic nature. He'd always been self-sufficient, the one in charge, never needing help from anyone.

But that was who he'd been before Jennifer died.

After her murder, he had begun to believe that love was a weakness. Why hadn't he realized sooner that loving Jenny hadn't been his weakness. It had been his grief that had come damn near close to destroying him. Grief that had manifested itself in uncontrollable rage and an unquenchable thirst for revenge.

He had rejected help from his friends, and had turned Lindsay away time and again. And why? Because he'd been afraid of caring about someone.

I'm sorry, Lindsay. I'm so very sorry.

After pouring himself a second cup of coffee, he yanked the phone off the base and dialed Griffin's Rest. He had a lot of fences to mend—starting with Griff and Lindsay. But first, he needed help.

Sanders answered on the fourth ring. "Powell residence."

"Sorry if I woke you," Judd said. "Is Griff up yet?"

"No, Mr. Walker, he is not."

"What about Dr. Meng?"

"She has not come downstairs this morning."

"Would you ask her to call me as soon as possible."

"Is it an emergency?" Sanders asked.

"Not exactly."

"Is there anything I can do for you?"

"Yeah, kick my butt."

"It would be my pleasure."

Judd chuckled. He wanted to ask to speak to Lindsay. He needed to hear her voice. But not yet. Not until he'd gotten his act together. Not until he could ask her to give him one more chance.

"Just give Dr. Meng my message," Judd said.

"Certainly."

When Judd started to hang up, Sanders said, "Wait just a moment, Mr. Walker." Then Judd heard the muffled sound of a conversation, as if Sanders had put his hand over the phone's mouthpiece while he talked to someone else. "Dr. Meng can speak to you now."

Before he had a chance to say thank you, he heard Yvette Meng's voice, "Good morning, Judd. What can I do for you?"

Tell her the truth. Just say it. "I may need help to stop drinking."

"Would you like for me to arrange for you to enter a clinic or—"

"Isn't there any other way?"

"You could come back to Griffin's Rest and put yourself under my care for the next few weeks."

"I'd rather not involve Lindsay in this."

"Lindsay isn't here," Yvette said. "She is on a temporary leave of absence."

"Where did she go?" Before Yvette could reply, he added, "Forget I asked. I know that wherever she is, she went there to get away from me." When Yvette made no comment, he said, "I'm going to try for a few days to do this on my own. If I can't make it solo, I'll come to Griffin's Rest by the end of the week."

Just as Griffin kept former FBI profiler, Derek Lawrence, on retainer, he also kept a talented sketch artist, Wade Freeman, on retainer. Wade was actually a painter and sculptor who lived in Maryville. He had an art studio in the downstairs of an old 1920 craftsman house and lived upstairs. Griffin owned several of Wade's paintings and bronze statues, some displayed at Griffin's Rest, others in the Powell Agency offices in downtown Knoxville.

Wade had arrived at seven this morning and had eaten breakfast with Griff and his other guests. Afterward, Yvette had joined Wade in the sunroom, so they could work together on the sketch of the man Barbara Jean had seen leaving her sister's apartment only moments after Gale Ann had been attacked.

Griff and Yvette had agreed not to tell Barbara Jean anything about either Yvette's unique ability to delve into other people's minds or that Wade Freeman was a sketch artist. For all Barbara Jean knew, Wade was simply an old friend who was visiting for the day.

During the first few hours after breakfast, Griff made several phone calls, the last one to his personal contact in D.C. It wasn't that he didn't have a conscience, that he didn't know how often he bent the rules, and occasionally broke the law. But sometimes the end did justify the means. At least, that was the way he saw things. Money was power. He'd always known that fact, but after becoming rich himself, he had realized exactly what money could buy.

It could buy a man's integrity.

It could buy information at the highest levels of government.

Griff used the power of his great wealth discriminately, but when he wanted something, he usually got it.

A soft rap on the den door ended Griff's mental efforts to justify to himself the reason he cut corners, bent rules, broke the law.

"Come in," he said.

Yvette entered, a sketchbook in her hand. "Wade has completed three different sketches of the man I described to him. One is exactly as Barbara Jean saw him, a profile of his face. One is Wade's interpretation of what the man might look like without his hat and sunglasses. The third is a full-face view, again Wade's interpretation."

Griff held out his hand. Yvette gave him the sketchbook. He looked at each sketch hurriedly, then studied each one for several minutes.

"An ordinary guy," Griff said.

"The only facial feature that might be considered unique is his rather large nose."

Griff shrugged. "Lots of men have big noses."

"Now that we have these sketches, what are you going to do with them?"

"I'll fax them to Nic Baxter." Griff smiled, thinking about Nic's reaction. "Once again proving to her that I believe in sharing. It will be up to her to decide how to best use these sketches." Griff stared at the first sketch, the profile of the possible BQ Killer. "You know, there's something familiar about his profile."

"Do you think you've seen a photograph of him or possibly seen the man himself?" Yvette asked.

"I don't know. I can't put my finger on it, but there's something there."

"It's possible that you've crossed paths with him, either in business or in a social setting. After all, the latest profile Derek compiled states that the killer is probably wealthy and Southern, which would easily put him in your circle of acquaintances."

Chartiece Woods hated her job as a maid at the Triple Eight Motel, but it kept her and her three kids off welfare. Her ex-husband sent money once in a blue moon, but she'd never been able to count on him, not even when they'd been married.

This morning, she had rushed through several rooms, doing the usual amount of cleaning, straightening, bed linens changed, and fresh towels put in place. One room had taken longer because the guest had apparently thrown a party. Beer bottles scattered around the floor and both the sink and bathtub contained dried puke. Teenagers!

Just as she unlocked the door to Room Ten, she checked her watch. Almost eleven. She needed to make up for the time she'd lost on Room Six, if she wanted to finish early enough to make it to her son's basketball game this afternoon.

Leaving her utility cart outside, Chartiece stepped into the room, flipped on the light switch, and gave the room a quick visual inspection.

Damn, there was someone still asleep in the bed. They must be passed out drunk or be high on dope not to have heard her enter.

"Sorry to have bothered you," Chartiece said as she approached the fully clothed woman lying in the bed. "I can come back—"

Two things happened simultaneously.

Chartiece saw that the woman's head was not connected to her body.

Then Chartiece let out a bloodcurdling scream.

Chapter 24

Only moments before dinner, Griffin received the call he had been anticipating, the call he had dreaded. He excused himself, left the dining room, and took the call in the privacy of his den. The Beauty Queen Killer had struck again. The woman's body had been found yesterday shortly before noon in a motel room in Bessemer, Alabama, outside Birmingham.

WBNN morning talk show hostess, LaShae Goodloe, had been decapitated.

Anger boiled inside Griff. Only years of mastering the art of meditation, as well as various other mental and physical arts, allowed him to gain control of his rage and channel it properly. But even now, there were times when he had to remind himself that the ultimate goal was justice, not revenge.

"The husband was questioned for hours," Griff's D.C. contact told him. "It seems they were separated and the husband has a notoriously bad temper."

"But he didn't kill his wife?" Griff asked. "You're sure?"

"LaShae Goodloe was a former Miss Birmingham, and she was still young and very attractive. Her talent was singing, so he chopped off her head and left a single red rose lying between her breasts. Sounds like our guy to me. Besides, the husband has an alibi. Confirmed."

"I suppose Nic is already on her way to Birmingham?"

"You suppose correctly."

With only the basic information, Griffin knew he needed to make some quick decisions that involved Lindsay and Judd. Sanders would handle the mundane necessities—seeing to it that the Powell jet was fueled and ready to take off, making hotel reservations in Birmingham, and arranging for a car. Rick Carson would do a background check on the principal players—the victim, her family, friends, and associates, as well as the detectives in charge of the case.

Knowledge was power. A different kind of power than great wealth, but equally important. And one could often be used to acquire the other.

Since Nic Baxter had already hightailed it to Birmingham, Griff saw no point in racing to Alabama tonight. Tomorrow would be soon enough. By then, the local police would know more than they did today, and Rick would probably have the name of a useful informant.

Griff didn't have to worry about dotting i's and crossing t's. That would be done for him by his employees. His one major decision was whether to involve Lindsay in this new BQK case. He could easily contact Judd himself or have Rick or one of the other Powell agents get in touch with him.

Lindsay needed a break—from the BQK cases and from Judd. The best thing he could do for her was leave her out of the loop this time around.

"Griffin?" Yvette stood in the den doorway. "Is everything all right?"

"I hope y'all didn't wait dinner for me."

"The others didn't," she replied as she approached him. "I thought perhaps your phone call was not good news."

"You're right. It wasn't. The BQ Killer has struck again."

Yvette nodded solemnly. "If only my special gifts included being able to see into the past and into the future. If I could go to a crime scene and see what had happened, I would be of more use to you."

Griff caressed her cheek with the back of his hand. "I wouldn't change anything about you, certainly not the very special gifts you have."

Yvette closed her eyes. To most observers, she would appear to be savoring Griff's touch, but he knew better. She was sensing his thoughts.

He lifted his hand from her face.

She looked up at him and smiled.

"Call Lindsay," Yvette said. "Send her to Judd. Tonight."

Griff glared at his old friend, disliking her advice. "Lindsay can't take more of the same. She's had enough. She needs—"

"She needs to be with Judd." Yvette's ebony eyes glistened with moisture. "And he needs her . . . as he needs the very air he breathes."

Griff glowered at Yvette. "What do you know that I don't know?"

She laid her hand on Griff's arm. "I know that neither of them is complete without the other. Send her to him. Call her now."

Griff huffed.

He wanted to argue with Yvette, but he didn't. He had never known her to be wrong. "Very well. I'll call Lindsay. But against my better judgment."

Sandi Ford locked the doors of her dance studio on Main Street in downtown Parsons, Louisiana, at precisely seventen and walked to her SUV parked out front. She had been taking private students three evenings a week, from six until seven, after her regular classes ended. Her twelve-year-old twin girls, Joy and Jeri, both needed braces; her eight-year-old, Shaun, had broken his leg playing soccer, and Earl Ray's insurance had a $1,500 per person deductible. While Earl Ray's paycheck had increased very little over the past five years, his insurance premiums had steadily increased and the benefits drastically dwindled. She had no choice but to earn some extra money. Despite the fact that she and Earl Ray both worked tirelessly, their debts kept mounting, and it hadn't helped that the raise her husband had been counting on had fallen through only last week.

Sandi opened the Tahoe's driver's-side door and climbed behind the wheel. They had purchased the used SUV three years ago, before gas prices had gone through the roof, and they simply couldn't afford to trade it in on another vehicle, not when they had only six months of payments left. Besides, she needed the room in the SUV, not only for hauling around her own three children and their friends, but for transporting the equipment for her dance troupe when they performed in contests.

The drive from downtown Parsons to their home on First Street took less than five minutes. The old Queen Anne Victorian she and Earl Ray had bought and lovingly restored in the first years of their marriage had been and still was Sandi's dream house. She just wished they could afford to fill it with the antiques she so loved.

Someday.

When the kids were grown and out of college.

She parked in the driveway behind Earl Ray's ten-year-old Ford pickup. They had planned to build a two-car garage, but just couldn't seem to work it into their budget. Their very tight budget.

Draping her bag over her shoulder, Sandi got out of the Tahoe, locked it, and headed straight for the backdoor. The minute she entered the kitchen, the wonderful aroma of tomato sauce, heavily laden with oregano, filled her nostrils. Earl Ray glanced up from where he was putting a tray of uncooked bread sticks into the oven and smiled at her. The first night they met—on a blind date fourteen years ago—she had fallen in love with his smile. At thirty-seven, Earl Ray's dark hair was beginning to thin and he had a small beer belly, but he was still good-looking, still sexy. If possible, she loved him more now than she had when they first married.

He closed the oven door and set the timer, then tossed the oven mitt on the counter. Sandi hung her bag on the coatrack near the backdoor.

"We're having spaghetti for supper," he told her. "Shaun is watching TV in the den and doing his homework. The girls are upstairs cleaning their room."

Sandi went over and put her arm around Earl Ray, hugged him, and then kissed his cheek. "It would seem you have everything under control."

He swatted her on the behind. She giggled.

"I've got a bottle of that wine you like chilling in the refrigerator," he said. "Maybe after the kids are down for the night, you and I—"

She kissed him again. Seriously. Putting a little tongue into it. He cupped her buttocks and pressed her into his erection.

"Ah, gee, I wish you two wouldn't do that," Shaun said as he entered the kitchen. "Stuff like that's liable to warp a little kid like me."

Laughing at their son's overly dramatic statement, Sandi and Earl Ray broke apart. Sandi walked over to Shaun and ruffled his thick auburn curls.

"One of these days, you'll want some girl to kiss you," Sandi said.

"Yuck. Not me. Not ever."

Glancing at her husband, she asked, "How soon will dinner be ready?"

"Give me ten minutes," Earl Ray said. "Why don't you go

sit down and rest until then?" He motioned to Shaun. "Run upstairs and tell your sisters to wash up and get ready for supper."

"Ah, do I have to?" Shaun whined.

"Go!" Earl Ray ordered.

Frowning, Shaun meandered out of the kitchen. The slow, steady clump, clump, clump of his athletic shoes hitting the steps as he climbed the backstairs echoed through the old house.

"Thanks, honey," Sandi said. "I've been on my feet all afternoon. I'd love nothing better than to sit down for a few minutes."

"I wish you hadn't had to take on those extra lessons. If my raise had come through—"

"That wasn't your fault. You can't help it if the union voted to accept the company's offer," Sandi said. "Besides, I'm enjoying giving these one-on-one lessons. Would you believe that one of my private students, Renae Yates, knew that I was once Miss Teen USA? It seems her mother was a student at Parsons State back when I was there."

An odd expression crossed Earl Ray's face. Fleeting. Momentary. If she hadn't been looking right at him, she would have missed it.

"What's wrong?" she asked.

"Nothing. It's just sometimes I wonder if you ever think about . . . well, if you've ever wished you'd done more with your dancing."

"I did. I own a dance studio, don't I?"

"You know what I mean. You have so much talent. If we hadn't gotten married—"

"I wouldn't change a thing. Besides, I never was as talented as you thought I was. Or my mother thought I was."

Earl Ray chuckled. "I believe your mother still blames me that you're not a prima ballerina with some high-falutin' dance company in New York."

Sandi blew her husband a kiss as she headed for the den. As a kid, she'd had high expectations. Her mother's dream for her to become a professional ballerina had somehow become her dream, too. She'd loved to dance, but by the time she was eighteen, she'd had to admit to herself that she lacked both the incredible talent and the relentless drive it took to succeed. Even now, her mother was convinced that Sandi had sacrificed herself for marriage and motherhood. No matter how many times she told her mother that she was happy, that she wouldn't trade her life for anyone else's, her mom refused to believe her.

Falling into the recliner in the den, Sandi sighed as she closed her eyes and let her mind drift. Not backward, but forward. To this fall when the Tahoe would be paid off. To next year when she would have socked away enough money for her and Earl Ray to take the kids to Disney World for a few days. To fifteen months from now when she could celebrate being cancer-free for five years.

Pudge listened as Pinkie told him, in detail, about luring LaShae Goodloe to her death. In the past, he had truly enjoyed hearing every grizzly detail, had loved hearing the excitement in his cousin's voice. But tonight was different. His mind kept fading out, thinking about how close they were to the end of their five-year game. The score was so close that either of them could win. But Pudge had no intention of being the loser. If he could find a redhead next . . .

"I can understand now why you've used that method several times. My God, it's exhilarating to take off someone's head. I had no idea that so much blood would shoot out halfway across the room."

"There are two major arteries in the neck that are severed when you take off someone's head," Pudge explained. "Did you touch her afterward?"

"Only to place the rose on her chest. Why do you ask?"

"Remember the Cotton Queen from Cullman last year? I laid my hand on her chest, after I'd cut off her head. Her heart was still beating. Slowly. Beating in tremors. Then in less than thirty seconds, it was over."

"Next time, I'll—"

"There probably won't be a next time for you," Pudge said. "Not unless your last kill is another singer."

Pinkie sighed heavily. "I wish we hadn't set a five-year time limit."

"We agreed that we would adhere to the rules. And that includes the stipulation that the winner takes all."

"I regret that we made such an unholy agreement."

"The game had become boring," Pudge reminded his cousin. "We had to up the stakes to keep the level of excitement high, to make it worth the effort."

"You're right. It's just I hate the thought of having to . . ." He gulped. "If I win, I promise that I'll make your penalty as quick and painless as possible," Pinkie said.

"If you win."

"I'm ahead now. LaShae Goodloe gave me ten more points. Even if you get a redhead next—"

"She'll be a redhead."

"You haven't already chosen her, have you? That would be cheating and—"

"No, certainly not," Pudge lied. Of course, he had chosen his next victim. But what Pinkie didn't know, wouldn't hurt either of them. Feeling quite self-satisfied, Pudge thought about the cute redhead from Parsons, Louisiana, practically in his backyard.

On the drive from Soddy-Daisy to the Walker hunting lodge in the next county, Lindsay had questioned her sanity. What was she doing? Why was she rushing to Judd this way?

When Griff had called an hour ago, she'd been playing Monopoly with Callie's kids, enjoying herself tremendously. During the past few years as a Powell agent, she had almost forgotten what real life was like. Regular routines, regular people living regular lives. No cloak and dagger. No murder mysteries to solve. No ruthless killers who couldn't be stopped.

"He's killed again," Griff had told her. "A former Miss Birmingham. He chopped off her head."

Lindsay pulled her Trailblazer to a steady halt in front of the lodge. To her surprise, lights burned brightly inside the house. That meant Judd wasn't sitting in the dark, as he so often did.

"Just as Derek predicted, our guy is killing more often. Not a month or two apart now, only a week or so," Griff had said. "The more frenzied he becomes, the better our chances of catching him, especially if he makes just one major mistake."

After getting out of her SUV, Lindsay yanked her coat off the passenger seat and put it on, then locked the vehicle and headed toward the front porch. As she approached the door, she thought she heard music.

Music? In Judd's house? Not possible. He didn't watch TV, didn't read, seldom listened to music, didn't do much of anything that was halfway normal.

"I thought twice about calling you," Griff had said. "I figured you'd had all you could take of both Judd and the BQK cases. But Yvette thought I should call you, allow you to decide for yourself. You don't have to do this. You can say no."

She could have said no, but both Yvette and Griff had known she wouldn't. When it came to anything to do with Judd Walker, she was shameless. Love could do that to a woman.

As she lifted her hand to knock, she heard the music again. Soft. Mournful. A heartfelt rendition of "Body and

Soul" floated from inside the lodge, like smoke in the night air. Hesitating, she dropped her hand and stood there on the porch, her pulse racing. Remembering. She had given Judd several jazz CDs for Christmas the year before last, knowing how much he loved jazz. He had tossed the decoratively wrapped gift aside without opening it.

Was this music off one of the CDs she had given him?

When she knocked several times, the tune changed to "Send in the Clowns." Soft, sweet, bluesy.

By the time she pounded her fist for the fourth time, the front door swung wide open. Lindsay gasped, not expecting Judd to respond so promptly.

They stood there staring at each other. Her heart sank. It was obvious that Judd hadn't shaved in days. His hair was tousled, needing not only cutting but combing. His golden eyes were bloodshot, his face haggard. He looked like hell.

Her first instinct was to put her arms around him and comfort him.

She didn't.

"What are you doing here?" he asked. His tone was neither hostile nor inviting.

He didn't sound as if he was drunk.

"May I come in?" she asked.

He moved aside and swept his arm out in an inviting gesture. "Sure."

When she entered the foyer, he closed the door behind her. The melancholy strains of piano, trumpet, and drums wafted out in the foyer from the sitting room on the left. She glanced through the open door and noticed a blazing fire in the massive stone fireplace.

Although she'd never been upstairs, she was quite familiar with the downstairs rooms: The two large sitting rooms flanking the foyer, the dining room, the kitchen, the three bedrooms, and a single bath with fixtures a good forty years old.

She noticed Judd had put his hands in his jeans pockets and his thumbs were hooked over the edge, nervously stroking the denim fabric.

"Want some coffee or maybe hot tea?" Judd asked.

Had she heard him correctly? Had he offered her something to drink? Had he actually been cordial?

"Nothing, thanks."

"Take your coat?" he asked.

She unbuttoned the coat and handed it to him.

"Go on into the parlor," he told her as he hung her coat on the hall tree in the foyer.

When she entered the sitting room on the left, she felt an odd sense of uncertainty. What was going on with Judd? Why was he being so nice to her?

"Have a seat," he said.

Startled that he was so close, only a couple of feet behind her, she gasped, then whirled around and faced him.

"Griff called," Lindsay said. "The Beauty Queen Killer has struck again."

Judd nodded, but said nothing.

"A former Miss Birmingham. He cut off her head."

Judd flinched.

"Griff's flying to Birmingham in the morning," she said.

"Okay." He nodded. "Should we drive down or should we see if we can catch a morning flight out of Chattanooga?"

She stared at him, puzzled by his calm, rational manner. "Want to tell me what's going on or should I assume you're an alien who has taken over Judd Walker's body."

His lips twitched. Was it possible that Judd had almost smiled?

He took a couple of hesitant steps toward her. Her breath caught in her throat.

When only inches separated them, Lindsay felt a sense of panic.

Run! Now, while you still can.

"You shouldn't have come here," he told her, his voice low and calm.

"I thought about not coming," she admitted. "Griff said he could call you or he could send Rick after you or . . . I had to come myself. You know that."

"Yeah, I know."

Placing her cupped hand over her mouth, she swallowed salty tears. She would not cry. Silly, silly woman! "I guess I'm like an old dog that keeps coming back after his master has kicked him for the twentieth time."

Judd stared at her, a peculiar expression on his face. When he reached for her, she jerked away, startled by his action. But she couldn't stop looking at him. He lifted his hand up and circled the back of her neck. Gently. When he pulled her closer, she didn't resist. Couldn't resist.

He lowered his head, bringing his lips in line with hers and whispered, "I'm sorry, sweetheart. You'll never know how sorry I am."

And then he kissed her.

Chapter 25

Other than his lips on hers, Judd didn't touch her, which somehow made the moment all the more poignant. Every nerve ending in her body tingled, alive with love and desire. She could no more stop loving him than she could grab a heavenly star and hold it in her hand.

He ended the brief, tender kiss, opened his eyes, and lifted his head. Lindsay looked up at him, staring into his face, unable to speak. He had taken her breath away with his gentleness. And the sincerity of his words.

I'm sorry, sweetheart. You'll never know how sorry I am.

He pressed his forehead against hers, his breathing heavy and erratic. Closing her eyes, she savored the sweet moment. She could feel the warmth of his breath mingling with hers, the scent of his body soap-and-water clean.

"I swear to God, Lindsay, if you can forgive me, I'll never do anything to hurt you ever again."

She sucked in air, so taken aback by his declaration, knowing in her heart that this time he meant every word. There was not one doubt in her mind.

He lifted his head again, then reached down and took

each of her hands in his. Loosely. No pressure. Holding her hands as if they were made of fragile glass.

"Any other woman would have given up on me a couple of years ago," he told her. "I've managed to methodically alienate every friend I ever had, including Cam and Griff. The only reason Griff has given me numerous second chances is because of you."

"Judd—"

"Shh . . . Let me get it all out while I can. Then you can say whatever you need to say. Okay?"

She nodded.

Continuing to hold her hands between their bodies, arms down in a relaxed manner, he said, "When Jenny died . . . when she was murdered . . ."

Lindsay squeezed his hands.

"I lost my mind. That's the only way I know how to describe what happened. I hurt so much. I couldn't bear the pain. You know how I was. You were there. You and Griff and Cam. Then day by day the agony grew worse until one day, there was nothing left inside me—no pain, no love, nothing except anger and vengeance.

"And no matter what I said, what I did, how I roared and bellowed, you were always there, trying to help me, caring about me when I wasn't worth caring about. I kept trying to push you away, but you wouldn't let me. Not until . . ."

Silence.

Their gazes met and locked. Lindsay thought she saw a shimmer of moisture glazing Judd's eyes, but quickly realized the tears were in her eyes, not his.

"You offered me love and I threw it back in your face."

"You couldn't help it that you didn't love me. We don't choose who—"

"I cared about you, Lindsay," he admitted. "That was the problem. I didn't want to care. I didn't want to feel anything, and there you were making me feel again, making me want and need again. I hated you for making me feel. And I hated myself for needing you so badly."

"Judd?"

He lifted her hands to his lips, kissed each in turn, then gently grasped her shoulders. "I'm a mixed-up mess, sweetheart. I don't know if I can straighten up and fly right or if I'm just a lost cause. But I . . . uh . . ." He swallowed hard. "I'm a real bastard for doing this, but here goes—I don't want you to give up on me. I need you. At least as a friend. Maybe . . . maybe more than a friend. I don't know."

She felt lightheaded, as if she were going to faint. It wasn't until she gasped for air that she realized she'd been holding her breath.

"You know how much I loved Jennifer. A part of me will always love her. There's nothing I can do about that. I don't know if I'll ever be able to come to terms with her death. If her killer is ever caught . . . ? Maybe not even then."

"You're not going to lose me," Lindsay managed to say, her voice quivering slightly. "I'll always be your friend. As for my being more than your friend . . . I love you."

He pulled her into his arms and held her. "I don't deserve your love. But God help me, I want it."

With her head on his chest, Lindsay wrapped her arms around his waist and held him as she had longed to hold him. Leaning down, he kissed the top of her head and when she looked up at him, he kissed her forehead.

This was a side of Judd she had never seen. The kind, caring man he must have been at one time, before Jennifer's murder.

He gently shoved her away from him, but smiled at her. "Let me work on cleaning up my act. And let me try this friendship thing. I used to be pretty good at it. Just ask Griff."

"He's told me. You two and Cam were dashing bachelors, partying together, dating the same women—"

"I guess he told you that we all three wanted Jennifer, and

that she dated both him and Cam before she dated me." Judd's smile vanished. "I'm sorry. I can't seem to stop talking about her."

"It's all right. She was your wife. You loved her. What kind of friend would I be if I didn't want to know everything about you, including your relationship with Jennifer."

Judd studied her for a few seconds. "You're a remarkable woman, Lindsay McAllister."

Smiling, she replied, "I've been trying to convince you of that fact for nearly four years."

He nodded toward the hallway. "I've got groceries. How about I whip up some soup and sandwiches for us, unless you've already had dinner."

"Callie and I ate a late lunch and the kids both had after-school activities, so she was just putting supper on the table when Griff called."

He grabbed her hand. "How about I fix the soup and you make the sandwiches?"

Nodding agreement, Lindsay's smile broadened.

As he pulled her along with him into the foyer and down the hall, he said, "I've got a box of shortbread cookies. The last time you bought groceries for me, you picked up some. I remember your saying they were your favorites. You said that they were great with coffee or with milk."

"Milk? Don't tell me you actually have milk in your refrigerator?"

"Sure do. And bacon and eggs and a fresh loaf of bread."

She paused when they reached the kitchen door. When she hesitated, he stopped, turned, and looked at her. "What?" he asked.

"Are you sure you're not an alien who's taken over Judd Walker's body."

He laughed. Honest-to-God laughter.

Lindsay's breath caught in her throat.

I don't know what's happened. I don't know if this miracle

*is permanent or temporary, but thank you, Merciful Lord.
Thank You.*

Sandi and Earl Ray rested on the sofa, their legs spread
out, her hips nestled between his thighs and his arms draped
around her. They had sent the kids to their rooms shortly
after dinner and had just finished off the chilled bottle of
white zinfandel. The mantel clock struck ten.

"We should head on up to bed," he told her. "Five-thirty
will roll around pretty quick." He nuzzled her neck. "Feel
like fooling around a little tonight?"

She sighed. "I'm tired, but . . ." She maneuvered her body
just enough so that she could raise herself up and kiss him.
"If you'll get on top and do all the work . . ."

"You've got a deal." He rubbed his hand over her buttocks. "All you'll have to do is lay back and enjoy yourself."

She jumped up off the sofa, planted her hands on her
hips, and glared at him. "Well, big boy, what are you waiting
for?"

He grabbed her, yanked her down onto his lap and gave
her a tongue-thrusting kiss. Just as they came up for air, the
telephone rang.

"Who the hell would be calling at this time of night?"
Earl Ray grumbled.

"I'll get it."

When she tried to stand, he held her down. "Let the machine get it."

She pulled free and stood. "It might be one of the mothers calling about the costumes for the recital next month."

After searching for the portable phone, she found it by
the fifth ring, on top of the magazine rack beside the recliner.
She picked it up, hit the On button and said, "Hello" without
glancing at the caller ID.

"Mrs. Ford?" a male voice asked.

"Yes, this is she."

"I'm Donald Holloway. My wife and I moved here from Tallulah, just last month, and Missy heard about your dance classes. Our girls were taking ballet and tap back in Tallulah and sure do miss it."

"Welcome to Parsons, Mr. Holloway." Two new students? Yes, yes, yes! "Are you and your wife interested in enrolling your daughters at my studio?"

"Yes, ma'am, we sure are, but we're both working and the only time we might get by downtown to see you would be at night. Is that a problem?"

"Why, no, I teach private lessons from six until seven three nights a week."

"Then would tomorrow night be all right? We could stop by between seven and seven-thirty. And after you see how talented our older girl, Melissa Lee, is, you might want to give her some private lessons. We don't spare any expense when it comes to our children."

Two more students, and one might take additional private lessons. This was great. Just when Sandi thought she had tapped all the potential students to be found in Parsons, new residents appeared like magic. How lucky was that?

Although she had planned to come home right after the last class at six tomorrow—Wednesday evening—so she wouldn't miss church services again this week, she knew the Lord would understand.

"I'll see you and your wife and daughters tomorrow evening," Sandi said. "My studio is downtown, on Main Street. You can't miss it. The building is pink, with a lavender front door and a ballerina painted on the display window, and there are costumes in the window."

"Yes, ma'am, my wife knows just where the place is. So, we'll see you tomorrow evening."

After Sandi hung up the phone, she whirled around and around. Earl Ray caught her and pulled her into his arms. "I thought you weren't going to work late tomorrow. We promised the kids we'd go to the Wednesday night service with them. We've missed the past three weeks."

"I know." Sandi stroked her husband's cheek. "But these are two potential new students and one might take private lessons. Do you know how much more money that could mean for us?"

Earl Ray frowned.

She ran her hand over his chest and down to his belt. "You can take the kids to church tomorrow evening, can't you? And I promise, I'll make sure I'm free next Wednesday night." She lowered her hand until it covered the zipper of his jeans.

Grinning, he laid his hand over hers and pressed it against his crotch. "Well, since you put it that way."

They laughed as they walked hand in hand out of the den and up the stairs, both of them eager to make love.

Pudge laid the prepaid cell phone on the bedside table, smiling to himself as he thought about his Oscar™-worthy performance as mild-mannered husband and father, Donald Holloway. Once again, the pretty flower he'd chosen was making things easy for him. He and Pinkie had occasionally discussed how trusting these women were, how easily fooled and manipulated. Apparently none of them were very bright. All were beautiful, but stupid.

He had driven through downtown Parsons this evening and noticed how desolate the place was after six o'clock. The old saying about the streets being rolled up certainly applied to this place. The only business other than the dance studio that stayed open after six was a mom & pop restaurant a block over from Main Street on Tipton Avenue. All the traffic lights in town went to caution yellow after six, except for the ones on Main. By seven o'clock, the town was dead. Tomorrow night nothing on the street where Sandi's Dance Studio was located would be open. A good eighty percent of the traffic would be near the three downtown churches, none of them located on Main.

Cutting off Sandi's feet would be so much easier if he could simply use a small chain saw, but they were such noisy tools. A sharp axe or meat cleaver should work just as well. Sandi was petite, with slender ankles. One good chop on each foot should do the trick.

He wanted to hear her scream. But could he risk someone else hearing her? It would all depend on where he could isolate her inside the studio. A backroom would be perfect. Doors closed and locked, lights dimmed, the mood set.

This would be one of his last kills. He needed to make every moment count before this game ended.

After feasting on thick ham sandwiches and potato soup, Lindsay and Judd sat at the kitchen table drinking milk and eating shortbread cookies. They had talked a bit during food preparation, sharing memories of childhood meals with their families.

"My mom was a great cook," Lindsay had said. "Every day when I came home from school, she'd have homemade cookies and a glass of cold milk waiting for me."

"My mother didn't know how to cook," Judd had said. "Of course, she didn't need to know how. She grew up with a live-in cook and so had my father. But my grandmother Walker knew how to cook, at least I recall when I was a small boy her preparing breakfast for me: Scones and orange marmalade. And she cooked quite a bit when we came here to the lodge. God, how I adored her."

"What did you call her, Grandmother?"

"I called her Mimi."

"How sweet. I don't remember either of my grandmothers, but I had a Pops. My father's father. He died when I was ten."

"Mimi died when I was sixteen. I didn't shed a tear. Not until almost a month later, then I broke down and cried for days."

Lindsay had known Judd for nearly four years, but tonight was their first "getting acquainted" conversation in all that time.

During supper, they'd talked very little, both enjoying sharing the meal. Lindsay had the oddest feeling that she was dreaming and would wake up at any minute. How often had she longed for an evening such as this?

When they finished off their cookies and milk, Judd stood, then stacked their dirty dishes. "I'll wash," he said, "if you'll dry."

"Okay." She picked up the silverware and followed him over to the old farmhouse sink.

"This kitchen needs overhauling. New stove, refrigerator, and definitely a dishwasher," Judd said. "Maybe one of these days, I'll remodel the whole place."

"It would make a wonderful home, out here in the country with all the woods and meadows and animals everywhere. You could get a couple of dogs—collies or golden retrievers. And you should put a swing on the porch."

Judd grinned at her. "The last woman who loved this old lodge was my mimi. She came out here with my grandfather on weekends, and believe it or not, she liked to hunt wild turkey."

"You're kidding?"

"Nope. She wouldn't have anything to do with deer hunting, but she was an expert shot. She's the one who had the flower garden put in out back. And in her day, there was also a herb garden and a vegetable garden. She loved flowers and fresh herbs and homegrown vegetables."

"So do I. Sanders and I have a herb garden at Griffin's Rest. And every spring we plant tomatoes in big pots on the deck."

Judd put a rubber stopper in the old sink, turned on the faucets and picked up the newly purchased bottle of dish detergent. "Mimi had a greenhouse built on the family property on Lookout Mountain. It's still there, but I believe it's empty now. When I lived there, Cook kept a herb garden in it."

Lindsay ran her hand across the lip of the oversized farmhouse sink. "If you ever redo the kitchen, you should leave this sink. It's in great condition and this type of sink is back in style."

Judd poured detergent into the running water, then set the bottle aside, and placed the dishes and silverware into the warm suds. "You grew up in Chattanooga, didn't you?"

"Sure did. Out in Lookout Valley. But both of my parents were originally from Sand Mountain, down in northeast Alabama."

"My family has been in Chattanooga for generations." He washed the first dish, rinsed it, and handed it to Lindsay.

They talked about this and that, the way friends would idly chitchat while doing a chore, and before long, the dishes, silverware, soup pot, and glasses were washed, dried, and put away.

"Did you bring a suitcase?" Judd asked as he took the dish towel from her and hung it over the edge of the sink to dry.

"An overnight bag," she told him.

"I'll have to put some linens on one of the beds downstairs. You can take your pick." He clenched his jaw. "I don't figure you'll want your usual room, the room where we . . ."

Closing his eyes, a pained expression crossed his face. "You should have let Griff horsewhip me for what I did."

Lindsay grasped his arm just above his elbow. He opened his eyes and looked at her. "I think maybe you've suffered as much from what happened between us that night as I have. If we're going to be friends, we both have to get past what happened."

"Can you do that?"

"Yes, I think I can." She released his arm.

"You might be able to forgive me, but I'm not sure I'll ever be able to forgive myself."

"All either of us can do is take things one day at a time," Lindsay said. "You're taking the first steps toward recovering from a horrible tragedy. I don't expect miracles overnight and neither should you."

He huffed. "Thank God, because I'm still a mess and I may always be screwed-up. I'll never be the same person I was before Jennifer was murdered, and I'm still the revenge-hungry, crazy guy I was last week. It's just . . ." He took Lindsay's hand in his. "You make me want to work my way back to being a decent human being again."

"I—I make you . . . ?" Lindsay nervously bit down on her lower lip.

He reached up and cupped her face with his open palms. "I have fought you tooth and nail, haven't I? I've done nothing to deserve your friendship or your love. I know that. But our good friend Griff made me realize that I've depended on you, needed you, wanted you, expected you to take all my shit, and keep coming back for more."

Blinking her eyes to dissolve the teardrops, Lindsay offered him a trembling smile. "Griff's good at giving come-to-Jesus talks, isn't he?"

"I can't promise you anything and I can't offer you anything. Not now. Maybe not ever."

She placed her hands over his where he held her face with

gentle force. "You have to know that when it comes to you, I don't have any pride. I'd do anything for you. I'd—"

He lowered his head and kissed her, all the while clasping her face with tender strength. She responded, opening her mouth for his invasion, savoring the moment. When they were both breathless, they broke apart and stared at each other. Judd let his hands drop away from her face.

"If I asked you to come to bed with me—"

"Ask me," she said.

"No. Not tonight."

"Oh." She felt as if he'd slapped her.

"It's not that I don't want you," he told her. "I do. God, sweetheart, I want you so bad it hurts."

"Then why—?"

"I don't deserve you." He stuffed his shaky hands into his jeans pockets. "I'm a crazy hermit, a vengeance-crazed renegade, and an alcoholic, too. I'm no prize for any woman and certainly not for you."

Lindsay released a long, deep sigh. Judd had just admitted not one horrible truth, but three. She didn't realize he knew, let alone would admit, that he had gradually become an alcoholic. Talk about major progress!

"You don't love someone because he's perfect. You love him in spite of his flaws," she told Judd. "Please, let me help you. Let me love you."

"And if I can't give you anything in return?"

You can. You will. Someday. "I'm not asking for anything, only that you open yourself up enough to let me in. As a friend, as a lover. Whatever you want or need."

"I want to do it right this time. Slow and easy. And wait until you don't have any doubts, when you won't be thinking about the last time. I want you to be able to trust me." He held out his hand.

She took his hand and went with him back into the front parlor. He restarted the CD player, and the moment the soft, melodic strands of a tenor sax and a guitar spread through the room, like warm molasses over hot bread, Judd pulled Lindsay into his arms.

"I used to be a pretty good dancer," he said.

She closed her eyes, laid her head on his chest, curved one arm around his waist, and lifted the other up to his shoulder.

If this was a dream, she hoped she never woke up.

Chapter 26

After looking at two of the three downstairs' bedrooms, deliberately avoiding the one where Judd had emotionally brutalized her, she chose the second room, knowing the minute she saw it that this had been his grandmother's room. A sturdy mahogany four-poster dominated the large space, the bed placed at an angle in one corner, taking full advantage of the long windows on the side and back walls. A ten-foot-high armoire, with massive doors and intricately carved trim, hugged the opposite wall, and a marble-topped dresser boasted a huge, beveled mirror.

"I'll take this one," Lindsay said.

Judd grinned. "This was Mimi's room."

"I thought maybe it was." She walked into the room, inspecting everything from the wool rug on the wooden floor to the twelve foot ceiling crowned with dark walnut molding that matched the mopboard, the windows, and the doors.

"She had the furniture moved here from the house on Lookout Mountain," Judd said. "It had belonged to my grandfather's parents and had been stored in the attic."

"Your house on the mountain must be incredible. Someday, you'll have to give me a tour."

"You might not like the house. Jennifer didn't like it any more than she liked this place." His smile disappeared. "Sorry. I keep—"

Lindsay whirled around and tapped his lips with her index finger. "Never apologize for talking about her."

Judd clasped Lindsay's hand and kissed her knuckles several times before releasing her. "I'll get some sheets and blankets and a couple of pillows. And if you'll give me your car keys, I'll bring in your overnight bag."

"You get the bed linens. I can get my bag."

He glanced at the dark, unused fireplace. "If you'd like, I can build a fire for you. As you well know, there's no central heat and air, and it can get downright cold here at night this time of year."

"A fire would be lovely. Thank you."

When Judd left, she explored the room, opening the armoire, looking at herself in the mahogany cheval mirror, wondering what Judd's mimi had looked like. Beautiful no doubt, as all wealthy society ladies were, then and now. As she made her way around the room, she spotted a small framed photograph sitting on the single bedside table. She picked up the photo and instantly knew that this was Mimi: Probably forty. Flame-red hair. Striking blue-green eyes. Freckles on her nose. A square face. Not beautiful. Not even pretty. But gorgeously alive. Vibrant.

A square jewelry box rested beside the five-by-seven-inch picture. Lindsay opened the top and music filled the air: Debussy's "Clair de Lune."

"That's Mimi," Judd said eying the frame she held. He stood in the doorway, his arms piled high with sheets, blankets, and pillows. "She told me that my grandfather told her, after they married, that the first time he saw her, he thought she was as plain as an old shoe. But that was before she spoke to him and smiled."

Judd came in, dropped the bed linens onto the bed, then walked over and took the photo from Lindsay. Staring at his grandmother's picture, he said, "I thought she was the most beautiful woman on earth. I loved her more than anyone."

He set the frame down and glanced at the fireplace. "I'll go get some wood, kindling, and matches and be right back."

Lindsay nodded, then went over to the bed, picked up the blankets and pillows and deposited them on top of the dresser. She shook out the sheet: Straight edges, no fitted bottom sheet. She whipped the first one apart and spread it over the bed. The sheets were clean, but smelled slightly musty, as if they'd been washed, folded, and then stored a good while ago.

By the time Judd returned with the firewood, she had made the bed and was stuffing the pillows into the hand-embroidered cases. Finishing the chore, she watched while he laid the wood inside the fireplace, arranged the kindling, and then lit the first match.

Judd had broad shoulders, a slender waist and narrow hips. He was long-legged and lean. His hair touched the edge of the moss green flannel shirt he wore.

When he rose to his feet and turned, their gazes connected.

She glanced away. "I need to run outside and get my bag."

"I'll do it for you."

"No, I can get it."

"Let me," he said. "I need to keep busy. I'm doing my best not to butt my head against the wall or drive to the nearest liquor store. I got drunk Sunday night, but haven't had a drop since. I'm nervous and edgy and . . ." He chuckled dolefully. "See, I told you I'm a screwed-up mess."

She rummaged in her pocket, retrieved her keys, and

tossed them to him. Despite his hand shaking, he caught them in midair.

"You know where the downstairs bathroom is," he said before he turned and headed up the hall.

Standing alone in the middle of Mimi's old bedroom, Lindsay thought about what had happened between her and Judd tonight. Just when she had almost given up hope . . .

He didn't make any promises.

He's afraid of hurting you.

He still loves Jennifer.

Three good reasons not to become sexually involved with him.

Yeah, right. She was already as emotionally involved as she could get. Hog wild in love. And she wanted him. Desperately.

Judd returned a few minutes later, brought her bag into the room, and placed it at the foot of the bed. "If you hear me wandering around half the night, don't worry about me. You know how restless I am. And trying to stay sober has made me beyond jittery."

"If you need me . . . if you want company at two in the morning, I'll get up and we can talk or have more cookies and milk."

Offering her a halfhearted smile, he nodded. "Good night, Lindsay."

"Good night, Judd."

Judd hadn't locked the doors here at the lodge since he moved in, but tonight he did. After all, Lindsay would be sleeping downstairs. He wanted to keep her safe.

He had thought his protective instincts had died with Jennifer. Apparently, they hadn't. They had simply been lying dormant.

But love had died with Jennifer.

Or had it?

I'm not in love with Lindsay.

I want her. I need her. But I don't love her. If I love anyone, I love Jennifer. On some level, I'll always love my Jenny.

But I thought love died with Jennifer.

He shook his head. Confusion plagued him. He had thought he knew himself, knew his own tormented soul, and had accepted the fact that he was an unfeeling son of a bitch. But Lindsay had reawakened his emotions, had made him reevaluate his life.

However, one thing had not changed, would never change. A part of him had died with Jennifer. The old Judd Walker had bled to death on the kitchen floor the night he held his butchered wife in his arms. The hull that had remained afterward turned into a vengeful, angry monster, a man who rejected every human kindness. And yet he had taken life-sustaining nourishment from Lindsay's kindness, her caring . . . her love.

Judd went from room to room, turning off the lights, then took the backstairs up to the second floor. His bedroom, the one where he'd slept as a boy and young man when he'd come to the lodge with his family, seemed darker, colder, and more empty than it had at any time since he'd made the place his main residence.

Knowing Lindsay was downstairs, resting in Mimi's old bed, a warm fire glowing in the fireplace, created a sense of loneliness in Judd, a loneliness that reminded him he no longer wanted to be alone.

Day and night. Alone. Lonely. Without human companionship.

For years now, he had existed from one day to the next, wallowing in self-pity and abject loneliness. It was a life he had chosen for himself and yet it was no life at all.

He walked over to the window, drew back the curtain and looked down onto the area where Mimi's garden had once produced not only lilies and marigolds and springtime daffodils, but delicious fresh herbs and an array of vegetables well into early fall. His grandmother and his father had loved the lodge, and even his prim and proper mother had enjoyed an occasional visit to the country.

He had loved and respected his mother and father, but it had been Mimi who had filled his young life with laughter and wonder. If he listened very hard, he could almost hear Mimi's laughter. The woman had known how to live, how to squeeze every ounce of joy from the simple things. She had loved her husband, loved her family, adored her only grandchild. When he and Jennifer had talked about having children, he'd told her how much he wished his mimi had lived long enough to see a great-grandchild.

But there was no great-grandchild. No wife. No future without . . .

Jennifer.

Darling Jenny.

Would you be jealous if you knew I cared about Lindsay?

I don't love her. I don't know if I'm capable of loving anyone. But Lindsay is important to me.

After sitting down on the bed, Judd removed his shoes and unbuttoned his flannel shirt. When he wiggled his toes, he glanced down and noticed a hole in his right sock. He hadn't paid any attention to little things like that in a long, long time. Grinning, he took off his shirt, tossed it to the foot of the bed, then unbuckled and removed his belt. He fell sideways onto the unmade bed and stared up at the ceiling.

It would be unfair to Lindsay if I went into a relationship with her knowing I could never love her.

But you do love her, an inner voice said.

He shot straight up and sat on the edge of the bed.

Yes, I do love her. But not the way I loved Jenny.

Jenny's gone. Lindsay is alive. She's here. And she loves you.

Judd got up, walked out of his bedroom, down the hall, and took the backstairs two at a time.

You have no right to take more from Lindsay than you already have. She loves you. If you go to her, she won't turn you away.

Judd came to a crashing halt in the middle of the kitchen, his hands balled into tight fists. He wanted to smash something to smithereens, to vent his frustration on some inanimate object.

God, he needed a drink. Needed it badly.

But there was no liquor in the house. He'd gotten rid of every half-empty bottle.

You can't get drunk.

But you can go to Lindsay.

She understood him, accepted him, and loved him.

He hadn't promised her anything.

Why should he fight what he wanted, what they both wanted?

He left the kitchen and walked down the hall. When he reached Lindsay's bedroom, he stopped suddenly, noting that the door stood wide open as if inviting him inside.

He took a single, hesitant step into the room before he realized that Lindsay was not in bed. She stood in front of the blazing fire, the outline of her body beneath her gown shadowed by the yellow-orange glow. As if sensing his presence, she turned around, looked right at him and smiled.

Lindsay had known that he would come to her. She had seen the desire in his eyes, had felt it in his embrace, in his kiss. He might not love her, but he needed her, and for now that would be enough.

"I thought you'd probably be asleep," he said, his gaze moving over her hungrily.

"I'm not sleepy."

"Neither am I."

They stood there, the width of the bedroom between them and simply stared at each other. Judd was in his sock feet and wore only his thermal undershirt and his beltless jeans. He looked delicious. Good enough to eat. All lean, luscious male.

She wondered how she looked to him. Plain and dowdy in her oversized pink sleep shirt that hit her just above her knees. Her face cleanly scrubbed, her curly hair tousled from combing through it with her fingers. Her feet encased in warm, fuzzy footies.

"I'm hungry," he said.

"You are?"

"I am."

"Do you want to share more milk and cookies?"

Shaking his head, he took several steps toward her. "I'm not hungry for milk and cookies."

"You're not?" Alive with anticipation, she swallowed nervously.

"I'm hungry for you," he told her.

"Judd . . ."

He spanned the space that separated them, and without saying a word, circled her neck with his big hand, lowered his head, and kissed her with an eager passion that matched her own. His other hand splayed open across her lower spine and eased her body into his, her mound against his erect penis. When she gasped, aroused by the feel of him, he thrust his tongue inside her mouth.

They kissed hungrily, their hands exploring each other. Touching, rubbing, caressing. She helped Judd remove his thermal undershirt. He threw it onto the floor, then lifted her sleep shirt over her head, and dropped it on top of his discarded undershirt. She shivered when the nighttime chill hit her bare skin, and her nipples peaked. He looked down at her, smiled, and cupped her breasts. His thumbs flicked across each nipple, eliciting a moan of pleasure from her.

"Lindsay . . ."

She loved hearing him say her name.

He knew he was making love to her. This wouldn't be just having sex for him. Lindsay wasn't like any of the others. She wasn't a substitute for Jenny.

Judd swept her up into his arms and carried her to the massive four-poster. After depositing her in the middle of the bed, he lifted her hips, and yanked her pink bikini panties down, over her legs and off. She lay there quivering, wanting him so badly that she couldn't bear another minute without him inside her.

When she held open her arms, he stripped off his briefs and tossed them aside, then climbed into bed. He came down over her, straddling her hips, bracing himself on his elbows as his lower body pressed into hers.

"I wish I could make this first time perfect for you," he told her as he looked into her eyes. "But I want you so much, need you so much . . ."

"I don't need any foreplay," she said. "Not this time. All I want is you inside me. Right now."

Judd grasped her hips and lifted her up to meet his first lunge. When he entered her, she cried out with the sheer joy of having him inside her.

"I love you," she whimpered. "I love you so much."

"Sweet, sweet Lindsay."

He took her in a frenzy of mutual need, hammering into her hard and fast. She moved in unison with him, quickly adapting to the frantic rhythm he set. With each moment that passed, each kiss, each thrust, each countermove, each sigh, each moan, she grew more and more aroused until her body exploded into climatic release only seconds before he came.

Quivering with fulfillment, she clung to him, kissing his

face as she bit her fingers into his tight buttocks. He shook and groaned as his orgasm hit.

Breathing hard and glistening with sweat, Judd rolled off her and onto his side, then pulled her into his arms. She nestled her head on his shoulder, every nerve in her body singing.

This was where she was meant to be.

She was born to love this man and only this man. Now and forever.

Chapter 27

The morning sun peered through the seams in the old wooden shutters that closed off the bedroom from the outside world. Shiny, yellow-white fingers of light crept across the wooden floor and room-size rug. The long tendrils spread out from the side and back windows and crisscrossed atop the four-poster bed. The fire had died out sometime in the early morning hours, leaving only glowing embers in the fireplace and allowing the gusting March wind to create a chill throughout the room.

But Lindsay didn't feel the cool air on her naked skin. All she felt was Judd's hot hands and even hotter mouth on her body. Caressing her. Licking her. She shuddered with release when he lapped deeply between her feminine folds, heatedly stroking her clitoris with the tip of his tongue. As wave after wave of pleasure flooded through her, Judd eased up alongside her, kissed her shoulder, and then rolled her over on top so that she straddled him.

Taking her by the waist, he lifted her up. While the aftershocks of her climax rippled through her, he brought her down over his erection, spearing deep and hard into her. She keened softly as he filled her. When she leaned her body forward, to give him access to her breasts, he immediately took one nipple into his mouth while he tormented the other with his thumb and forefinger.

He stroked her buttocks as she rode him, the tempo of her lunges steadily increasing. He grunted once, twice, then sucked greedily on her breast as he came. She slowed, then went still. When his shudders ended, he urged her into movement, and with him still semi-erect inside her, she managed to climax quickly.

Panting, physically drained, her whole body zinging with the aftereffects of her second orgasm, she spread out on top of him, her naked flesh adhering to his with their mutual musky perspiration. He stroked her back, then moved down to her buttocks, his caresses lingering.

She lifted her head enough to kiss his shoulder from neck to arm before melting into him and sighing contentedly.

"I could stay right here like this forever," she told him.

He chuckled. "We'd eventually get hungry and I'd have to carry you to the kitchen for more milk and cookies."

Closing her eyes, she savored the moment, knowing that she could no more make these hours she'd spent with Judd last indefinitely any more than she could actually stop time. During the years she had known Judd, she'd never heard him joke around, never heard the sound of laughter in his voice.

I might not be his love, but I am his lover. I make him happy. I know I do.

And she was willing to take what she could get.

"We don't have to go to Birmingham," she whispered, uncertain how he would react.

"Yeah, we do." He rolled her off him and onto her back, then leaned over and kissed the tip of her nose. "We've been off in our own private world. Now, it's time to come back to reality."

Sighing, she nodded.

He caressed her cheek, then kissed her, robbing her of breath.

When he lifted his head, she looked up at him. "Does reality include the two of us being together?"

He sat up in the bed. "That depends on what you want . . . what you're willing to settle for."

Her chest tightened. There would be no declarations of love, no promises of forever after. That was their reality.

"I'll take whatever you have to offer," she told him as she sat up and scooted to the edge of the bed.

He reached out and placed his hand on her shoulder while she had her back to him. "You deserve more than I can offer you."

"You know that. I know that. But, unfortunately, my heart has a mind of its own."

He squeezed her shoulder. "Then it is what it is. Friendship and sex."

Don't cry. Don't you dare cry.

"Friendship and sex," she repeated his words.

"Why don't you take a shower while I fix us some coffee," Judd said. "Then I'll shower while you whip us up some breakfast."

Forcing a smile, she glanced over her shoulder. "One night of wild, passionate sex together and you're already expecting me to prepare your meals. What next, master, fetching your slippers and pipe?"

Keep things light. Make this easy for him. He's taken a giant step. Meet him more than halfway.

Judd chuckled. "I don't smoke a pipe, so just fetching my slippers will be quite enough."

She stood, totally at ease with her nudity. After all, there wasn't an inch of her body that Judd had not only seen, but touched and explored.

"I'm going to soak in the claw-foot tub this morning," Lindsay said. "Bring me a cup of coffee while I'm soaking and I could be persuaded to make French toast for breakfast."

"If you'll make French toast, I'll not only bring you coffee, but I'll scrub your back."

"Coffee will be enough, thank you. If you scrub my back, you might wind up in the tub with me." She winked at him as she lifted her overnight bag from the floor at the foot of the bed.

"I could be coaxed into taking a bath with you," he told her, his tone playful.

"If we're going to make it to Birmingham this morning, we won't have time for more hanky-panky."

He climbed out of bed, gloriously, delectably naked.

God, she could eat him with a spoon.

"You're drooling, sweetheart," he told her.

"Can't help it. You're gorgeous."

He eyed her from head to toe. "So are you. Every sweet inch of you."

"Coffee," she reminded him. "Then breakfast. And after that, we'll hit the road and you can call Griff while I drive."

"You're a bossy little thing."

"That's nothing new."

"Yeah, but my liking it is new."

She laughed, hoisted her bag over her shoulder, and hurried out of the bedroom and down the hall to the bathroom.

Two hours later, after coffee, baths, breakfast, and a quickie on the kitchen table, they locked up and headed toward Whitwell. Soon after hitting Interstate 24, they connected with Interstate 59, which would take them directly to Birmingham.

While Griff and Powell agent, Maleah Perdue, had checked into the Wynfrey Hotel, Rick Carson had set up meetings at different times with three potential informants. All three worked for the Bessemer PD in some capacity, although only one of them was directly involved with the LaShae Goodloe case. He'd been one of the first patrol officers on the scene when the motel manager had reported a murder in Room Ten.

Griff had personally telephoned the lead detective, Jeremy Watson, who had been cordial but standoffish at first. But the detective's attitude had changed when Griff had made comments about how this really should be Watson's case, and how unfortunate it was that the FBI had swarmed in so soon and taken over. His subtle hints that working with a wish-she-was-a-man female agent like Nic Baxter made a guy look all but emasculated to the press had worked like a charm on the he-man Watson.

Having a preliminary background check on Lieutenant Watson in his hand as he spoke to the detective gave Griff a definite advantage. It seems that Watson had been married to a man-eating, hot-shot Realtor who had left him for a wealthy client. Strike one against the female sex. And four years ago, he'd been passed over for a promotion, which had gone to a younger officer—a woman with less experience than Watson had. Strike two.

Griff grinned, knowing that it was highly likely that Nic Baxter's kick-butt-and-take-names attitude had already pissed off the detective.

Strike three?

"Look, Jeremy . . . I can call you Jeremy can't I?" Griff asked in his good-old-boy voice.

"Sure thing. But make it Jere. That's what my friends call me."

"And you call me Griff."

"Yes, sir, it would be my pleasure," Watson said.

"Well, Jere, it's like this, I know you can't officially include me in your investigation and I certainly don't want to interfere in any way. But us guys have to stick together, don't we?"

"Damn straight."

"I know Special Agent Baxter is just doing her job—"

"Yeah, and running roughshod over me and my whole department in the process. She's even taking over the press conference this afternoon." Watson grumbled a few choice curse words under his breath. "You know the type. Hell, you know her personally, don't you?"

"Yeah, I've had to deal with her on every Beauty Queen Killer case." Griff lowered his voice, adding a soft chuckle before he said, "The woman's a real ballbuster."

Watson let out a belly laugh. "Look, I've got to go. She and her flunky, Friedman, are motioning for me to join them. They've brought in the night clerk from the Triple Eight Motel. Even though I took his statement yesterday, that wasn't good enough for her. She's got to question him herself. She won't learn nothing new. He saw one guy go into Room Ten last night and another guy come out."

"If that's the case, you've got yourself an eyewitness?"

"Yeah, sort of. Problem is he couldn't give us a decent description of either guy."

Griff managed to keep his voice calm and level. "Thanks for the info."

"You didn't hear it from me." Watson added, "Nothing official mind you, but why don't we meet for drinks later today. Give me your number and I'll call you."

Griff called off the digits to his cell number, then said, "Thanks, man. I'll owe you one."

With a lead detective as cooperative as Watson, they might not need an informant, but Griff believed in covering all his bases. It wouldn't hurt to have more than one source of information.

* * *

Nic had picked up Detective Watson's animosity the moment they'd met. He was one of those old-fashioned police officers, despite not being a day over forty-five, who thought women should stay at home, barefoot and pregnant. No doubt, at sometime in his life, some woman had kept him pussy-whipped, making him resent all aggressive females. Well, tough shit. She didn't have the time, patience, or inclination to care.

Suck-it-up had been her motto for a long time.

As a professional courtesy and in the spirit of cooperation, she had invited Lieutenant Watson to join her and Josh when they questioned Randy Tidwell, the night clerk from the motel where LaShae Goodloe's body had been found.

Nic and Josh had arrived in Birmingham late yesterday and gone straight to the Bessemer Police Department before checking into their hotel. Four other members of the BQK task force had come in this morning and were at present doing their jobs, just as she and Josh were.

Ever since she arrived at headquarters at eight o'clock today, she'd been expecting to see Griffin Powell. He was like a bad penny, he kept showing up. But so far, he hadn't put in an appearance. Was he waiting so he could show up at this afternoon's press conference? Probably. He seemed to like nothing better than harassing her. One of these days, he was going to step over the line and give her a legitimate reason to arrest him.

She hated to admit that she lived for that day.

"Watson's waiting for us," Josh whispered for her ears only. "Ready to go in?"

"Uh, yeah, sure." She offered the Bessemer detective a curt nod, then opened the door to the interview room and marched in, Josh and Watson following her.

The motel clerk sat alone in the small room, reared back

in one of the chairs at the table, arms up, his fingers locked behind his head. The guy certainly appeared to be relaxed.

"Mr. Tidwell, I'm Special Agent Baxter, with the Federal Bureau of Investigation." She walked over to him and held out her hand.

He shot up out of the chair and shook her hand. "Are you the one in charge?"

"Yes." She inclined her head to the side, where Josh stood. "This is Special Agent Friedman." She glanced behind her and said, "And I believe you've already met Detective Watson, with the Bessemer PD. You spoke to him briefly yesterday."

Tidwell's gaze moved around the room, from one person to another, then he focused on Nic. "When my boss called and told me that LaShae Goodloe, from WBNN, was murdered at our motel, I didn't know the killer had been one of the guys in Room Ten. Either the one who rented the room or the other one."

"Tell me what the one who rented the room looked like," Nic said.

"Well, he had shaggy blond hair and blue eyes. He was average height and just a bit on the stocky side. Not fat, just solid."

"Would you recognize him, if you saw him again?" Nic asked.

"Probably."

Nic narrowed her gaze. She got some odd vibes from Tidwell, nothing sinister, just slightly off. She had a feeling he was the type who liked the idea of being a key witness.

"You wouldn't give Lieutenant Watson any details about either of the men you saw when he questioned you earlier. Why not?"

"I didn't want to waste my time with an underling." Tidwell grinned. "I was saving my story for the top dog." He pointed at her. "That would be you."

She knew that comment stung Watson's masculine pride.

"Okay, so you saw this blond guy go into Room Ten, but then you saw another man come out a few hours later."

"Yeah, that's right. I had stepped outside to get a Pepsi from the machine in front of the office and I saw this other guy sort of sneaking out of Room Ten. He didn't think anybody saw him. But I did."

"What did that man look like?"

"About five-nine or ten, thick build, but not overweight. It was dark, so I couldn't make out the color of his eyes, but his hair was brown. Dark brown, I think."

Hair color and eye color could be easily changed in a matter of minutes with contact lenses, hair dye, or wigs. Her gut instincts told her that the blond man who entered and the dark-haired man who exited Room Ten were one and the same. Average height, stocky build.

Nic motioned to Josh, who removed copies of three sketches from his briefcase and handed them to her. Lieutenant Watson glared at the sketches she held, then looked up, and frowned at her.

"I have some sketches that I'd like you to look at and tell me if any one of them resembles either man you saw." Nic laid the sketches out on the table, one by one. "Take your time."

While Tidwell studied the sketches, Lieutenant Watson gradually maneuvered around behind Nic so that he could get a better look.

"None of them are the blond guy," Tidwell said. "And I'm not sure, but this one—" he tapped his fingers against the profile sketch that Griffin Powell's artist had drawn.

She hadn't been surprised when she had received the sketches, via e-mail attachments, a couple of days ago. After all, Griffin had been sharing information with the FBI ever since Judd Walker hired him to search independently for Jennifer Walker's killer. Nic hated to admit that sometimes he'd gotten hold of info they hadn't.

"Was the man you saw leaving Room Ten wearing a hat or sunglasses?" Nic asked.

"Nope, but I saw him from the side, just like in this picture and this looks like the guy."

"Thank you, Mr. Tidwell." She turned to Josh, who nodded his understanding. She then spoke to their eyewitness again. "Special Agent Friedman is going to ask you a few more questions, and take your official statement, then you may go. And thank you for your cooperation."

When she exited the interview room, Lieutenant Watson followed her, but before he could speak to her, Officer Deaton, Watson's partner called out to him.

"Can I see you a minute, Jere?"

"Excuse me, Ms. Baxter," Watson said, totally disregarding her official title and using the word "Ms." as if it were a slur.

Something was up. She could feel it in her bones. Watson and Deaton talked quietly, each occasionally glancing her way as if she were the topic of conversation. After a couple of minutes, Deaton headed off and Watson walked over to her, a defined reluctance in his step.

"The crime scene boys have a key piece of evidence that they're going to turn over to your people." He was doing his duty, but she could tell that it stuck in his craw.

"Why haven't you mentioned this evidence before now?"

"Because until the crime scene team gave it a thorough once-over, we didn't know it was all that important."

"Okay, I'll buy that explanation. So, tell me what this key piece of evidence is."

Watson bristled. "We found LaShae Goodloe's purse at the scene, but didn't figure it would amount to anything, not even when we saw the compact tape recorder."

Nic eyed the detective inquisitively.

"Well, she was a TV reporter. Sort of. So it made sense that she'd have a tape recorder. We turned the purse and everything in it over to the crime scene boys. They rewound and played the tape this morning. There was part of an interview on it with some poor bastard talking about how he'd been sexually abused by his minister when he was a kid. And . . ." Watson paused for effect.

"And?"

"And the tape picked up the killer telling the victim exactly how he was going to kill her. The tape didn't pick up every word he said, but it's clear enough for voice recognition if we had a voice to compare it to."

Chapter 28

Within half an hour of their arrival in Birmingham, Griff knew that things had changed, not only between Judd and Lindsay, but with Judd himself. It wasn't that he'd done a complete about face overnight, but anyone who had known him for any length of time would have picked up on the subtle differences. And Griff had known Judd pre-Jennifer, during his marriage, and post-Jennifer. Although the man who had arrived at the Wynfrey less than an hour ago was neither of those Judds, Griff recognized the fact that traits of both remained. The intensity was still there and the jitteriness from badly needing a drink, but Judd appeared to be less sullen and definitely wasn't as hostile or volatile.

"I'm on my way to meet up with Detective Watson," Griff said to Judd. "Why don't you come along with me."

While Judd looked at him inquiringly, Lindsay asked, "Am I not invited?"

Griff shook his head. "Afraid not. Neither you nor Maleah. It seems the lieutenant prefers dealing with men." He grinned at his newest female Powell agent, a petite blonde with big brown eyes and a wet-dream kind of body. The lady also had a degree in criminal justice, was an expert marksman, and a killer poker player. That last bit of information had come straight from Rick Carson, who'd lost his shirt in a recent game with the lady.

"Oh, I see." Lindsay pursed her lips and nodded. "Leave it to you to find out just how to play the odds. I swear, Griffin Powell, you've got a chameleon personality that can change on a dime."

"That kind of talent is priceless in my line of work."

Lindsay rolled her eyes upward and shook her head.

Griff winked at her. "While we men are out doing all the hard work, why don't you girls arrange for dinner in my suite for all of us—Rick and Holt, too. We'll have a powwow and compare notes."

Maleah glared at Griff. Grinning, Lindsay shook her index finger at him.

"He's halfway kidding," she told Maleah. "But just so you know, the big boss is definitely an equal opportunity employer, but he's also a bit of a male chauvinist."

"I believe that's what's known as a backhanded compliment," Griff said.

"You boys go on." Lindsay waved them off. "Maleah can bring me up to date on anything I need to know."

Five minutes later, Griff and Judd were on their way from the Wynfrey to the bar in Bessemer where Lieutenant Watson had told Griff he'd meet him.

"I've got some very interesting info for you," Watson had said. "A new development in the case."

He hadn't pressed Watson for the info over the phone, knowing the lieutenant was probably the type who preferred getting his pats-on-the-back in person.

As Griff entered Highway 459, he gave Judd a sideways glance. "So, are you going to tell me?"

"Tell you what?" Judd asked, as if he had no idea what Griff meant.

"Exactly what's going on? What happened between you and Lindsay?"

"We're okay now. Really okay."

"Meaning?"

"We're working on figuring out our relationship."

"Is that right? Well, while you're figuring it out, don't you dare hurt her again," Griff warned.

"If I do, it won't be intentional."

Griff grunted.

"I . . . uh . . . I'm not sure about anything," Judd admitted. "I've been in a dark hole for years and now I'm trying to drag myself out of it. I may make it. I may not."

"If you're not careful, you could drag Lindsay down into that dark hole with you because she's going to hang onto you for dear life and try to singlehandedly pull you out."

"Don't you think I know that?"

"Do you? That woman would die for you and all you've done for the past four years is—"

"You were right about my needing her."

Griff exited 459, following Lieutenant Watson's directions. He didn't respond to Judd's comment until he pulled up at a red light, then he looked directly at his old friend.

"What can I do to help you?" Griff asked.

Griff saw hope in Judd's nervous smile. "The first thing I need is help to stop drinking." He swiped his hand over his mouth. "I haven't touched a drop in days and it's getting harder, not easier."

"Come back with us to Griffin's Rest. Let Yvette—"

"I've already spoken to her and she offered to work with me. But I don't want to involve Lindsay, and if I go to Griffin's Rest, she'll be there. I want to do this one thing on my own, without her being anywhere around." Judd looked at Griff, man to man.

"I understand. We'll find you the best rehab clinic in the South."

"Thanks. And I don't want to put it off. I want to check in as soon as we see what's what with this new BQK case."

"Look, I'm meeting Lieutenant Watson in a bar," Griff said. "If I'd known you were trying to stop drinking, to go cold turkey—"

"Don't turn around and take me back to the hotel," Judd said. "I want to hear what this guy has to say. I need to be a part of this."

"You're already sweating just thinking about—"

"I'll order a Coke and if I even act like I'm going to drink anything stronger, kick me on my ass."

"You can count on it," Griff told him.

It took less than fifteen minutes for Maleah to make all the arrangements for dinner in Griff's suite for six people and for Lindsay to contact Rick and Holt to inform them of Griff's plans for an evening work session.

"So, we seemed to have taken care of that pretty quickly," Lindsay said as she looked at Maleah, smiling, and doing her best not to stare at the new Powell agent.

Maleah had hired on a few months back, right before Christmas and had only recently completed the mandatory six-week training session that each new Powell agent had to take. No exceptions. No matter what a new employee's background—be it law enforcement, military, mercenary, or someone fresh out of college—Griff sent them off to his own special boot camp. Some made the cut. Some didn't.

For the life of her, Lindsay couldn't understand why a woman with Maleah's looks and brains would want to be a P.I., even if Powell agents were the best in the business.

"I guess you know this is actually my first field assignment," Maleah said. "I was surprised that Mr. Powell brought me along and called in another agent to help Angie guard Ms. Hughes."

"Griff likes to give new agents a variety of assignments so he can grade them on their abilities in various areas. That way he can decide what they're best suited to do within the agency."

"You seem to have worked exclusively with him on the Beauty Queen Killer cases. Is that right?"

"Pretty much. I've done an odd assignment now and again, but my main job is working with Griff on the BQK cases."

"I've heard quite a bit about Mr. Walker from the other agents, and I have to say he's not what I expected. He doesn't seem the beast I've heard he can be." As if realizing she'd said something she shouldn't have, Maleah clenched her teeth in an "oh, crap!" gesture. "Sorry, I spoke before I thought. It's one of my weaknesses. I know you're personally involved with—" Maleah shook her head. "God, I'm sorry. I'm nervous and talking way too much."

"It's okay," Lindsay assured her. "I'm sure some of the agents have filled you in on my history with Griff and Judd. Probably Angie, since you two have been working together at Griffin's Rest."

"She wasn't gossiping. Honestly, she wasn't."

"Don't sweat it. It's no secret that I joined the Powell Agency for one reason only—to help Griff track down the Beauty Queen Killer. And my motivation was personal. Not only was I partnered with the lead detective on Jennifer Walker's murder case when I worked with the Chattanooga PD, but I've been in love with Judd for quite some time."

Gazing at Lindsay with a look of admiration in her big brown eyes, Maleah said, "I think I'm going to like you. You're straightforward and honest."

"Well, I think I'm going to like you, too."

"Friends in the making?" Maleah held out her hand.

Lindsay took her hand and they shook on the friendship deal.

"Look, there's something I've been wanting to bring up to Mr. Powell," Maleah said. "But since I'm new at the agency, I wasn't sure if it was appropriate. Would you mind if I run it by you?"

Curious, Lindsay indicated with a hand wave that they should sit down on the sofa there in Griff's suite. "Come on. You can fill me in on whatever it is."

"You sit," Maleah said. "I've got to get something out of my briefcase, then I'll join you."

Lindsay sat. Maleah grabbed her briefcase off the desk by the windows, took a seat by Lindsay, deposited her case on her lap and popped it open. She lifted out a file folder. "Take a look at these. Newspaper and magazine clippings and a detailed report about this woman."

Lindsay took the file folder, opened it and stared at the glossy magazine photo of an attractive, petite blonde. She scanned the article, which focused on the former Miss UT, who was now an actress, playwright, and director. Paige Allgood was relocating to the Knoxville area and planned to open her own theater after she established a little theater group whose members would enact her plays and the plays of her writer friends. Ms. Allgood was a widow who had inherited a sizable fortune from her much older husband, thus enabling her to fulfill a lifelong dream.

"This is interesting, but I don't see—"

"Take a good look at her," Maleah said. "Don't you see the resemblance?"

Lindsay looked at the photo again, then flipped through the newspaper clippings, but didn't pick up on any significant resemblance to someone she knew.

"Sorry, I don't—"

"This woman—this former Beauty Queen—could pass for my sister, or yours for that matter. She's petite, blonde, pretty, and about our age. She's thirty. I'm twenty-nine."

Lindsay had never thought of herself as pretty. "So?"

"If we could get her—this Paige Allgood—to cooperate with us, I could take over her identity for a few weeks, at least until after April first and maybe . . ."

"Shit! You're talking about a setup, using yourself as bait to capture the BQ Killer."

"I realize we have no way of knowing if he'd take the bait, if he'd actually come after me, but—"

"Griff would never agree."

"You know him a lot better than I do, but are you sure?"

"Yes, I . . ." Lindsay studied the pictures of Paige Allgood. Actually, she resembled this woman as much if not more than Maleah did. They had the same slender, small-breasted shape, where Maleah was bosomy and more hourglass shaped. And former Miss UT or not, the woman was not as pretty as Maleah. With the right makeup and hairstyle, maybe a wig, and a different wardrobe, Lindsay could easily pass for Paige Allgood with people who didn't know her personally.

"You're awfully quiet," Maleah said. "I can almost see the wheels in your brain spinning. What are you thinking?"

"I'm thinking several things. First of all, it wouldn't be easy to persuade Griff to go along with this idea. The second thing is that we don't know if Paige Allgood would agree to cooperate with us. And third—I'm the obvious choice to impersonate Paige, not you." When Maleah opened her mouth to protest, Lindsay held up a restraining hand. "No arguments." She shoved the glossy photo of Paige into Maleah's hand. "She and I have the same body type. Besides, I've got seniority as a Powell agent and experience as a police officer. I'm better equipped to do this job than you are."

"And you have a personal stake in this, don't you?" Maleah clenched her teeth and whined, "Sorry. I did it again. I'm a pro at putting my foot in my mouth."

"No, you're right—I do have a personal stake in this. If

we can stop the BQ Killer Judd might finally be able to put some closure on his wife's brutal murder."

"You'd do anything for him, wouldn't you?"

"Yeah, I would."

"Even risk your life? We both know that no matter what precautions we take, something could go wrong."

"There's something you should know. The FBI has already tried a sting operation twice in the past three years and our guy didn't take the bait either time. They've used FBI agents with fake backgrounds as former beauty queens, but our guy passed them by, if he ever noticed them to begin with."

Maleah threw up her hands. "And here I thought I'd come up with a brilliant plan."

"It's a good plan. Just not original."

Maleah smiled. "So, do we talk to Mr. Powell or—"

"Let me talk to him. I'll tell him you did the research and came up with the plan, but that I want to be the one to impersonate Paige Allgood."

"What do you think he'll say?"

"I think he'll say no way in hell."

"But?"

"If I decided to do it on my own, would you help me?"

"You really think Mr. Powell will nix the idea?"

"I don't know, but if he does—"

"I'll help you," Maleah said.

And in that moment Lindsay knew what she had to do, whether the plan worked or not, she had to try. For Judd's sake. If she could lure the BQ Killer into a trap . . .

The only thing remotely Irish about O'Brien's Pub was the name and a couple of Irish ales on tap. Typical of most bars, the music was loud, the air filled with smoke, and the

customers a mixture of races, sexes, and ages. When Griff
and Judd entered the place, Griff surveyed the bar area first
and then ran his gaze over the tables.

"Just ask Pete, the bartender," Watson had told Griff.
"He'll point you to my usual table."

Griff knew what Watson looked like, but he certainly didn't
share that info with the detective. Rick had done a background check on Watson, along with other key players in the
LaShae Goodloe murder, and each report had contained a
photo.

"That's him, over there." Griff inclined his head in the direction of a back table where a lone man sat nursing a beer
bottle. "Wait here and I'll go ask the bartender to point out
Watson." Griff grinned.

A couple of minutes later, Griff and Judd approached the
detective, who, when he noticed the two men heading
straight toward him, stood up and watched them.

"Lieutenant Watson?" Griff held out his hand.

"Yeah. You Griffin Powell? You've changed a lot since
you played for UT."

"Twenty years will change a man." Griff shook hands
with Watson, then introduced Judd. "This is Judd Walker, an
old friend of mine. His wife was a victim of the BQ Killer
nearly four years ago."

Watson shook Judd's hand. "Sorry for your loss. We're
going to get the son of a bitch."

When the three men sat down at the table, Watson motioned
to a waitress and asked, "What do you guys want to drink?"

Griff's gaze met Judd's for a split second, then Griff
looked at Watson and grinned. "We're hooking up with some
mighty fine ladies later, so we'll just take a couple of Cokes.
We want to wine and dine our dates properly. Too much
liquor can keep a guy down, if you know what I mean."
Griff's smirking expression implied that he and Judd wanted
to stay sober enough to be able to get it up later.

Watson chuckled and slapped Griff on the back. "Lucky you." He looked at Judd. "You, too. Me, I'm going home to a microwave meal and my remote control."

"A guy like you ought to be out there pleasing the ladies," Griff said.

Watson grinned.

When the waitress showed up, Griff ordered two Cokes, then turned back to Watson, who ordered another beer.

As soon as the waitress was out of earshot, Watson said, "You didn't get this information from me. I can rely on you not to mention my name, right?"

"Absolutely," Griff assured the detective.

"Like I told you earlier today, we got ourselves an eye-witness." Watson looked from Griff to Judd. "The night clerk at the motel, a guy named Tidwell, saw one man going into Room Ten the night of the Goodloe murder and another one coming out." Watson leaned in closer and lowered his voice. "That Baxter gal thinks I didn't figure out that the two men Tidwell saw were probably the same man, just wearing different disguises. She thinks I'm just a local yokel."

"Special Agent Baxter likes to think she's smarter than most men." When Griff spoke, Judd gave him a you're-so-full-of-shit look.

"She showed Tidwell some sketches she had," Watson said. "Probably done by one of their FBI sketch artists from a description another witness gave them."

"Is that right?" Griff said.

"Did this Tidwell guy see any resemblance between the man he saw, in either disguise, and the man in the sketches?" Judd asked.

"Yeah, as a matter of fact, he did. He said the profile sketch of the man in a hat and sunglasses looked like the man who'd left Room Ten on the night of the murder."

Judd and Griff exchanged glances.

"I've got another little gem for you, Mr. Powell," Watson said, a cocky glint in his eye

"Ah, come on now, Jere, didn't I tell you to call me Griff?"

Watson chuckled. "Yeah. Yeah, you did." He took a couple more swigs from his beer bottle. "Well, Griff, this bit is top secret and not a word of it can leak out. Understand?"

"Nobody will hear it from us," Griffin said.

The waitress returned with a beer and two Cokes.

As soon as she placed the drinks on the table and left, Watson motioned for Griff and Judd to huddle closer. "This LaShae Goodloe did a morning talk show here in Birmingham. She interviewed people all the time." He paused, looked right and left as if he thought someone might overhear him, then continued. "We found one of those mini-tape recorders in her purse, but we didn't think much about it, considering what she did for a living. But the crime scene boys listened to the tape, and guess what they heard?"

Griff looked directly at Judd, who suddenly went stiff, his facial muscles tight.

"This Goodloe woman must have had the recorder on because it taped this guy telling her how he was going to kill her. Our CSI team says that it's clear enough to make a match, if we had a voice to compare it to."

"I don't suppose there's any way you could get me a copy of that tape, is there?"

Watson blew out a long, huffing breath. "I'm afraid not, Griff. I'd like to oblige you, but I'd get my ass in big trouble doing something like that."

Griff patted him on the back. "I understand, Jere. Don't give it another thought."

Half an hour later, when Griff and Judd were heading back to the Wynfrey, Griff said, "I'm going to find a way to get a copy of that tape."

"Why bother? It's just more worthless information about

a phantom killer. The voice on the tape is useless without a suspect's voice for comparison."

"Look, I'm going to tell you something, but I don't want you to get all bent out of shape about it."

"What?" Not just a question, but a demand.

"The sketches that Nic Baxter showed the motel night clerk—I sent them to her."

Judd glared at Griff. "I take it that Barbara Jean Hughes finally managed to remember enough to work with a sketch artist."

"Yeah, Barbara Jean is where we got the information." Griff wasn't lying; he was simply protecting Yvette. "Counting the motel clerk, we now have three witnesses who agree on an ID."

"That's great, but it amounts to nothing. One big monster-size zero. The sketch shows the guy in sunglasses and a hat. Big freaking deal. And you've got the killer's voice on tape. Yippee. A vague description, a sketch of a guy wearing a disguise, and a taped voice that can't be compared to squat. What good is any of that?"

"When I first saw the sketches after Wade Freeman finished them, I realized that there was something familiar about the man's face."

"What the hell do you mean?"

"I think I've seen this guy somewhere before, but I haven't been able to figure out the when, where, or who. My mind can't seem to see beyond the disguise."

Chapter 29

Sandi Ford checked her watch: Seven-twenty. She had hoped the Holloway family would show up earlier instead of later, but apparently not. No sense wasting time, not when she could be doing something productive while waiting on her potential students and their parents. A new shipment of costumes had come in this afternoon, right in the middle of her four-to-five-year-olds' ballet class. The postal carrier had, as she always did, simply left the boxes on the floor just inside the front door. The spring recital was only a few weeks away, so the sooner she unpacked the costumes, fitted them to each child, and allowed time for alterations the better off she'd be. This past year she'd waited until the last minute and wound up paying for an overnight delivery.

After cutting off all the lights except the one florescent in the middle of the ceiling that she left burning twenty-four-seven, Sandi went to the front of the store and inspected today's shipment. Just as she picked up the first of five large but not heavy boxes, she heard a strange noise that sent shivers up her spine.

What was that?

Clutching the box to her chest, she stopped dead still and listened.

Quiet.

It wasn't the first time when she'd been here alone at the studio that she'd heard odd sounds. After all, this was an old building, built around 1910, and old buildings had a way of creaking and moaning. Old wooden floors and rafters. Ancient water pipes. The wind whistling down the two chimneys. Former owners had closed off the two fireplaces, one downstairs and the other upstairs, but when she and Earl Ray had renovated the place and turned it into a dance studio, they had reopened both fireplaces.

Ignoring her nervous reaction to the noise, she carried the box to the storeroom at the back of the studio, turned on an overhead light, and set the box on a long wooden table. Then one by one, she brought the other four boxes to the storeroom, lining them up on the table.

She had a couple of box cutters around here somewhere. *Think, Sandi.* Oh, yes, they were in the Lost-and-Found box on the top shelf of one of the molded plastic Dollar Store bookcases she used to keep miscellaneous items. Knowing she couldn't reach the top shelf, she shoved one of the two folding chairs at the table over to the bookcase and climbed up on the chair seat. Even then, she had to stand on tiptoe to reach the box.

Why on earth had she put it up so high?

To keep little hands from being able to reach it, that's why.

Just as she managed to grab hold of the box's edge, a male voice inexplicably said, "Need some help?"

She practically jumped out of her skin. Gasping, her hands shaking, she dropped the box, which fell to the floor with a whopping flop.

Sandi stared at the man who had somehow made his way into the doorway. Medium height, a bit on the stocky side.

Brown hair and eyes. Dressed in dark blue work clothes, the kind maintenance employees and mechanics often wore.

"Ma'am, I'm sure sorry I scared you." He smiled warmly. "Are you all right?"

Sandi swallowed her initial uncertainty. "Are you Mr. Holloway?"

"Sure am. I'm running a bit late. I apologize."

When Sandi started to climb down off the chair, Donald Holloway rushed over and offered his assistance. She braced her hand on his arm and stepped down, then turned to him and held out her hand. They exchanged a cordial shake.

"Where's your wife and daughters?" she asked.

"The girls are out in the car," he said. "I'm afraid Missy couldn't make it. She had to work an extra shift over at the packing plant."

"Oh, I see." *There's no reason to be nervous just because you're alone in the back storeroom with a man you don't know. He's a husband and father. He has a pleasant smile and a friendly attitude.* "Well, why don't we go out into the studio. I have a brochure you can take to show your wife. Those and the application forms are in my desk up front."

When he turned toward the door, Sandi breathed a sigh of relief.

But he didn't walk through the open door. Instead he closed it and turned back around to face Sandi.

"What are you doing?" she asked, then realized how stupid her question had sounded. She marched toward him, determination in her walk. "Please, open the door, Mr. Holloway."

"I'm afraid I can't do that, Sandi."

His smile altered. No longer a good-old-boy grin similar to Earl Ray's and her daddy's and most of the men in Parsons, but a sinister smirk.

Oh, God, she was in trouble!

Sandi's heartbeat accelerated. Real fear radiated through her, prompting her body to send out a distress signal.

When Donald Holloway moved toward her, she eased backward very slowly. There was a back entrance to the building, just a few feet behind her. The heavy wooden door opened up into the alley, but she kept it locked. Damn it, her keys were in her purse, on her desk, in the studio, along with her cell phone and her can of pepper spray.

Damn! Damn!

This can't be happening.

"I'm glad you made it so easy for me," Mr. Holloway said. "I had wondered if there was a backroom where we could be alone."

With a rush of adrenaline surging through her, Sandi tried to remember the basic self-protection tactics she'd seen on television. Go for the eyes. Go for the groin. Try to break the guy's nose. Any of those would mean getting up close, which she really didn't want to do. But it was going to happen. He was going to rape her unless she found a way to stop him.

"I know what you're thinking," he told her. "You're thinking of ways to fight me, hoping you can escape." His eyes narrowed into evil slits, his mouth twisting into a snarl. "The harder you fight, the worse it will be for you."

"Don't do this. Please."

"Ah, Sandi, Sandi." He moved slowly toward her. Not rushing. As if he had all the time in the world. "Don't you understand. I have to. You're worth twenty points and I really need those points if I'm going to win."

Puzzled by what he said, she stared at him. "I don't understand."

He reached out and grasped a lock of her chin-length hair. Cringing, she tried to pull away, but he yanked on her hair. She yelped.

"You're a redhead. Such beautiful auburn hair. That makes you worth twenty points."

"Are you playing some sort of sick game?" Did he assign

various scores to the women he raped according to their hair color?

When Donald Holloway laughed, the sound sliced through her like razor blades.

Their gazes locked in combat. Sandi decided right then and there that she was not going down without a fight. The fight of her life.

When he manacled his meaty hand behind her neck, she stood on tiptoe and head-butted him. Hollering in pain, he released her immediately. She slid around him and headed for the door.

"You'll pay for that, bitch!" Just as she clasped the doorknob, he grabbed her by her hair. Yanking her backward, he dragged her across the room and slammed her into the wall. Her face hit the old plaster wall with a resounding thud, and she knew instantly that her nose was broken. Blood gushed from her nostrils.

Suddenly, without warning, he jerked her around and covered her bloody face with a foul-smelling rag. Within seconds everything went black.

By the time Sandi came to, Pudge had arranged everything in the back storeroom to his satisfaction. He had also locked the front door to the studio. How long would he have before Sandi was missed, before her husband got worried about her and came by to check on her? Thirty minutes? Forty-five? No matter, this wouldn't take long.

She opened her eyes. When she saw him standing over her, staring down at her where she lay on the wooden table, she let out an ear-piercing scream. Back here, so far away from the street, no one could hear her, even if there had been anyone on the sidewalk in front of the studio. But there wasn't. All of Main Street, except for an occasional vehicle passing through, was empty. Dead as dead could be.

Pudge stroked her flushed cheeks. "Aren't you the spunky little fighter."

She tried to get up, but quickly discovered that she was spread-eagled on the table, her arms and hands bound so tightly they were quite immobile.

"Just go ahead and rape me," she told him. "Or have you already—"

"Rape you? Don't be silly. I have no intention of raping you."

"Then what are you . . ." Realization dawned. She screamed again.

"No one can hear you," he told her.

"Please, dear God, please don't kill me. I have three children . . ."

Drowning out her pitiful pleas with thoughts of the shiny new axe he had brought with him when he'd entered the studio, Pudge visualized hacking off her lovely feet. He had stored the axe in a large box, wrapped with twine, and set it near the front entrance. At present, that effective chopping tool rested against the foot of the table.

He walked around the table to the end, reached out, and caressed first one of her feet and then the other. She squirmed and whimpered.

"Such pretty little feet. A ballerina's feet."

He lifted the axe. Sandi's eyes widened in fear. She opened her mouth, but only a hoarse wail came out.

As he clutched the axe and lifted it up, positioning it for the first strike, an incredible sense of power shot through him, like an instant high from drugs, only stronger and sweeter. So much sweeter.

He could all but taste Sandi's fear. The sound of her whimpers, her cries, her pleading gave him a hard-on. He brought the axe down across her right ankle. The sharp, heavy blade severed her foot from her calf.

Sandi screamed in pain.

Pudge lifted the bloodstained axe and repeated the process, hacking off her left foot. Sandi screamed again. His muscles tensed. His nerve endings burned.

Pudge ejaculated.

As Sandi's dying screams echoed in his ears, he shivered with release.

It didn't happen all that often. He usually didn't come when he killed a woman, only later, when he relived the moment looking at the photographs he always took at the scene.

Still clutching the blood-soaked axe, he stared at Sandi, who apparently had fainted from the pain. It wouldn't take long for her to bleed to death.

Before he actually realized what he was doing, Pudge lifted the axe again and brought it down over Sandi's left knee. It took three tries before he separated her calf from her thigh.

Excitement flooded through him. Then he took off her right calf at the knee.

God, what a feeling!

Laughing from the sheer joy of possessing such godlike power, Pudge brought the axe down repeatedly, hacking away, taking off Sandi's hands and arms. Blood soaked the table and dripped down onto the floor. And Pudge kept laughing as he swung the axe over and over again.

Chapter 30

Resting in the hotel bed, Lindsay stretched languidly, savoring the memory of Judd's lovemaking. They were sharing a room at the Wynfrey, so Griff and the Powell agents all knew. So what? Everyone already knew she loved Judd.

When she turned over, expecting to see Judd lying next to her, she found an empty bed. Her heart skipped a beat. Where was he?

"Judd," she called.

"Be right there." His voice came from around the corner. He was either in the bathroom or out in the hall.

She heard the mumble of voices, then a soft click-clack. She felt around near the foot of the bed, searching for her nightshirt, but couldn't find it. After shoving back the covers, she scooted to the side of the bed and looked at the floor. There it was. She reached down, grabbed her nightshirt, and pulled it over her head. Just as she got out of bed, Judd rolled a white-tablecloth-covered cart into the sitting area of their small suite.

"Breakfast is served." Judd smiled at her.

"You ordered breakfast?" She padded across the floor. "Thank you. For some reason, I'm starving this morning."

He snaked his arm around her waist and pulled her close. "Vigorous lovemaking builds up an appetite."

She looked at him, knowing full well that he could see all that she felt at that precise moment shining in her eyes. Love beyond reason. Mindless. Obsessive.

"Our being together is good for both of us, isn't it?" *That's it, Lindsay, wear your heart on your sleeve. You're practically begging Judd to confess his feelings.*

He sat down in one of the two armless chairs in the room, then reached up, grabbed her wrist, and pulled her down into his lap. She put her arm around his neck and looked directly at him.

"It's good for me, sweetheart, but I'm not so sure it's good for you. Ever since we've known each other, I've been the taker and you've been the giver. That's not fair to you. In the past or now."

She dotted kisses all over his face. "I don't mind being the giver, just as long as you'll take what I offer. Love and friendship and understanding and—"

He kissed her. She sighed, loving his mouth on hers.

"I'm going away for awhile," he told her.

She felt as if all the air had been knocked out of her. "What? When?"

He caressed her hip, then took her right hand, brought it to his lips, opened her palm, and planted a kiss in the center. "This afternoon. Griff's sending Holt Keinan with me back to Griffin's Rest, then Dr. Meng will accompany me to the clinic. The rehab clinic."

"When was all of this decided?" *Without me? Why wasn't I involved in the discussion and the decision?*

"I spoke to Griff about it yesterday and then last night he told me Yvette had made the arrangements and I could check myself in whenever I was ready."

"I'll go with you," Lindsay told him.

"No."

"But why not? You need me. You—"

"I need you to let me do this without you."

She looked away from him, not wanting him to see how upset she was.

"Lindsay?"

"Huh?"

"Stay with Griff. Be my eyes and ears during this investigation. You can do that for me, can't you?"

She nodded.

"If I'm lucky, I'll be gone only a few weeks." He grasped her jaw, her chin cradled between his thumb and index finger, then forced her to face him. "I'm an alcoholic. I've been sober less than four days and I've wanted a drink the entire time.

"I can lick this thing on my own, but just temporarily. The clinic Griff found is the best in the South and after the first few days, they'll allow Yvette to work with me, as my personal psychiatrist."

"Judd, are you saying—?"

"I'm saying that I've needed grief-counseling ever since Jennifer died." He laid his forehead against Lindsay's and closed his eyes. "I'm finally going to get the help I've needed." He whispered the next words against her lips. "Because of you."

His admission filled her heart. A timid joy. Accepting. Nondemanding. Realizing that he couldn't tell her that he loved her. Not yet. But someday. If she were patient.

"Can I call you while you're in rehab?" Lindsay asked.

"Probably not the first week," he said, opening his eyes and lifting his head. "But I'll call you as soon as they'll let me."

She cuddled in his embrace.

While you're fighting your demons, I'll be laying a trap

*for Jennifer's killer and hopefully catching him. It will be my
gift to you. Closure.*

Griff called in his troops that afternoon—all four Powell
agents and Judd. He hadn't told them anything except to be
in his suite at two-thirty. Everyone would be on time, if they
knew what was good for them. Griff hated tardiness. It was
one of his pet peeves.

Lindsay had spent part of the morning devising what she
and Maleah believed was a very persuasive plan to present
to Griff. If they could get Paige Allgood to agree for Lindsay
to assume Paige's identity—temporarily—then Lindsay would
move into Paige's home and Maleah would pose as her personal maid.

Judd had spent most of the morning making his plans to
go to the rehab clinic near Atlanta. Phone calls to his attor-
neys, one to Yvette, and another to his old friend Camden
Hendrix. He had told her that Cam had been surprised to
hear from him, but that they had talked about fifteen minutes
and agreed to meet once Judd came out of rehab.

"I've lost too much these past few years," Judd had told
her. "Jenny was taken from me. The rest, I threw away."

Lindsay and Judd arrived at Griff's door only a couple of
minutes before Holt Keinan, a long, lean cowboy from
Texas, who wore boots and a Stetson, and had the manners
of an old-fashioned gentleman.

When they entered the suite, they found Maleah and Rick
already there.

Griff motioned for them to enter. "Come on in."

Once they were all seated around the dining table, stan-
dard in the VIP suites, Griff placed a small cassette player in
the center of the table.

"Is that what I think it is?" Lindsay asked.

"If you think it's a copy of the tape from LaShae Goodloe's purse the night she was murdered, then you'd be right," Griff replied.

"I would ask how you got hold of it, but I assume palms were greased and money exchanged hands," Lindsay said.

"Quite a bit of money," Griff admitted. "I haven't listened to the tape since Rick brought it to me, so we'll all be hearing it for the first time together." He eyed Judd. "If you'd rather not listen to it . . ."

"Play it," Judd said.

Griff hit the Play button.

The room went quiet and still.

They listened, first hearing a woman's voice—obviously LaShae Goodloe—and then a man's voice, soft, low, almost hushed. Timid.

"I'd very much like for you to come on my show and talk about what happened to you," the woman said. "Even if you don't want to name your rapist—"

"Reverend Boyd Morrow," the man blurted out.

Griff stopped the tape. "My guess is there is no Reverend Morrow, but we'll check out the name to make sure."

He restarted the tape.

"I know how much courage that took—to tell me the man's name. If you decide to press charges against this Reverend Morrow, I and WBNN will stand by you and help you in every way possible."

The conversation continued with the man asking her to promise not to desert him.

She promised.

A few minutes later, the man asked, *"Are you all right?"* To which she replied, *"Yes, I–I think so. I feel odd. A bit dizzy."*

"The son of a bitch drugged her," Rick said.

"He probably put something in her Coke," Maleah added.

For several minutes, they heard no more conversation on the tape, only faint noises, nothing really identifiable. Then, sounding as if it came from across the room, a man's voice said, *"Don't fret, my lovely LaShae. You'll never grow old and ugly. I'm picking you before you wither, while you're still fresh and beautiful."*

Lindsay's gut clenched. She looked at Judd. He'd gone ashen, his eyes glazed, his jaw tight. She knew what he was thinking. Wondering if the killer had spoken similar words to Jennifer the night he killed her.

The man's voice continued, *"I've been practicing, so I should be able to take off your head with one powerful chop. I don't want you to suffer."*

Lindsay reached between them and grabbed Judd's hand. Cold as ice. And trembling.

As they continued listening, hearing only the man's voice, Griff made an observation. "Apparently he had her gagged. All I've heard are her whimpers."

"There's music in the background," Rick said. "There are no radios in the motel rooms at the Triple Eight. Our guy must have provided his own musical accompaniment to murder."

"If you lie still, it will be easier for me to take off your head with one chop. If you keep squirming, it might take several tries. We don't want that, do we? You don't want to suffer and I don't want you to suffer."

Judd squeezed Lindsay's hand so tightly she almost cried out. But she didn't say anything. Dear God, the pain he must be suffering.

"I've never chopped off a head before, but I decided that since time was running out and the game would soon end, that I should try it. On a human, that is. I've practiced numerous times on various animals. Cats and dogs mostly."

Judd released Lindsay's hand abruptly, jumped up, knocking his chair over in the process, then ran toward the door.

Griff shut off the tape. Lindsay shoved back her chair and stood.

No one said a word when she rushed out the door after Judd.

She caught up with him where he had stopped and doubled over, about halfway down the hall. When she reached him, she didn't touch him, just stood nearby.

"Judd?"

"Leave me alone." No hostility, just overwhelming sadness.

"I shouldn't have let you listen to that tape."

"You couldn't have stopped me."

"I should have tried."

He lifted his head and glared at her through damp eyes.

My God, he actually had tears in his eyes!

"I need to be alone," he told her.

"Judd, please, let me help you."

"You can't. Not right now."

She desperately wanted to put her arms around him.

"I'm sorry. I . . ." He turned around and walked away.

"Judd!"

He was going to the nearest bar. Liquor could dull the pain, if only for a few hours. *Go ahead, drink until you pass out. Do whatever you need to do to stop the pain.*

Startled when a big hand came down on her shoulder, she gasped and jumped, then looked over her shoulder and up into Griff's ice-blue eyes.

"I'll send Holt to find him and stay with him," Griff told her.

"We shouldn't have let him listen to that tape."

"He had to listen to it."

Blinking the tears from her eyes, she whipped around and faced Griff. "You know what he was thinking, what he was feeling, what he was seeing inside his mind."

"Yeah, I know."

"I'm going after him. Tell Holt—"

"Damn it, Lindsay, don't go. Let him do whatever he's going to do. If you get in his way, he could wind up hurting you."

"I don't care." Tears trickled from her eyes.

Griff grabbed her and pulled her into his arms. She fell apart, sobbing, clinging to him.

In the end, Holt had gone to find Judd and Lindsay had gone back into Griff's suite. Rick and Griff had made themselves scarce for a while, leaving Lindsay alone with Maleah.

Did Griff think she'd open a vein and bleed all over the place, just because Judd had walked out on her? Did he think she needed another woman to talk to? Or maybe to guard her?

As she paced back and forth, Lindsay mumbled to herself.

"Go ahead and kick something," Maleah told her. "Or break something. Then when you've worked off a little of your frustration, do something positive."

Lindsay stopped and glared at Maleah.

"It's obvious you want to do something for Judd, so do what you can—talk to Griff about our plan."

It took Lindsay a few seconds to wrap her mind around what Maleah had said: Do something positive. She couldn't help Judd right now by going after him and trying to stop him from drinking. But if she could give Judd his wife's killer . . .

"You're right. I can't stop Judd from getting drunk. I can't make him want me with him. But I can use myself as bait to lure Jennifer Walker's killer into a trap."

"That a girl."

"Where's Griff?"

"I'm not sure where Mr. Powell and Rick went, but I'll

call Mr. Powell's cell phone and tell him we need to talk to him."

Thirty minutes later, while Judd was God-only-knew where, doing God-only-knew what, Lindsay and Maleah presented their plan to Griff, who listened patiently, a scowl on his face.

"No way in hell," Griff told them.

"Don't be unreasonable," Lindsay said.

"I'd be with her all the time, posing as her maid," Maleah added.

"If you're with her all the time, our killer won't show up," Griff said. "He's not an idiot."

"He wouldn't know I was there. We can figure out a way to make him think Lindsay is all alone and yet we'd be keeping an eye on her."

Griff grunted. "The FBI has already tried this ploy twice and the BQ Killer didn't take the bait. What makes you two think he'll—?"

"I need to do this," Lindsay said.

"Hell, why don't I just put a gun in your hand and help you hold it to your head and pull the trigger?" Balling his big hands into fists on either side of his body, Griff snorted. "There's no guarantee our guy will take the bait. And if he does and anything happens to you, what do you think will happen to Judd?"

She stared at Griff, startled by his question.

"You hadn't thought about that, had you?"

"Nothing will happen to me. We'll work out all the details and then put our plan into motion. The BQ Killer is smart, but not so smart that we can't outwit him."

"And if I refuse to be a part of this?" Griff asked.

Lindsay and Maleah exchanged glances.

"Yeah, I know," Griff said. "You're going to try to pull this off, with or without my help."

"Then help me. Please."

He didn't say anything for several minutes, just stood there frowning as he studied her. "I'll work out the plan." He glanced from Lindsay to Maleah. "And you both will follow my orders to the letter. Understand?"

"We understand," they replied simultaneously.

Shortly before ten that evening, someone knocked on Lindsay's hotel room door. Hurrying barefoot across the room, she peered through the viewfinder and saw Judd and Holt Keinan standing in the hallway. She flung open the door.

"I've been drinking." Judd walked into the room. "But I'm not drunk, at least not drunk enough."

"I tried to get him to sleep in the other bed in my room," Holt told her. "But he insisted on coming back here to you."

"Thanks, Holt," Lindsay said. "You can go on now. I can take it from here."

"Yeah, you can go now, Holt, old buddy." Judd waved him away. "Lindsay will take good care of me. She always does."

"Are you sure?" Holt asked her.

"I'm sure." Lindsay walked Holt to the door, then turned around and marched back to Judd. "Would you like some coffee or hot tea or maybe another drink? Scotch? Bourbon? Name your poison."

He leered at her, a silly grin on his face. "I'd rather have milk and cookies."

"Would you now?"

"Yep. And afterward, I want you." When he reached for her, she sidestepped him. "Ah, come on. Don't be that way."

"Judd, you're drunk."

"Just a little."

"No, you're very drunk."

"Don't be mad at me. You know why . . . Drowned my sorrows. Feeling no pain."

She glared at him. "Is that right? No pain. Sorrows all gone. Poor Judd."

He staggered toward her. "I'm sorry. I tried. I tried really hard."

She lifted her hand and patted his cheek. "I know you did."

"Don't leave me, sweetheart." He wrapped his arms around her and rested his chin on her shoulder. "Don't you leave me, too."

She slid her arm around his waist and led him to the bed. "Sit down. I'll help you get undressed."

He sat. When she unbuttoned his shirt, he grabbed her hand. "Thank you."

She offered him a forced smile, then continued removing his clothes until she had him down to his briefs. When she turned him around and pressed her hand against his chest, urging him to lie down, he didn't fight her. She lifted the sheet and comforter and covered him.

He gazed up at her. "Did I say thank you?"

"Yes, you did." She brushed the loose strands of his overly long hair away from his face, then leaned over and kissed his forehead.

He closed his eyes and sighed heavily. Within minutes, Judd was fast asleep.

Lindsay went into the bathroom, changed into her nightshirt, then came back and crawled into bed beside him. She lay there looking at him, watching as his chest rose and fell with each breath.

"God help him," she said. "God help us both."

Griff sat alone on the sofa in his suite, his jacket off, his shirt sleeves rolled up to his elbows. With his feet propped on the coffee table, he stared at the television, catching a word or two of the CNN late night newscast while his eyelids drooped. It had been a long day. One that had started out with promise and ended on a sour note. At least for Judd and Lindsay.

Ever since he had agreed to spearhead Lindsay and Maleah's scheme to capture the BQ Killer, he'd had a great many second thoughts. Too many things could go wrong. Using Lindsay as bait put her life in danger. No two ways about it. No matter how meticulous the details . . .

He knew why Lindsay wanted to do this. Everyone involved knew why. She hoped that capturing Jennifer's killer and bringing him to justice would give Judd closure and allow him to move on with his life. A life with her.

What would it be like to have a woman love me the way Lindsay loves Judd?

Griff harrumphed.

Love wasn't for him. He didn't want or need anyone. Certainly not some woman willing to sacrifice everything for him. He sure as hell would never . . .

His cell phone rang. Who the fuck? It had to be past eleven.

He felt on his belt for his phone, then remembered that he'd taken off his belt and laid it and the phone on the bed.

Let it go to voice mail.

You'd better get it. It could be important. Nobody calls without a good reason at this time of night.

Griff got up, lumbered into the bedroom, and managed to answer one ring short of voice mail picking up. He didn't bother checking caller ID.

"Powell here."

"He's killed again," Griff's D.C. contact told him. "A red-head in Parsons, Louisiana."

"His last kill was only days ago."

"This kill was different."

"How so?" Griff asked.

"The lady was a dance instructor."

"So?"

"So normally, he'd cut off her feet or chop off her legs."

"And this time, what did he do?"

"He took off her feet and her legs. And then he hacked off her arms and her head and . . . Hell, Griff, he chopped her to pieces."

Chapter 31

"You're awfully quiet," Maleah said. "Are you all right?"

Lindsay's intense focus on the road ahead—Interstate 59—combined with thoughts of those last moments with Judd this morning had kept her occupied since she and her fellow Powell agent left Birmingham around seven this morning, shortly after Judd left with Holt Keinan.

"I'm okay. Just preoccupied."

"I know you wanted to go with him, but he'll be okay. He's doing a very brave thing, going into rehab."

"Yeah, I'm very proud of him. And so thankful that he's finally asking for the help he's needed. It's just . . . I won't be there to look after him, to protect him."

"No, but you will be doing something that could help him more than anything else. Finding this murdering son of a bitch will help Judd and everyone else who has lost a loved one to the BQ Killer find closure."

"Maybe."

"Are you having second thoughts about—"

"No." Lindsay cast a quick glance at Maleah. "I'm fully

prepared to step into the role of Paige Allgood first thing to-morrow."

"I still can't believe that Mr. Powell was able to set things up so quickly." Maleah talked with her hands, which moved constantly when she spoke. "In less than twelve hours, he not only persuaded Ms. Allgood to go along with our plan, but as we speak, there are people pulling everything together for us at her home and the building she's renovating for a theater. And she's off to Paris for three weeks, going there incognito."

"Money talks."

"Is he as rich as people say he is?"

"Probably richer," Lindsay said.

"I wonder why a guy that rich would want to head up a P.I. firm in Knoxville, Tennessee?"

"You'd have to ask him."

"Never. Mr. Powell intimidates the hell out of me."

Lindsay smiled. "Griff is definitely a take-no-prisoners type, but I truly believe that he's one of the good guys."

"You really like him, don't you?"

"I like him. I respect him. But I don't really know him. I don't think anyone does, other than Sanders. And possibly Dr. Meng." Lindsay maneuvered her Trailblazer through the interstate traffic into the far right lane.

"You know there are rumors about you and Mr. Powell," Maleah said. "You're the only Powell agent who lives at Griffin's Rest full time and—Crap! I'm talking too much. I'll be quiet now."

Silence.

"Lindsay, I'm sorry. It's none of my business. I'm afraid I'm the inquisitive type. Actually, I'm just plain nosy."

"It's okay. I don't mind telling you since there's no truth to any of the rumors. Griff and I are friends. Nothing more."

"That's what I thought. I mean it's obvious you're in love

with Judd Walker." Maleah groaned. "God, why don't I just shut up!"

"Stop apologizing all the time," Lindsay said as she steered the SUV into the lane that connected I-59 to I-24. "We're going to be spending a great deal of time together for the next few weeks, so we'll have to adapt to each other's personalities. And if you say anything that offends me, anything I don't like, I'll tell you. Okay?"

"Okay." Maleah released a deep breath. "I promise I'll be quiet now."

Lindsay kept her eyes on the road ahead as her mind replayed once again those final moments this morning when she said good-bye to Judd. No tears. No pleas to go with him. Only heartfelt hope. And a tender kiss.

"I wish you would keep talking," Lindsay said. "It helps keep my mind off other things."

"Oh. Sure. What do you want to talk about?"

"Anything other than Judd, Griff, and the BQ Killer."

"Well, let's see. I hear hemlines are shorter for spring, doctors now say both coffee and chocolate are actually good for us, and there's a possibility that George Clooney will eventually run for president."

Lindsay laughed. "Oh, yes, you and I are definitely going to be good friends."

Griff and Rick Carson had flown into Parsons, Louisiana, early in the morning. While Griff had checked them into a local B & B, taking over the entire ten-room establishment, Rick had set to work checking out the lay of the land. Rick's first phone report came in at eight-thirty.

"Nic Baxter and her task force haven't arrived yet. They're due in any time now. It seems there was some initial confusion at first as to whether or not this latest murder was a BQK case, so that delayed things."

"And why was that?"

"The woman's entire body was chopped to pieces, which was not our guy's MO."

"Was there a rose left at the scene?"

"Yeah. A yellow one. Sandi Ford was a redhead. But it seems the rose wasn't found right away. It wasn't on or near the body, which was lying on a table."

Griff parked the rental car a block over from Main Street, then walked to Sandi's Dance Studio. A swarm of police, reporters, and curious townsfolk blocked his view. He checked his watch: Ten after nine. Scanning the crowd, he searched for Nic and Josh. No sign of either.

Being a large man, his size alone intimidated others, so he had no problem making his way past the horde to reach the yellow crime scene tape where a police officer stood guard. The young man wasn't a day over twenty-one.

"Who's in charge here?" Griff asked.

"Chief Crowell," the officer replied.

"Is he here?"

"Yes, sir."

"I'd like to speak to him." Griff whipped out one of his business cards and handed it to the boy, who took it, looked at it and grinned. "Hey, I've heard of you. You used to play for UT. And you're some big hotshot P.I. now, aren't you?"

Griff grinned.

"Look, the chief's sort of been expecting you. He said that you show up at all the Beauty Queen Killer murders and he'd lay odds you'd show up here in Parsons today."

"He was right," Griff said. "So, would you mind telling him that I'm here and I'd appreciate a few minutes of his time."

"Sure thing, Mr. Powell."

Within five minutes, Griff was having coffee with Chief Crowell at the bookstore/coffee shop three doors down from Sandi's Dance Studio.

"I've never seen anything like it," the chief said. "Worst goddamn slaughter you could imagine." He shook his head. "That poor woman. A wife and mother. A good Christian woman."

"Is there anything you can tell me, unofficially, of course? I understand you weren't sure at first if this was the work of our BQ Killer."

"Yeah, that's right. From what I knew, the BQ Killer didn't chop his victims into pieces." The chief swallowed. "Sandi Ford had been butchered. And nobody noticed the rose at first. Apparently, it had fallen off the corpse and onto the floor. One of the first officers at the scene actually stepped on the damn thing and left bloody footprints all over the place." The chief's gaze met Griff's. "That's definitely an unofficial statement. Stuff like that makes the department look bad."

Griff nodded. "Who found the body?"

Crowell huffed. "The husband. The poor guy had been at Wednesday night church services with his three kids and when he got home and his wife wasn't there, he came downtown to the studio to see what was keeping her."

"Then the husband called the police?" Griff asked.

"Actually, one of their kids did. It seems Earl Ray Ford came out of the studio screaming hysterically. One of their daughters called nine-one-one. When the officers arrived on the scene, they found the wife's body."

"Then what?"

"I was contacted immediately. Something like this has never happened in Parsons."

"I understand."

"I called in the state boys immediately. I knew we weren't equipped to handle a murder case, especially one like this. Hell, we haven't had a murder in Parsons in five years."

"So the state took over the case? That's their people working the crime scene?"

"Yeah, that's right. But I was informed this morning that the FBI would be handling the investigation here on out, as soon as they show up."

Since Griff and Chief Crowell sat at a table in the front of the coffee shop, near the front door, Griff couldn't miss seeing the door swing open and a woman enter. He grinned.

"I believe they've just arrived," Griff said.

"Huh?"

Nic Baxter marched toward the table, hell's fury in her dark eyes. She stopped, planted her hands on her hips and looked directly at Chief Crowell. "I hope you haven't been discussing Sandi Ford's murder with this man."

A puzzled expression crossed the chief's face. "Ma'am?"

"Chief Crowell, let me introduce you to Special Agent Nicole Baxter," Griff said. "She heads up the FBI's BQK task force. In other words, she's the man in charge."

Nic whipped around and glared at Griff. "I don't have to remind you that this man is a private detective." Although she was speaking to Chief Crowell, she was looking at Griff. "He is not, in any way, a part of the official investigation. If he has used persuasion or coercion to obtain information from you, I need to know right now."

Chief Crowell shoved back his chair, stood, and tapped Nic on the shoulder. She froze momentarily, then turned to face him.

"Ma'am, I know I'm just a small town police chief, but I'm not an idiot. Mr. Powell here has been nothing but a gentleman. There's been no persuasion or coercion going on this morning. We were just sitting here having us some coffee and talking about football."

Griff barely managed to hold in his laughter.

Nic bristled. "Very well. Thank you." Ignoring Griff completely now, she focused on the chief. "As soon as you've finished your coffee break with Mr. Powell, I'd like to speak to you. Privately."

"I don't know what happened to me," Pudge said. "I swear, it was as if someone else was hacking away at her, as if I were watching it being done."

All the while Pinkie listened to his cousin telling him about how he'd gone berserk when he had killed Sandi Ford, he kept thinking about the fact that Pudge had scored twenty points and they were now neck-and-neck, heading toward the finish line.

"It was the most exhilarating experience of my life," Pudge said. "The whole thing was surreal, but utterly glorious."

Pinkie knew he had to move fast to get ahead. He couldn't allow Pudge to score more points. The consequences would be deadly. Although he strongly suspected that Pudge had cheated and chosen Sandi Ford as his next victim before Pinkie had killed LaShae Goodloe, he hadn't pressed the issue, hadn't called foul. No, instead, he'd done a little cheating of his own. He had already found a lovely blonde, a former Miss Memphis, who had been a twirler. A baton twirler. Now, there was a talent for you.

"By the time I finished, I was bathed in blood." Pudge sighed. "If I hadn't been concerned that someone might see me that way, I wouldn't have washed off there in the restroom at the studio. I rubbed her blood into my hands and my face. It was like a satiny smooth lotion."

Pinkie thought about how he would kill the blond-and-beautiful Sara Ann Stewart. Cut off her hands? Chop off her arms?

Even after listening to Pudge's exuberant retelling of Sandi Ford's murder, Pinkie knew he would not derive a similar pleasure from butchering a victim. Of the two of them,

Pudge was by far the more brutal, bestial type of killer. Pinkie preferred being less dramatic, but equally effective. After all, dead was dead.

Why not beat her to death with a baton? a wicked inner voice with a sense of humor suggested.

Absolutely divine idea. And so appropriate. Something new and unique.

"Our game has gone on far too long," Pudge said. "Admit it, you had become as bored as I had with doing the same old things time and again. Chopping little Miss Sandi into pieces invigorated me."

"I'd think knowing we're in the last days of our game would create enough excitement for both of us," Pinkie replied.

"Getting worried, Cousin?"

"Not at all. I have every confidence in myself. But if you're concerned, I'm willing to renegotiate terms."

Pudge's laughter irritated Pinkie in a way it never had. "You find that amusing?"

"Yes, as a matter of fact, I do. You see, dear cousin, I know you're concerned that I shall be the winner and you the loser. Otherwise, you wouldn't be all but begging me to change the rules this late in the game."

"I was not begging. I was simply offering to give you a way out."

"What's wrong—you aren't afraid of death, are you?"

"No more than you are."

Chapter 32

Today was March thirty-first. The end of the month, the end of the week. And the Beauty Queen Killer had struck four times in the past sixteen days. Sara Ann Stewart in Memphis, Tennessee. A blonde. Beaten to death with a baton. Audrey Smallwood, Macon, Georgia. Hacked to death as brutally as Sandi Ford had been. A brunette. Kalindy Naramore, Columbus, Mississippi. Hands cut off. Another brunette. Whitney Webster, Bowling Green, Kentucky. A blonde. Doused with kerosene and set afire.

Every other murder gruesome to the extreme.

How many points had each woman been worth to him?

"He's on a killing spree," Griff had said. "It's as if he's gone into a murderous frenzy right before April first."

Derek Lawrence had advised Griff that it was highly possible that the killer planned to end his game on April first and knowing the end was near, he was murdering as many women as he possibly could, as quickly as he could.

Why hasn't he come after me? After Paige Allgood? Lindsay had been living the other woman's life for a couple of weeks now, wearing a platinum, shoulder-length wig, contact lenses, and expensive designer clothes she hated. However, it was the jewelry that created the biggest problem for her. In every photograph of the wealthy former Miss UT, she was wearing several bracelets, heavy gold necklaces, a broach on her lapel or collar, and two sets of earrings dangled from the twin holes in each ear.

For a woman whose idea of jewelry was diamond studs and a wristwatch, being decked out in gold and jewels on a daily basis irritated the hell out of Lindsay. How did anyone function weighed down by so much clutter?

But for now, Lindsay sat, completely uncluttered, wearing a pair of jeans and an oversized cotton sweater, on the sofa in Paige Allgood's den. Since Paige was notorious for sleeping until noon every day, Lindsay had her mornings free. Her afternoons were spent at the downtown building the real Paige planned to convert into a theater—the old Woodruff Building. Powell agents posed as contractors, designers, and investors, assisting her in bringing her role as Paige Allgood to life. The only question was did they have an audience? An audience of one.

Was the BQ Killer out there, watching and waiting? Or had he not even noticed a high profile, young, attractive, blond, former beauty queen who was ripe for the picking?

Deep in thought, Lindsay jumped when the phone rang. God, she hadn't realized how jittery she was. Day after day of playacting while they waited and waited and waited was beginning to take a toll on her nerves.

Maleah, sans the black wig and glasses she wore in her disguise as the maid, came into the den, the portable phone in her hand. "Ms. Allgood, there's a gentleman who'd like to speak to you." She covered the mouthpiece with her hand. "No name on the caller ID, just a number. But he said his name is Allen Posey. He's interested in supporting local actors with a sizable donation to the little theater group you're founding."

Lindsay nodded. "Call Powell's and run a check on this guy, then grab the other phone and listen in."

"Will do." Maleah handed Lindsay the phone.

"Hello, Mr. Posey, this is Paige Allgood."

"Ms. Allgood, this is such an honor," the distinctively Southern voice said. "I've been reading all about you recently, and I must say that I'm simply dying to get in on the ground floor of your little endeavor."

"Are you really? Well, color me delighted. As you know, I don't really need investors, but I don't want to be selfish and not share with other like-minded philanthropists."

"Then you're not adverse to my making a sizable donation, are you?"

"My goodness, no."

"I do have one small request." He chuckled softly. "Well, actually two. First, my daughter, Cynthia, is a very talented girl. I'd like to see her cast in the first play you produce."

"I . . . uh . . . I believe that could be arranged, especially if she's very talented."

"And my second request is that I'd like a private tour of the building you're converting into a theater."

"Oh, well . . . uh . . . certainly. That shouldn't be a problem. I'll have my assistant meet you at your convenience—"

"No, no, my dear. You don't understand. I'd like for you personally to give me a tour."

A red warning signal popped up in Lindsay's mind. "Uh . . . I believe that can be arranged."

"Splendid. Shall we make it for tomorrow evening. Around six?" he asked, absolute glee in his voice.

A voice that sparked shivers along Lindsay's nerves.

"Six tomorrow evening at the front entrance. Let me give you the address and directions on how to—"

"No need. I'm familiar with the area."

"Then you're from Knoxville?"

"Yes, of course. I thought surely you'd heard of me." He

sighed dramatically. "Would I be presumptuous in asking you to have dinner with me tomorrow evening, after the tour?"

Dinner? Hmm . . . Either this guy was on the up-and-up or he was giving a great performance. Lindsay wasn't sure which, but her instincts told her it was the latter. She couldn't quite pinpoint what it was about Mr. Posey, but there was definitely something "off" about him.

"Dinner? Well, all right. That sounds nice."

"Until six tomorrow."

Lindsay hit the Off button, then tossed the phone down on the sofa. Maleah, who'd been standing by and listening to most of the conversation on the portable extension, lifted her brows in a wasn't-that-interesting expression.

"What do you think?" Lindsay asked.

"Could be our guy."

"We know he's an expert at luring intelligent women into his web. Derek has told us that he probably creates a different scenario for each victim and invents a personality for himself that for some reason appeals to the victim."

"Makes sense." Still holding the extension phone in her hand, Maleah sat down on the sofa with Lindsay. "What would appeal more to Paige than a refined gentleman interested in local theater?"

"We have a little over twenty-four hours to set things up. But first we have to find out all we can about Allen Posey. If there really is an Allen Posey."

As if on cue, Maleah's cell phone rang. She removed it from her shirt pocket and flipped it open. "Yes. Uh-huh. I see. Okay, I'll tell her." She closed her phone and turned to Lindsay. "That was the office. They ran a quick check and found that there is an Allen Posey. He's a rich old codger. A native of Knoxville. Old family. Old money. And he has two daughters: Cynthia and Tracy."

Lindsay nibbled on her bottom lip. "Then either our

caller is on the up-and-up or he's assuming the real Allen Posey's identity and is guessing that Paige Allgood wouldn't know the difference."

"I say we contact Mr. Powell right away."

"I'll handle contacting Griff."

"All right." Maleah got up. "I'm in the mood for a Caesar salad for lunch. How does that sound to you?"

"Fine."

"I'll let you know when it's ready."

As soon as Maleah exited the den, Lindsay put in a call to Griff—on his private cell number.

Judd hadn't told Lindsay when they spoke this morning that he was being released from the clinic around noon today. Before he went to Griffin's Rest tomorrow to surprise her, he wanted to go home to Chattanooga first, get a haircut and a manicure, then look through his closet and find some decent clothes. He had already contacted his housekeeper and told her to get his old rooms prepared and to have his Porsche serviced and ready for him to drive. The first step in reclaiming his life was to return to the life he'd known before Jennifer's murder and go from there. Yvette had made him see that he'd find some things from the past comforting, just like stepping into a favorite pair of old shoes. And other things from his former life would no longer fit him and would need to be discarded.

"You'll build a new life for yourself," Yvette had told him. "It will take time and effort, and it won't be easy. But the day will come when you'll be glad that you're alive."

He didn't kid himself. He knew he had some rough times ahead of him, that for every step he took forward, he might wind up taking two backward. But as long as he had Lindsay at his side, he'd make it. God, how he'd missed her. After more than two weeks of intensive rehab, including brutal sessions twice a day with Yvette, Judd was now clean and sober. And prepared to face months of continued grief-counseling.

"Are you ready to leave?"

Judd nodded to Yvette, who stood in the open doorway to his private room. "I'm ready."

"Are you sure you want me to drop you off in Chattanooga?" she asked.

"Yeah, I'm sure." He picked up his duffel bag, hoisted it over his shoulder, and walked toward Yvette. "When you get to Griffin's Rest, don't tell Lindsay that I've been released. I want to surprise her tomorrow afternoon."

"I won't say a word," Yvette promised.

Griff sat alone in his den that evening, a glass of bourbon resting on the desk blotter, and the sketches Wade Freeman had drawn of the possible BQ Killer lay side by side below his drink. As he studied the man's face, he reached over and tapped the Play button on the mini-recorder.

"I've never chopped off a head before, but I decided that since time was running out and the game would soon end, that I should try it. On a human, that is. I've practiced numerous times on various animals. Cats and dogs mostly."

Troubled by the fact that there was something oddly familiar about the faces in the sketches and the voice on the tape, Griff had spent the better part of the past two hours trying to figure out if he actually recognized either, or if his mind was playing tricks on him.

Did he know the BQ Killer? Was this monster someone in his social circle, someone he'd shaken hands with on various occasions? *If so, why don't I know who he is? Why can't I make the connection?*

Griff knew hundreds of people well enough to call them by name. If he were acquainted with the BQ Killer, then both the face in the sketches and the voice on the tape were somehow different than the man Griff knew. Disguised? The face, yes. But why would he have disguised his voice since he wouldn't have known he was being recorded? Not disguised, just slightly different. Altered by excitement, by the mental and emotional thrill of the moment?

Rubbing the back of his neck with one hand, he reached out with the other and picked up his glass of bourbon. By this time tomorrow, it was possible that none of this would make any difference. Whoever had called Lindsay claiming to be Allen Posey was an imposter. Griff had telephoned and spoken to the real Allen Posey—at his villa in Italy where he'd been for the past three weeks.

Chapter 33

All Pinkie needed to win was this one last kill. Today. April first. Pudge couldn't allow that to happen. He had played by the rules for most of the past five years. But recently, he had come to realize that he could not lose this game. He wasn't ready to pay the ultimate price and forfeit everything to his dear cousin. When he had suggested adding the death-of-the-loser clause to the rules of their game, he had never actually considered the fact that he might lose. After all, as brilliant and devious as Pinkie was, he was the lesser man. Not quite as smart. Not quite as diabolical. And where Pinkie had the ability to actually love, Pudge did not. He respected his cousin, found him a worthy opponent and would miss the game playing in which they had indulged since first meeting in their teens.

But I've never loved anyone, never cared deeply for another human being. And that one ability alone makes me far superior.

He had tried every way possible to worm the name of his chosen victim from Pinkie, but his cousin had refused to divulge her identity. Arranging everything would have been so much easier if Pinkie wasn't so stubborn. Nonetheless, there were ways to achieve every goal. He had been keeping close tabs on Pinkie, knew where he was and what he was doing at all times.

Although he didn't know the time Pinkie had chosen for his next kill or the victim, he did know where the event would take place. Somewhere inside the old Woodruff Building in downtown Knoxville.

Pinkie had acquired the original blueprints to the building yesterday, and Pudge had followed him there last night when the place had been deserted. No doubt, he'd been mentally setting the scene, preparing for the last kill.

Where inside the building had Pinkie chosen for the sacrificial altar?

Pudge parked his get-away car—a rental—a block away, removed the suitcase in which his rifle was stored, and walked up the alley to the back entrance of the old building. He checked his watch. High noon. All he had to do was be patient and wait. Sooner or later, Pinkie would show up with his former beauty queen in tow, believing that with her death, he would win the game. But what he didn't know was that he, not she, would be the final victim.

Judd drove to Griffin's Rest in his antique Porsche, a car he'd loved since his father had given it to him for his eighteenth birthday. Of all the vehicles he'd owned, this one was his favorite. Something about driving this car made him feel like a teenager again, his whole life ahead of him, a blank canvas. He parked the car, hopped out, and ran toward the front door, a sense of anticipation zinging through him. He could hardly wait to see Lindsay, to surprise her, to lift her off her feet, swing her around in his arms, and then kiss her. He didn't know exactly where their relationship was going, but they'd figure it out along the way. The one thing he did know for certain was that she was a part of his future as surely as Jennifer had been a part of his past.

Judd rang the doorbell. *Hurry up. Hurry up.*

Sanders opened the door. "Good evening, Mr. Walker. How nice to see you."

Judd breezed past Sanders, straight into the foyer. "Good evening to you, too. Would you please tell Lindsay that she has a guest."

Sanders cleared his throat. "I take it that she wasn't expecting you."

"I wanted to surprise her."

"I see, sir. Won't you come in and wait in the living room."

"Is Griff around? I want to talk to him before Lindsay and I leave."

"No, sir. Griffin is in Knoxville."

While Sanders disappeared down the hall, Judd meandered into the living room. He had made late dinner reservations at an exclusive restaurant in Knoxville and booked a suite in a four-star hotel where he intended to spend the night making love to Lindsay. He planned to begin his new life tonight—with the woman he loved.

And he did love Lindsay.

Not the way he had loved Jennifer, but in a different way.

"Love is never the same," Yvette had told him. "That doesn't mean one love is greater or less than another."

Judd walked through the living room to the far side, stood by the wall of windows and looked outside. Springtime had finally arrived. Rebirth. The trees were beginning to fill out with green leaves, flowers were blooming, grass was growing.

He wanted to plant a garden at the hunting lodge, as his mimi had done years ago. Fresh herbs, a few vegetables, and even flowers.

For Lindsay.

With Lindsay.

From now on, Lindsay would be a part of everything in his life.

"Judd?" Yvette Meng's voice called out clearly.

He turned and saw her standing several feet behind him. She had entered the room so quietly that he'd been unaware of her presence until she spoke his name.

"Good evening. Lovely evening, isn't it," Judd said.

Sanders walked over and stood by Yvette.

Instantly, Judd knew something was wrong.

"What's going on?" he asked.

"Lindsay isn't here," Sanders said. "She's in Knoxville."

Tension curled tightly around Judd's gut. "Is she on an assignment with Griff?"

"In a way," Sanders replied.

Judd glanced from Sanders to Yvette, then back at Sanders. "I want to know what you're not telling me and I want to know now." Judd practically growled the demand.

Sanders hesitated. "I'm sorry, Mr. Walker . . ."

Judd stormed across the room, an unknown fear clawing at his insides.

"Stop." Yvette's calm yet commanding voice got through to him in a way a harsher tone wouldn't have.

"For God's sake, what is it?" Judd looked pleadingly at Yvette.

"Tell him," she said to Sanders.

"Are you sure?" Sanders asked.

She nodded.

Sanders explained about Lindsay and Maleah's plan to trap the BQ Killer, giving Judd the condensed version, then continued speaking during Judd's outbursts, completely ignoring his rage.

"And Griff agreed to this? He enabled her? Damn it, what was he thinking, putting her out there like that, using her as bait?"

"Griffin is protecting her," Sanders said. "Lindsay is doing this for the same reason she has done everything else for the past four years—for you. She would have done it with or without Griffin's cooperation."

"I never asked her . . ." Judd slammed his fist into the wall, bursting a hole in the Sheetrock. "This is all my fault. If anything happens to her . . ."

"Griffin is close by, along with six Powell agents. Holt Keinan is a former SWAT sharpshooter. They set everything up a few hours ago. Lindsay will be surrounded by protection."

"Exactly where is this coming down and when?"

"This evening," Sanders said. "She's meeting this man at six o'clock."

Judd checked his watch: Five-fifteen.

"Where?"

"Tell him," Yvette said to Sanders. "But only—" she grabbed Judd's arm "—only if you agree to let me go with you."

Judd glared at her. "Agreed."

Pinkie looked at himself in the mirror and smiled. He was years younger and pounds heavier than the real Allen Posey, but with the gray wig and mustache, he could pass for a man in his fifties. If only he could have gotten into the Woodruff Building last night, he could have prepared everything for tonight. But he had memorized the original blueprint and knew the perfect area. In the basement. She could scream her head off and no one would hear her. After removing the small vial from his pants pocket, he studied it for a moment, then replaced it, along with a plain, white cotton handkerchief. A couple of whiffs of this stuff and she'd be out like a light. Easy to lift and carry. If there was one thing he hated, it was a struggling victim. He patted his back, where a sheathed, nine-inch, hunting knife, attached to his belt, lay hidden beneath his lightweight overcoat. The knife was for the kill. The gun in his coat's outer pocket was simply a precaution. Just in case there was any trouble.

After the kill, he would return here to the motel, remove his disguise, shower, and get a good night's sleep. Tomorrow, he would fly straight to Louisiana, to Pudge's plantation with evidence of his kill. Photos taken with his tiny digital camera.

And then he would kill his cousin.

Pinkie sighed.

He truly hated the thought of killing Pudge. But rules were rules. He would allow his dear friend, his beloved cousin, to choose the method by which he wished to die. Poison? A single gunshot to the head? Strangulation?

All decked out in her Paige Allgood garb, Lindsay arrived at the old Woodruff Building at precisely two minutes to six. Ms. Allgood had given her consent for the Powell Agency to use her Bentley, which was being driven this evening by Rick Carson, dressed as her chauffeur. When he pulled the car up to the curb, he surveyed the area around the front entrance.

"He doesn't seem to be here yet," Rick said.

"No, but he could be watching and waiting."

Rick got out, opened the backdoor, and helped Lindsay onto the sidewalk. "Be careful," he whispered.

She smiled, squared her shoulders and tilted her chin. A show of confidence or false bravado?

Rick drove off, but Lindsay knew he would circle two blocks and then park in the alley behind the building and join Griff and the others inside.

Straightening the fur-trimmed cashmere sweater she wore, Lindsay walked toward the front door, pausing every few steps to glance around, the way anyone would if they were expecting to meet another person.

When she reached the double entry doors, she turned and

faced the street. Glancing at Paige's heavy eighteen-karat gold watch on her wrist, Lindsay noted that it was now one minute past six.

Act normal. Keep a pleasant expression on your face. Don't appear to be worried. If he's watching, he might pick up on the least hint of anxiety.

But how could she act naturally when she knew that very soon she would come face to face with a brutal murderer? *Do the best you can,* she told herself. *Remember, not only will catching this bastard save lives in the future, but it will help Judd put the past to rest.*

Five minutes later, still waiting, Lindsay twisted the gold bangle bracelets on her right wrist. God, how did Paige Allgood stand these damn things? Stay calm. Just because he isn't punctual doesn't mean he isn't going to show.

She glanced up the street, left, then right. There he was! Her pulse raced as a man of medium height and medium build came up the sidewalk, drawing closer and closer. His hair was steel gray, neatly styled, and she knew immediately that it was a really good hairpiece. With only streetlights and the interior lights from the Woodruff Building's marble-floored foyer for illumination, Lindsay wasn't able to see the man's face clearly at a distance.

"Ms. Allgood," the man called when he was a couple of yards away.

"Yes," she replied. "Are you Mr. Posey?"

"That I am, my dear."

She met him halfway, each of them pausing when only a couple of feet separated them. They stared at each other. He smiled. She returned his smile.

There was something familiar about his face. His eyes. Not the color, but the expression. And the mouth. Did she know this man? Had they met at sometime in the past? Even with the gray hair and mustache, she could tell he was not fifty, nowhere near it.

He grasped her arm gently, his fake smile unsettling her.

The instant he touched her, every nerve in Lindsay's body came to full alert.

Don't panic. Go inside with him. You won't be alone. Griff has Powell agents stationed throughout the building. You're as safe as you can possibly be—on the arm of a serial killer.

"I'm eager for you to see the potential in this building," Lindsay said. "And if after the tour, you're still interested, I'll bring along my architect's plans for the renovation when we go for dinner later. I have a copy of the plans in the office here."

"And as eager as I am to tour the building and take a look at the architect's plans, I'm even more eager for us to have dinner together," he told her. "I hope you don't mind, but I've made early dinner reservations, so we can dine first and then come back here later for the grand tour."

Lindsay knew instantly that something had gone wrong. Why had he changed their plans? Why had his grip on her arm tightened significantly? And why was he hauling her closer to his side?

He had walked right into a trap! How could he have been so stupid? No, he wasn't stupid. How could he have known?

Although she resembled Paige Allgood, this woman was not the former Miss UT that Pinkie had met on several occasions over the years.

He knew this woman, but she wasn't Paige.

She was Lindsay McAllister. A very special Powell agent.

He had seen her with Griffin Powell a few times in the past three years.

If he walked into the Woodruff Building with her, what would be waiting for him? Griffin Powell? Judd Walker? Powell agents, all with weapons loaded and aimed right at him? And if he tried to run away? No, running wasn't an option.

She knew something was wrong. The moment he changed plans on her, she had become suspicious. Getting her into his car on the pretense of going to dinner probably wasn't going to work.

Think, damn it, think! Think fast. Get yourself out of this mess any way you can.

Was he truly in a no-win situation?

There had to be a way out.

And if not?

He had no intention of going down without a fight. He might be able to outsmart his opponents. But if all failed, then, by God, he would go out in a blaze of glory. And he wouldn't go alone.

"I have my car waiting," Pinkie said. "Shall we go, my dear?"

The fake Paige replied, "I'm sorry, but I really prefer showing you the building now and going out for dinner later, as we originally planned."

She wasn't buying it, which meant she must know he wasn't the real Allen Posey. Pinkie eased his hand into his overcoat pocket, gripped the 9 mm and shoved it into her side. "I'm afraid there's been a drastic change in our plans, Ms. McAllister."

Chapter 34

Ms. McAllister. Ms. McAllister. Lindsay's own name reverberated inside her head. This man, whoever he was, knew her. Knew her name.

Snapping her head around, she stared at him, trying to figure out who he was, where she'd seen him.

His sneering smile seemed vaguely familiar.

"I'm afraid I can't oblige you by walking into Griffin's trap," he told her.

Don't panic, Lindsay. Stay calm and as much in control as possible. He's not going to shoot you here and now. He knows what awaits him once he walks into the Woodruff Building, but he has to realize that he can't run. You're his hostage, his only bargaining tool. He has to keep you alive.

At least for the time being.

It's not as if Griff doesn't know what's going on. That's the reason he made you wear a wire. Just in case something went wrong.

So what now? Play dumb? Pretend not to know what this guy was talking about? Buy Griff some time to figure out how to handle the situation?

Barely managing to constrain the panic gripping her, Lindsay asked, "What's wrong with you, Mr. Posey? I'm Paige Allgood, not someone named McAllister."

"You are not Paige Allgood. Although the real Allen Posey has never met Paige, I have. Several times."

Lindsay's heart stopped. Crap!

"I can't imagine why you'd think such a crazy thing," she said, hoping she could bluff her way out of this. "I most certainly am Paige Allgood." She jerked on her arm, but he held steadfast. "If you'll release me, I can show you my driver's license, my credit cards, my—"

He chuckled, the sound so eerily maniacal that it sent shock waves through Lindsay. "I must admit that there is a resemblance, though only superficial. If you and I had never met, I probably wouldn't have realized so quickly that you weren't Paige, and Griffin's little trap might have worked."

Lindsay swallowed. "You and I have met before? When? Where?"

He eyed her speculatively. "Are you wired, my dear?" He surveyed her from neck to knees. "Of course you are. Which means you can hear me, can't you, Griffin?" He chuckled. Cold chills raced through Lindsay. This man knew he now had nothing to lose.

"There is no way out for you," she said. "No matter what you do to me, you can't escape."

He pressed his mouth against her ear and whispered softly, "Before Griffin can turn his sharpshooters on me, we're going to take cover. If you fight me, I'll kill you instantly. Do you understand? Just nod. Don't say anything."

She nodded.

He pulled her along with him toward the corner of the building, which faced a side street. "Down!" he ordered when they reached a row of concrete steps that led below street level to what had once been an entrance to offices housed in the basement.

Lindsay realized that he held her in a protected area, out of range of any sharpshooter, with only two ways to reach them—either through the basement door or directly down the steps leading from the sidewalk. Either way, her captor would be able to kill her before being overtaken.

Not allowing his personal feelings for Lindsay to immobilize him, Griffin instantly issued orders, taking into consideration the fact that even if they had the Beauty Queen Killer trapped, Lindsay's life was too high a price to pay for capturing him. And yes, his decision to cooperate—up to a point—with the killer was a decision based on the fact that he loved Lindsay.

Griff kept two men inside the building, on the mezzanine level, able to see anyone entering or leaving. He sent one to the basement to secure the area, the others outside, with Holt Keinan in charge of finding Lindsay and her abductor's location.

"If there's anyway you can take him out, do it," Griff ordered. "I want Lindsay safe. Understood?"

Griffin couldn't allow his concern for Lindsay to cloud his judgement, but at the same time her safety was of paramount importance. If he contacted the local authorities, their very presence might push the BQ Killer over the edge. He had set this sting operation into motion and it was up to him to see it through to the end.

Lindsay, damn it, why did I let you talk me into this?

Heaven help us all if Judd loses you to the same maniac who killed Jennifer.

Judd!

Yvette had phoned him ten minutes ago to apprize him of the situation, that she and Judd were on their way to the Woodruff Building. Griff had bristled at the news, his angry why-the-hell-did-you-tell-him? question met with Yvette's trademark calm.

"You have always trusted my instincts," Yvette had said. "Trust them now. I believe Judd needs to be there."

Griff flipped open his cell phone and called Yvette.

When she answered, he said, "Keep Judd away from here. We have a problem. The BQ Killer realized we had set a trap for him. He's taken Lindsay hostage."

The moment Yvette closed her phone and turned to Judd, he knew it was bad news. "What?" he asked.

She hesitated, her dark eyes focused on him, but said nothing.

Glancing back and forth from her face to the downtown street traffic, he swallowed hard.

"Please, stop the car," Yvette said. "Pull off the road as soon as possible. We must talk."

A foreboding sensation gripped Judd, tightening his muscles and creating a buzzing hum inside his head. Within minutes, he turned into the first parking area he saw, this one adjacent to a local bank. Leaving the Porsche's engine idling, he looked directly at Yvette.

"Do you trust me?" she asked.

What did him trusting her have to do with anything? "Yeah, sure. As much as I trust anyone."

She reached over, grasped his arm and said, "The trap set for the BQ Killer . . ."

Judd closed his eyes as emotional pain radiated through him. "What went wrong? Is Lindsay . . . ?"

Yvette squeezed his arm. "You will not lose another woman you love to this evil man."

Judd's eyes flew open. He glared at Yvette. "You really can

read minds, can't you?" He flung off her arm. "Just tell me. Now!"

"The BQ Killer somehow realized he had walked into a trap. He has taken Lindsay hostage."

Judd couldn't breathe. Couldn't think. Agony so intense he felt as if he were dying consumed him completely.

"Damn Griff for letting her put her life on the line!"

"Griffin wants us to stay away and wait. Can you do that?"

"No way in hell. I can't just wait."

Yvette nodded. "Griff loves her, too, and will do all within his power to save her."

"Griff may love her, as a friend, as a sister, but she isn't his life," Judd said.

"And she is yours. I understand."

"You can't get away," Lindsay told him. "There's nowhere to run."

He smiled at her, his expression eerily sinister. "Perhaps you're right, but before I'm captured or killed, I can kill you."

"Killing me would serve no purpose. You need me. I'm all that is standing between you and a firing squad. If you think for one minute that Griffin Powell will allow you to live if you kill me—"

His deranged laughter echoed all around her, in her, through her. A death knell warning her of impending tragedy.

"Do you know how many women I've killed?"

She understood the question was rhetorical and required no response.

"I admit that simply shooting you would give me little pleasure, but . . ." He glanced at the closed door behind them, an exterior entrance to the basement. He whispered in her ear again, so that the wire she wore wouldn't transfer his voice directly to Griff. "If I can get that door open and we can find a little privacy inside, I can show you exactly who you're dealing with, who you thought you could so easily ensnare in your trap."

"The door's locked," Lindsay told him, loud and clear. She had no idea if the door was locked or not, but if he managed to take her inside, she couldn't be a hundred percent sure there would be a Powell agent on the other side, waiting to rescue her. After all, she didn't know if Griff knew exactly where she was. "And if you risk moving closer to the basement door—"

He slapped her soundly across the face. Reeling from the force of the blow, Lindsay staggered backward and might have fallen against the concrete wall behind her if he hadn't held onto her with his other hand. By the time her ears stopped ringing and she licked the blood from her busted lip, he had the gun pressed into her ribs again.

Using his free hand, he reached up under her cashmere sweater, grasped the wire taped to her chest and ripped it from her flesh. Groaning, she glared at him, her mind shifting into overdrive. She couldn't wait for Griff and the other agents to rescue her. She had to act now, before it was too late.

Just as she made her move, her captor's strong arm manacled her neck as he pressed a foul smelling rag over her nose.

No, damn it, no!

From his strategic hiding place, Pudge heard voices, running feet and the shout of orders. He had come to the Woodruff Building intending to kill his cousin Pinkie before Pinkie had murdered his latest victim and won their five-year dying game. But much to Pudge's surprise, he had been trapped here inside once a crew of gunmen had descended upon the place. Overhearing bits and pieces of conversation while he managed to keep hidden from them, he surmised that Griffin Powell had set a trap for Pinkie, using one of his female agents as bait. If he hadn't been caught in the middle of the sting operation, Pudge would have found this development highly amusing. As it was, he could do nothing but wait and let the scenario play out in front of him, then escape at the first opportunity.

But it was so unfair that someone else would take Pinkie's life, and that was bound to happen. His cousin wasn't the type who would surrender. Like he, Pinkie would rather die than be taken alive.

Since the woman Pinkie held captive was not a former beauty queen, that meant no matter what the outcome-whether she lived or died-Pinkie had lost the game. Today was April first. The deadline for the final kill. Pudge had more points, which made him the winner. It was only his right to claim the prize.

There might be a way . . .

Lindsay's eyelids flickered as she tried to open her eyes. What had happened? Where was she? How long . . . ? That bastard had knocked her out with something, maybe ether? She didn't know. It didn't matter.

Had he been able to open the basement door? Was that where they were now?

When she finally managed to open her eyes fully, she realized they were in the building, which meant he had gotten inside, somehow, someway. But they were not in the basement.

As she gazed up, she saw the three-quarter moon, a few twinkling stars, and the vastness of the dark evening sky. Startled at first, then puzzled, she tried to sit up, but found that her hands and feet were bound. Struggling to move up and into a sitting position, Lindsay heard a man's self-satisfied chuckles.

Before she could do more than roll side to side, her captor placed his foot down on her chest. "Be still. I wouldn't want you rolling off the edge of the roof and onto the street, six floors below us."

"The roof?" She gulped the question.

"The basement door was unlocked," he told her. "I managed to carry you inside and straight to the freight elevator before anyone figured out where we were or what I was doing. I imagine that by now, they're running around in circles trying to figure out what happened to us."

"Griffin will find me. He'll stop you!" She tried the ropes binding her wrists. Tight. And the more she struggled, the tighter the knots became.

"By the time Griffin finds you, I will be gone. And you, my lovely little Lindsay, will be quite dead."

Shivering involuntarily, she tried to make out his face in the semi-darkness. He stood several feet away, in the shadows.

"Since Paige Allgood is known for her voice, for her singing and acting abilities, I had planned to slit open her throat and hack away at her vocal chords."

What's that in his hand?

Oh God! He held a knife with a long, serrated blade. A hunting knife.

"But since I can do whatever I want with you, I'm thinking about slicing here and there—" he brandished the knife over her face, down her arms, over her belly "—and letting you scream your head off. I love hearing women scream in agony. It gives me such a feeling of power and superiority."

Please, Griff, find me. Find me soon. Before it's too late. And if you don't make it in time, tell Judd . . . Tell him that I love him.

* * *

Judd and Yvette entered the Woodruff Building, per Griff's instructions, walking directly into the grand rotunda: Gray marble floors, white marble pillars, walnut wainscoting, huge crystal chandelier. A split staircase that spiraled right and left, leading to a banister-encased open mezzanine. Magnificent in the way only buildings from a bygone era were.

Without touching Judd, Yvette sensed the increasing tension in him and around him, especially as Griffin approached. His solemn expression cautioned them.

"What's happening?" Judd demanded, barely able to control his rage.

Yvette kept sending him subliminal messages, doing her best to connect with his mind without him being aware of what she was doing. Her ability to soothe savage beasts was, at best, minimal, depending on the circumstances and the beast involved. Judd was a man on the edge. One false move and he would fall headlong into uncontrollable mania. He had already lost one woman to a sadistic madman. She knew that everything within him was determined not to let history repeat itself.

"We've traced his movements," Griffin said. "If I had it to do over again . . ." He sucked in a deep breath. "He's got her on the roof." Griff glanced up. "The elevator goes all the way up to the sixth floor, then there's a short set of stairs leading from there to the roof. The door locks from the inside, but if we rush through the door, he'll kill her for sure. And if we try to go in with a helicopter, same thing."

"Tell me you have a plan." Judd glowered at Griffin. "If not—"

"We have a plan." Griffin glanced at Yvette. She gave him a telepathic assurance that Judd was at least temporarily under control.

Barely.

"I'm going up there and talk to him through the closed door and do my best to distract him, at least long enough for Holt to get positioned on top of one of the buildings across the street. With this building on a corner and the building beside it only five stories high, the two directly across are the only ones that will give Holt the ability to zero in on our killer and take him out. But in order to get into position, Holt will be partially visible if the killer is looking that way."

"You need someone who can not only keep the BQ Killer distracted, but put him in the line of fire. Right?"

"Right."

"I'll go," Judd said.

"No. Not you. If you fuck up . . . This is Lindsay's life we're talking about."

"Don't you think I know that."

Griffin glanced at Yvette again. *You must let him do this.*

"Okay," Griffin said.

Judd heaved a deep, silent groan. "Let's go."

Lindsay did not want to die.

God, please don't let it happen. Not now. Not this way. If the Beauty Queen Killer murders me, mutilates my body, it will destroy Judd completely. He almost didn't survive Jennifer's death. If I die at the same monster's hands . . .

The BQ Killer loomed over Lindsay where she lay on the rooftop, curled into a fetal position. Her hands and feet might be bound, but she would not lie still and make it easy for this lunatic to cut her up into little pieces.

"Is your life flashing before your eyes?" he asked. "I'll give you a few more minutes to make your peace. And feel free to beg me for your life. I get off on hearing my victims beg. They all do it, you know."

"I won't."

"Oh, you will. Once I make the first few cuts and the pain becomes unbearable. You'll beg, tough girl. You'll beg and plead and scream, just like all the rest of them."

"You're insane."

"And you're scared."

"How does someone become as evil as you are?" *Griffin where are you? My time is running out.*

The cold springtime wind blew across the rooftop, chilling Lindsay, reminding her that she was still alive, could still feel.

How much would it hurt? To be stabbed and sliced? To be tortured? To be left to bleed to death?

"Are you trembling because you're cold?" he asked, ignoring her comment about him being evil. "And have you finally realized that no one can save you?"

"If you kill me—"

He laughed in her face. "If I thought Griffin would make a deal with me, I would release you, but we both know that he would be willing to sacrifice your life in order to capture the Beauty Queen Killer."

Before Lindsay even thought of a reply, a loud, deep voice called out through the closed door that led from the rooftop to the staircase leading down to the sixth floor.

"Griffin may be willing to sacrifice her, but I'm not," the voice shouted. "I'm Judd Walker. I'll make a deal with you. Name your terms."

Chapter 35

Lindsay gasped.

Judd was here? How was that possible? He was still in Atlanta, at the rehab center.

Startled by Judd's unexpected presence just beyond the closed door, Lindsay's abductor spun around and glared at the barrier between him and the voice that had offered him a way to escape certain death.

"You're Jennifer Walker's husband," the killer said. "The man who sicced Griffin Powell on me four years ago."

"Let's talk," Judd shouted. "Let's make a deal."

"Why should I trust you?"

"What have you got to lose?"

The man laughed.

God, how Lindsay hated his eerie laughter.

"Talk to me," Judd told him. "I'm your only hope of coming out of this alive. You have to know that if you harm Lindsay, you're a dead man."

"I'm a dead man regardless."

"Not necessarily."

"You have nothing to offer me."

"That's not true. All you need to do as a first step in our negotiations is exchange hostages. It will be my life for Lindsay's, just in case anything goes wrong. Let me talk to you face to face. Let me open the door—"

"No way in hell!"

"I'll come through the door very slowly, with my hands on my head. If I make one false move, you can shoot me, that is if you have a gun."

"I have a gun, wise guy. And I know how to use it. But I also have a knife that I've already used on Lindsay."

No, no! He's lying, Judd. Don't listen to him. Lindsay's heart wept. *Damn you, you evil son of a bitch. Don't do this to Judd. Don't conjure up memories of what you did to Jennifer.* "Judd, he hasn't—" Her voice was so weak she doubted Judd heard her.

Without any warning, the killer aimed his pistol at her and fired. The bullet sliced through the top of Lindsay's shoulder. She moaned with pain.

"I shot her. Do you hear me? And if you try anything, I'll kill her right now. I swear I'll do it."

"Lindsay!" Judd cried her name.

"He must love you if he's willing to swap places with you," the killer said to Lindsay as he walked over to her and kicked her in the ribs. "Knowing that will make killing you all the sweeter." Surveying her trembling body, he waved his weapon over her, from her head to her feet.

With his attention focused on Lindsay where she lay at his feet, the killer didn't react quickly enough when the rooftop door swung open. He spun around to face the raging force storming toward him. Too late, he realized that he had lost control of the situation. He pointed his gun at Judd, then back at Lindsay. Everything happened so quickly, almost simultaneously, so Lindsay really didn't know what occurred first. Judd attacked, using his body like a battering ram. As he knocked the BQ Killer backward, the man fired his pistol, but she didn't know if he had hit Judd or if he had shot her again. Suddenly, the crack of a rifle shot rang out, and then another, both echoing loudly in Lindsay's ears. Pain sliced through her stomach as if a sharp sword had pierced deep and wide, and she knew she had taken a second bullet. As she lay there staring at her abductor, only a few feet away from her, she saw blood trickling from a single hole in his head and from another in his neck. He slumped to his knees, and then toppled over, face down onto the rooftop.

Lindsay opened her eyes. The morning light was much too bright. Her head ached and her mouth felt dry. Wondering where she was, she glanced from right to left. Closed white blinds covered the windows. Sunlight peeked through the cracks. The walls were light green, the ceiling white. The bed was narrow, the linens soft. A packet of some kind of IV solution stood by the bed, with a long tube leading from the packet to her hand.

She stared at the top of her bruised hand. A needle was embedded in a vein, tan tape crisscrossing the tubing to hold it in place.

I'm in a hospital.

I'm not dead.

What happened? *Don't you remember?* an inner voice said. *The Beauty Queen Killer shot you twice. And someone shot him.*

Judd! Oh, God! If Judd hadn't distracted her abductor . . .

Lindsay thrashed about, wanting Judd, needing Judd.

Two large, gentle hands stroked her shoulders, soothing her. "Lie still, sweetheart. Everything's all right. You're going to be just fine."

She quieted and gazed up into Judd's beautiful golden eyes.

"Judd." Her voice sounded like it belonged to a croaking frog.

"Hello, beautiful."

"Where . . . ? What . . . ? How long . . . ?"

"You're in the hospital recovering from a nasty bullet wound. Cary Maygarden, the Beauty Queen Killer, shot you."

"Cary Maygarden? The eccentric millionaire from Nashville was the BQ Killer?"

Judd nodded.

"He shot me. Twice," Lindsay said, slightly dazed by the realization that Judd, Griffin, and she had interacted socially with the killer only recently. No wonder he had seemed so familiar.

"One bullet grazed your shoulder and the second hit you in the lower right side of your abdomen. But the doctors patched you up and you'll soon be good as new."

"Cary Maygarden was the BQ Killer," Lindsay repeated, barely able to believe it.

"He's dead. And his death was far too easy. Two shots. One in the head, the other in his neck. If there were any justice, he would have died a slow, agonizing death. I would like to have taken him apart, piece by piece for what he did to you . . . for what he did to Jennifer."

Lindsay lifted her IV-free hand. Judd grasped her hand, brought it to his face and held it against his cheek. That's when she noticed his heavy beard stubble.

"You need a shave," she told him. "How long—?"

"Four days," he said. "Four of the longest days of my life."

"I'm thirsty."

He poured her a glass of water, then pushed the button to raise the head of her bed enough so that when he put the glass to her lips, she was able to take several sips through the straw.

After he put the glass on the bedside table, he eased down and sat on the edge of the bed. "That was a damn fool thing you did, using yourself as bait to trap the Beauty Queen Killer. If anything had happened to you . . . God, Lindsay, when I thought I might lose you, too . . ."

Using all the strength she could muster, she brought her hand up and laid it on his arm, then squeezed weakly. "It worked. We got him, didn't we? It was worth the risk."

"Not if I'd lost you." He clasped her hand again with the utmost tenderness. "Lindsay . . ."

"How did you know where I was and what was going on? I know Sanders never would have told you."

"As a matter of fact, he did. But only at Yvette's urging. Before we left Griffin's Rest, she called Griff to let him know we were coming into Knoxville and that she'd make sure I didn't do anything stupid."

"Apparently, she wasn't able to do that."

Judd frowned. "When I heard that first shot, I thought he'd killed you. At that point, I didn't care what happened to me." He leaned over carefully and kissed her lips. She sighed. He lifted his head and smiled at her. "I love you."

"Please, say that again."

"I love you, Lindsay McAllister."

Tears flooded her eyes. She blinked repeatedly, but several stray drops hit her cheeks. "I love you, too, but you already know that. And I want you to know that it's all right if you're never able to love me the way you loved Jennifer. And I don't care if you still love her and always will."

He kissed her hand, then held it against his chest as he gazed down at her. "While I was in rehab, Yvette was allowed to work with me, to take me through a crash course of grief-counseling. She made me realize something very important about love. I can love Jennifer for the rest of my life and I can love you, too. Jenny will always have a place in my heart. She'll always be my first real love. But you, Lindsay, are the woman I want to spend the rest of my life with, the woman I'll grow old with, the woman who was meant to be mine. You're my last love, sweetheart. My true soul mate."

* * *

Griff was more than surprised when several hours ago, he received a telephone call from former FBI Special Agent Curtis Jackson inviting him to meet him at Cary Maygarden's ancestral mansion outside Nashville.

"Nic's officially in charge of the BQK cases, but since I headed up the original task force, they're allowing me to be in on the conclusion," Jackson had said. "Our people have been going over the guy's house with a fine-tooth comb for days, searching for memorabilia from his kills."

"And?"

"And nothing. Not until this morning. That's when our guys found a secret room in the basement."

"And inside?"

"Not a damn thing, but just when we'd given up, guess what we found?"

"Another secret room."

Jackson chuckled. "Yes, sir. And I thought since you're the one who actually caught the BQ Killer, you should be allowed to take a look at Maygarden's trophy room."

"How does Nic feel about that?"

"Not happy, but she's not going to bar you from entering. Strictly as a favor to me, her old mentor."

And that's how Griff wound up with Nic Baxter, Josh Friedman, and Curtis Jackson inside Cary Maygarden's gruesome secret chamber, the walls lined with photographs of beauty queens. Photos of them as contest winners, with their crowns and roses, alongside shots of the same young women after they had been murdered. Photo after photo of hacked, chopped, butchered, slaughtered wives, mothers, daughters, sisters. Each one a woman loved by someone, missed by someone, mourned by someone.

Griff stopped at the photograph of Jennifer Mobley Walker the night she was crowned Miss Tennessee. So young. So beautiful. So full of life.

When he stared at the snapshot of Jenny sitting on the

floor in the kitchen where she had died, her hands hacked off and lying on either side of her, Griff whispered her name.

"That's Judd Walker's wife, isn't it?" Nic said as she came up beside Griff. "She was a beautiful woman."

Griff nodded.

"I wonder why he chose to display pictures of these particular women," Nic said.

"What?" Griff was still thinking about Jennifer, remembering the vibrant, vivacious woman she had been.

"Look at the photos, each one of them," Nic told him. "Don't count the pictures themselves, but count the number of women represented here."

"Is there some reason you want me to play this numbers game? We know how many women he killed, so there should be—" Griff stopped rattling as his gaze swept up and down the snapshot-covered walls.

He went back to the first photo and began counting—the women, not the pictures. Nic followed him to the end of the long, narrow room and back up on the other side.

"I'll be damned. He displayed photos of only half the women he killed," Griff said.

"Odd, don't you think?"

Griff nodded. "There's probably some simple explanation. Maybe he rotated the pictures for some reason or other. After all, he was playing a sick game where with each murder he racked up points, so it wouldn't be a huge stretch to imagine he liked to change out the photos of his victims according to the month or the season or whatever."

"You're probably right."

Griff studied Nic, noting the tilt of her lips. Not a smirk. Certainly not a smile.

"What are you not sharing with me?" Griff asked.

She shrugged. "What makes you think . . . Oh, all right. You'll find out soon enough when your sharpshooter— what's his name?"

"Holt Keinan."

"When Mr. Keinan is notified that although he did shoot Cary Maygarden, it may not have been his bullet that killed him."

"What?"

"According to our medical examiner's report, the bullet that entered Maygarden's body first hit him in the neck, severing a vital artery. Keinan's bullet hit him in the head, probably seconds before or after. Either one could have killed him."

"So Holt shot him twice."

"With two different rifles?"

"Two different . . . ?"

"The bullets removed from Maygarden's body came from two different rifles, which means—"

"He was shot by two different people."

"Did one of your other agents shoot Maygarden?" Nic asked.

Griff didn't reply.

"If not, then it seems we have a mystery shooter on our hands. Someone who managed to slip onto the rooftop of a nearby building without being seen. Someone with a motive to kill Cary Maygarden."

"Is the FBI going to actively search for another shooter?"

"No, not at this time."

"What are you going to tell the press?"

"Only the basic facts. No details. But I intend to go over every aspect of this case, from A to Z, until I figure out who other than your agent, might have killed Maygarden and why."

"And you told me about this so that I could help you solve the mystery," he said sarcastically, knowing full well that he would be the last person on earth Nic would ask for help.

"No, Mr. Powell, I told you because I want you to think about it, ponder over every detail, worry yourself crazy, and try your damnedest to put the puzzle together. You see, I didn't give you all the pieces, so if anyone is going to be able to put the puzzle together, it won't be you."

Pudge drove all night, staying wide awake without a problem. For him, killing was like a massive shot of adrenaline, sending his heart racing and his pulse pounding.

He had known that Pinkie would get the final kill, the April Fools' Day kill that would commemorate their first kill and end their game. If his cousin had won, then he would have lost. Lost more than the game. After all, the stakes had been high. The loser would forfeit his life at the hands of the winner.

Pudge had thought for sure he'd win. After all, despite Pinkie's knack for murder and mayhem, Pudge was the more intelligent of the two, with an IQ that bordered on genius.

Then when the end drew near, Pudge had known what he had to do. He had kept tabs on his cousin and followed him to meet his last victim. That's when he'd realized poor Pinkie had walked right into a trap. Being careful not to be seen, Pudge had managed to go up a flight of backstairs and station himself on the rooftop of a building across the street from the Woodruff. If Pinkie had been taken into custody, he would have sung like a bird, implicating him, naming him as a co-conspirator.

If he'd known in advance that Griffin Powell had stationed his own sharpshooter on another rooftop, Pudge could have saved himself the trouble. But even if it hadn't been his bullet that ended Pinkie's life, at least he had gotten the satisfaction of seeing him lose the game in a most spectacular way.

When the medical examiner discovered that there were two bullets from two different rifles in Pinkie's body, the FBI would no doubt investigate. But since there was no way to trace the rifle to him or any reason to suspect him of having been involved, he was in the clear.

As it stood now, the Beauty Queen Killer would be laid to rest and the case closed, leaving him free to start a new game. A game of murder.

Epilogue

Spring raced by, rushing headlong into summer, which melted into early autumn, bringing chilly nights and the first frost of the season. And Lindsay's wedding day. She and Judd had married in a simple private ceremony, with only the closest family and friends in attendance. Her cousin Callie had been her matron of honor. Griff had been Judd's best man. Their very special guests had included Cam Hendrix, Sanders, Barbara Jean Hughes, Yvette Meng, Maleah Perdue, Rick Carson, and Holt Keinan.

Judd had offered her a honeymoon anywhere on earth, reminding her that she had married a very wealthy man and could have anything her little heart desired.

"My heart desires you," she'd told him. "And a honeymoon at the hunting lodge."

So they had driven one county over to the Walker lodge outside Whitwell for what was supposed to have been a two-week honeymoon. That had been nearly two months ago. After just three weeks there, they had decided to contact an architect and a contractor and make plans to renovate the place, after the first of the year.

Judd hadn't decided if he wanted to return to practicing law or if he wanted to be a gentleman farmer. Lindsay didn't care. Whatever made her husband happy was fine with her. After all, she had everything—well, almost everything—she'd ever want. And come late summer next year, she would have everything.

Side by side, Lindsay and Judd worked in Mimi's old flower garden, planting the tulip and daffodil bulbs that would bloom in March and April. A row of bronze and yellow mums they had planted in early October grew in profusion along the back walkway. The next heavy frost would probably get them, but they would simply die down and then be reborn next fall.

Judd helped Lindsay to her feet, their gloved hands clasping. He put his arm around her waist and looked up at the cloudless blue sky. "It's a wonderful day."

Standing on tiptoe, she kissed his cheek. "Everyday with you is a wonderful day."

"How would you feel about living here permanently?" he asked.

"Do you mean it?"

"If you'd like to. If it's what you want."

She threw her arms around his neck and hugged him. "It's exactly what I want. You know I love this place. I love fishing in the creek and skinny-dipping in the pond. I love our long walks in the woods and working in the garden together and . . ." She looked him square in the eyes. "And I can't think of a better place to raise our little girl."

"Our little girl?"

"Well, she could turn out to be a he, but—" Lindsay laid her hand over her still flat belly "—somehow I just know our first child will be a girl."

"You're pregnant?"

"Uh-huh. I picked up a pregnancy test at the drugstore in Whitwell yesterday and when I took the test this morning—"

Judd lifted her off her feet and swung her around and around, then eased her down his body, holding her close.

"I want to name her after your mimi," Lindsay said. "But you've never told me what her given name was."

"Emily," Judd told her. "Mimi's name was Emily."

"It's lovely." She looked questioningly at Judd. "So, is it all right with you if our little girl is Emily Walker II?"

Judd glanced heavenward, then kissed Lindsay playfully on the nose. "Have I told you today, Mrs. Walker, just how much I love you?"

She squirmed against him. "Not since this morning before breakfast, so maybe you'd better tell me again."

"I love you," he said, then laid his open palm over her stomach. "And I love our little Emily II. Or possibly Judson VI."

Savoring the joy of the moment, Judd and Lindsay embraced, and their laughter carried far and wide on the cool November wind.

Nic Baxter recognized the caller ID and thought twice about answering her phone. But curiosity got the better of her.

"Hello, Mr. Powell, what can I do for you?"

"Happy Thanksgiving," Griff said. "Are you anticipating a lovely day with family or friends or do you have to work?"

"Why are you calling?"

"I'm driving down to the Walker hunting lodge to spend the holiday with Lindsay and Judd and I got to thinking about you, wondering if you were all alone."

"Either tell me why you really called or I'm going to hang up."

"Ah, you're no fun."

Nic groaned.

"There were two of them," Griffin told her.

"What did you say?"

"You probably figured that out about the same time I did that—Cary Maygarden had an opponent in his sick little Dying Game—but you've kept that information to yourself. Otherwise the bureau wouldn't have closed the BQ Killer case."

"It's just a guess," she said. "I have no proof."

"Yeah, it's just gut instinct with me, too. But you know what that means, don't you? Out there somewhere, there's still a serial killer on the loose."

"That well may be, but there hasn't been another BQ murder since Cary Maygarden was killed."

"That's because that game ended when Maygarden died. Who do you think our other shooter was that day at the Woodruff Building?"

"Maygarden's opponent."

"Bingo. And once a serial killer, always a serial killer. I'd say it's only a matter of time before this guy kills again, if he hasn't already . . ."

Dear Reader,

Many of you have contacted me to tell me that you enjoy reading books with connecting characters and are interested in learning about Knoxville P.I., Griffin Powell. Griff has appeared in several of my novels as a secondary character. From the moment I first introduced him, I found him fascinating and knew he had a horrible secret past. In *The Dying Game*, I gave you glimpses of the man he is now and hints about those ten missing years of his life, hopefully whetting your appetite for his book. You were reintroduced to Sanders, Griff's mysterious right-hand-man, and introduced to the exotically beautiful Dr. Yvette Meng, each a dear friend from Griff's lost years. And you met FBI Special Agent Nic Baxter, one lady who hasn't succumbed to Griff's irresistible charm. In fact, Nic intensely dislikes Griffin Powell, both professionally and personally. And the feeling is mutual.

As you know, Pudge still remained on the loose at the end of *The Dying Game*. That's because he's going to be back in my next thriller, ready to play a deadly new game—a game of murder. As the clever Game Hunter Killer, Pudge specifically chooses his victims—all women who are both physically and mentally superior. In his sick game, he is the hunter and they his prey. Having outsmarted the FBI and the Powell Agency once before, Pudge finds it amusing to play catch-me-if-you-can with Nic and Griff. When he contacts each with clues and dares and threats, they have no choice but to join forces in order to stop him from killing again and again. But no one knows just how personal the killer's game will become for Nic and Griff—not until it's too late.

Look for Griffin Powell's book in February 2008. In the meantime, I always enjoy hearing from readers. You may contact me through my Web site at *www.beverlybarton.com*, or by writing to me in care of Kensington Publishing.

Warmest regards,
Beverly Barton

Prologue

I am not going to die! Damn it, I refuse to give up, to let him win this evil competition.

Kendall Moore pulled herself up off the ground where she had fallen, face-down as she ran from her tormentor. Breathless and exhausted, she managed to bring herself to her knees. Every muscle ached. Her head throbbed. Fresh blood trickled from the cuts on her legs and the gashes in the bottoms of her calloused feet.

The blistering August sun beat down on her like hot heavy tendrils reaching out from a relentless monster in the sky. The sun was her enemy, blistering her skin, parching her lips, dehydrating her tired, weak body.

Garnering what little strength she had left, Kendall forced herself to stand. She had to find cover, a place where she had an advantage over her pursuer. If he caught up with her while she was out in the open, he would kill her. The game would be over. He would win.

He's not going to win! Her mind screamed orders—run, hide, live to fight another day. But her legs managed only a few trembling steps before she faltered and fell again. She needed food and water. She hadn't eaten in three days and hadn't had any water since the day before yesterday. He had been pursuing her from sunup to sunset for the past few days, apparently moving in for the kill. After weeks of tormenting her.

The roar of his dirt bike alerted her to the fact that he was nearby, on the narrow, rutted path to the west of her present location. Soon, he would come deeper into the woods on foot, tracking her as he would track an animal.

At first she had been puzzled by the fact that he had kidnapped her, then set her free in the middle of nowhere. But it hadn't taken her long—only a matter of hours—before she realized that she wasn't free, no more than a captive animal in a game reserve was actually free.

Day after day, he stalked her, hunted her down, and taught her how to play the game by his rules. He'd had more than one opportunity to kill her, but he had allowed her to live, and he'd even given her an occasional day of rest. But she never knew what day, so she was forced to stay alert at all times, to be prepared for yet another long, tiring match in what seemed like a neverending game.

Pudge parked his dirt bike, straightened the cord holding the small binoculars around his neck and the leather strap that held the rifle cover across his back. Kendall didn't know it, but today was the day she would die. He had brought her here to this isolated area three weeks ago today. She would be his first kill in this brand new game that he had devised after several months of meticulous planning. Only recently had he decided that he would hunt his prey for three weeks, then go in for the actual kill on the twenty-first day.

After his cousin Pinkie's death on April first of this year, he had discovered that he missed his one-time opponent and lifelong best friend more than he'd thought he would. But Pinkie's death had been inevitable. After all, he had been the loser in their "Dying Game" and the consequence of losing was forfeiting one's life.

You'd love this new game, dear cousin. I am choosing only the finest female specimens, women with physical prowess and mental cunning. Only worthy adversaries.

Kendall Moore holds an Olympic Silver Medal in long-distance running. Her slender, five-ten frame is all lean muscle. In a fair fight, she might actually win the game we're playing, but whenever did I fight fair?

Pudge chuckled to himself as he dismounted from the dirt bike.

I'm coming for you. Run. Hide. I'll find you. And then I'll kill you.

As he stomped through the woods, Pudge felt a surge of adrenaline rush through his body, heightening his senses. He had missed the thrill of taking a human life, of watching with delight the look of horror in a woman's eyes when she knew she was going to die.

Soon, he told himself. The first victim in The Murder Game is only a few yards away. Waiting for you. Waiting for death.

Kendall knew that if her captor chose to kill her, her chances of escape were nil. He had proven to her several times that she was powerless to stop him from tracking her and finding her. He had pointed his rifle at her, dead center at her heart, more than once, then grinned with evil glee, turned and walked away. But the time would come when he would not walk away. Was today the day?

She heard his footsteps as he crunched through the underbrush, drawing closer and closer. He wasn't trying to sneak up on her. In fact, he seemed to want her to know that he was approaching.

You have to keep moving, she told herself. Even if you can't get away, you have to try. Don't give up. Not now.

Kendall ran for what seemed like hours, but probably wasn't more than ten minutes. Her muscles ached, her heart raced. Out of breath and drained of what little energy she had left, she paused behind a huge, towering tree—and waited.

Keep moving!

I can't. I'm so tired.

He's going to find you. And when he does . . .

God, help me. Please, help me.

Suddenly, as from out of nowhere, her captor called out her name. Just as she turned toward the sound of his voice, he stepped through the thick summertime foliage surrounding them. The trickle of sunlight fingering down through the ceiling of sky-high treetops hit the muzzle of his rifle, which he had aimed directly at her.

"Game's end," he said.

He's never said that before, Kendall thought.

Breathing hard, she lifted her head and stared right at him. "If you're going to kill me you son of a bitch, then do it."

"What's wrong Kendall, are you tired of playing our little game?"

"Game? That's all this is to you, isn't it? Some sick perverted game. Damn it, this is my life."

"Yes it is. And I hold the power of life and death—your life and death—in my hands."

His cold, self-satisfied smile sent shivers through her.

"Why me?"

"Because you're so very perfect."

"I don't understand."

"You don't need to understand. All you need to do is die."

She swallowed hard. He's actually going to kill me this time. Icy fear froze her to the spot. "Do it, damn you, do it!"

The first shot hit her in her right leg. Pain. Excruciating pain. She grasped her bloody thigh as she fell to her knees. The second bullet hit her in the shoulder.

She stared at him through a haze of agonized tears and waited for the third shot.

Nothing.

"End it," she screamed. "Please, please . . ."

The third shot entered her chest, but missed her heart.

The pain enveloped her, taking her over completely, becoming who she was. No longer Kendall. Only the torment she endured.

As she lay on the ground, bleeding to death, her captor approached. When she felt the tip of the rifle muzzle pressing against the back of her head, she closed her eyes and prayed for death.

The fourth and final bullet answered her prayer.